Varik glanced at her. "I'm trying to apologize. *Again.* I want us to work past this. I want us to—"

"To what? Get back together? Not gonna happen."

"Why not? We loved each other once."

"Loved—past tense."

"Can't you just let it go?"

She shook her head. "Let it go? Varik, you—"

"It was an accident. Damn it! You know I would never intentionally hurt you."

"You almost fucking killed me!"

The Corvette drifted across the centerline into oncoming traffic. A horn blared, yanking Varik's attention back to the road. He jerked the wheel, and the car regained its lane seconds before colliding with a minivan.

"Stop the car!" Alex demanded.

Varik pulled into the parking lot in front of an abandoned storefront and screeched to a halt.

Alex pitched forward. The seat belt tightened across her chest, pinning her in place, and she hissed as pain raced through her arm.

"Ah, shit." Varik unbuckled his own safety belt and twisted in his seat to face her. "Are you okay?"

"No, I'm not okay," she said through clenched teeth. She batted away his hand. "You show up here and suddenly all hell breaks loose. You say you're here to help with the investigation, but then you start pulling this 'let's get back together' crap."

"Alex—"

"Three vampires and five humans are dead. At least a dozen more are injured, and I've been shot." Her voice cracked. "No, Varik, I'm definitely *not* okay."

BLOOD
LAW

JEANNIE HOLMES

■ A DELL BOOK | NEW YORK

A Dell Mass Market Original

Copyright © 2010 by Jeannie Holmes
Excerpt of *Blood Secrets* copyright © 2010 by Jeannie Holmes

This book contains an exerpt from the forthcoming book *Blood Secrets* by Jeannie Holmes. This excerpt has been set for this edition only and may not reflect the final content of the forthcoming edition.

ISBN 978-0-553-59267-2

Cover design: Dreu Pennington-McNeil
Cover art: Don Sipley

Printed in the United States of America

www.bantamdell.com

2 4 6 8 9 7 5 3 1

For Daddy

acknowledgments

Writing can be a solitary path, but no writer is ever truly alone. There are usually many supporting characters who work tirelessly to see a book created and to keep an author sane. I'm no exception, and would like to pay heartfelt tribute to the following people.

Thanks to Carolyn Haines for her guidance, friendship, encouragement, and hours of reading various rough drafts. You saw something in those early pages and helped me find my voice. Alex, Varik, Tasha, Harvey, Darryl, and the other residents of Jefferson wouldn't exist had it not been for your support.

I want to give a huge thanks to my wonderful agent, Marian Young, for not only being completely awesome in every way but also answering hundreds of questions, guiding me through "the process," and most important, taking a chance on a new author with a crazy idea to have vampires running amok in the Mississippi backwoods. I couldn't have asked for a better champion, and I'll never be able to fully express the depths of my gratitude.

Thanks to my truly amazing editor, Danielle Perez. While I may have started with a good story, you've made it leaner and meaner with your insights, suggestions, and questions. Like Marian, you took a chance on a new author, and your support has been incredible. "Thank you" doesn't begin to cover my appreciation for all of your hard work.

To my equally incredible publisher, Nita Taublib, thank you for your wisdom, insights, and support. Huge thanks to the Dell art department for creating such an outstanding cover. (I've been left speechless, which is virtually impossible for a Southerner!) I'm truly honored by the dedication of everyone at Dell who worked to bring *Blood Law* to fruition. Many thanks!

I would also like to thank some very special people for sharing their knowledge and expertise. Thanks to D. P. Lyle, M.D., for providing forensic information, and thanks to Ron O'Gorman, M.D., for answering some of my medical questions. Thanks to the members of the underground vampire communities (names withheld by request) who shared their personal experiences. Thanks to the members of law enforcement who responded to my questions on various Internet forums, e-mail lists, and in person. I wish I could name you all individually. Please know that I appreciate everything you do on a daily basis and thank you so much for your insights! Any errors or acts of creative license involving the aforementioned individuals or groups are my own.

Special thanks go to all the students who passed through the University of South Alabama's fiction writing workshops, read various incarnations of this book, and offered their feedback and suggestions. Extra-special thanks go to Michelle Ladner and Kim Robertson for slogging through the full complete manuscript. More special thanks go to Annmarie Guzy, Ph.D., for helping me to understand that gore isn't always the way to go. Sometimes it's the slow and steady creeping shadow that is the most effective. And to the USA Horror Club I pay special tribute for their constant and unfaltering support that is not unlike a crazed machete-wielding maniac or a horde of rabid zombies—y'all rock!

Finally, I want to thank my friends and family—Carolyn W., Ricky, Sarah, Robert, Mary, Mike L., Steve, Dan, Bobbie, Thomas, Joe, Debra, Joey, Lauren, Crystal, Jim, Nicole, Brent, Lucy, Chris, Liz, Dave, Brent, Jr., Theresa A., Theresa B., Heather, Athena, Alexis, and Mike Z.—for their patience, support, and willingness to share mass quantities of caffeine and chocolate. If I've forgotten anyone, it wasn't intentional, and you know who you are and how much I appreciate you. However, the most special of thanks are reserved for two people.

Mom—thanks for encouraging me from a young age both to be creative and to understand the value of having "a real job." You were my earliest reader, critic, and supporter when I was a kid and making up my own stories—complete with dialogue for you! You're the best, and I love you!

Mark—you've stuck by me through the shadows as well as the light. I could never name all the ways in which you supported me and this book. You read pages. You cooked. You looked after the cats. You brought me mochas when I needed a boost and flowers when I forgot to stop and smell the roses. You saw me on the bad days as well as on the good, and you're still here. I couldn't have gotten this far without you. Thanks, babe, and I love you!

BLOOD
LAW

prologue

SIX LIFELESS EYES FOLLOWED HIM, SILENT WITNESSES WHO would never share their stories, never reveal his secrets.

He tried to ignore their accusing stares by turning his back to them, but six pinpoints of heated malice bore into him as he swung the hammer. Each strike drove the sharpened cross through layers of flesh and bone to pierce the still heart of his latest victim.

No, he shouldn't call it a victim. It was nothing to him. It wasn't even human. It, and others like it, would pay for their crimes. Crimes committed against him, his family, and against God himself.

Those bastards would pay for what they had done to Claire. He would see to that.

The final blow landed, and the hammer fell to the blood-soaked cement floor with a dull thud, splashing drops of congealing blood onto his already stained work boots. He stared at his handiwork. It was perfect, just like the others. He wiped a bloody hand across his sweating brow and smiled.

"That bitch'll never figure this out," he said, turning to his mute audience. "Not until it's too late, anyway."

Six lifeless eyes stared at him in adoration. Three mouths opened in a silent chorus, singing his praises, as he waltzed to a tune of his own design with the memory of his beloved Claire.

october 13

ALEXANDRA SABIAN HATED CEMETERIES. DURING HER
twenty-plus years as an Enforcer with the Federal Bureau of Preternatural Investigation, she'd been in far
too many. Some thought cemeteries were calm and
peaceful places, but for her it was like stepping into a
waking nightmare.

Blue and white emergency lights strobed across the
landscape, casting strange shadows on the ground.
The pulsing wash created the illusion of movement in
the corners of her eyes, which relentlessly searched for
the shadows that moved against the direction of the
light.

Crime scenes attracted both the living and the dead,
and it was her job to listen to both.

She pulled her shoulder-length auburn hair into
a crude ponytail and secured it with a paper hair cap
similar to what surgeons would wear in an operating
room. She carefully stepped into a disposable Tyvek
jumpsuit and slipped paper foot coverings over her

boots. Preservation of the scene was vital, especially with outdoor sites. In today's world of forensic science, a stray hair or fiber could make or break a case, and this was one case she wanted to get right. The protective gear she donned was to prevent cross-contamination and had the added benefits of rendering the wearer androgynous, giving the appearance of multiple Pillsbury Doughboys prowling the scene.

She signed in her name and badge number with the communications officer responsible for keeping track of everyone who entered and left the scene. Steeling herself against what awaited her on the other side of the yellow tape barrier, she ducked under the barricade and picked her way through the headstones, snapping a pair of latex gloves into place as she walked.

"Murder, my ass," someone said in a raised voice from a group of uniformed officers huddled in the darkness. "Killing vampires should be considered a public service, if you ask me."

Alex recognized the voice as belonging to Harvey Manser, Nassau County's duly elected sheriff and all-around jackass. His dislike of vampires, and even more so of her, was well documented, and the feeling was mutual. Tonight, however, she wasn't in the mood to respond to the obvious bait he provided. She ignored the comment and kept walking.

Even though it'd been forty years since vampires—her people—had revealed themselves to humanity, relations between the two species remained tense. Progress had been made in educating the human population about the difference between real vampires and those portrayed by Hollywood, but some of the old fears remained and combined with the new. She could understand their fear. Suddenly waking up to discover that humanity wasn't the only intelligent life on the planet must have been quite a shock.

Floodlights illuminated the scene, and she blinked against their glare as she joined the group of similarly attired detectives and officers surrounding a freshly discovered body. Centuries of evolution had made her entire race photophobic—a misnomer because they didn't actually fear light. Instead, they experienced varying degrees of eye discomfort or pain, depending on the amount of brightness. Like most vampires, she thought wearing sunglasses during the day was a fair trade for the superior night vision she gained. Not that it helped her much under the glare of police spotlights.

"Alex." A short Doughboy wannabe with a round caramel face broke from the group. "I'm sorry to call you out in the middle of the night like this."

Alex shrugged, already focusing on the scene before her. "Night. Day. Doesn't really matter. It's not like killers punch a time clock, right?"

Lieutenant Tasha Lockwood sighed. "No, I guess not."

As the liaison officer between the human-operated Jefferson Police and Nassau County Sheriff's departments and the FBPI, Tasha had worked closely with Alex for the six years Alex had been living in the tiny southwestern Mississippi town. While neither of them would categorize their relationship as a friendship, they'd built a level of mutual respect and understanding that both found comfortable.

Alex indicated the body with a thrust of her chin. "So, what've you got for me?"

"Same scenario as before," Tasha answered, leading her around the scene's perimeter. "Caucasian male vampire, nude, no signs of defensive wounds on hands or arms, no blood present at the scene, cross-shaped stake driven through the heart, and—"

"No head," Alex finished as they stopped beside a tombstone, in front of which the body lay.

The corpse lay on its back with its arms stretched out at shoulder height, feet bound with bright yellow nylon rope, in a classic crucifix position. The ragged neck stump abutted to the sleek black granite tombstone, so it appeared as though the marker itself was the body's head.

The image of another body, bloodied and lying crumpled beside a gravestone, pushed its way into her consciousness. She closed her eyes and forced the memory to retreat into the darkness of the past once more. Opening her eyes, she looked over the scene and noted the leather pouch draped around the arms of the cross-stake. "Who called it in?"

"Anonymous tip came into the main switchboard at JPD," Tasha answered. "The nine-one-one system automatically logs the numbers of calls received. Switchboard doesn't."

"Photos been taken?"

"Yeah, it's all yours."

Alex skirted around the tombstone, careful not to

disturb the body's position, and knelt beside it, inhaling deeply. A vampire's sense of smell was ten times that of a human, and she found a complex kaleidoscope of scents: the cleanness of pine from the trees hidden in the darkness beyond the floodlights. The earthy smells of a nearby freshly dug grave. The stink of sweat mixed with adrenaline from the humans moving at the periphery of her vision. Leaning close to the corpse, she inhaled again and fought the urge to sneeze. "Body smells of decay and a faint trace of ammonia."

"Ammonia?" Tasha echoed. "Didn't you say the same about the other bodies?"

"According to the ME's report, our killer scrubbed the bodies with an ammonia mixture, presumably to limit the amount of evidence we could gain. It also keeps initial insect activity to a minimum."

"Crap. Well, that makes our job all the more difficult."

"Yeah, but it also tells us that our subject has at least a working knowledge of forensics, which is one more reason for us to be careful when handling the scene." Plucking the leather pouch from the cross-stake, Alex pried the cords open and dumped the contents into her gloved hand. A golden wedding band. A Mississippi driver's license. Two bloodstained pieces of what appeared to be ivory.

"Are those teeth?" Tasha asked, peering over Alex's shoulder.

"Fangs," she said, poking them with her gloved finger. Disgust rose within her. Vampires didn't grow fangs until puberty, when hormonal changes forced the body to undergo its physical transformation from child to adult, and they were permanent dental fixtures, not the retractable kind favored by film and fiction. Until that time, human and vampire children were virtually indistinguishable. Defanging a vampire was the equivalent of forcibly castrating a human—a brutal practice that was reported all too frequently.

She dropped the fangs back into the leather pouch and examined the ring. It was a plain golden band with no inscription or other identifying marks. She checked the corpse's left hand and saw a clear delineation in the skin coloration of the third finger that matched the width of the band. "Our victim was married," she said, and added the ring to the pouch.

"Interesting," Tasha said. "Our last vic was single."

Four days prior, Alex and Tasha had worked a similar scene across town. The body of Grant Williams, an employee of Phancy Photos Studio and Video, was discovered in a loading bay at Kellner Hardware. Williams had been positioned in the same manner, and the pouch draped over his cross-stake contained fangs, a blood-smeared photo of the victim and his girlfriend, and his driver's license. A tattoo on his lower back had helped them confirm his identity.

However, Williams wasn't the first body. Nine days before, a startled security guard at a rest stop north of town had found the body of an as-yet-unidentified vampire in one of the men's room stalls.

Alex held the new license in her hand, turning it toward the light. "Eric Stromheimer, age ninety-seven, address is four thirteen Cork Lane." She glanced at Tasha. "He's local, just like Williams."

"You'll notify the family?"

"I hate this shit." Alex slipped the driver's license back into the pouch. Notifying families that a loved one was dead was never easy, and when that loved one had been murdered, it was even worse. She stood and slowly began searching the ground around the body for anything that appeared out of place.

"Evening, ladies," a young man pulling a gurney said as he approached.

"Hey, Jeff," Alex replied without glancing up.

"May I be the first to say that the marshmallow-man look is not flattering on either of you?" Jeffery Stringer, assistant medical examiner for Nassau County, announced with a broad grin.

Tasha launched into a lecture about proper conduct at a crime scene, to which Jeff alternately smirked and chuckled, and Alex rolled her eyes. Twenty-three, long-limbed and skinny, and with delusions of being a ladies' man bouncing in his head, she knew Jeff was more talk than action, and even though his comments often bordered on inappropriate, she just as often found he brought a much-needed levity to an otherwise gruesome occasion.

"Besides"—Tasha was wrapping up her lecture and glancing at her watch—"how can you possibly be so damn chipper standing in a graveyard on a weeknight?"

Jeff grinned as he laid out a black body bag next to their victim. "Caffeine, sugar, and sex. Not necessarily in that order."

Tasha groaned and shook her head.

Alex snorted and paused in her search. "That's more information than I needed, Jeff."

He shrugged and worked a pair of latex gloves over his long fingers. "The lieutenant asked."

Alex chuckled and resumed her search of the surrounding area. She circled the perimeter marked by the tape and on each subsequent pass moved closer to the center point—Eric Stromheimer's headless body.

Jeff whistled softly as he squatted beside the headstone for a closer look. "Another decap for your collection, huh, Alex?"

"I'd prefer the collection to end with three, thank you."

"So would Doc Hancock." Jeff rose and grabbed a large case from the gurney. "By the way, I called him, and he's not going to be happy if this interferes with his New Orleans plans this weekend."

"Granddaughter's wedding?" Tasha asked.

Jeff nodded. "He said if he misses seeing her walk down the aisle, then he was going on strike. In the meantime, he'd be able to take a look at your latest acquisition in the morning."

"Great," Alex muttered. "That means he should have the autopsy done by the time the cavalry arrives."

"Cavalry?" Tasha faced her. "What cavalry?"

"I called FBPI headquarters after Doc Hancock gave his findings on our last victim. A couple of forensic techs and a mobile lab will be here tomorrow. Once they arrive, we'll be able to process evidence quicker."

"Thanks for the heads-up." Irritation added a hard

edge to Tasha's words. "As the liaison officer between the Bureau and local enforcement, I'd like to know these things in advance."

Alex frowned at the detective. "Sorry, Tasha, but between notifying the Williams family, tracking suspects, and all the corpses piling up, I guess it slipped my mind."

"You don't have to be snarky. I'm asking for a little communication, that's all."

Alex could understand Tasha's annoyance, but not telling her of the mobile lab's arrival earlier had been an honest mistake. She'd been surprised by Chief Enforcer Damian Alberez's willingness to send the lab to Jefferson. The Bureau had three mobile labs, and all were precious commodities, usually assigned to large or high-priority cases. The fact that he'd agreed to send one to Jefferson for only two bodies—now three—made her uneasy and left her wondering what Damian knew that she didn't.

Her footsteps slowed and then stilled as something in the grass beside an adjacent tombstone caught her eye. She squatted beside the marker for a closer look and called to the others over her shoulder. "I need tweezers and a small evidence envelope."

Tasha appeared at her shoulder. "Find something?"

Alex accepted a tiny manila envelope and a pair of long tweezers that looked more like small tongs from Jeff. Kneeling down, she pointed to a wad of paper and waited as he snapped a series of pictures with a digital camera before seizing the tiny ball with her tweezers.

She held it up for closer inspection. "Looks like a gum wrapper."

"A gum wrapper isn't that unusual," Tasha said. "Considering we're in a publicly accessible area, it could belong to anyone."

Alex moved it below her nose and inhaled.

"Smell anything?"

"No, but this is the one thing close to the body that was also near the others."

"Are you thinking the killer dropped it?"

"It may be nothing, and it may be just the thing we need to break the case." She slipped the wad into the envelope, sealed and labeled it, and handed both to Jeff.

Alex stifled a yawn but was unable to avoid a full body stretch as she stood. Even though the night was young and dawn hours away, she could see the subtly shifting colors along the eastern skyline and feel the changes in the air.

Microcurrents swirled around her. Their molecules vibrated in response to the gradual changes in the sun's and moon's positions in the sky. Shadows faded from black to gray in tiny increments too faint for human eyes to detect.

One shadow danced along the edges of her vision, drifting against the slight breeze that caressed her cheek. The shadow elongated, seemed to take on more mass, then quiver and fade, becoming less distinct. It moved away from the floodlights, returning to the darkness.

Alex recognized the shadow as one of the unquiet spirits haunting the cemetery. Most were harmless and unseen to human eyes. But she wasn't human, and her own close encounter with death six years previously had heightened her awareness of the spirit realm. She often wondered if she'd be able to see them at all if it weren't for her innate empathic abilities and her talent for psychometry—the ability to gain knowledge and visions of past events through physical contact with objects, including bodies such as the one she now left behind her—a gift she'd possessed since birth, and a rarity among vampires. More than once she'd wished for the ability to control her talents, to direct them and use them to aid in her work as an Enforcer. Unfortunately, control was something she lacked, and her visions of the past came at random and in disjointed fragments, leaving her to muddle through the interpretations.

She pushed all thoughts of the shadows aside, and watched Jeff as he placed paper bags over Eric Stromheimer's hands to preserve any trace evidence that might be present. However, a cursory look earlier had shown no visible signs of trace under his fingernails. She could only hope that once the mobile lab arrived, the techs would be able to find something usable.

Alex rummaged through Jeff's kit and found two small plastic evidence bags. Once again she opened the leather pouch that had been draped around the cross-stake and inserted Stromheimer's driver's license into one bag and his wedding ring into the other. The fangs remained in the pouch and would be sent on to the ME's office with the body. As she labeled the bags to establish a chain of evidence, her stomach rumbled loudly and she sighed.

"Sounds like someone's in need of a break."

Jeff's voice carried more than a hint of humor, and Alex blushed. "Yeah, I guess so."

The wind shifted and carried the smell of blood to her. Her eyes found and lingered on the bloody stump that once supported a head, and she licked her lips. Her gaze shifted from the body to Jeff, locking onto the young man's neck and the pulsing vein beneath the surface. Her stomach rumbled again.

"Whoa." Tasha's voice intruded into Alex's mind as plainly as the woman's hand now latched on to her arm. "I think it's time for you to go."

Alex focused on Tasha's face. The detective's caramel skin pulsed with life, and Alex's eyes slid involuntarily to the woman's neck. She pulled away, forcing herself to look at the ground. "Yeah, I think you're right."

"I'll wrap things up here."

Alex nodded, picked up the two plastic bags containing the driver's license and ring, and headed for the yellow tape barrier. She removed her protective gear as she made the trek back to the scene's entry point. She dropped the clothing items into a bag provided by the communications officer and signed out, indicating that she retained possession of the two items now nestled in the inner pocket of her leather jacket.

Human officers huddled in the strobing wash of blue and white lights, stealing furtive glances and whispering as she passed. Being the only Enforcer assigned to police Jefferson's vampire population made her a minor celebrity, as if her name alone wasn't enough.

She was the youngest child and only daughter of

Bernard Sabian, whose brutal murder in the spring of 1968 in Louisville, Kentucky, had led to vampires announcing their presence to humanity after centuries of secrecy. She'd been five when her father's decapitated body was found with a wooden stake through his heart. Bernard Sabian had become an instant martyr to the vampires, and the community as a whole had taken up the rallying cry of "Never again." They offered up Alex, along with her older brother and their mother, as the paramount image of lives shattered by violence, ignorance, and hatred.

But seven years later, the Braxton Bill, named for the senator who introduced it to Congress, passed and vampires became legally recognized citizens of the United States. Once the human government finally gave them equal protection under the law, the Sabians were forced out of the spotlight. Bernard Sabian and his family had served their purposes. The vampire community gave them pats on the back and quietly shuffled them off to relative obscurity, which suited the Sabians just fine. Seven years after Bernard's death, his family had finally been allowed to grieve, but Alex's father's murder still haunted her.

She hurried past the final group of officers. The scent of fear and adrenaline drifted up from the crowd and spiked her oncoming blood-hunger. Holding her breath, she trotted the last few yards to her Jeep and climbed inside.

Her hands shook as she reached into the glove compartment. It'd been three days since she'd properly slaked her blood-hunger. If she didn't do it soon, the tremors would worsen. Her concentration would start to slip. The hunger would gnaw at her until it consumed her thoughts, and the spiral would deepen, drawing her down, down, down, into madness.

A triumphant cry escaped her lips when she shook the carton she'd pulled from the glove box and she heard the distinctive rattle within. She ripped open the carton and dumped the single vial into her hand.

Thick liquids—one clear and the other a pale pink—sloshed within the tube. She applied enough pressure to the tube to rupture the thin gelatin barrier between the liquids and shook it to combine them. The mixture turned a dark red, and the chemical reaction warmed the new compound until it matched her body's temperature. She ripped the black stopper from the tube and greedily drank its contents.

The fluid coated her tongue and throat like oil. A metallic tang failed to completely cover the bitter taste of chemicals.

Alex sucked the last drop from the tube and then exhaled loudly, like a swimmer surfacing from a deep dive. She hated Vlad's Tears, the synthetic blood product vampires used as a stopgap measure when a human donor was unavailable. It wouldn't rid her of the blood-hunger, only delay it for a time. She shoved the drained tube back into its box. At least her hands had stopped trembling.

She cranked up her Jeep and rolled down her window, allowing the cool air to permeate the suddenly warm interior. The scent of pines, adrenaline, and blood wafted to her on the night breeze, and she felt a sharp hunger pang in her belly.

"Damn it," she muttered, and threw the SUV into gear. Only when she was out of the cemetery and away from humans did she allow herself to breathe freely.

Varik Baudelaire peered through the window inset in his Victorian-style home's front door and swore softly before thumbing the latch on the dead bolt. The door swung open and he stared at the huge black mass standing on his porch. "What the hell do you want?"

"Nice to see you, too," Damian Alberez, Chief Enforcer for the Federal Bureau of Preternatural Investigation, said in a rumbling bass voice. "You going to invite me in?"

"Do I have a choice?"

"Not really."

Varik stepped back, holding the door wide, and gestured for the vampire to enter.

Damian ducked his bald head beneath the stained-glass transom and entered the foyer. Standing a few inches over seven feet with a barrel chest and biceps nearly as large as Varik's thighs, he was an imposing figure long before he ever flashed his fangs. He tapped the edge of a file against one meaty palm. "We need to talk."

"Well, I didn't think you were here for milk and cookies." Varik closed the door, slipped around his oldest friend, and passed through an open archway leading to the front parlor.

He'd been slowly restoring the Victorian manor on

the outskirts of Louisville in the five years since his retirement from the Bureau. Working on the house gave
him something to do besides dwell on the past and the
woulda-coulda-shouldas of his life. While much of the
first floor was complete, the second floor was in varying
stages of demolition and reconstruction.

On the first floor, he'd retained the original mold-
ings around the dormant fireplace and high ceilings
throughout, and the heart-of-pine wooden floors would
glow a warm gold in the sunlight. Much of the home's
color scheme remained true to the Victorian era, but
the walls of the front parlor were painted a light gray
and the furnishings a mixture of burgundies, grays, and
creams—colors that brought him comfort.

Comfort he wished he felt as he settled into a wing-
back chair and watched as Damian perched on the edge
of a sleek burgundy leather sofa. "So, to what do I—"

Damian slid the file he held across the glass-top coffee table to Varik.

He stared at the FBPI seal emblazoned on the folder
but made no move to pick it up. He met Damian's steady
gaze and shook his head. "I'm not—"

"Pick it up. Look at it."

Varik sighed and grabbed the file. He flipped it open
and was greeted with a full-color photo of a decapitated
corpse—legs bound with yellow nylon rope, arms outstretched, and a cross-shaped stake driven through its
chest. More photos followed. Wide-angle shots of a loading bay. Close-ups of the cross-stake. Another wide view
of the scene, with a woman standing beside the body, a
mix of horror and recognition on her face. A yawning

pit opened beneath him, threatening to devour him, and he closed the file. "When were these taken?"

"Four days ago."

Varik glanced at the folder in his hands. His heart now pounded in his chest, and it sounded like a drumbeat in the stillness of the room.

"*She* needs you," Damian said softly.

"Did she ask for me?"

"No, she asked for a mobile lab and two forensic techs."

Varik smirked. "Then she doesn't need *me*."

Light from a tableside lamp seemed to be absorbed by the blue-black of Damian's ebony skin, giving him the appearance of a humanoid black hole. He nodded toward the file. "That was the second. The first showed up over a week ago, and another body was discovered about an hour ago in a cemetery."

"You can't possibly think this"—Varik held up the folder—"has anything to do with Bernard's murder."

Damian shrugged. "A good investigator doesn't rule out anything."

Varik tossed the file onto the table and rose to pace to the archway. When he turned, he spread his arms wide. "Alex hasn't asked for me. After—" He paused, fighting the flood of memories that crowded his mind. He pulled in a deep cleansing breath and released it slowly. "After what happened between us, she *wouldn't* ask for me, even if she did think I could be of some use."

"She's in over her head."

He threw his hands up in frustration. "I'm *retired*!

Don't you understand that? I don't work for you any-more."

Damian drew himself up to his full height and pro-duced a silver badge and identification card from a pants pocket. He set them both on top of the file. "I took the liberty of reinstating you with full pay and benefits—Director of Special Operations assigned to the Jefferson, Mississippi, field office."

"Damian—"

"Mobile lab leaves from Bureau headquarters in two hours." Damian rounded the coffee table and strode toward him. He paused as he drew even with Varik and gave him a meaningful stare. "I expect you to be there and ready to go to Jefferson tonight," he said, and then continued toward the door.

"Do I have a choice?"

Damian's coal-black eyes settled on him, and the vampire smiled, showing the full extent of his fangs. "Not really."

The door closed behind Damian, and Varik crossed to the coffee table and slid the folder from under the badge and ID card. He pulled out the photo showing the entire crime scene, dropped the file on the table, and sank onto the sofa as he studied the woman in the picture.

Alexandra Sabian stood beside a vampire's corpse, wind billowing her hair around her face, a moment frozen in time. Her emerald-green eyes, visible in the wash of lights from the loading bay, seemed to stare back at him. He knew all too well that the past had a habit of intruding on the present. Sometimes it was for the best, but more often it was better for the past to remain in the past.

Now he had an opportunity to atone for some of his past by intruding on Alex's present, something he'd sworn he'd never do unless she asked for him, which she hadn't. But if by going to Jefferson he kept part of her past where it belonged, he owed it to the Sabian family to try.

"Ready or not, here I come," he said, and shoved the photo back into the file before heading upstairs to pack.

october 14

"I'M SORRY FOR YOUR LOSS," ALEX SAID, RETURNING THE evidence bag containing Eric Stromheimer's wedding ring to her jacket's inside pocket.

Natalie Stromheimer hid her face behind her hands and sobbed.

Alex looked away from the woman's grief. It was a raw, private emotion not meant to be viewed, but she'd seen others in the same state. They all reminded her of her own loss, a constant ache deep inside her that never went away.

She studied the tidy family room adjacent to a spotless kitchen. Plush carpet felt springy beneath her hiking boots. Floral pillows added a touch of brightness to the mocha-colored sofa upon which a distraught Mrs. Stromheimer wept. The neutral beige walls were lined with photos: A black-and-white photo of Eric and Natalie on their wedding day. Natalie holding an infant in her arms. Snapshots of ball games, birthday parties, and vacations. A portrait of the Stromheimers with a gangly teenage son and a shaggy dog at their feet. Evidence of the all-American suburban family who thought violence was something that happened to "other people."

She'd seen another example of domestic bliss shattered by violence in the small town—the only unsolved case on her books. Claire Black had been killed a couple of years after Alex arrived in Jefferson. She had worked the case, exhausted all her leads, until the trail fell cold.

Irritated with herself, she turned her attention back to the new widow in front of her and was startled to find that a grayish-white mist had settled beside Natalie and seemed to enshroud her thin shoulders. Natalie appeared not to notice the wispy fog surrounding her, and then Alex understood. The spirit of Eric Stromheimer had found its way home. Natalie couldn't see or feel the mist around her, but later, when her mind gave out and she fell into an exhausted sleep, her subconscious would replay the message being imparted now. Alex was witnessing a husband's final farewell.

"Mrs. Stromheimer," she said softly. She cleared her throat and leaned forward in her chair. "I know this is a difficult time, but I need to ask you a few questions about Eric."

The mist quivered and roiled like a gathering cloud as Natalie shifted her position, smoothing her dark hair away from her reddened face. "Of-of course," she sniffled. "I'll d-do what I can."

"When was the last time you saw your husband?"

"Two days ago, when he left for work." Natalie brushed a tear from her cheek. "He works offshore as a roughneck on an oil rig."

"Is that why you didn't report him missing?"

"He usually called when he reached the platform, but sometimes, if the weather is bad, I may not hear from him for a few days. I just assumed—" Her voice cracked, and fresh tears leaked from the corners of her closed eyes.

The spirit-mist beside Natalie shivered. Alex gave the woman time to compose herself and studied the undulating vapor. Its edges rippled, lengthened, and took on a vaguely humanoid form before shuddering and returning to a translucent cloud.

She wondered, not for the first time, if her father had visited her mother in the same way after his death. Had he come to her? She remembered the bizarre dreams that had plagued her sleep soon after her father's funeral. Endless mazes. Hallways filled with doors. Strangers begging for her help. Then one night, the dreams stopped.

"I don't understand how this happened," Natalie whispered, pulling Alex's thoughts back to the present. "Why would someone do this to Eric? He worked hard. He was kind and gentle. He never harmed anyone!"

Alex watched the cloud slip from the sofa and drift on an invisible breeze to hover over her and Natalie's heads.

"Eric was a good man," Natalie said, anger creeping in to replace the sorrow. "He was a terrific father—oh, God." Her anger evaporated as quickly as it had manifested. "Marshall."

"That's your son?"

"He's at Mississippi State studying engineering."

Natalie's head dropped into her hands once more. "What do I tell him? How do you tell a child his father is dead, murdered?"

Alex clenched her teeth as the memories surfaced. Sunshine. Butterflies. Blood-splattered tombstones. A child's scream.

She forced the memories into the darkness of the past and focused on the spirit of Eric Stromheimer floating overhead. The mist pulsed, thinned, and finally dissipated, leaving her alone with a sobbing widow in what was once a cheery family room, and desperately trying to hold back her own tears.

"Whoo-eee," a brunette waitress whooped. "Are you single?"

Varik Baudelaire groaned inwardly, and the two men entering the Waffle House diner behind him snickered. They'd been driving for several hours straight and had finally reached the southern side of Memphis, but they still had a long way to go.

After Damian's visit, he'd packed and left a message with a neighbor that he would be out of town for several days. He'd then driven to FBPI headquarters to meet the mobile lab and the forensic techs, Freddy Haver and Reyes Cott, a duo he'd quickly nicknamed "Beavis and Butt-Head."

Freddy had displayed a level of hero worship upon meeting Varik by stating he'd read all of Varik's case files—a statement he'd found hard to believe, since most of the cases he'd worked before his retirement in 2004 were still considered classified, according to FBPI standards. Despite his fondness for gushing, Freddy seemed to recognize that his behavior overstepped boundaries and had backed off.

However, Reyes had annoyed him from the start by drooling over Varik's Corvette and asking, "Dude, how many hoochies have you scored with this thing?" when they were introduced. His behavior progressively worsened during their travels, to the point that Varik found himself entertaining violent thoughts toward the younger vampire.

Damian assured him that Reyes was one of the Bureau's best trace evidence and latent print analysts. He was willing to trust Damian's judgment, but his patience was wearing thin and he wasn't in the mood for the aggressive flirtations of a middle-aged human waitress. Nonetheless, he continued to the elevated bar, eyes on the woman who'd addressed him. The other men settled in a booth on the opposite side of the small diner.

The waitress grinned as he approached, folding her arms on the bar and leaning forward, which effectively tightened her gray uniform's too-small shirt over her too-large bosom.

He mirrored her stance, glancing at her prominently displayed name tag. "Well, Rachel, that depends on who's asking."

She puffed out her chest to the point that Varik believed the buttons on her shirt would litter the floor. "Oh, that would be me, dahlin'," she drawled.

"I see." He slowly removed his denim jacket, aware of the way she stared at his flexing biceps beneath his black button-down shirt. He laid the jacket on one of the raised stools beside him and ran a hand through his long ebony hair, draping it over his shoulder so it brushed the top of his jeans.

Rachel's gaze followed his movements and drifted over his chest, down to his waist, and stopped. "Hey, are you a cop or something?"

He patted the silver badge clipped to the front of his belt. "Enforcer, actually."

Her eyes widened, and her spine straightened.

Varik smiled, showing a hint of fang.

Rachel blanched and fell back two steps.

Freddy and Reyes in the booth across the diner roared with laughter.

Varik snapped his fingers and pointed at them without taking his eyes off the frightened waitress. The laughter ceased, and he picked up his jacket. "So, Rachel, how about a round of coffee, black, for my friends and me?"

She nodded silently.

The forensic techs snickered when he slid onto the bench opposite them a moment later. "Shut up."

"Sorry, sir." Freddy coughed and grew somber.

"First it was those hoochies in the Porsche in Louisville," Reyes said, and used his fingers to keep count. "Then it was the clerk at the gas station in Nashville. Now the waitress here." He shook his head. "Dude, does this happen every time you go somewhere?"

Varik studied the laminated menu on the table before him and tried to ignore the thought of slamming

Reyes's head through the plate-glass window, which played through his mind like a film reel.

"I bet it's the hair," Reyes whispered to Freddy, nudging him in the ribs. "Chicks dig the hair."

"Shut up, Reyes." Freddy nudged him back.

"Have you noticed that *Monsieur* Baudelaire still has a hint of Paris in his Kentucky drawl? Between the hair, the accent, and the car, he's *got* to be getting laid regularly."

"You're talking out of your ass again."

"What do you think, Freddy? I could grow out my hair and fake the accent. Then all I need is the car."

Varik sighed. It was time to end the madness. "You can do all that, but you still won't get the attention."

"Why not?"

"Well, to put it bluntly, Reyes, you're just plain ugly."

Reyes's jaw dropped, revealing a crooked left fang, and his overly large eyes bulged out farther from their sockets.

Varik shrugged. "Sorry, dude."

Freddy cackled, and Reyes slumped in the booth like a man who'd been dealt a death blow.

Rachel arrived with their coffee. She hurriedly set three steaming mugs in front of them and scurried away.

Satisfied to have silenced Reyes at least for a time, Varik sipped his coffee and reveled in the warmth the bitter liquid infused in him as it slid down his throat.

Freddy settled into the corner of the booth as he slurped his coffee, winced, and reached for the container of sugar. He kept his eyes on Varik while pouring sugar into his coffee. "So, what do we know about this case?"

"Not much at this point," Varik answered. "Jefferson is a small town, roughly six thousand in population, and an estimated third to half that number are vampires. The forensic team is limited to a few trained members of the local police department." He took another drink and leaned back with a sigh before continuing.

"At approximately five thirty a.m. on October ninth, the body of Grant Williams was found in one of the loading bays of a hardware store. The positioning of the corpse suggested a ritualistic-style slaying. A similar scenario played out at a rest stop on September thirtieth, only that victim has yet to be identified. Due to the limitations of the local forensic team and now the discovery of a third body, Enforcer Sabian has requested additional personnel in order to conduct a proper investigation. That's where you two lab rats come in."

"Enforcer Sabian?" Reyes echoed, reviving from his momentary stupor. "As in Alexandra Sabian? Bernard Sabian's daughter?"

Varik nodded.

Reyes whistled softly.

Varik folded his arms in front of him. "Do you know her?"

"Only by reputation, and I saw her picture in a Bureau newsletter once. It was part of an article on how she'd busted up a major Midnight ring in Jefferson."

Varik sipped his coffee. He remembered seeing the article. Midnight was a powerful drug that had plagued the vampire population for years. A combination of the human street drug Ecstasy, aspirin, garlic, and animal blood, vampires addicted to Midnight were often violent and highly erratic in their behavior. No one knew how the drug first came to be created, but its effects were undeniable. Aspirin and garlic thinned a vampire's blood and allowed for the Ecstasy to have a greater hallucinogenic effect.

However, it was the animal blood that posed the greatest threat. A genetic quirk left vampires unable to generate enough psychic energy to sustain themselves. Thus, they relied on the residual psychic energy within human blood to keep them from going insane. Animal blood, because its residual energy was more primitive and instinctual in nature, could transform an otherwise healthy vampire into a horror-story lunatic. Combining it with a hallucinogen like Ecstasy was the equivalent of standing in the center of a bonfire while playing Russian roulette. The outcome was guaranteed not to be pretty.

Reyes continued to speak of Alex and slapped Freddy on the shoulder. "Wait until you see her. She's smoking-hot, dude. Red hair, green eyes." He shook his head. "I've always been a sucker for redheads. I may just have to—"

Varik's hand seized the front of Reyes's shirt and pulled him forward. Hot coffee spilled from Reyes's overturned mug and poured over the side of the table. Varik tightened his grip, and his voice was a low snarl. "Let's get something straight here and now. You will show Enforcer Sabian the proper respect once we arrive in Jefferson. If I hear you make *any* inappropriate remarks, I'll rip your fangs out with my bare hands."

Reyes gulped loudly, and Freddy stared at them both with wide eyes.

"Do we understand one another?"

"Yes, sir," Reyes gasped.

Varik shoved him back in his seat. He noticed the diner's employees watching them with a combination of shock and terror. He drained the rest of his coffee and grabbed his jacket as he slid out of the booth. Placing a twenty-dollar bill on the counter beside the register, more than enough to cover the price of their order, he left the diner without saying another word.

Cold air slammed into him, sucking his breath away. He shrugged into his jacket and crossed the empty lot to his black Corvette parked next to a large tour bus–sized RV that served as the FBPI's mobile forensic lab. He leaned against the car's trunk and bowed his head.

Another breeze rustled the dried leaves of a nearby sycamore tree and whipped through his hair. Thoughts of the past swirled through his mind. Memories of his and Alex's life together, the life they should've had, taunted him.

He remembered the hours they had spent with each other during her training. The thrill he'd felt with their first kiss was as fresh to him now fifteen years later as if it'd happened only moments ago. He smiled at the memory of her reaction when he'd asked her to be his wife.

He turned his attention to the night sky. A waning crescent floated in the dark heavens, casting little illumination on the world. Streetlights flooded the darkness and drowned the natural glow of the stars, and he sighed. He and Alex had once enjoyed stargazing as they made plans for their future—a future that had ended six years ago when Alex left Louisville.

The wind continued to whirl around him and for a moment he thought he could still smell her scent, a heady combination of jasmine and vanilla. His skin prickled as he remembered the brush of her fingertips along his back as they made love.

Raised voices from across the parking lot interrupted his thoughts and signaled the approach of Freddy and Reyes.

He pushed the remote button to deactivate the Corvette's alarm. Sliding behind the wheel, he consulted the global positioning display on his cell phone. They were south of Memphis, a few miles into Mississippi, in the town of Horn Lake. From there, the journey was a straight drive south on Interstate 55 to Jefferson, about five to six hours.

Tossing his cell phone onto the passenger seat, his gaze met his own eyes in the rearview mirror, and he sighed.

"You screwed up. She moved on. Deal with it," he said to his reflection.

Freddy and Reyes waved to him to indicate their readiness to depart as they boarded the mobile lab. Moments later, the rumble of the RV's engine penetrated the Corvette's interior, and the muscle car's engine roared to life.

Varik pulled out of the parking lot in front of the mobile lab, gunning his engine as he headed toward the interstate. The car responded, announcing its confidence to all. As he pulled onto the interstate, his only wish was for the butterflies in his stomach to cease their mad dancing long enough for his own confidence to return.

Stephen Sabian's bright blue Dodge pickup glowed beneath the halogen bulb of a streetlamp outside Crimson Swan. Alex hadn't been certain he'd returned from his business trip to Natchez, a town about fifty miles to the west. Seeing his truck eased the rising tension in her shoulders. She could always rely on her brother to chase away the demons that haunted her after visiting a victim's family.

Natalie Stromheimer had been in no condition to be left alone. After asking her a few more questions, Alex waited until a family friend arrived to stay with the widow before leaving. She'd made her way through the quiet town, barely aware of the homes and businesses she passed. Now she killed the Jeep's engine and paused to stare at the brown-and-redbrick structure before her.

Jefferson's only blood bar was designed to resemble a neo-Gothic church and was the vampire community's sanctuary. No humans were allowed inside except for the on-staff donors, a few employees, and those serving as private donors to vampires. The first floor was the actual bar, but the second floor was Stephen's spacious loft-style apartment.

The central cathedral, which would've normally housed the sanctuary and altar within a church, sported a high peak and heavy red-and-black double doors. Two narrow arched windows flanked the entrance and allowed for the only natural light within the bar. Above the entrance, a large round rosette window fed light into the interior of Stephen's apartment. A smaller single-story cathedral stood to the left and held the bar's storeroom, office, and the private blood donor rooms.

The nonfunctional bell tower to the right of the central cathedral held another smaller apartment that Stephen often rented to donors but which she'd occupied for the past two weeks since a fire at her apartment complex had left her homeless. While her unit hadn't been burned, it had sustained heavy smoke and water damage. The complex's manager estimated it would be at least a month before she could return home.

Alex locked up the Jeep and shoved her hands into the pockets of her leather jacket. Aside from her vehicle and Stephen's truck, the bar's lot was deserted, as were the lots of the two adjacent restaurants and the strip mall across the street. Her footsteps echoed in the darkness, punctuating the emptiness she felt within her soul.

She opened one of the massive wooden doors and entered Crimson Swan. High-backed booths with red-and-black leather-upholstered cushions lined the walls. Wooden tables with cherry- and mahogany-inlaid tops were clustered throughout the space. Stained-glass chandeliers hung over every booth, and smaller matching lamps sat in the center of each freestanding table, adding a warm glow to the wood when lit. The large common room was dark and still, with only a single light shining behind the bar opposite the doors.

The vampire behind the bar watched her intently as she strode toward him, eager to satisfy the craving that now consumed her thoughts. He raised one blond eyebrow when she sat down in front of him. "You look like shit."

"Bite me."

Stephen laughed and produced a glass vial filled with blood from beneath the counter. He poured the thick liquid into a shot glass. "Freshly squeezed, just the way you like it."

Alex seized the glass and swallowed the tepid blood in a single gulp. A shudder ran through her as its warmth slid down her throat and across her chest. Her fingertips tingled, and she felt a slow blush warm her cheeks. Her heart skipped a beat, then began to race as adrenaline pumped into her system. She closed her eyes as the flood of memories locked within the blood washed over her.

She heard the laughter of friends and family at a child's birthday party. She smelled the sweet dampness of hay mingled with manure as hands bigger than her own groomed a large gray horse. The hairs on the back of her neck stood on end as the memory of the unknown donor's first kiss filtered through her mind.

The images faded, and Alex licked the last traces of blood from her lips, savoring the salty metallic taste.

"Been a while, huh?" Stephen's drawling voice acted like a balm to her irritated mind and brought her back to the present.

"Three days," she whispered hoarsely, grinding the heels of her palms against her eyes.

"I'm surprised you made it that long."

"I was using Vlad's Tears." Alex folded her arms on the bar and rested her forehead against them. The surge of adrenaline from the blood was already fading. Sleep pulled at her, enticing her to follow it.

"Vlad's Tears is synthetic blood, Alex. It won't stop the hunger, only delay it."

Sleep danced away with his words. Sitting up, she glared at her brother. "I'm well aware of that, but I didn't have a choice."

"You need to take better care of yourself. Take a break once in a while."

"Tell that to the three bodies lying in the morgue."

"Three?"

She nodded.

"Shit."

"Yeah," Alex sighed. "My thoughts exactly."

"All the same as Dad?"

"Nearly identical."

The siblings lapsed into silence, lost in their own memories.

Stephen finally shook himself and asked, "Have you been to see the family?"

"Wife and a son in college. She doesn't know how she's going to tell the son."

"She'll figure it out. Mom did."

"I don't like this, Stephen. I've got a really bad feeling about these murders."

"You think they're related to Dad's?"

"I don't know, but I can't rule it out, can I? There are simply too many coincidences, and you know how I feel about coincidences."

Stephen grabbed the drained glass and turned his back. The glass rattled loudly as he dropped it into a small sink. An uncomfortable silence settled between them.

Resting her chin in the palm of one hand, she yawned and drummed the fingers of her other hand on the bar. She didn't believe in coincidences. She'd seen too much in her career as an Enforcer to accept chance as a rationalization for events. Combine experience with her innate talents and coincidence swiftly became an invalid explanation for her.

Despite her efforts to maintain a tight control of the facts regarding the murders, rumors had spread quickly through the vampire community. Even though news of Grant Williams's decapitation had spread throughout the town, speculation surrounding the similarities to her father's murder had remained within the vampire population. While they shared media outlets with humans, vampires were not as forthcoming with details of community happenings, especially crime. Only the populace's intense desire for privacy kept it from spreading. Vampires were like Las Vegas: what happened in the community stayed within the community. She counted on their private nature to keep the information from the human media, at least for now.

Her gaze slid along the bar's gleaming black granite top to the far wall. A black-and-white poster of Bela Lugosi, dressed as Count Dracula, descending a winding stone stairway, hung over the silent coin-operated juke-box. Other framed images of classic movie monsters—a shared love between her and Stephen—decorated the Swan's walls, but Lugosi was her favorite. The tuxedo-wearing actor reminded Alex of her father. Her eyes drooped closed as she thought of him.

Bernard Sabian had smelled of the chalk he used during his history lectures at the University of Louisville, tobacco from the cigars he smoked in his campus office but never at home, and coffee, which he drank black. He'd been born in southern Ireland in the early 1400s, and even after centuries of living in the United States, he'd never lost his accent.

Like many older vampires, especially those who worked closely with humans, her father had filed down and capped his fangs so as to appear human. She re-membered the weekly trips to the local hospital to ob-tain a covert blood supply drawn from patients and when he passed out at the hospital's back door. While he'd never worn a tux or an opera cape that Alex could remember, her father had possessed the same grace and charismatic presence captured in the classic Lugosi image, and she'd loved him unconditionally.

"Hey," Stephen said, gently shaking her shoulder.

"Hmm?" Alex glanced at her surroundings, momen-tarily forgetting where she was.

"If you're going to snore, you should go up to bed."

"I don't snore." Alex hid a yawn behind her hand and then checked her watch. "You're up late."

"That's because I didn't get back from Natchez until about an hour ago."

"A meeting with potential investors ran until the wee hours of the morning?" Stephen worked hard to build Crimson Swan into a success and was now looking to expand it into a franchise. Investors would go a long way in helping him realize his newfound dream.

"It does when the investors want to negotiate over the blackjack table at a casino."

"Lucky you."

"Five hundred bucks and three investors lucky."

"That's great," Alex yawned.

"Dealer was cute, but I guess my luck ran out."

"Lucky for Janet."

He grinned, and his pale blue eyes sparkled mischievously. "She thought so when I left her place."

Stephen had been dating one of the part-time bartenders at Crimson Swan, Janet Klein, for only a few months, but Alex thought her brother was truly smitten with the dark-haired human, despite his jests. He visited her regularly and even picked her up and drove her home most nights she worked, just to spend a few minutes "off the clock" with her.

Alex rolled her eyes and slipped off her stool. "Whatever. I'm going to bed."

Stephen began wiping down the bar. "All right. I'll be up soon. Just need to finish a few things in the office."

She nodded, trying unsuccessfully to stifle another yawn. "G'night."

He waved to her as she rounded the bar and entered a restricted area of the building.

Two staircases branched from a central foyer accessible from a back door in the bell tower. The stairs to the left led to Stephen's loft, and those to the right to the tower apartment. Alex trudged up the tower stairs, removing her jacket as she climbed. Four flights of steps twisted back on themselves before revealing a single door at the top. She fished her keys from her pocket and entered the apartment.

She draped her jacket over the back of a rented leather sofa and hung her keys on a peg beside the door. The switch for the floor lamp she'd borrowed from Stephen clicked on. She squinted against the light and looked around at her temporary home.

Clothes spilled from boxes strewn around the combination living and dining room. A folding card table and two collapsible metal-and-cloth chairs in the dining area separated the living space from the tiny galley kitchen. Her bed—another rental, with the head abutted to the half-wall separating the kitchen from the bedroom—was half hidden by a shoji screen. The only other walls in the studio-style apartment encased the bathroom on the far side of the bedroom.

A warm, furry body brushed against her legs, followed by a large black-and-tan Maine coon cat appearing on the back of the sofa beside her. He brushed his head against her belly, leaving a swath of stray hairs across her black shirt.

"Hey, Dweezil." She scratched behind his ears with one hand and brushed at the hairs with the other. The cat leaned into her hand and purred in response. "Did you hold down the fort while I was gone?"

Dweezil yawned and stretched before jumping off the sofa and trotting behind the screen.

Alex followed, shedding clothes as she walked. Depositing her sidearm and badge on the table beside the bed, she noted the cat's obvious comfort as he lay curled in a tight ball on her pillow. "Keep it warm for me," she said, as she padded naked into the bathroom.

Dweezil half opened one eye and flicked an ear in her direction.

She brushed out her auburn hair and prepared for bed. Slipping an old University of Louisville T-shirt over her head, her hand grazed the long jagged scar on her neck. Her fingers traced the old wound where it ran diagonally from her left ear to her collarbone. The edges nearest her collarbone were puckered, but the remainder was a slick hardness, a constant reminder of a past better left forgotten.

She forced her hand away and exited the room. She turned off the floor lamp and crept through the darkness to the bed.

Dweezil chirped his annoyance at having to share the space.

Alex wrapped the cat in her arms and curled her body around him. His warmth and the vibrations of his purring relaxed her, driving away the memories that threatened the edges of her consciousness. She released her breath in an explosive puff, and sleep claimed her as soon as she closed her eyes.

three

THE NASSAU COUNTY MUNICIPAL CENTER COVERED AN entire city block in the heart of downtown Jefferson. The multibuilding complex housed the metro police force as well as the sheriff's department and the central jail, although county and metro detainees were housed in separate areas. In addition to law enforcement, all courts and official government offices for the city and county were encompassed by the multiplex. The sun's morning rays filtered through the bare branches of the massive live oaks that lined the downtown streets and defined the city center as the green jeweled heart of the growing town. Lieutenant Tasha Lockwood had always loved the charm and grace inherent in the older buildings and wide streets surrounding the Municipal Center.

Having been born in Jefferson and growing up in the era after the vampires went public, Tasha considered herself fairly open-minded toward vampires, but that didn't mean she wasn't cautious around them. She refused to allow fear to rule her life, which was why she'd volunteered to act as the liaison officer between human law enforcement and the FBPI when Alexandra Sabian moved to Jefferson. Over time she'd gained a great deal of respect for Alex, and the two had settled into a comfortable working relationship.

She stood alongside several members of both the metro police force and sheriff's department on the Municipal Center's steps and watched the largest RV she'd ever seen try to navigate the turn off a side street into the complex's parking lot. The other officers either watched mutely or laughed and joked about the "crazy damn vamps and their big-assed tour bus."

Tasha kept her arms folded in front of her and hoped no one noticed the sweat that beaded her upper lip. Alex had said only two forensic techs were coming, but the mobile lab that settled into a corner of the parking lot looked as though it could easily house a dozen or more.

She couldn't help but feel that her job as liaison officer was about to become much more difficult.

A sleek black Corvette bounced into the lot behind the RV, earning whistles and murmurs of appreciation from many of the men, and pulled into a space near the steps that was reserved for official vehicles. The door swung open, and even from a distance, Tasha could tell the driver was a vampire. She could feel his gaze sweeping the crowd on the steps from behind his dark sunglasses. He seemed to pause when he came to her, and a chill slithered down her spine. Even the officers around her who'd been laughing and talking moments before had grown quiet.

The mobile lab's air brakes hissed loudly. Tasha and several others jumped, startled by the sudden fracturing of the silence. The Corvette's driver smirked and walked toward the lab. His movements were the fluid motions of someone accustomed to authority and power combined with a predator's grace. Two men emerged from the far side of the RV and met him.

"Who the fuck is that?" Harvey Manser asked from beside her.

Tasha glanced up at the balding man. "Beats the hell out of me. Alex said the Bureau was sending techs. She didn't mention the other one."

Harvey took a drag on his cigarette. Smoke billowed from his thin lips as he spoke. "I told you before, Lieutenant, vamps aren't to be trusted."

She waved away the smoke that drifted into her face. "Maybe Alex doesn't know about him."

"Why would they keep one of their own in the dark?"

Tasha shrugged. She didn't know how to respond to that.

"Think about it. Sabian lied about the number of bloodsuckers the feds were sending. Who's to say she's not lying about a bunch of other shit?"

"Well, you'd know a thing or two about lying, wouldn't you, Harvey?"

He puffed on his cigarette. "I don't know what you mean."

"Don't play innocent with me. The fire at Oak Tree

Apartments, the one that damaged Alex's unit—I know you know more about that than you've reported."

"I've told you everything I know."

"You were the first officer on the scene. How is it that you beat both metro and the fire department there?"

Harvey dropped his cigarette butt to the brick-lined walkway and ground it beneath his heel. "Just lucky, I guess."

Tasha's eyes narrowed. "Lucky, my ass."

She'd known Harvey for a long time and had never known him to arrive first on a scene. The fire had broken out in an unoccupied apartment and spread quickly to several surrounding units. Until the fire marshal ruled on a cause for the blaze, Tasha had only suspicions and no evidence to support them.

"You may want to watch that ass of yours, Lieutenant, because here comes your new vamp." He winked at her, jogged down the Municipal Center steps, and disappeared around the corner that led to his department's parking lot.

Tasha watched the vampire striding toward her. Long black hair fell over one shoulder to brush the waistband of his jeans as he moved. A streak of gray along his left temple marked him as a vampire who'd seen at least one century pass. Alex had told her once that vampires started "going gray" only after they'd reached at least one hundred years. He removed his sunglasses as he mounted the stairs, revealing eyes the color of dark chocolate rimmed in gold, and her breath caught in her throat.

"Lieutenant Lockwood?" The man's voice was low and held a seductive silkiness.

Tasha nodded, unable to speak.

"I'm Enforcer Varik Baudelaire," he said, showing his silver badge and identification while extending his opposite hand in greeting. He smiled and showed a hint of fang.

Shaking herself out of her trance, Tasha clasped his hand. Even though she stood in a public area surrounded by other officers, she could feel her skin crawling in response to an old fear. "I wasn't aware that Alex was bringing in another Enforcer."

"Enforcer Sabian doesn't know that I'm here." He dropped her hand. "Yet."

Tasha forced herself to look into his eyes and not to stare at his fangs. Her heart rate increased sharply, and she knew he could hear it as well as smell the adrenaline leaking into her bloodstream. "I see."

"The FBPI is interested in solving these murders quickly, which I'm certain you can appreciate."

The fight-or-flight response gripped her body, and she struggled to remain calm as she nodded.

"My superiors sent me here to check on the investigation's progress and lend whatever assistance I can."

"You mean they sent you here to spy on Alex."

Another smile tugged at the corners of his mouth. "That's one way of looking at it, yes."

Tasha didn't know much about the inner workings of the vampires' federal watchdog agency, but she'd been a cop long enough to know that sending an unannounced "assistant" to an active investigation meant trouble. She fought through her nerves to ask, "Is the Bureau planning to replace Alex?"

"Not at the moment, but we do have growing concerns about the case. Due to the nature of death and the obvious violence shown in the commission of the crimes, you can understand why we can't afford to let this investigation become a political hotbed."

"Hate crimes will always be a political hotbed."

"All the more reason to resolve the matter quickly."

Tasha eyed the Enforcer, making mental notes. She decided that he wasn't handsome. He was beautiful. His features didn't hold the rugged look of some men but maintained a youthful softness. The slight graying of his hair gave him the appearance of someone in his mid-thirties, and his physique was that of someone who took pride in his appearance. She could see the muscles rippling beneath his clothing—muscles that could easily tear her limb from limb if he desired. "So, why come to me first?"

"I was hoping that you could fill me in on the latest before I spoke with Enforcer Sabian. Has an autopsy been performed on the victim found last night?"

"Not yet, but I doubt that we'll learn anything beyond what we already know."

Varik toyed with the buttons of his denim jacket. "Postmortem decapitation and staking with no discernible cause of death."

"Exactly."

"How is the killer incapacitating his victims?"

"That's the part we don't know." Tasha crossed her

arms in front of her. "But I have to be honest, Enforcer Baudelaire, I'm not very comfortable with the idea of going behind Alex's back on this investigation. I would feel better about discussing this with you if I had her approval. She's put in a hell of a lot of hours, even risking blood-hunger—"

"Was she on-scene at the time?"

"Yes."

A pained expression crossed his face like a dark cloud. "Would you happen to know where I can find her?"

"Since her apartment was damaged in a fire—"

"Any connection to the murders?"

"None that we've found. The fire marshal is still investigating it as a possible arson. However, Alex is probably at her brother's place. He has a small studio apartment he rents out from time to time, and she's been staying there."

His skin paled noticeably. "Her brother's place?"

"Crimson Swan. He owns it. You know him?"

Varik nodded. "I've known Alex and Stephen for many years."

"So, you and Alex have worked together before?"

"I was the one who trained Alex when she became an Enforcer."

Tasha's eyebrows rose slightly. The Bureau had sent not only a surprise assistant but Alex's mentor. Never a good sign.

Varik pulled a small notepad and pen from his jacket pocket. "I've taken up enough of your time, Lieutenant. If I could trouble you for directions, I'll be on my way."

Tasha took the pen and paper and scribbled directions to Crimson Swan. She handed it to him and gestured to the mobile lab with a nod. "What about your friends?"

Varik glanced over his shoulder. "They need a couple of hours to prep the lab before they can start processing evidence."

"You're just going to leave that thing parked here?"

"Have you got a better place to put it?"

Tasha looked from the lab to the Municipal Center and back to Varik, who smiled as he replaced his sunglasses.

"Don't worry, Lieutenant. They had blood this morning and have enough on hand in the lab to keep them happy."

"I wasn't—" Tasha allowed her protest to die. She *had* been thinking of the vampires' close proximity to the predominantly human workers within the multiplex. She felt her face burning as she looked away.

"Thanks for the directions," Varik said, and turned to leave.

A sudden thought occurred to Tasha. "Wait." She shuffled her feet as he looked up at her from several steps below. "You know, it's funny. I've known Alex ever since she came to Jefferson, and she's never mentioned you."

"I'm not surprised. We didn't exactly part on the best of terms."

"Professional or personal?"

"Both." A muscle along his jaw twitched as he bowed slightly. "Thanks, again, for your time, Lieutenant."

Tasha watched as he slipped behind the wheel of his Corvette and left the parking lot. Once the car was out of sight, she snatched her cell phone from her pocket. Alex rarely spoke of her past, and when she did, it was usually because someone else broached the subject. She didn't know the history of Alex's relationship with the man who was now driving through town, but as she dialed the number she'd memorized long ago, she'd be damned if she'd allow Alex to face him unprepared.

Alex walked through endless rows of weathered gravestones, searching for something, for some*one.* She paused in her dream's quest, looking around at the sparse trees and distant homes. She knew this cemetery, knew for whom she searched, knew he was near.

"Alexandra," a voice whispered her name on the wind.

Dread slithered down her spine. She forced herself to move past one row. Two. She followed the phantom voice until the scent of fresh blood, pungent in the rising breeze, made her steps falter.

"Alexandra."

She halted. She knew this place and didn't want to continue. "No," she whispered, and closed her eyes.

"Alexandra," the voice called again, closer and more insistent.

"Go away."

Wind brushed her cheek, a gentle caress, startling her, and she opened her eyes to a remembered horror.

A crumpled body lay on its back a few yards away. Blood had splattered across the gravestones and soaked into the ground, turning the budding grass black. What had been a white shirt was now a splash of crimson against the darkness of a suit. A single brightly colored butterfly fanned its wings on the end of a wooden stake.

A scream welled within her but lodged in her throat as the dreamscape shifted. The cemetery morphed into a barren plain stretching beneath a seething sky. Movement to her right drew her attention.

Hundreds of orange-and-black monarch butterflies swarmed around her, lifted and carried her up into the darkening sky. The motion of their wings sounded like distant and distorted voices whispering to her. They carried her higher and higher, and the black-and-gray clouds rolled and tumbled above her, mirroring the butterflies' aerial dance.

Wind buffeted her and tore at her carriers' delicate wings. Their whispered messages increased, trying to compensate for the wind's growing howl. The breeze became a vortex, and a familiar smell of sandalwood and cinnamon enveloped her. "Varik," she murmured, but her voice was lost in the storm.

The churning tornado ripped the butterflies away one by one. Her heart beat against its bony cage. The storm stripped the last butterfly of its wings, and she felt herself suspended in the air for a moment. She screamed as she fell and the roaring wind became the first crashing notes of Beethoven's Fifth Symphony.

Alex sat up, gasping for breath. Sandalwood and cinnamon clung to her, cloying in their spicy sweetness. She looked around her, uncertain if she was awake or still in the dream. Music sounded from nearby. Her cell phone.

She searched for the phone on the bedside table, knocking over a half-empty glass of water. "Damn it."

Beethoven continued to play. Dweezil chirped his annoyance from his perch on top of the half-wall separating the bedroom from the kitchen.

Cursing, Alex stumbled from the bed, searching the previous day's clothing scattered on the floor. She finally located the phone in the pocket of her jacket and flipped it open to silence the symphony. "Sabian," she said hoarsely, dropping onto the sofa and resting her head in her free hand.

"I've been trying to reach you for the past ten minutes," Tasha said.

"Sorry, I was asleep." She rubbed her eyes and yawned. "What's up?"

"I just had an interesting visitor and wanted to warn you before he shows up at Stephen's."

Nervous energy burned in the pit of her stomach, reminding her of the dream. The image of a tall black-haired vampire came to her mind along with a fresh infusion of sandalwood and cinnamon. "Varik," she whispered, and the butterflies in her stomach spun faster.

"Yeah, how did you—"

"He's in town?"

"Came in with the mobile lab."

Alex stared at the ceiling. She'd heard Varik had retired, settling down in Louisville in the house that would've been theirs if she'd stayed. Questions raced through her mind. Why was he in Jefferson? Had Damian sent him? Her hand strayed to the scar on her neck. Or was he finally coming for her?

"Alex?" Tasha asked quietly. "Are you—"

"I have to go."

"But—"

Alex flipped her phone closed and ended the call. She could sense Varik's presence vibrating in her mind like a suddenly remembered melody. There would be no point in hiding, since she knew he was equally aware of her presence. She hadn't seen or spoken to him in six years, but a mix of anticipation and dread closed around her. Part of her wanted to reclaim her place in his arms, and part of her wanted to escape, tear a hole in the apartment's wall and run away.

"Running isn't an option," she muttered. She looked down at her University of Louisville T-shirt and bare legs. He would be there soon.

She raced through the apartment, throwing off the shirt as she ran for the shower. Within moments, hot water coursed over her shoulders but did little to ease the tension building in her muscles. She showered in record time and hurried to dress while Dweezil watched her with what appeared to be amused detachment.

An image filled Alex's mind as she pulled on her boots, and the force of it made her gasp. Stephen, his face twisted in rage, stood in front of Varik, shouting at the taller vampire. "Ah, shit."

She clipped her sidearm and badge to her jeans, grabbed her cell phone and keys, and ran from the apartment. Angry voices rose through the bell tower's stairwell. Opening the door leading into the bar, she saw Stephen's fist connect with Varik's jaw. "Stephen!"

"You stay the fuck away from my sister!" Stephen shouted, straining against the two vampire patrons holding him back from the stunned Enforcer now lying on the floor. Other customers scattered, heading into corners or out the front doors. "Get the hell out of my bar!"

Alex stepped between Stephen and Varik as the intervening patrons cleared out. "Stop it!"

The irises of Stephen's blue eyes had changed to bright amber. He pushed her aside. "Stay out of this, Alex."

She grabbed Stephen's shirt in both fists and shook him, forcing him to look at her. "You lay one more hand on him, and I'll charge you with assaulting an officer."

Stephen's mouth opened and closed a few times before his words finally tumbled out. "You wouldn't dare. Not after what he did!"

"Try me."

"You're going to defend *him*?"

"Stephen—"

"He deserved it"—his eyes shifted to Varik—"and worse."

"Back off, Stephen. I'm not going to—"

"He's right," Varik said, as he climbed to his feet.

Alex looked over her shoulder at him.

He brushed a trickle of blood away from the corner

of his mouth and studied his hand. His dark eyes swirled like tiny maelstroms, the irises bleeding into the color of molten gold. "I deserved this one, but that's your one freebie, Stephen. Next time I won't be so charitable."

Stephen lunged forward, and Alex pushed him back against the bar. Glasses beneath the counter tumbled onto the floor and shattered with the force of their impact. "I said, *back off*." She glanced at Varik. "You! Get the hell out of here."

"We need to talk."

"Outside."

Varik turned on his heel, slipping on a pair of sunglasses. "Later, Stephen," he shot over his shoulder as he left.

"Damn it! Let me go." Stephen squirmed between her and the bar. "I'm gonna kill that son of a bitch."

She waited for the door to close before she released him and stepped back, still blocking his path. "You will over my dead body."

"How can you protect him after what he did? How?" Stephen glared at her, breathing heavily, his eyes still bright amber.

"Because, like it or not, it's my job. He's an Enforcer."

"But he—"

Alex raised her hand to stop him. "I know what he did, Stephen. I was there, remember?" She stepped closer to him, laying her hand on his shoulder. "I don't even know why he's here, okay? Until I know what's going on, I need him alive." She smiled wryly. "After that, *then* you can kill him. String him up by his balls and use him as a piñata, whatever you want."

Stephen scoffed and brushed her hand away.

"But until then, leave him alone."

"Fine, as long as he stays out of my bar."

Alex nodded. "Agreed. Now I better go see what Señor Asswipe is doing in town."

"Be careful," Stephen called after her.

She raised a hand in acknowledgment as she stepped out into the midmorning sunlight.

Harvey Manser ground the butt of his cigarette into the overfilled ashtray. "Shit, Bill, empty this damn thing, will you?"

Bill Jenkins glared at him but swept the tiny metal tray off the truck-stop diner's counter.

Harvey looked around at the few patrons huddled over their meals. Maggie's Place wasn't much to look at, but it offered some of the best food in town, if you didn't mind extra grease and burned toast. Mismatched tables and chairs crowded the floor between the counter where he sat and a bank of tattered Naugahyde booths.

A couple of truck drivers occupied one booth, silently eating their stacks of pancakes and sausage links. A woman sat at a table, reading the paper and absently munching on a salad of iceberg lettuce that had seen better days. The only other customer was the man seated next to him at the counter, Martin Evans, who was busy chasing a piece of pork chop around his plate with a fork.

Bill dropped the ashtray. It spun in a wobbly circle before coming to a rest. "What the hell's going on, Harvey?"

He lit another cigarette. He'd known this conversation was coming, and now that it was upon him, he found himself reluctant to engage. It wasn't out of fear or a lack of enthusiasm but because he was tired of arguing with Bill. The man needed to decide to either shit or get off the pot. It was that simple. Smoke billowed from his mouth as he spoke. "With what?"

"The vamps." Bill's voice dropped to a whisper. "I heard they found another body last night."

"Yeah."

"Well, who's behind it?"

Harvey rolled his shoulders. "How should I know? Vamps aren't my jurisdiction."

"But people are scared. I hear them talking. Rumor has it that these killings are two rival Midnight gangs offing each other so they can expand their territory."

"Where'd you hear that?" Martin asked.

"Tubby Jordan came by this morning. He told me."

"As long as they're killing vamps, what difference does it make?" Martin stuffed a forkful of mashed potatoes into his mouth.

"Think about it," Bill said. "Half of the town's population is fucking bloodsuckers. That drug hypes them up, makes them crazed. A couple of dead vamps would be the least of our problems if the gangs take over."

"I haven't seen or heard anything that would support that rumor," Harvey said. "Besides, we've got bigger problems."

The two men quieted.

He took a long draw on his cigarette and released his smoky breath slowly. "Sabian's brought in more Enforcers."

"Shit." Martin wiped his mouth with the back of his hand. "How many?"

"Three, and two of them are forensic experts with a mobile lab."

Bill emitted a low whistle, and Martin mouthed curses.

"In order for our plan to work, we're going to have to be damn sure we cover our tracks."

"How are we supposed to do that?" Martin pushed his plate aside. "I don't know crap about that stuff, and neither do either of you."

Harvey tamped out his cigarette. "That's why I'm going to have Darryl stop by the meeting tonight."

"Darryl?" Bill scoffed. "What can he do?"

"Hopefully, keep us out of Parchman Penitentiary, for starters."

Martin and Bill exchanged glances. "What's Tubby say about him?" Bill asked.

"Tubby doesn't have anything to say. He knows we need Darryl."

"Well, if Tubby's okay with it, then count me in." Martin stood and stretched. "I got to get back to the Feed 'n' Seed."

They all muttered their good-byes, and Martin left the diner after giving one final wave at the door.

"Are you sure about this, Harvey?" Bill asked after a moment had passed. "Especially after what happened at Oak Tree."

Harvey lit another cigarette and shook his head. "No, but it's the only way to reclaim our town. Besides, Oak Tree was a trial run to get Sabian off her game. That's why we need Darryl, to make sure we get the big event right."

Bill nodded. He hesitated, as if he would say something more, before finally moving to the grill, and began scrubbing away the cooked-on remnants of someone's meal.

Varik leaned against the trunk of his Corvette, arms folded across his chest and dark sunglasses hiding his eyes. He'd taken off his denim jacket, and the black dress shirt he wore clung to his broad shoulders and accentuated his well-toned biceps.

He watched Alex exit the bar, and his pulse quickened as the sunlight turned her auburn hair into a fiery veil. She hesitated and then walked toward him. He could see her eyes, could tell they were a mix of amber and emerald. She pulled a pair of sunglasses from her pocket and slipped them over her hypnotic gaze. The urge to sweep her into his arms was almost overwhelming, but the ache along his jaw reminded him that he no longer had a place in her life.

"What are you doing here?" She stopped a few feet in front of him and folded her arms beneath her chest, mirroring his stance.

"Getting the hell knocked out of me, apparently." He raised his hand to gently touch the cut in the corner of his mouth.

"It'd take more than one punch to knock the hell out of *you*."

Varik smiled, then winced. Stephen had caught him off guard, but he'd make certain it didn't happen again. He reached his hand out to her, then let it fall when she pulled back. "It's good to see you, Alex."

"That doesn't answer my question."

He took a deep breath and jammed his hands into the front pockets of his jeans. "The Bureau sent me to check on the investigation's progress."

"I thought you were retired."

"Not anymore, thanks to Damian."

"Why did he send you?"

"He seems to think you need my help."

"You mean he sent you to spy on me."

"That's the second time today I've been accused of spying. If you want to see it that way, then so be it, but I *am* here to help."

"You can help by getting in your car and leaving. I'm doing just fine, thank you."

"Is that so?" Varik leaned forward, looking at her over the top of his shades. Her sunglasses reflected his molten-gold eyes. "Then why were you risking blood-hunger on-scene?"

"Where did you hear that?"

"Lieutenant Lockwood was very accommodating."

Alex scowled. "I was under control."

"Rii-ight"—he drew the word out—"sure you were."

He looked around the parking lot and the surrounding area. Cars turned into a strip mall across the street. A white Cadillac had to brake hard to avoid crashing into a small red pickup that darted into an empty space in front of one of the shops. Varik shook his head and turned back to Alex. "If you don't have time to take care of yourself, then you can't very well care for the investigation. You *know* that. Hell, I taught you that."

"*You're* going to lecture *me*?" Alex laughed and tucked a strand of windblown hair behind her ear, showing the edge of a jagged pink scar. "I'm not the one who killed dozens of people."

"I was following orders." He pushed away from the car and stalked a few steps toward the bar.

For centuries, human parents had ruled their children with tales of the bogeyman hiding in the closet. Vampires were no different, but instead of the bogeyman, they had threatened their misbehaving children with the Hunters, vampires who punished those who broke vampiric law, and the only punishment had been death. Varik had been a bogeyman to generations of vampire children. But that was all in the past, before— He turned back to Alex. "Yes, I killed people. Yes, I was a Hunter, but it was a different time then, Alex. Humans didn't know we existed. Secrecy was our only means of survival. We kept the peace through force."

"Don't try to romanticize it, Varik. You were nothing more than a hired assassin."

"When are you going to understand that what I did was a long time ago, a hundred years before you were even born? I'm not that person anymore. I haven't killed anyone in over fifty years."

"Good for you."

He charged forward, and she immediately dropped into a fighting stance, fists held in front of her chest. He stopped, watching her, not moving so as not to provoke her any further. "Don't think yourself to be so high and mighty. Enforcers are nothing more than Hunters dressed up in political correctness to please the humans."

"Enforcers don't kill people."

He laughed.

"We uphold the law."

"Believe what you want. I can't change the past, no matter how much I may want to. I'm tired of trying to explain myself to you, Alex." He propped himself up against the trunk of his Corvette, staring at his boots.

They stood in silence, looking everywhere but at each other. The first notes of Beethoven's Fifth Symphony broke the silence, and Alex jumped. She fumbled with her jacket and retrieved her phone. "Sabian," she answered breathlessly.

Varik strained to hear the conversation. He managed to catch part of it, enough to know it was the coroner calling.

Alex glanced at her watch. "Okay, I'll see you at two." She snapped the phone closed.

"Autopsy. Sounds like fun."

"Damn your ears."

He smirked. "Listen, I think we've gotten off on the wrong foot here."

"No shit."

"We're going to have to find some way to work together." He heard Alex's stomach grumble loudly. "Why don't we go grab a bite to eat? My treat."

She shook her head. "I have things to do."

"Damn it. Does everything have to be an argument with you?"

She pulled her keys from her pocket. "No, not everything. The Bureau sent you to check on the progress of the investigation. I told you it's under control and I don't need your help. No argument there." Turning on her heel, she walked away. "Good-bye, Enforcer Baudelaire."

Varik watched her climb into her Jeep and then slam it into reverse. She zipped past him, and tires squealed and horns blared as she darted into traffic, nearly causing a three-car pileup. Picking up his jacket, he watched her speed away from the bar. "Good going, Varik," he said to himself. "Next time, try *not* pissing her off for a change."

four

"NEED A RIDE?" HE SHOUTED THE QUESTION THROUGH the passenger-side window.

The vamp that'd been walking along the side of the road stopped and approached the open window. "Yeah," it said. "My car broke down a ways back." It nodded toward the deserted country road. "My house is another couple of miles up. You mind taking me there? I'll pay you for your trouble."

"Don't worry about that. Hop on in."

The vamp climbed into the truck's cabin. "Thanks. I appreciate this. My boss is going to kill me for being late."

He checked the rear mirrors and pulled onto the asphalt road once more. He glanced at the speedometer and the picture of Claire tucked in beside it. Her dark eyes glittered up at him, alight with anticipation for what was to come. "Where do you work?"

"Here and there. Mostly construction."

He nodded, listening to the thrum of the tires over

the asphalt and wind whistling through the partially opened window. The two combined into a hypnotic pulse that relaxed him. He could feel himself slipping into that familiar peaceful state, the calm of the hunter's mind before he unleashed his fury and pounced.

A rock in one of the tires clicked rapidly against the pavement and created a steady musical score for the fantasy playing in his mind. *Kill it. Kill it. Kill it.*

"My place is the next drive on the left," the vamp said, pointing to a partially obscured gravel entrance.

Rocks crunched under the tires and pinged against the truck's bottom. Large red oaks and pines surrounded the small brick house and nearby wooden storage shed. He pulled the truck through the circular drive and stopped in front of the house.

"Thanks again," the vamp said, opening the truck door. "Sure I can't pay you something?"

"No, the Lord works righteousness and justice for all the oppressed."

"Uh, right. Well, like I said, thanks for the ride."

He nodded.

The vamp closed the door and crossed the drive in front of the truck, heading for the house.

He glanced at Claire's photo. Shadows covered her face, but her eyes bore into him. He reached below the seat, pulled out the hidden nine-millimeter Sig Sauer P250, and killed the truck's engine. The vamp was already inside the house, in its lair, but that made no difference. He knew he could take it down the same way he had the others.

Alternating sunlight and shadows danced before him as he quietly walked up to the front door. He thumbed off the gun's safety mechanism and peered into the home. No sign of the vamp in the furniture-devoid first room. The metal storm door squeaked faintly as he opened it and moved inside.

A door to the right opened to a kitchen, and another to his left led into a narrow hallway. He paused by the front entrance, allowing his eyes time to adjust and the storm door to close. The scuffling of feet in the hall-way gave away the vamp's location.

It entered the front room and jerked to a halt, star-ing at him. "What the fuck—"

He'd practiced a quick-draw kill, and now he raised the Sig Sauer and fired. The bullet streaked from the gun's barrel and exploded into the vamp's heart.

The vamp stumbled back into the hall, staring at the scarlet stain spreading over its chest. It slid to the floor and left a wide red stain on the white plaster wall.

The joy that overcame him was rivaled only by the joy he'd felt the day he and Claire had married. He stalked toward the vamp, keeping the gun trained on its motionless body. He tapped its foot with his toe and re-ceived no reaction. Everyone knew vamps were devious creatures, demons with golden tongues and a host of mind-bending powers. He had to be certain it was dead before he moved the body.

The report of the gun echoed like an explosion within the confines of the small hallway. Blood and fragments of bone and brain sprayed the wall behind the body. It fell over onto its side, a gaping hole in its head to match the one in its chest. Satisfied, he inhaled a cleansing breath and gagged from the stench of gunpowder and blood permeating the still air.

To escape the smell, he entered the kitchen and breathed an inaudible curse as a new odor assaulted his senses. Boxes of empty vials crowded the counters. Large clusters of garlic bulbs hung from the ceiling, filling the air with their pungent aroma. Huge bottles of aspirin were scattered over a table along with bags of other brightly colored pills. Guessing what he'd find, he opened the refrigerator and his stomach turned when he saw the rows of jars filled with blood.

Everything needed to make Midnight, the drug responsible for taking away his beloved Claire, was present.

Anger overtook him. He slammed the fridge closed and fired several rounds into the door. Sparks popped from the dying motor and dark red liquid oozed from the broken bottom seal. Roaring in a primal fury, he overturned the table, smashed the various pills to powder beneath his heels. He ripped the garlic from the hooks from which it hung and hurled it through the kitchen window.

A breeze entered the kitchen, cleansing it of the overpowering smell of garlic and blood, and carried away his anger.

Sickened by the mess before him, he returned to the empty first room, where the air was marginally cleaner.

A vision of Claire smiling at him glided into the room through the front door. "Claire ..." He smiled and reached for her.

The vision faded, and he found himself staring into emptiness, left behind once again, but he and Claire would be reunited soon. Once his tasks were finished and justice had been served, he would join Claire, and nothing, not even death, would tear them apart.

Alex dodged an outbound eighteen-wheeler and swerved around a stationary minivan to pull into an open space in front of Maggie's Place. Her encounter with Varik had left her in a foul mood and in desperate need of coffee and food. The truck-stop diner wasn't the best place for either, but it was the closest to Crimson Swan.

She sat for a moment behind the wheel of her Grand Cherokee trying to compose herself. Her temples throbbed with every heartbeat. She ripped her sunglasses off and tossed them on the seat beside her. "Damn it," she mumbled, grinding her fingers into her closed eyes. "Damn *him*."

Varik had always been able to push her buttons, but she'd thought that she'd left him in the past, where he could no longer hurt her. Time hadn't completely erased her feelings. She'd suppressed them, denied their existence, but seeing him had brought on a rush of memories.

One now drifted up from her subconscious, a brief image of Varik. His eyes were the color of molten gold. Blood covered the front of his shirt and hands.

"Get a grip, Alex," she whispered, fingering her scar. She couldn't afford to show weakness with Varik in town. His assurances that he was there to help meant nothing. Damian had reinstated him. She knew how the Bureau worked. By sending her former mentor to aid her without warning, they showed a lack of confidence in her abilities.

A new surge of determination to see the case through to the end filled her. "Fuck 'em," she said to her reflection in the rearview mirror. Her normally pale cheeks were flushed and her eyes were bloodshot, but at least they'd returned to a normal color. Her hair didn't look too bad, a little mussed from the wind but presentable. Varik's sudden appearance may have unnerved her, but that didn't mean she had to let it show.

Her stomach growled in protest of her delay. With a heavy sigh, she opened the Jeep's door.

Interstate traffic whizzed by on the nearby overpass. Big rigs and family vehicles were a constant stream through the combination diner and gas station. Parents yelled at their children to avoid the moving cars. Men gathered around the tailgates of their pickups, watched the commotion with feigned disinterest, and commented on the weather. The steady rumble of idling eighteen-wheelers mingled with the noise of interstate traffic and vibrated the ground beneath Alex's feet.

A car horn blared in the distance. She looked to the interstate in time to see a sedan accelerating around a red pickup that had pulled to the shoulder on-ramp. Even small towns had bad drivers. She shook her head and entered the diner.

The mismatched tables and chairs and tattered Naugahyde booths of Maggie's Place were a dramatic contrast to the unblemished environment of Crimson Swan. Backless stools bolted to the floor in front of a chipped Formica counter and facing the open grill showed the same amount of wear as the booths. The dingy and cracked laminate flooring had pulled away from the concrete slab beneath some of the tables. A clock and two unframed and faded posters of Elvis Presley and Hank Williams Jr. added little cheer to the poorly painted green walls.

Slow country music played from an antique jukebox tucked into the corner beside the restrooms. The smell of burning bread, rancid grease, and stale cigarettes filled the air and seemed to cling to Alex as she wound her way around the tables.

Sheriff Harvey Manser and a few other men occupying several of the counter stools glanced over their shoulders at her. Two frowned and said muted words to their companions before rising and leaving the diner.

Alex ignored the dark looks they directed at her when they passed and the whispers from the family of six seated at the largest booth. She knew she was encroaching on a predominantly human restaurant, but her hunger dictated her actions for the moment. Their discomfort at having a vampire in their midst would be short-lived. She didn't intend to stay.

A short man with salt-and-pepper hair looked up at her from his position in front of the grill when she sat down at the counter, scowled, then turned back to his work.

She plucked a laminated menu from between a sugar container and a napkin holder. Scanning the limited offerings, she made her choices and checked her watch. The autopsy was scheduled to begin in about an hour, so she had plenty of time to eat. Her leg bounced anxiously as she watched the traffic through the grease-fogged windows. Half of her hoped to see Varik's Corvette pulling into the parking lot, but she knew him too well. He wouldn't follow her. He'd wait and ambush her at the autopsy. Glancing at her watch again, she wondered if she could convince the coroner's office to bump up the time.

"What're you having?"

Alex started at the sound of the waitress's voice. She hadn't heard the woman approach and stared at her.

The woman cocked her hip and scratched at the stiff beehive hairdo piled on top of her head. "You deaf?"

"Large coffee and a bacon-and-egg sandwich, extra mayo. To go. Please."

The waitress turned away, shaking her head, and Alex pulled her cell phone from her pocket. She'd call Jeff and have him try to convince Doc Hancock to move up the autopsy. She was halfway through dialing the number when a voice beside her brought her up short.

"Didn't think you vamps needed to eat," Harvey said, smoke pouring from both his mouth and the cigarette he cradled between two fingers. "Thought you all got by on just blood."

Closing the cell phone, Alex half turned to face him. Harsh fluorescent light made his skin appear sallow. The wisps of hair he normally combed from left to right in an effort to minimize his spreading baldness stood on end, as if someone had soaked them with hair spray during a windstorm. Gray eyes stared at her through the smoky haze with undisguised hatred. Alex glanced over his shoulder at the men who had taken a sudden interest in their conversation. She smiled, showing her small fangs. "Just popped in for a quick bite."

The men turned away, and Harvey frowned. "If you're planning to eat anyone here—"

"No, that would be rude."

"Kind of like leaving your pet detective to deal with the new crop of bloodsuckers that wheeled into town this morning."

"First of all, Tasha isn't my pet. Secondly, I didn't leave her to deal with anyone. Except maybe you."

"I'd watch that attitude if I were you. Folks with bad attitudes in this town have a way of getting burned."

"Burned, huh?" She cocked her head. "Confessing to that apartment fire, Harvey?"

All conversation in the diner stopped, only the slow melody of a country-music ballad disturbing the silence.

Harvey ground the remains of his cigarette into an already overflowing ashtray and stood up. His hand rested on the butt of his service revolver as he leaned over Alex. "You accusing me of something, vamp?"

She met his angry glare without flinching. "What's the matter, Sheriff? Feeling the prick of a guilty conscience?"

"The only thing I feel guilt over is playing nice with the likes of your kind because some governmental bureaucrats forty years ago didn't have the ability to understand the consequences of setting monsters loose on our streets."

"You think the world would be better if humans had never known of us—"

"Damn right."

"—and that humans and vampires shouldn't live together?"

"The good Lord may make the lion and lamb lay down together one day, but the lion is still a killer."

"Who are you to say the lamb isn't?"

A greasy paper bag dropped to the counter in front of Alex, cutting off Harvey's reply. "Five fifty," the waitress said, setting a large paper cup beside the bag. "To go."

Alex stood and began searching her pockets. She laid out a five and three ones on the counter. "Keep the change."

The woman snatched the money and flicked her eyes to Harvey. "Can I get you anything, Sheriff?"

"Coffee," he said, pulling a pack of cigarettes from his uniform's pocket. He tapped the filtered end of one on the counter's edge. "Guess if you ever manage to track down the killer, then we'll see who has more blood on their hands—the lamb or the lion."

Alex shrugged. "Doesn't really matter. Either way, someone is going to answer for these deaths."

"Since we're on the subject, any luck finding those heads?"

"Yeah, I'm taking out lost-and-found ads in all the newspapers within a three-county radius. 'Missing heads. Reward for their return. No questions asked.'"

She picked up the grease-stained bag and coffee cup. "Now, if you'll excuse me, I have an autopsy to attend."

She left the diner, balancing the bag and coffee in one hand while fishing for her keys in her pocket with the other.

As she rounded the side of her Jeep, she heard the gunshot an instant before she felt the burning pain.

Emily Sabian compared the price of two brands of tomato sauce and picked up three cans of the on-sale brand. Moving down the grocery store's aisles, she picked up other canned vegetables, fruit, and a box of pasta. She checked her list and tallied the prices she'd marked next to each item. She'd picked up almost everything and was well within her budget.

At the deli, she added a boxed pecan pie to her cart. A little treat now and again never hurt anyone, and pecan pie was her weakness. If it weren't for her naturally high vampire metabolism, her waist would've thickened to the point of no return by now. However, she tried to take care of herself and secretly prided herself on maintaining a curvy size-twelve figure. She didn't even mind the fact that silver shot through her once-golden curls. Her blue eyes still sparkled, and she was happy, despite losing Bernard. His death had been difficult, but her children had kept her going.

She sighed as she stopped in front of the Vlad's Tears display. The synthetic blood tasted horrible, and she rarely used it. Louisville had become known as the Vampire Capital of America in the years after Bernard's death, and donors were never in short supply. Regardless of her personal preferences, she liked to keep a supply on hand for guests.

"Emily!" a woman called from behind her.

Suppressing a groan, she smiled at the rotund woman wheeling toward her. "Hello, Pearlie. How are you?"

Pearlie Marker stopped her motorized shopping-cart scooter next to Emily's cart. "Oh, all right, considering my knee's been bothering me a good bit lately." She rubbed her right knee with a pudgy hand and used the other to smooth the close-cropped white hair on her head, pressing it down so it conformed to the contours of her rounded face. "There must be a cold front moving in."

Pearlie had lived a few doors down from the Sabians for years and had known them before she knew they were vampires. In the days after Bernard's murder, Pearlie had been one of the few humans who'd stuck by the family and accepted them regardless of their bloodsucking nature. At the time, Emily had thought Pearlie a godsend, but she'd quickly learned that the woman loved to gossip, and her ardent support was often motivated by a desire to be in the center of the latest neighborhood scandal.

Emily nodded in sympathy and grabbed two twelve-pack containers of Vlad's Tears. "I hate to hear that you're having troubles, Pearlie."

She waved away the comment. "Just the price we humans pay for getting old."

Emily laughed nervously as she dropped the synthetic blood into her cart.

"I'm so glad I caught you," Pearlie said. She twisted the handle of her shopping scooter and inched it forward. "I've been meaning to call and see how you were holding up."

Emily's brow furrowed in confusion. "Fine. Why would you be asking?"

"Well, with all that unpleasantness down in Jefferson—isn't that where Stephen and Alex moved?" She plowed ahead, not giving Emily an opportunity to respond. "Of course it must be. How many towns in Mississippi can be named Jefferson, after all? Anyway, with those awful murders going on, I thought you might be—"

"Murders?" Emily's voice was louder and shriller than she'd expected. A few nearby shoppers turned and looked at her. "What murders?"

Pearlie blinked rapidly, and her jowls flapped as she tried to get the words out. "Three vampires were killed. Staked and beheaded."

Emily gasped and had to clutch at her cart to keep from swaying on her feet. Her mind reeled and raced in circles. When had she last spoken to Stephen or Alex? Were they okay? Was Alex investigating? Were these murders somehow connected to Bernard's? When had Stephen last called her, one or two weeks ago?

"Are you okay? You don't look so good." Pearlie patted Emily's arm. Her eyes widened, and her hand flew to her mouth. "Oh, my stars. You didn't know, did you?"

Emily shook her head, unable to speak.

"My grandson works for one of the television stations in Memphis. He told me about it. I just assumed, with Stephen and Alex being there, that one of them would've told you about it. Alex is an Enforcer, right? Why wouldn't she tell—"

"I'm sure Alexandra has her reasons," Emily said quietly. A shiver traced down her spine, jolting her into action. "I have to go." She pushed her cart away, heading for the line of registers at the front of the store.

"I'll call you later," Pearlie shouted.

Emily hurried to the checkout stand, searching her purse for her cell phone before she realized she'd left it at home to charge the battery. She had to get home. She had to know if Stephen and Alex were okay. Her foot tapped the floor and her fingers drummed the handle of her cart as she waited for the cashier to ring up her purchases.

If something had happened to one of them, she would've been notified, she thought. No one had knocked on her door. No one had phoned her. Uneasiness quivered in her belly. She had to be certain her family was safe.

She snatched the receipt from the cashier's hand and rushed for the door with images of caskets and flower-draped funeral homes flashing through her mind.

Tasha reached Maggie's Diner and was greeted with a chaotic scene of ambulances and fire trucks, as well as police cars from city, county, and state agencies. Medical personnel scrambled across the parking lot, performing triage on the wounded. White sheets stretched across temporary posts dotted the pavement and marked the victims who wouldn't be needing transport to Jefferson Memorial Hospital. Sheets were no longer draped over bodies in order to avoid cross-contamination of forensic evidence.

In total, she counted five dead on the scene and at least a dozen more wounded, including the most critical, who'd already been taken away.

Harvey Manser, shouting orders and chain-smoking, stood in the center of it all.

She made her way over to him, mindful to step carefully around the pools of blood that seeped from beneath the makeshift fences and filled cracks in the deteriorating asphalt. "What the hell happened?" she demanded once she'd reached Harvey's side.

"Gunman parked on the side of the southbound on-ramp," he answered, pointing toward the interstate with the glowing tip of his cigarette. "Damn fool shot into the crowd. It's a miracle none of the gas tanks exploded."

"Call came across the wire with an officer down."

Harvey nodded, drawing on his cigarette. "Sabian took one in the arm."

Tasha glanced around at the remaining ambulances. "Where is she now?"

"Inside. All this blood was bound to set her off, so I had a couple of my deputies haul her in there for the EMTs to check her out. Didn't want her attacking the survivors."

She couldn't believe her ears and gaped at him.

"Don't give me that look. She's a fucking vamp. I wasn't going to stand by while she either attacked the survivors or fed off the dead."

"Are you stoned or just stupid, Harvey? I can never tell."

"Excuse me?"

"It's ignorant bastards like you who create events like this in the first place," she shouted, flinging her arms wide.

"Now wait just a damn minute. You can't—"

"Oh, shut up, Harvey." Tasha stormed away. "Just shut the fucking hell up!"

Officers stopped in their tracks to stare at her. Harvey hurled obscenities at her back, but she kept her eyes focused on the entrance to Maggie's Place as she walked. Her hands shook, and she curled them into fists at her sides.

Drive-by shootings. Mass murder. Beheadings. These were crimes associated with larger cities, with *somewhere else*. With the exception of the rare suicide by handgun, the only shootings recorded in Nassau County for nearly fifteen years were hunting accidents. Senseless violence on the scale they were now experiencing wasn't supposed to happen in Jefferson. Not in her hometown.

Tasha entered the diner and found Alex seated at a table with a paramedic at her side. She passed the two deputies who stood to either side of the door and kept their hands on their service belts, sidearms within easy reach.

Alex looked up as Tasha approached the table. Her

normally green eyes were dark amber, and small specks of dried blood dotted her face. Her gaze flicked over Tasha's shoulder and back. "I don't suppose you can convince Harvey to call off his goons."

"He seems to think you're going to start biting people."

Alex snorted and rolled her eyes. "If I did, he'd be the first."

Tasha heard the two deputies shifting behind her. She pulled out a chair and sat opposite Alex. "How badly are you injured?"

"Just a scratch."

The paramedic rummaged in his kit for more gauze. He glanced at Tasha. "She needs to go to the hospital for stitches but refuses."

Tasha peered over the paramedic's kit. A long, seeping gash cut diagonally across Alex's right biceps. She met Alex's gaze, silently questioning her apparent decision to forgo further medical attention.

"The bullet only grazed me," Alex said softly. "It looks worse than it is. I'll be fine in a few days."

Vampires didn't heal instantly, as they did in the movies, but they did heal quickly. A broken arm would have a human in a cast for a minimum of six weeks. A vampire's body would mend the same break in one. If Alex said she'd be as good as new in a few days, Tasha believed her.

Alex winced as the paramedic applied pressure to the wound and began the process of dressing it.

Raised voices outside drew their attention. Tasha

stood and stepped toward the door as Varik burst through it with a red-faced Harvey on his heels.

"Who the fuck do you think you are?" Harvey demanded. "You can't—"

"Varik Baudelaire," the vampire shot over his shoulder. "Director of Special Operations, Federal Bureau of Preternatural Investigation."

Tasha's eyes widened. Varik had neglected to give his full title to her during their first meeting. She glanced at Alex, but the wounded Enforcer kept her own gaze resolutely on the tabletop in front of her.

"I don't give a shit if you're the fucking Pope," Harvey shouted. "You can't waltz into an active crime scene and claim it as yours!"

Varik reached Alex's side as the paramedic was applying the final strip of tape. He glared at Harvey with eyes the color of molten gold. "I just did."

Harvey squared his shoulders and puffed out his chest. "Those are humans lying under those sheets out there. You don't have jurisdiction in this matter"—he jabbed a finger at Alex—"and neither does that bloodsucking whore!"

The diner erupted in a flurry of movement and shouted curses. Varik lunged for Harvey. The bewildered paramedic sprinted for the door as Alex sprang to her feet. She grabbed for Varik's arm, but he moved too fast and avoided her grasp. His hands closed on Harvey's shoulders and his momentum carried the two of them across the room, where they crashed into the jukebox.

"Get your claws off me!" Harvey fought to free himself.

Tasha found herself scrambling to intercept the two deputies reaching for their guns. "Secure your weapons! Do *not* draw your weapons!"

"Her name is *Enforcer Sabian*, and you *will* respect her," Varik snarled.

"Damn it, Varik," Alex said, as she tried to separate them with one hand. She grabbed a handful of Varik's hair and pulled. "Let him go!"

Harvey stumbled away from the two vampires, glaring at them and groping for his sidearm.

Tasha stepped between the sheriff and the vampires. "Harvey, no!" She held her hands in front of her to ward off his advance. "Don't do it. Don't do something you'll regret."

Unbridled hatred and anger contorted Harvey's features. "Attacking humans carries a death sentence. Believe me, I won't regret a damn thing."

"Death only applies if the human is bitten," Alex said from behind Tasha. "And you aren't."

"She's right," Tasha agreed softly. "Unless you're willing to draw down on two Enforcers and open up a whole new world of trouble for yourself, I suggest you walk away right now, Harvey."

"I'm not giving up the scene to fucking bloodsuckers."

"A federal officer has been shot," Varik said. "You don't have a choice."

"You have proof she was the intended target?" Harvey countered. "I don't, but I do have five dead humans. I say that beats a clipped arm any day of the week."

"You stubborn son of a—" Varik began, and Tasha cut him off.

"Harvey's right. There isn't anything indicating Alex was the shooter's target. She may have simply been in the wrong place at the wrong time."

"I agree," Alex said, and earned an exasperated sigh from Varik. "Until there's hard evidence showing either that I was targeted or that this is somehow related to the other murders, this isn't our rodeo."

"Fine," Varik said, and headed for the door. "I'll be outside when you're ready to leave."

Tasha watched him exit the diner and felt the tension level drop once he was gone. Harvey remained on edge beside her, but he no longer had his hand on the butt of his revolver. The deputies, at a silent command from Harvey, followed Varik outside, no doubt to keep an eye on him and prevent him from tampering with any evidence.

Alex picked up her jacket from where it'd been draped over a chair's back. She met Harvey's hard stare with one of her own. "I'll send you the write-up of my account ASAP."

"Yeah, you do that," Harvey muttered, and lit a cigarette.

"Alex," Tasha called to her as she turned away. "Are you sure you're going to be okay with that guy?" She nodded toward the parking lot, where she could see Varik pacing beside his Corvette.

Alex smiled wanly. "There was a time when I would've questioned it myself, but given recent events, I think I can honestly say that my staying with Varik is in the best interest of all of us right now."

Tasha didn't know how to respond and stood silent beside Harvey as Alex joined Varik outside. She caught a glimpse of Varik holding the passenger-side door of his Corvette open for Alex, and moments later, the two Enforcers were gone.

"Good riddance, if you ask me," Harvey said, tamping out his cigarette's remains in a tin ashtray. "We don't need their kind around here anyway."

"'*Their* kind'?" Tasha repeated. "We could've used their help. They're cops, same as you and me."

Harvey wagged his finger in her face. "No, they most certainly are *not* like you and me. It's time you understood that their kind don't always play by our rules."

"What are you talking about?"

"They're vampires. Sure, they claim to follow our laws, but they have their own. Humans are nothing more to them than forbidden fruit waiting to be plucked." He stepped closer. "If you asked my opinion—"

"I didn't."

"—I'd say one day soon someone was going to put those uppity demons in their place."

Tasha's eyes narrowed. "What is that supposed to mean?"

"Nothing. Just a prediction on my part."

"What happened to your oath to protect and serve *all* citizens of Nassau County?"

"I safeguard the good God-fearing humans." He backed toward the exit. "The vampires can all go to hell."

"With talk like that, you could make someone won-
der if you aren't a member of the Human Separatist
Movement."

Harvey smiled, his hand on the door. "Maybe I'm just
someone who sympathizes with their point of view."

"Are you telling me you buy into their 'separation by
any means necessary' bullshit?"

"Take a look outside here, Lieutenant, and ask yourself what you would think if that was one of your loved
ones lying under a sheet."

Tasha made no move, but something stirred within
her. A familiar tightness uncoiled in her belly. Fear slithered up her spine and made her shiver.

"Ask yourself that, and then you tell me it doesn't
make sense."

The blaring whoop of a siren assaulted her as Harvey
opened the door and slipped out. She watched as another ambulance sped away, carrying the wounded to
the hospital. She stood in the center of Maggie's Place,
staring at the congealing drops of Alex's blood on the
floor and wondered when her world would stop spinning out of control.

five

AS VARIK DROVE HER THROUGH THE STREETS OF JEF-ferson, Alex thought of when she moved to the tiny Mississippi town. The population had been roughly half of what it boasted now, and more human than vampire. It was the destruction of New Orleans and the Mississippi Gulf Coast that swelled the ranks of vampires in the town, as many sought to escape the hardships post–Hurricane Katrina. She was the first Enforcer ever assigned to the region, and gaining acceptance hadn't been easy.

The vampire community had welcomed her, especially since she'd moved quickly to close several small Midnight drug-manufacturing operations in the county that sprang up as a result of the rapid influx of new inhabitants. The largest bust she'd made was two years ago. Working in conjunction with a task force from the Drug Enforcement Agency, she'd shut down a major supply line for the region and arrested more than a dozen manufacturers, transporters, and street dealers.

Even though the main distributor had evaded her grasp, it had been a boost to her career and to her popularity among Jefferson's vampires.

However, the humans hadn't been so open.

Stephen had left his job as regional manager for the Vlad's Tears Corporation when construction began on Crimson Swan. Humans had circulated petitions to protest the bar's opening. Picketers tried to block construction crews. Threats were made against Stephen and the bar. She'd investigated all the threats, made a few arrests—both humans and vampires. She'd worked with the Jefferson Police Department to minimize the disruption caused by the protesters.

In the end, Crimson Swan had been built and opened in May. By working with the JPD and the DEA, she'd solidified her position as an Enforcer willing to work with both vampires and humans to keep the fragile peace between the two communities. However, that tenuous harmony hadn't come without a price. She'd pissed off a lot of people, on both sides of the argument.

"Don't be mad at me," Varik said, as they paused at a red light.

Alex sighed and shifted in her seat, pulling her mind out of the past. She flexed the fingers of her right hand, trying to loosen the stiffening muscles in her arm. "I'm not mad."

"Yes, you are."

They were on their way to meet with Doc Hancock regarding Eric Stromheimer's autopsy results. She'd left her Jeep at Maggie's Place as part of the crime scene. The investigators would need all vehicles to remain in position until they'd documented their locations to aid in the reconstruction of the shooting. Until she was able to reclaim the SUV, she would have to rely on someone else for transportation, and at the moment, that someone was Varik. "I'm not mad at you. I'm mad at the son of a bitch who shot me."

"Is that why you're giving me the silent treatment?"

"Okay, maybe I'm a little pissed off with you." The light turned green, and they slowly accelerated through the intersection. "It's hard to gain the respect of a lot of the humans in Jefferson. The vampire community is growing, but it's still a small town. Change doesn't come easily. Having Harvey in an uproar doesn't help matters, either, so when you started in on him, I knew it was only going to make my job that much harder once all this is over."

"I realize that now, but that's not what I was talking about."

"Then what?"

"When you left Louisville—"

"Don't." Alex shook her head and altered the position of her arm to lessen the pain. She glanced at him over the top of her sunglasses. "I'm not having this conversation. Not now."

"Why? Why don't you want to talk about what happened?"

"What's the point? There's nothing else to say."

"The point is that you haven't said anything at all. You left Louisville without so much as a good-bye or kiss-my-ass."

"Would it have made a difference?"

"You could've at least given me a chance to explain what happened."

"I think what happened was pretty damn obvious."

Varik glanced at her. "I'm trying to apologize. *Again.* I want us to work past this. I want us to—"

"To what? Get back together? Not gonna happen."

"Why not? We loved each other once."

"Loved—past tense."

"Can't you just let it go?"

She shook her head. "Let it go? Varik, you—"

"It was an accident. Damn it! You know I would never intentionally hurt you."

"You almost fucking killed me!"

The Corvette drifted across the centerline into oncoming traffic. A horn blared, yanking Varik's attention back to the road. He jerked the wheel, and the car regained its lane seconds before colliding with a minivan.

"Stop the car!" Alex demanded.

Varik pulled into the parking lot in front of an abandoned storefront and screeched to a halt.

Alex pitched forward. The seat belt tightened across her chest, pinning her in place, and she hissed as pain raced through her arm.

"Ah, shit." Varik unbuckled his own safety belt and twisted in his seat to face her. "Are you okay?"

"No, I'm not okay," she said through clenched teeth. She batted away his hand. "You show up here and suddenly all hell breaks loose. You say you're here to help with the investigation, but then you start pulling this 'let's get back together' crap."

"Alex—"

"Three vampires and five humans are dead. At least a dozen more are injured, and I've been shot." Her voice cracked. "No, Varik, I'm definitely *not* okay."

Varik reached for her and then stopped. "I just wanted to talk. That's all. I never meant to hurt you. Ever. The blood-hunger was too strong. I couldn't control it."

"But the fact remains that you would've killed me if Stephen hadn't stopped you. You would've drained me, Varik. Bled me dry." Her hand slipped beneath her hair to touch the jagged scar between her left ear and shoulder. "And I would've let you. I don't want that to happen again."

"It won't."

"How can you be so sure?"

He hung his head. "I can't. All I can say is I'm sorry."

"What's done is done, Varik, and we can't change it."

"I know, but couldn't we at least try?"

Part of her wanted to give in to him, the part that still loved him. She'd hidden that part away, tucked it into the shadow-filled recesses of her mind, but now that he was in Jefferson—sitting next to her—she couldn't deny it any longer. She couldn't deny its existence, but she could resist it. "It's over, Varik."

He sighed, slumping into the seat.

"I'm sorry." And the part of her that still cared for him genuinely meant it.

"So am I. I'd just hoped that we could—"

Beethoven's Fifth Symphony filled the cloistered confines of the sports car. Alex struggled to retrieve her jacket from where she'd thrown it on the floorboard between her feet. She finally extracted her cell phone from the tangled leather and groaned when she saw the number on the display. Flipping the phone open, she took a steadying breath before speaking. "Hi, Mom."

"Why didn't you tell me?" Emily Sabian asked by way of greeting.

"Tell you what?"

"About the murders." The sound of a drawer opening and closing punctuated her statement.

Alex closed her eyes and rested her head against the seat. "I didn't want to worry you."

"And letting me find out from Pearlie Marker that my daughter has been investigating murders similar to her father's was your solution to not worrying me?"

"It wasn't like that, Mom. How did Pearlie find out, anyway?"

"Her grandson, the one who works for a TV station in Memphis."

"How did he—"

"I don't know, Alexandra."

She heard a zipper being secured, and her mother grunted as though she was moving something heavy. "Mom, what are you doing?"

"Packing. I'm coming to Jefferson."

Alex felt the blood drain from her face. She glanced at Varik. "Mom, I don't think your coming to Jefferson is such a good idea right now."

Varik shook his head in silent agreement.

"Why not?" her mother huffed.

"I'm in the middle of an investigation."

"Maybe I can help. After all, you *are* the only Enforcer—"

"Varik's here," Alex said softly. Silence filled her ear and she checked the display on her phone to be certain the call hadn't been dropped. "Mom? Are you still there?"

"Yes," she replied. "It's just—I thought he retired."

Alex gave Varik a lopsided half-smile. "Damian reinstated him."

"I see. Has he been able to help you?"

"Depends on your definition of help."

Her mother sighed. "I'm coming to Jefferson."

"No, Mom."

"Alexandra, I'm coming. End of discussion."

Anger bubbled within her. Having Varik in Jefferson was stressful enough, but if she had to worry about her mother's safety as well, she didn't know if she could handle that much pressure. "You can't—"

"There's an evening flight, and I can rent a car once I get to Jackson."

"Will you listen to me? You can't come here."

"Don't take that tone with me, young lady."

"I can't run a murder investigation and find the son of a bitch who shot me *and* babysit you all at the same time!" Alex heard her mother's sharp intake of breath and realized the moment she said it that she shouldn't have. "Mom—"

"You were shot?" Panic nibbled at the edges of her mother's voice. "And you didn't—"

"The bullet barely grazed me."

"My baby's been shot," her mother groaned.

"Mom, it's not that bad."

"Is Varik there? I want to speak with him."

"Mom, please—"

"Now, Alexandra!"

Alex sighed and handed the phone to Varik.

Varik's eyes never left her face. "Hello, Emily."

She could hear her mother's muffled voice speaking rapidly in French, and she frowned. Her mother knew Alex had never learned to speak Varik's native language, an advantage her mother had often employed when she wanted to covertly impart instructions or gain information.

Varik nodded. *"Oui."*

"What is she telling you?"

He simply shook his head and continued to listen to her mother. He wasn't going to tell her anything.

"Damn it, Varik," she hissed.

He smiled as her mother's voice rose sharply. "Emily says you shouldn't curse."

Alex snarled and slumped in her seat. The movement sent another ripple of pain through her arm, and she gritted her teeth.

"Je m'en occupe." Pause. *"Bien sûr."* Pause. *"Oui. À bientôt."* Varik closed the phone and handed it to her.

"What did she tell you?" Alex demanded, snatching the phone from his hand.

He turned in his seat and reached for the ignition key. "She asked me to keep you out of trouble."

"Sounded like more than just a simple request to me," she muttered, as he guided the car into traffic and they continued on their way.

"Keeping you out of trouble is anything *but* a simple request."

Alex grunted and turned her attention to the passing cityscape. Her mother was coming to Jefferson. They hadn't seen each other since she moved from Louisville, had barely spoken outside of holidays and birthdays, and even those conversations had been strained.

Her mother believed she should've stayed in Louisville and worked on her relationship with Varik. Alex's hand drifted to the scar on her neck. What was there to work on? Their relationship had been destroyed. She closed her eyes and gave herself over to the memory.

She stood in the tiny kitchen, staring at the tiled floor that'd been scrubbed clean of any traces of her blood. The scent of bleach was still strong and made her nose burn.

The ring he'd given her glittered on her finger as she'd raised her hand. They'd been engaged for only two months. She hadn't had time to make any plans or pick out a dress. She slipped the ring off her finger, laid it on the kitchen counter next to the coffeepot, and walked away.

Now, six years later, he'd walked back into her life. Resting her head against the seat back, she inhaled deeply, and Varik's natural scent of sandalwood and cinnamon combined with her own of jasmine and vanilla to create an intoxicating mixture that stirred her soul.

"You're awfully quiet," Varik said. "You awake?"

Alex didn't answer and kept her eyes closed, feigning sleep. Perhaps if she kept them closed, when she finally opened them, the nightmare of the past few weeks would've dissipated.

She could only hope.

It'd been four years since Claire was taken from him. He paused at the threshold separating the porch from the house's interior. He still wasn't accustomed to the sound of a silent home.

Floorboards popped under his weight as he stepped into the dark living room. He closed the door and reached for a light switch.

The soft glow of a floor lamp across the room illuminated a small television resting on top of an overflowing bookcase. His battered recliner with its equally shabby side table faced the television. The room was a jumbled mess of papers, books, empty plates and glasses, and a row of boxes stacked along the wall beside the door leading to the kitchen. The boxes contained what remained of Claire's clothing and personal items. He'd packed them up months ago but didn't have the heart to get rid of them. He couldn't bear the idea of parting with them, of parting with her.

Only one section of the room was free of clutter—the area next to the boxes containing a small mosaic-tiled table he and Claire had purchased on their honeymoon in Mexico. On the table was a silver tray that held Claire's gold wedding band and diamond engagement ring, her hairbrush, and a bottle of her favorite perfume. The room's walls were bare except for the enlarged portrait of Claire in her wedding dress that hung over the table.

He paused in front of the table and photo. He kissed his fingertips and transferred the kiss to her lips. "Hi, sweetheart. I'm home."

The ornate golden frame made the blond highlights in her hair sparkle. Her brown eyes held all the warmth and excitement he remembered from their wedding day. She wasn't smiling, but she wore a serene, dreamy expression, like that of a lover waiting for her first kiss. An elaborate tattoo of a vine-covered cross was visible on her elegant neck. The white veil trailing over her bare shoulders stood in stark contrast to the dark tan of her skin.

He inhaled deeply, recalling the smell of cocoa butter and suntan lotion. Claire had taken great pride in maintaining her summer glow all year. He teased her about her mid-winter trips to the tanning beds, but he'd loved her skin. He'd loved everything about her, except her job.

"Goddamn vamps." He frowned and looked away. "I never understood why you wanted to work at that blood bar."

Claire had worked as a waitress and part-time donor at a blood bar in Natchez. She claimed the tips she received were worth the drive, but he'd hated her being on the road late at night. If only she'd listened. If only he'd been more insistent. If only—

Something heavy crashed to earth in the rear of the house. He sighed and glanced at the portrait before setting out to investigate the source of the noise. He didn't have to go farther than the kitchen.

A bracket holding up one end of a wooden shelf above the back door had given way. A set of antique cast-iron trivets that had been Claire's lay scattered on the tile floor. He picked up the trivets and set them on the counter. Beneath the remains of the shelf, two of the tiles now sported large cracks.

He saw movement from the corner of his eye. A shadow darted from the hallway that led to the bedrooms, slipped behind the refrigerator, and into the living room. "Damn it," he muttered, retracing his steps into the other room. "I don't have time for games, Claire."

The shadow hovered beside the boxes before passing over the table and disappearing behind the portrait. Claire's eyes, full of heat and accusations, stared at him from the photo.

"I'm going to take care of it." He stood before her and stroked the broken halo of her hair. "Don't worry. I made a promise, sweetheart. I won't rest until those bastards have paid for what they did."

It had taken him the better part of a year, but he'd tracked down those most likely to be responsible for Claire's murder. He'd gotten the names of all the vamps that'd been in the Natchez blood bar when Claire left work. He'd searched for them. Some were in other states, beyond his reach, but a few were in Jefferson, and he'd done what that Enforcer bitch hadn't been able to do. He'd found justice for Claire.

He thought of the two vamp bodies awaiting him in

his workshop behind the house. One was the vamp he'd killed earlier. The other was tonight's project. He glanced at the blood smeared across his clothes. Moving a corpse was dirty work. He was amazed that vamp blood was the same color as human blood. One would think demons bled black acid, but the dark red always surprised him.

He checked his watch. He didn't have time to start preparing the vamp before tonight's meeting. The Human Separatist Movement had been trying to find a way to rid Jefferson of the vamps. While he was content to hunt them down one by one, he knew it was impractical. He needed an alibi—or at least a set of scapegoats. Sooner or later, no matter how careful he'd been with potential evidence, that Sabian bitch would figure out who was behind it. Then she'd come looking for him.

And he'd be ready.

The elusive shadow slipped from behind Claire's portrait and passed over him. A hint of lavender filled the air, surrounded him, and left him feeling giddy and excited. Claire gave him the smell of her perfume only when she was pleased with him.

He smiled up at her photo and was elated to find her smiling back.

Harvey propped his feet on the corner of his desk and cradled the phone between his ear and shoulder. A coffee-stained mug rested on the apex of his large rounded belly. A thin ribbon of blue smoke rose from the cigarette that bobbed on his lips as he spoke.

"Thanks for calling, Jeff. I appreciate it." He slipped the receiver into its cradle and leaned farther back in his chair.

The news from the coroner's office wasn't good. Total number of dead from the shooting at Maggie's Place was now seven, with six more injured, including Sabian. He had to admit, however, that it could've been a lot worse.

He absently rubbed his shoulder where the new Enforcer had grabbed him. He could feel the tenderness of the forming bruise, and it throbbed in time with his heartbeat, but he'd never give those uppity vamps the satisfaction of knowing they'd hurt him.

He'd toyed with the idea of reporting the incident to the Bureau but decided against it. The only witnesses, aside from two of his men, had been Sabian and Lockwood. He was certain Sabian would back up whatever story the other Enforcer concocted, but Lockwood was a wild card. She was the liaison officer. He could never tell which side she was on.

A knock on his door brought him out of his musings. "Yeah," he called. "What is it?" he asked when Deputy Justin Case slipped into the office.

"All the vehicles from Maggie's Place that were hit with bullets have been moved to the JPD impound lot," Deputy Case said.

"Good. I want slugs dug out of each one. I want to know what kind of rifle the shooter was firing, and then I want a list of all registered owners of that model in the county."

"Yes, sir."

"State troopers have any luck with finding that truck reported leaving the scene?"

"Nothing yet."

Harvey took a draw from his cigarette. "Was Sabian's vehicle brought in?"

Deputy Case shuffled his feet and looked sidelong at the door. "I'm not sure."

"Green Grand Cherokee."

Recognition lit the deputy's face. "Yes, sir. Now I remember. It had the back glass shot out."

Harvey nodded. "Good." He drew on his cigarette again, a plan forming in his mind. His gaze flicked to Deputy Case. "Anything else?"

"No, sir."

"Then why are you still here?"

Deputy Case opened his mouth to respond, thought better of it, and scurried away under Harvey's steely stare.

Harvey's thoughts returned to his plan. If he could pull it off, he'd be hailed as a town hero for generations to come. Vamps thought they were so smug, so perfect. They paraded around Jefferson like humans owed them penance. Any break in their holier-than-thou façade was priceless to the Human Separatist Movement.

HSM, unlike some of the other anti-vamp organizations, believed in the complete separation of human and vampire communities, and was willing to exploit any means necessary to accomplish that goal. It employed lawyers and lobbyists to bend the ears of politicians in state and federal government. It established independent schools, usually attached to an HSM-controlled church, for human children. The group worked within the laws to accomplish what it could, but "by any means necessary" didn't always stop at the borders of the courthouse or capitol building.

Violence, though not officially advocated, wasn't discouraged among group members. HSM had more legal influence than other groups, because of its willingness to work within the law's confines. If any members turned violent and were caught, HSM offered them free legal representation in exchange for the members' promise to behave for a minimum of six months to one year, if whatever charges the member faced were dropped, which they often were.

He might need those very services if the fire marshal discovered that the blaze at Oak Tree Apartments wasn't an accident. The blaze was set in an unoccupied apartment, using a deliberately shorted electrical outlet as the point of origin. However, they hadn't counted on the fire spreading so quickly. Who could've known that newly installed carpet was so flammable?

Regardless of how the fire marshal's investigation concluded, metro police would still have to tie the crime to someone, and given HSM's history and his own reputation, Harvey didn't need to worry too much about the what-ifs. If he was caught, he'd call on his good standing to raise public support for his release. If that didn't work, he'd call on the Human Separatist lawyers. It wasn't like his affiliation with HSM was a secret. He simply neither denied nor confirmed it.

Whether or not he was ultimately implicated in the Oak Tree fire or the group's carefully laid upcoming plans, he'd tear Sabian down and take the whole blood-sucking community with her.

A slow smile curved his lips as he blew a stream of smoke from his nostrils. The smoke curled around him, encircling his shoulders like a ghostly lover's arms. Those damn vamps would be out of town by the end of the week, and Jefferson would return to its rightful owners—the good God-fearing human citizens of Nassau County.

His smile turned to a chuckle and then to a full-bellied laugh.

six

ALEX TOYED WITH THE ZIPPER OF HER JACKET AND glanced at her watch. The original time for their meeting to find out the results of Eric Stromheimer's autopsy had been two o'clock. They were two hours behind schedule, and her arm was hurting again.

"Here, take these." Varik shoved a bottle of water and two white tablets into her good hand.

"I said I was fine."

"Bullshit. I promised your mother I would watch out for you. Now be a good girl and take your medicine."

"I knew you two were conspiring against me." She popped the aspirin into her mouth and swallowed them dry. She struggled to open the water bottle with one hand. Finally conceding defeat, she handed it to Varik to open.

He grinned and twisted the cap free. "We weren't conspiring. She was merely asking that I keep an eye on her headstrong, impetuous daughter until she arrived."

Alex gulped down half the water before answering.

"I still can't believe she *likes* you, even after what happened between us."

He leaned against the cinder-block wall opposite her. "Emily and I understand one another. We're older, from a different generation, as the humans would say."

"Are you saying that someone as headstrong and impetuous as me is incapable of understanding the world as you do?"

"Not at all." He pulled a small clear plastic tube from his pocket. "I'm saying someone as young as you has a different way of viewing the world than Emily and I." He bent the tube until she heard a barely audible *snap* and then shook it. Dark liquid sloshed within its confines.

Alex's eyes widened as she recognized the vial. "Varik!"

He stopped in mid-shake. "What?"

"You're going to do that here? Now?"

"Yes."

Alex watched, speechless, as Varik tore the seal from the tube's stopper and drank half of the synthetic blood in one gulp. His eyes closed, and he shuddered. When he opened his eyes again, they were an odd mixture of dark brown and gold that reminded her of the cooling lava flows she'd seen on television. "I can't believe you just did that." She looked up and down the corridor in which they stood. "What if someone had walked in and seen you?"

"What's the matter? Afraid to let a human see us for what we really are?" His voice was thick and breathy.

"No, it's just that—never mind." She waved a dismissive hand. Even though she'd grown up in the years after humans had learned of vampires' existence, she'd been counseled not to flaunt her reliance on blood or Vlad's Tears, because it made many humans uncomfortable. "I thought you didn't like Vlad's Tears."

"I don't." He cleared his throat and looked at the tube in disgust.

"Then why are you using it?"

"It was a long drive from Louisville. Freddy, Reyes, and I were able to catch a few hours of sleep at the hotel, but unlike them, I didn't have time to find a donor this morning. Since I seem to be banned from Crimson Swan, it's this or nothing."

Alex felt a sharp stab of guilt when she looked at the healing bruise along his jaw. It had been hours since Stephen punched him. Instead of the bright bluish-purple of a recent injury, it was the sickly green-and-brown color human bruises turn after about a week. "Yeah, well, Stephen was right. You deserved it."

"That may be true, but that doesn't make it hurt any less." He saluted her with the tube. "Cheers." He drained the rest of the liquid and shuddered again, stamping his foot as he swallowed.

Alex couldn't contain her chuckle. "You look like a kid being forced to take cough medicine."

"That's what I feel like." He tossed the empty tube into the trash bin. "You'd think they could at least make the stuff taste better."

"You want them to make it cherry-flavored or something?" She sipped her remaining water.

"That would be nice, or grape. I always liked grape.

Just think"—he adopted an exaggerated commercial voice-over tone—"Vlad's Tears: now in thirty-two delicious flavors, including watermelon, butter pecan, and chocolate chip."

She laughed.

Varik grinned. "It's nice to hear you laughing again."

Her laughter died. "Don't start, Varik."

"With what?"

"The whole 'let's rekindle the flame' thing." She tossed her empty water bottle into the recycle bin.

"I wasn't. I was merely stating a fact."

"Whatever."

He held his hands up in mock surrender. "Could we please call a truce until after the autopsy?"

Alex nodded and stared at the faded linoleum floor. She knew she was being too sensitive, but Varik's sudden appearance coupled with everything that'd transpired—the disturbing dream she'd experienced that morning, her argument with Harvey, the shooting at Maggie's Place—had left her feeling off balance.

She hadn't had time to analyze her dream, but the cemetery had been Saint Michael's in Louisville, where they'd buried her father. Her childhood home had been only a few blocks away, and she knew the cemetery well. She and Stephen had often played there during the summer months, hiding among the gravestones and climbing the trees. Life had been much simpler then. Her thoughts drifted to the past, to her father.

It was Valentine's Day 1968, only a month before he was killed. He came home from work with a dozen red roses for her mother and a single white rose for Alex. He swept Alex up into his arms and gave her the flower with a peck on the cheek. "For Princess Alexandra," he said, "the fairest in the land."

She giggled as the stubble of his beard tickled her face. He smelled of coffee, tobacco, and the chalk he used while teaching classes at the University of Louisville. His scent mingled with the sweet perfume of the rose. "Love you, Daddy," she said, as she hugged him.

He smiled, showing his perfectly human teeth. His strong arms held her tightly and he whispered, "I love you, too, Princess."

"Hey," Varik's voice and hand on her shoulder brought her back to the present. "They're ready for us."

Alex shied away from his touch and entered the autopsy room. Even though she'd been there before, she was still struck by how closely it resembled an emergency room. Cabinets lined one wall and housed a large stainless-steel sink. Rolling tables were pushed up against the far wall, and shelves containing instruments, jars, and other containers filled yet another wall.

Dr. Philip Hancock sat on a raised stool on the other side of the autopsy table, making his final notations. His bald head gleamed under the harsh fluorescent lights when he looked up at her. "Ah, Alex." He smiled warmly and pushed his soda-bottle glasses away from the end of his hooked nose. "Good to see you again."

Alex could hear the creaking and popping of his joints as he moved. "You, too, Doc."

The thickness of his glasses magnified his brown eyes and gave the doctor the look of a perpetually surprised owl. He shifted his larger-than-life eyes to Varik. "Who's your friend?"

Before Alex could answer, Varik stepped forward, extending his hand. "Enforcer Varik Baudelaire."

Dr. Hancock shook Varik's hand limply, his gaze traveling over the tall vampire. He glanced at Alex and jerked his head toward Varik. "He helping or hindering?"

"That remains to be seen," she said.

"I see." The doctor sat down on the stool with a loud groan. "You'll have to forgive me for sitting, but I'm not as young as I used to be. The bones can only take so much." He sighed heavily before fixing Alex with a somber stare. "How's your arm?"

"It's been better, but I'll heal."

"You should have a sling on it to keep it from bouncing around too much. Didn't they give you one at the emergency room?"

"She didn't go to the ER," Varik answered. "She refused."

"The hospital had enough incoming wounded without me adding to the chaos. Add in the five dead—"

"Seven, actually," Doc Hancock corrected. "One was DOA at the hospital and another died on the operating table. Four—including you, Alex—were sent home with minor injuries, and two more are listed in critical but stable condition in the ICU at Jefferson Memorial."

"I hadn't heard the updated numbers," Alex whispered. "That makes thirteen."

"Any idea who the shooter was?"

"None, and it's not our case. Sheriff Manser," she sneered, "is handling it."

Doc Hancock rocked back on his stool. "Oh, my God in Heaven. Well, that's going to be a clusterfuck if I've ever seen one."

Alex never expected to hear profanity from the man in front of her. She knew the shock registered on her face when he winked at her.

He picked up his notes and tapped them on the side of the metal table. "Guess you want to know about Mr. Stromheimer."

Alex stepped up to the waist-high steel table. The body lying on it was completely covered by a white sheet, but standing beside it, she could smell copper and the faint aroma of veal. It was the scent of blood and flesh, of fresh death. Forcing herself to look at Dr. Hancock instead of the body, she swallowed the bile rising in her throat and realized she still hadn't eaten. The coffee and sandwich she'd purchased were casualties of the shooting.

"You okay?" Dr. Hancock's owl eyes blinked at her. "You look a little green."

Alex nodded. "I'm fine."

Dr. Hancock watched her for a moment, then launched into his findings. "Well, this one's not much different than Grant Williams or the first victim, John Doe Vampire. Death by exsanguination." He looked up at Varik. "He bled out."

Varik stood silently with his arms folded over his chest.

Flipping through his notes, Dr. Hancock continued.

"Decapitation occurred postmortem, as did the staking. Judging from the damage to the neck tissue and spine, it appears the head was removed with a large blade, something like an ax or machete."

"What about the discoloration around the stake?" Alex fixed her gaze on the white sheet. Had it just moved?

"Tattooing," Dr. Hancock answered, reading his notes, "caused by unburned gunpowder hitting the skin."

"The victim was shot?" Varik shifted as he spoke. "And then staked?"

Dr. Hancock's eyes focused on him, and then he looked at Alex. "He's a bright one, isn't he?"

"Top of his class."

The doctor grunted and continued. "Judging from the patterns and fragments I found inside the chest cavity, I'd say it was fired within a few feet of the victim's chest. Most likely a nine-millimeter."

"Why use a stake if the victim's already dead?" Varik brushed past Alex as he moved to the head of the table.

"Cover," Alex whispered, staring at the white mass spread before her. The sheet seemed to rise and fall with a phantom breath. Fear slithered up her spine, wrapped around her chest, and restricted her breathing. "Most humans still believe the only way to kill us is with a stake. Use both and make sure the vamp is dead while also covering your tracks."

"She's right," Dr. Hancock said. "The stake followed the track of the bullet, for the most part."

"Why didn't you find this with the other two?" Varik lifted the edge of the sheet, peering underneath.

The cloth fluttered, and Alex gripped the side of the table. Her stomach churned, and she felt dizzy. Little pinpoint starbursts danced before her eyes.

"We didn't know to look for it, but I went back to the other bodies after seeing this one. There's no indication of tattooing or residue on the victims, and I didn't find any bullet fragments in the chest cavity when I opened them up the first time. I checked again to be certain, but the stakes covered the bullet track, so it's hard to tell how much damage is caused by the stake and how much is bullet-related." Dr. Hancock turned to Alex. "You sure you're okay?"

The table shifted, and the victim's hand sprang from beneath the sheet, brushing her fingers. She screamed and pulled away from it. The cold numbness of the grave iced her blood, freezing her in place.

"Alex!" Varik grasped her shoulders as Dr. Hancock hurried around the table.

Alex watched as the headless corpse sat up. She whimpered and struggled against Varik's grip. The sheet slipped to the floor, revealing the gaping hole in the corpse's chest and the crudely stitched Y-incision spanning its torso. "Let me go," she whispered. "I have to go."

Varik tightened his grip. "What's wrong? What do you see?"

The corpse swung its legs over the side of the table and stood.

Alex pulled one shoulder free, but her feet remained frozen. "He's coming for me."

"Who? Who's coming for you?"

"Alex." Dr. Hancock's voice was low and steady, soothing. "There's nothing there."

The corpse raised one arm, reaching for her. Air whistled through the gaping chest wound as it drew a ragged breath.

"Alexandra," the phantom voice of her father whispered to her.

"Alex." Varik shook her gently. "Who's coming for you?"

The pinpoint starbursts returned, and the room grew dim. Her legs gave way and she fell against Varik as darkness closed around her. "Daddy."

Tasha's unmarked squad car rocked with the force of her slamming the door shut. She gripped the steering wheel and stared at the throng of crying families gathered in front of Jefferson Memorial's emergency entrance. They deserved answers. Unfortunately, she didn't have any to offer.

Harvey had sent her to the hospital to interview the victims who weren't critically injured. They'd all said essentially the same thing. "I didn't see anyone. I don't know why anyone would do something like this."

Maggie's Place was outside the town's corporate limits, and investigating the shooting fell to the sheriff's department. He'd requested additional manpower from metro police, since his department was understaffed due to recent budget cutbacks. The JPD had suffered decreased funding as well, but they'd retained their forensic team.

The irony was that Alex, as an FBPI Enforcer, had the best funding of any law enforcement in the area and access to a state-of-the-art mobile forensic lab. However, Harvey refused to entertain the thought of cooperating with her after Varik's display in the diner.

"Varik," Tasha muttered. She didn't trust him, and it was becoming obvious that relying on Alex for information about him would prove futile. Even though she knew Alex was tight-lipped about her past, Tasha couldn't help but think there was more to their prior relationship than mentor and trainee. The only other person in Jefferson who would know and who might be willing to talk to her was Stephen.

She made her decision and started the car. She lifted the microphone for her police radio and spoke into it. "Lieutenant Lockwood to Dispatch."

"Dispatch," a woman's voice crackled over the radio. "Go ahead, Lieutenant."

"I'm heading to Crimson Swan to follow up on some information with Stephen Sabian. If anyone needs me, page my cell phone."

"Ten-four," the woman responded.

"Lockwood, out." She returned the microphone to the clip attached to the side of the radio. Pulling out of the hospital's parking lot, she turned west and headed for Crimson Swan.

She wove through the narrow one-way downtown streets and passed through Old Towne, the historical residential neighborhood of Jefferson that was a strange mix of antebellum mansions, Victorian manors, and 1930s bungalows. Majestic oaks lined the wide streets, casting their graceful moss-laden shadows over perfectly manicured lawns and pristine wrought-iron fences.

Tasha had been born and raised in Jefferson and had always admired Old Towne's illusion of slower, simpler times. However, that's all it was—an illusion. A single right turn and two stop signs brought her to Jefferson Boulevard, the commercial heart of the town. She turned left onto the divided four-lane street, and three traffic lights later, she pulled into Crimson Swan's parking lot.

Stephen's blue Dodge pickup was one of several vehicles in the lot. Most of the customers would be those vampires who lived in the rural areas of Nassau County but worked within the town's corporate limits. Even though several hours of daylight remained, as the day drew to a close, more vampires would begin congregating at the bar before going home to their families for the night.

She suppressed a shudder as she reached for one of the wrought-iron handles on the blood bar's massive double doors. Even though she'd grown up after vampires had gone public, the fact that she was willingly going into the lion's den still unnerved her. Taking a deep breath to steady herself, she threw the door open and entered.

Heads turned and conversations died. Tasha estimated at least a couple dozen eyes in varying shades of yellow staring at her. All vampires' eyes changed to a variation of gold when they were under the influence of either blood-hunger or an intense emotion, such as anger. Judging from the hard glares directed at her, she could safely assume an even mix of the two in the bar's patrons.

She walked forward, hoping her legs weren't shaking too badly for anyone to notice. A few humans, including a dark-haired woman behind the counter, watched her with curiosity before turning back to their vampire companions and conversations. Bars always made her feel vulnerable, regardless of whether they served humans or vampires. Ever since she stopped drinking ten years ago, she hadn't set foot in a bar outside of official business. Her visit to Crimson Swan was official business—at least that's what she told herself. Looking around at the dim lights, classic movie monster décor, and silent vampires, she wondered again if she was doing the right thing.

Stephen emerged from the back of the building carrying a heavy beer keg in each hand as easily as she'd carry a six-pack of soda. The kegs thumped against the wooden floor when he set them down, and conversation returned although at a much lower volume. He saw her and waved her over. "Tasha, I'm so glad you're here. I heard about Alex and the shooting. I tried her cell phone, but she didn't answer. No one at the hospital will give me any information. I'm going out of my mind here."

"She's fine. The bullet just grazed her arm."

He sighed and slumped against the bar's counter,

head resting on his arms. He remained there for several seconds before straightening and running a hand through his thick curls. "That's a relief. Thanks for stopping by to let me know."

"You're welcome, but actually, that's not why I'm here."

"I see." He grinned, showing sharp white fangs that were larger than Alex's. "I paid my speeding tickets. I swear."

"I need some information."

"About the shooting?"

"Not exactly. Think you could help me?"

Stephen shrugged. "I can try."

She looked over her shoulder and then back to him. "Is there somewhere we can talk in private?"

One blond eyebrow arched, but he gestured for her to follow him. "Janet," he addressed the human woman manning the bar. "I'll be in my office for a while if you need me."

The woman nodded as she filled a large glass with a mixture of blood, vodka, and hot sauce while an anxious-looking vampire watched.

Tasha quickened her step, eager to place some distance between herself and the vampires who continued to surreptitiously stare at her. She and Stephen entered a narrow hallway lined with doors. As they passed, she thought she heard moaning coming from behind a few.

Stephen seemed to notice a question on her face and answered before she voiced it. "Private donor rooms," he explained. "It's only when I hear screaming that I worry."

She stopped in mid-stride, mouth agape.

He laughed. "Relax, I'm joking." They'd reached the end of the hall, and he opened a door that was next to last on the right side. "See for yourself."

Unable to suppress her curiosity, she peered around the doorjamb, and most of the tension left her body.

A male vampire who looked as though he could easily bench-press a small car sat in front of a wall of flickering black-and-white monitors.

"Josh," Stephen said, leaning against the opened door and gesturing to the other vampire, "monitors all the private rooms as well as the common bar area and parking lot. Nothing happens in or around Crimson Swan without us knowing."

Josh nodded to her as his fangs crunched through a Doritos tortilla chip. "Everything's quiet, boss," he slurred, spewing a few bright orange crumbs as he spoke. He waved another chip at the monitors. "Only three rooms in use, and they're all behaving themselves. No signs of the HSM nuts, either."

Stephen straightened. "Good." He reached for the door and began closing it. "Let me know if you do see any."

Tasha saw Josh salute them with one more chip before the door closed completely. "Having some kind of trouble?"

Stephen crossed the hall to the last door on the left and opened it. He flipped on the light and sighed. "Tubby Jordan and some of his people were here this morning. I was getting ready to call the cops to remove them when they suddenly packed up and left."

Nathaniel "Tubby" Jordan was the founder and pastor for Holy Word Church, a nondenominational congregation with questionable affiliations—several of the church's members were known associates of various vampire hate groups, including Blood Brothers and the Human Separatist Movement. He'd gained the "Tubby" nickname after acquiring a large belly as a result of too many Sundae Revival Ice Cream Socials at his church.

She'd known Tubby ever since he'd moved to Jefferson from out west a few years ago. While she didn't agree with many of his beliefs, she respected him as a community leader who'd done a lot of good in the town in a short amount of time. Even so, his antics were nothing new to her, and it was out of a relationship born of mutual respect that she'd convinced Alex not to arrest Tubby and some of his followers when they chained themselves in protest to the bar's framework while it was under construction.

Since that time, Tubby and his "flock" continued to regularly protest both the existence of Crimson Swan, which they called a "mockery of God's house" because of its resemblance to a church, and vampires in general. Unless they became physically violent or otherwise damaged property, which they never had, the First Amendment protected their right to speak their minds. Even so, she knew the source of their anger, and a tiny part of her agreed with their mockery charge.

However, Tubby wasn't the reason why she followed Stephen into his office.

Wood paneling and certificates of outstanding achievement in sales from the Vlad's Tears Corporation covered the walls. She'd forgotten that Stephen was once the southwest Mississippi regional sales manager for VTC. Once she became accustomed to thinking of someone in a certain way, it always seemed like a minor shock to either be reminded of some element of their past or discover something new. Like Alex's relationship with Varik Baudelaire.

"So," Stephen began, as he sank into a leather executive's chair behind a pristine desk, "what kind of information are you in the market for?"

Tasha eased into a chair opposite him, avoiding the overstuffed leather sofa. "I need to know whatever you can tell me about Varik Baudelaire."

A change swept over Stephen. His smile disappeared, and his mood visibly darkened. "Why?"

"Because I don't trust the son of a bitch."

"You shouldn't. Varik's after one thing and one thing only—Alex." He eyed her for a moment, rubbing the knuckles of his right hand. "Is Alex still pissed at me?"

"Why would she be pissed at you?"

"She didn't tell you that I punched Varik?"

"Alex hasn't been in a talkative mood today."

"Doesn't surprise me. Varik's a bit of a touchy subject where she's concerned."

Tasha propped her elbow on the chair's arm and cupped her chin with her palm. "Alex wasn't real clear on their connection, aside from Varik being her mentor when she joined the Bureau."

"It goes deeper than that, much deeper. They were engaged."

"That would explain why Varik roughed up Harvey when he called Alex a bloodsucking whore."

"Varik's protective of Alex. All male vampires are protective of females. It's ingrained in our genetic makeup to be protective."

"A real alpha-male syndrome."

"Yeah, you could say that." Stephen swiveled his chair so she saw only his profile. The overhead lighting, although dim, bounced off the framed certificates along the wall and brought out the lighter platinum highlights in Stephen's golden curls.

Tasha watched him, waiting, and thought it was easy to forget he was a vampire when he wasn't staring at her. He was just another handsome guy until he smiled and showed his fangs. "Look, Stephen, I don't know what is happening with Alex, but Varik seems intent on keeping me out of the loop."

"He's good at that sort of thing."

"I'm just trying to understand what's going on."

"I really shouldn't—"

"Varik looked like he was getting awfully chummy with her when they left Maggie's Place together." She hated to manipulate Stephen, but she needed to know what was going on between the two Enforcers. If either of them did anything to compromise the investigation, the FBPI would want answers from all those involved, including her, and she didn't intend to find herself on the wrong end of a vampire inquisition.

Stephen gripped the arms of his chair tightly, and Tasha could hear the wooden frame groaning beneath the leather. When he finally swiveled back to face her, his eyes shone with a controlled anger. "What I'm about to tell you can never leave this bar. Do you understand?"

She nodded.

"If Alex finds out I told you, she'll roast me alive. Not to mention the fact that I'm breaking a host of community taboos by talking about this with a human."

"You have my word that I'll never repeat anything you tell me."

"You've seen the scar on Alex's neck?"

How could she miss it? It was a jagged slash cutting diagonally across Alex's skin, extending from just behind her left ear to the top of her collarbone. Tasha had estimated once that it was about six inches in length and nearly a quarter of an inch at its widest point. "Yeah."

Stephen took a deep breath and said in a rush, "Varik attacked Alex."

Tasha's eyes widened. She'd expected to hear about a bad breakup, maybe a public no-holds-barred argument, but this scenario had never crossed her mind.

"Damn near killed her, actually. If I hadn't shown up when I did, he probably would've succeeded."

"Why would he—what caused—"

"He'd been injured that day during a raid on an illegal donor operation. He needed blood but was too stubborn to admit it." Stephen picked up a pen from his desk and began toying with it. "Alex was at home. She'd taken the day off and was cooking when Varik came in. They were both in the kitchen, talking, and Alex accidentally cut herself."

Tasha's stomach felt as though it were performing cartwheels.

Stephen tossed the pen aside and rubbed his eyes as if trying to wipe away the memory. "The smell of fresh blood sent Varik over the edge. I think Alex would've let him drain her if I hadn't shown up. She barely survived as it was."

Tasha had seen what an out-of-control vampire was capable of doing. A shoot-out she'd been part of as a rookie had been the final result of a domestic violence dispute between two vampires. A husband killed his wife and then tore through town. She'd pulled his car over for running a red light. He'd pulled a gun and shot her three times. Luckily, two of the bullets were deflected by her body-armor vest, but the third had struck her leg. She'd shot him twice before her leg gave out and she fell to the ground. Drawn by her blood, he'd been moving in to bite her when her backup arrived.

Fear coiled around her spine and made her shiver. She swallowed, forcing the memories to retreat and willing herself not to vomit. "So, that's why Alex left Louisville?"

"I'd already moved here to take the job as regional sales manager with VTC. I'd gone home for a visit but stuck around after the attack so I could keep an eye on her and make certain Varik stayed away from her while she was in the hospital. Once she was finally out, Alex packed up and we left town together."

Tasha felt cold, numb. "She never told me any of this."

"Like I said, Alex doesn't like to talk about it."

"But if Varik needed blood, why didn't he just find a donor?"

Stephen shrugged. "I've asked myself the same question. All I know is that Alex is the only reason I didn't kill that son of a bitch then. And she's the only reason I didn't kill him when he showed up today."

"You think Alex still has feelings for him?"

"I'm sure of it, and not because of the blood-bond, either."

"The what?"

"Because Varik took so much of Alex's blood, there's a psychic connection between them. It's hard to explain."

"You mean Varik can read Alex's mind?"

"That's part of it, yeah. Right after the attack, he was able to track her, sense where she was, that sort of thing. She could do the same to him. She had to learn to put up mental barriers to keep him out of her head."

"Can they still do that?"

"Probably," he said with a shrug.

"But it's been six years!"

"Doesn't matter. Once two vampires share blood, a permanent bond is forged. They feel what the other feels. If one has blood-hunger, so will the other. Every emotion is amplified, and unless they learn to control it, they could lose themselves in the bond. And if they continue feeding off one another, the connection grows stronger, to the point that if one dies then the other could die as well."

"Shit," she whispered.

"Now that Varik's in town, my concern is that he's going to try to find a way to strengthen the bond again."

"How would he do that?"

"Either bite her or find a way to have her drink his blood. Time and distance weaken the bond, but it never goes away."

Tasha's brain worked to comprehend what Stephen was telling her. She'd suspected a bigger connection between the two Enforcers, but this was beyond anything she could've imagined.

A knock on the door made her jump in her chair and Stephen smile. "Come in," he called.

The woman from the bar, Janet, poked her head around the door. "Sorry to interrupt, but I need more vodka out front for the Bloody Marys."

Tasha took the interruption as a sign that it was time for her to leave. She stood and nodded to Stephen. "I've got to get back to the station. Thanks for the information."

"Anytime," he replied, as he rose from his chair.

She passed the bartender with a polite nod.

"Tasha?" Stephen called.

She stopped with one foot in the hallway and waited for him to continue.

"Be careful around Varik." Stephen's eyes were slowly bleeding over to amber. "If he sees an opportunity to get Alex back, he'll take it and won't care who gets in the way."

"I'll keep that in mind."

"Tell Alex to call me."

"Will do," she said over her shoulder and hurried

down the hallway, leaving Stephen and Janet alone in the office.

She hurried through the less crowded bar and outside into the cool new darkness. Once she was in the car and moving, she cranked the heater up and turned onto Jefferson Boulevard, trying to chase away the cold that had crept into her bones.

seven

ALEX DRIFTED ALONG INVISIBLE CURRENTS WITHIN THE darkness. The sensation of being carried aloft by thousands of hands gnawed at her. She fought against the unseen hands, tried to work against the forward movement, to no avail. Time slowed as she dipped and spun through the void.

"Alexandra," a voice called to her from the surrounding gloom.

"Who are you?" she asked the voice, twisting within the void to search for its source.

A light in the distance sliced through the unending blackness.

"Alexandra."

The voice floated to her along the currents flowing from the light. The stream through which she drifted seemed to swell into a rising wave, rushing her toward the growing brightness. She tumbled and fell, rolling into the light, and found herself in a wide-open field. Trees dotted the landscape, and sunlight glinted off the surface of a nearby pond. Gentle wind ruffled her hair, and she smoothed it away from her face. She turned in a slow circle, searching for a clue to tell her where she'd landed.

In the distance, beyond the pond, a form moved. She watched for a time while it shambled forward, stopped, seemed to quiver and disappear only to reappear a moment later in a different location, but always advancing steadily toward the pond and her.

Seeing no other signs of life, she walked in the direction of the pond. The voice that had called her name in the nothingness through which she'd fallen was now silent. She frowned. In fact, the world was *too* silent. Although she felt a breeze brushing against her, she heard no rustling of leaves from the scattered trees. Her footfalls were devoid of sound.

She stopped. Whoever or whatever she'd seen earlier had disappeared completely. Where could it have gone?

Uneasiness roiled her stomach and prickled her skin. A blast of frigid air sluiced up her back. She spun and instantly recoiled, feet backpedaling from the headless corpse standing before her.

Its swollen and discolored hands reached for her. Sound returned to the world as a wheezing voice issued from the bloodied neck stump. "Alexandra . . ."

Alex turned and fled. She ran toward the pond, glancing over her shoulder at the motionless corpse.

A low rumble sounded from below the ground, and the earth pitched to one side.

She tumbled, rolled, and regained her footing.

The ground trembled and undulated beneath her.

Stone monoliths sprung from the dirt, blocking her path.

She changed direction and more stones appeared, cutting off her escape, hemming her in.

The sky darkened with storm clouds. Windblown debris pelted her, but she continued to run, following the monoliths as they sprang up around her, shifting her path whenever one appeared to block her.

She'd lost sight of the headless corpse long ago. Her sides began to ache from the strain of running. The earth continued to rumble. She heard the groaning of more stones breaking to the surface and sliding against one another in the distance.

Part of her mind realized she was running blindly through a maze and if she didn't slow down, she could easily miss a turn that would lead her out of it. However, her rational mind had given up control to the primitive part of her brain that was ruled by fear.

Her heart slammed inside her chest. Her breath came in short, ragged gulps. Her pulse beat in her ears and temples. Her legs became lead pistons that churned mechanically. On and on she ran through a seemingly endless labyrinth. She turned a corner and skidded to a halt.

The path before her was blocked, a dead end. The corpse she'd been trying to escape stood with its back to a wall of monoliths, its arms outstretched as if awaiting an embrace.

Breathing heavily, Alex backed away. A now familiar rumble grew louder. She fought to keep her balance while the earth pitched and moved like a living creature. A monolith rose beneath her feet, and she was forced to dive out of its way.

All movement ceased, and silence descended once more. She looked up at the stone that had risen beside her. It had effectively boxed her in with the corpse.

"Alexandra..." the corpse wheezed.

"Who are you?" she asked, picking herself up off the ground where she'd landed on her knees. "What do you want from me?"

Shadows appeared in the makeshift room's corners. Time skipped, and the shadows slithered forward. A high keening wail pierced the silence, forcing her to cover her ears and close her eyes. The keening softened gradually, fading to a fluttering of invisible wings. When she looked again, the original corpse had been joined by two more.

Alex stepped back in surprise. All three were nude and had gaping wounds in their chests, which rose and fell in time with the sound of air whistling through the ragged openings of their necks.

Staring at the lead corpse, the one she'd first encountered, she no longer felt overwhelmed by fear. A feeling of recognition and kinship had replaced her terror. "What do you want from me?" she repeated.

Whispering voices rose from the trio.

"We..."

"...are..."

"...trapped."

"Trapped where? Why?"

"Void..."

"...limbo..."

"...forgive."

"I don't understand."

"Alexandra," a voice called from behind her.

She turned and gasped. Before her stood a tall vampire, his nearly snow-white hair short and neatly styled. A streak of bright copper, the only remnant of his original hair color, slashed through the silver bangs above his dark-green eyes. Stubble from a beard that would never grow softened the squareness of his jaw.

"Daddy?"

"You shouldn't be here," Bernard Sabian said. "You aren't ready."

"How is this possible?" Numbness crept into her limbs, and she felt heavy, as if an immense weight was bearing down on her shoulders. "What's going on here?"

"Go home, Alexandra."

Darkness closed around her, stealing the light. It devoured the headless corpses and nibbled at her father. She felt the shadows pulling her into their embrace once more. She reached for the light, trying to hold on to it, on to her father. "Daddy!"

Her father and the light vanished, and she fell screaming into emptiness.

Alex lay motionless on the small paisley couch in the morgue's employee lounge. All color had drained from her normally pale skin. Varik watched as Dr. Hancock finished his exam and rose to face him.

"She passed out," he said, and removed his glasses to

wipe his brow with a handkerchief. He replaced his glasses and blinked. "Want to tell me what the hell was going on in that room?"

Varik shrugged. "You were there. You know as much as I do."

"Seemed to me that you know more than you're letting on, though."

"Will she be okay?"

Dr. Hancock sighed. "Keep her warm and she should come out of it soon. You're not going to tell me, are you?"

Varik moved to the couch and draped his denim jacket over Alex, tucking it under her chin.

"Right," Dr. Hancock mumbled, and shuffled to the door. "Let me know when she wakes up."

Varik placed a chair from the single table in the room next to the couch. The chair creaked as he sat down and brushed a stray lock of hair from Alex's face. His fingertips traced the line of her jaw. "I need you to wake up, baby," he whispered.

He could feel her mind pressing against his. The blood-bond they shared, though weakened from time and lack of contact, had become more noticeable since his arrival. He was certain that with minimal effort he could slip into her mind, share whatever dreams were plaguing her. He settled for holding her hand.

Sharing a blood-bond with Alex wasn't something he'd planned. It'd been an accident, the result of primal instinct overtaking the rational consciousness, and not a day passed that he didn't regret his inability to control himself. He'd seen nearly two centuries pass. He should've known better. He'd been stupid and careless, and he'd lost Alex because of it.

But what was done was done, and he couldn't alter the past. He could only hope to improve on the future.

The loud techno beat of a cell phone echoed through the room, jarring him from his thoughts.

Varik pulled the phone from its carrying case on his hip and checked the caller identification. "Not now," he groaned. He answered the phone as he walked toward the door. "I'm not alone. Hang on a second."

With a final glance at Alex, he stepped into the hallway. "Go ahead," he said into his cell phone.

The deep voice of Damian Alberez rumbled through the phone. "What's Sabian's status?"

Varik rubbed his forehead with his free hand. "The investigation is progressing normally."

"Bullshit. If it were progressing normally, I wouldn't be hearing reports of seven dead humans and six others wounded, including one Enforcer."

Varik closed his eyes and mouthed a silent curse. He should know better than to lie to Damian. The man could smell a lie told two states away. "There's been a complication."

"You call a mass shooting a complication?"

"No, of course not, but the Nassau County Sheriff's Department is handling the shootings."

"I wanted to have the best investigator in the Bureau on these murders. Now I'm beginning to question my decision to pull you out of retirement. The lead Enforcer in a murder investigation is gunned down in broad daylight, and you just hand it off to the nearest human!"

"There's no evidence to suggest that Alex was the target or that the shooting is in any way connected to our murdered vampires."

"*Find* a connection!"

"And how do you suggest I do that? Pull a shiny object out of my ass to distract these dumbass rednecks while I poach their case?"

"I don't care how you do it. I only care about the results."

"Then fuck off and let me do my job!"

Damian didn't respond, and Varik inhaled deeply, trying to rein in his temper. "There's something else," he said slowly. "Alex has been..." Varik's voice trailed off.

"Has been what?" Damian grumbled.

"*Affected* by the investigation."

Damian was silent for several seconds. "How badly?"

"I don't know yet." Varik propped his forearm on the wall and rested his head on his arm. He briefly explained what had happened during the autopsy review.

"Is she still unconscious?" Damian asked.

"Yes."

A heavy sigh filtered through the phone. "I hoped it wouldn't come to this."

Varik shook his head. "You can't do it, Damian. Don't make me do it."

"If Enforcer Sabian isn't able to continue, then you'll have to take over as primary investigator."

"And if I refuse?"

"I'll send someone else."

Alex resisted his involvement, but anyone else would

have twice the resistance and the case would suffer until Damian was forced to replace them both. He couldn't allow that to happen. He had to find a way to keep her on the case.

Damian's voice softened. "I know how you feel about her, Varik, but policy is policy."

"I know." He pushed away from the wall and paced down the hall.

"Just be glad things aren't like they were back in the old days, before all this bureaucratic crap."

"Don't go there, Damian."

"If a Hunter was compromised back then, he'd be dead before the next sunrise."

Anger chilled his words. "Is that supposed to make me feel better?"

"I'm trying to set things into perspective."

"You're doing a lousy job."

"I don't expect you to revert to your old methods—"

"Good."

"But I do expect you to relieve Enforcer Sabian of her duties, *if* she should prove incapable of continuing this investigation." Damian's tone shifted back to one of authority. "Am I making myself clear, Enforcer Baudelaire?"

"Yes, sir, perfectly clear."

"And I expect regular status reports on your progress with Sabian."

"Yeah."

The call ended, and Varik slipped the phone into its carrying case. He'd known Damian for a long time, well over a century, and considered him a good friend. However, he thought Damian still had a lot to learn about relating to others.

When vampires announced themselves to the world, their Hunter division was quietly absorbed into the Special Operations unit of the FBPI. Varik had been made director of the unit when Damian was promoted to Chief Enforcer.

Damian knew of his and Alex's prior relationship, knew that Varik would be able to determine better than anyone if she was reaching a breaking point. He could see the logic in Damian's decision to send him to Jefferson. He'd been a Hunter of Hunters. Now he was being forced into a similar role, and he hated it.

He scrubbed his face with his hands and breathed deeply. The lingering scent of jasmine and vanilla, Alex's personal scent, on his hands brought a memory to the surface.

It was August 13, 2003. He and Alex had been together for several years, and he'd finally worked up the courage to propose. A knot had formed in his stomach, twisting his insides and making his heart race.

Alex was asleep, lying on her stomach with her left hand resting on the pillow beside her head. He took a deep breath to steady his nerves and his hand. He slipped the two-carat pink diamond ring onto her finger. She mumbled something in her sleep and her hand closed, clenching the pillow, but she didn't wake up.

He snuck out of the bedroom they shared and walked down the hall to the kitchen. The knot in his stomach refused to go away as he began cooking bacon and brewing coffee. Questions ran through his mind:

Would she say yes? Would she say no? Would she want scrambled or fried eggs for breakfast?

Several minutes passed before he heard the floorboards in the bedroom creak. His hands shook as he tried to pour the coffee. He had once been capable of killing someone without batting an eye, but proposing marriage was turning him into a nervous wreck.

Quick footsteps in the hall announced Alex's approach. She entered the kitchen wearing a faded red terry-cloth bathrobe and holding her left hand in her right. The pear-shaped diamond sparkled as brightly as the captured tears on her lashes, but she was smiling.

"I made coffee," he said, offering the mug with the most liquid.

She took the cup and set it aside before she jumped into his arms. She wrapped her own arms around his neck and her legs around his waist. He stumbled back with the force of her attack and crashed into the counter, knocking jars from the spice rack beside the stove. Her breath was warm on his ear as she spoke. "It's beautiful."

The knobby terry cloth felt rough against the palms of his hands as they cupped her bottom, supporting her weight. "The coffee?"

"The ring, you jackass."

Varik smiled, and the knot in his stomach eased. "So, can I take this as a 'yes'?"

A scream erupted from the employee's lounge.

"Alex!" he shouted in return, and sped down the corridor.

———————

After talking with Stephen, Tasha had returned to the Municipal Center, intending to speak with Harvey, only to be told he wasn't there. She'd turned over her notes from her interviews with the victims at the hospital to Deputy Case. When she asked for an update, he'd evaded her question, saying they'd "be in touch" if they required any more assistance from the metro police.

Fuming at being shut out of the shooting investigation, she went to her office to review the items gathered from the Eric Stromheimer scene only to discover the two forensic techs Varik left in the mobile lab had commandeered all evidence from Stromheimer, Grant Williams, and John Doe Vampire. They'd cleaned out the temporary command post Alex had established in one of the police department's interview rooms and had even grabbed the photos and files Tasha had on her desk.

Her fuming exploded into rage. She'd been halfway across the Municipal Center's parking lot when her cell phone rang. The precinct's radio operator had patched through an urgent call from Joe Parsons, the night-shift foreman for Morrison Distribution. He'd stated he was concerned about a missing employee—a vampire named Gary Lipscomb—and asked to meet with her. She aborted her encounter with Varik's Enforcers in favor of pursuing a potential lead, which was why she now sat in Parsons's office, waiting.

Tasha rocked back and forth on the uneven legs of a threadbare office chair. The glassy eye of a largemouth bass, frozen in mid-struggle, seemed to bore a hole into her forehead as she stared up at it. Dust covered the fish's back, and a spider had made a small web in the corner of the gaping mouth. She hated animal trophies, but at least the fish kept her from staring at the deer-head-turned-hat-rack mounted on the wall beside her.

A short, wiry man entered the office along with the sounds of diesel engines, the high-pitched warning beeps of forklifts, and the shouts of warehouse employees. "Sorry to keep you waiting, Lieutenant," the loading dock supervisor said as he closed the door, effectively blocking out much of the noise. "Can I get you anything? Coffee? Water?"

"No, thank you, Mr. Parsons."

He sank heavily into the tufted imitation-leather executive's chair behind the battered desk. "Now, where were we?"

"You were telling me about Gary Lipscomb."

"Ah, yes. Well, Gary's been driving a forklift for about six months, since he moved here from Natchez, and he's always been a model employee. At least he was until about two weeks ago."

"What happened two weeks ago?" she asked, scribbling notes on a small notepad.

"Gary began acting strangely—coming in late, taking long lunches, leaving early. I tried talking to him about it. He said he was having a lot of personal problems. I asked if there was anything I could do to help, but he shut down, refused to talk."

"Do you have any idea what these personal problems may have been? Trouble at home? Work?"

"I don't know about his home life. Gary wasn't the most talkative guy, but then again, he's a vamp. One thing I've noticed about them is that it's easier to squeeze blood from a turnip than convince them to share information." Parsons chuckled at his own joke but quickly sobered when Tasha didn't react. He cleared his throat and continued. "As for work, he's not the only vamp working here, but we've never had any major problems. The occasional flare of tempers, nothing unusual about that."

"No threats?"

"No, no, I can't—wait, there was an incident about a month ago." Parsons sat forward. "Gary was loading pallets on a truck. He was almost done, only had a few left, when the truck's driver started raising holy hell." He ducked his head. "Pardon my language. Anyway, he ranted about a 'damn bloodsucker' loading his truck. The guy stood on the dock and blocked Gary's lift, wouldn't let him finish. I had to get one of my other guys to do it."

"What did Mr. Lipscomb do?"

"He shrugged it off and went back to work. He said he just wanted to forget the whole thing."

Tasha scribbled more notes. "Do you know the driver's name and who he works for?"

Parsons nodded. "Oh, yeah. He's a regular through here. Name's Owen Gibson, hauls for Fast Freight Trucking, an independent company out of Natchez. He's in here five or six times a month."

Tasha nodded. "When was the last time Mr. Gibson picked up a load?"

"Been a couple of weeks now, I guess."

"Is that unusual?"

Parsons shrugged. "Can't really say. Sorry. I just assumed he was on vacation or assigned to a different route."

Tasha made a few more notes. "Has Mr. Lipscomb ever called in sick?"

"No, never. I mean, he's a vampire, right? They have pretty stout immune systems, so it's not like he's going to catch the flu or anything."

"Mr. Parsons, what you've told me is interesting, but I don't see why any of this would lead you to believe Gary Lipscomb is involved in these murders."

"Well, that's it, Lieutenant. Gary hasn't shown up for work in several days. When that body was discovered last night, I feared the worst." He opened a drawer and pulled out a small zip-top bag. "I heard you'd identified the body as this Stromheimer guy. That's when I got really concerned."

"Why is that?"

"I checked Gary's records, and he listed Eric Stromheimer as an emergency contact. So, when I heard the news and Gary still didn't show up for his shift today, I searched his locker, thinking maybe I'd find something to explain his behavior, and found this." He dropped the bag on the desk in front of her.

Tasha stared at the small vial. Dark liquid coated its sides. Some of it had leaked around the cross-threaded cap and dried in a corner of the bag. She plucked a tissue from the container on Parsons's desk and carefully used it to lift the bag. She turned it so she could

see the vial's top. A crudely drawn teardrop superimposed over a crescent moon adorned the cap. "Midnight," she muttered.

Parsons was nodding. "Morrison Distribution has a
zero-tolerance drug policy, and we randomly test em
ployees every month. Gary's presented clean tests four
times. That's why I was shocked to find that in his
locker."

"You said he began working here six months ago. He
was *randomly* selected four times?"

Parsons flushed. "Well, uh, as I said, the tests are random. I don't, uh—I mean, the orders for who is tested
and who isn't come from the manager. I'm just—I just
follow—"

"Mr. Parsons, save your breath. I'm not interested in
Morrison Distribution's drug-screening selection process."

The foreman slumped in his chair, looking both relieved and guilty.

Tasha wrapped the tissue around the bag and vial
and tucked them both into her pocket. Midnight users
were incapable of rational thought and were prone
to aggression and violence. The murders of Grant
Williams and Eric Stromheimer were too clean and me-
thodical for her to believe any vampire on Midnight
could be responsible. However, given the connection between their latest victim and a currently missing vampire, it was a lead she couldn't ignore. There was also
the issue of the unidentified first victim. She checked
her watch. She needed to get this new information and
evidence to Alex as soon as possible.

She slipped the notebook and pen into the inside

pocket of her jacket as she stood. "I think that will do for now, Mr. Parsons. If you hear from Mr. Lipscomb or think of anything else"—she held out a business card—"please give me a call."

Parsons stood with her, accepting the card, and extended his other hand. "Sure thing, and if you hear anything from Gary, you'll let me know?"

Tasha shook his hand. "Of course."

The phone rang, and Parsons sighed. "I can have someone see you out, Lieutenant, if you don't mind waiting," he said, reaching blindly for the phone.

"I can find my way."

The cacophony of the loading dock seemed to pulsate around her. She skirted the perimeter of the warehouse, taking care to stay clear of the forklifts and the heavy pallets of freight they moved.

She glanced at her watch again as she exited the building. If she hurried, she could issue a BOLO for Gary Lipscomb and Owen Gibson. She wanted to talk to the trucker, get his side of the story.

As she closed her sedan's door and reached for the ignition, she saw Mr. Parsons burst through the door she'd exited, waving madly and running toward her.

He was huffing by the time he reached her open window. "I—I thought of something." He paused to suck down a few breaths. "Gary's car. Would that help you find him?"

"It might. You know where it is?"

Parsons nodded and half turned, pointing across the expansive parking area. "Rusted Town Car in the corner. Been here since he went missing."

Emily Sabian tugged on the handle of her single carry-on bag, and it tumbled from the plane's overhead storage bin. The flight from Louisville to Memphis had been a rough one. She'd tried to find a nonstop flight from Kentucky to Mississippi, but none existed, at least not on short notice.

Storms were moving through the region and threatened to delay many of the connecting flights. Passengers hurriedly gathered their belongings and impatiently inched along the narrow aisle to the exit. Once they broke into the relative openness of the terminal's walkway, several ran ahead as they grumbled about both the weather and the slower exiting passengers.

Emily stepped out of the semi-dark tunnel into a blinding world of fluorescent lights. She paused near a cluster of chairs to gain her bearings and allow her eyes to adjust to the sudden brightness. She found a bank of monitors and checked the status of her connecting flight to Jackson, Mississippi. Thunder rumbled ominously as she saw that her flight was delayed due to the storm bearing down on the Memphis International Airport.

She bought a coffee and croissant from a café and resigned herself to a potentially long wait. Autumn thunderstorms were unpredictable. They could last moments or hours. Either way, she wasn't going anywhere for a while.

She made her way to her next gate, which thankfully wasn't crowded. Judging from the noise level coming from the nearby food court, she surmised that many travelers had decided to take advantage of the delay. She found a seat at the gate in front of a low-volume television but with a view of the flight status monitors, the service desk, and a runway. If any more delays were going to occur because of weather, she should be one of the first to know.

Emily extracted her cell phone from her bag and pressed a preprogrammed button to dial Stephen's number. She broke off a piece of her croissant as she listened to the ringing in her ear.

"Your call has been forwarded to an automated voice messaging system," a computerized female announced. "Please leave your message after the tone."

"Stephen, this is your mother. I'm in Memphis, on my way to Jackson, and my flight's been delayed, so I'll be late getting into Jefferson. As soon as I have a better idea of when I'll be arriving, I'll let you know."

She paused before continuing softly. "Stephen, I know Varik's in Jefferson, because I've already spoken with him. I know how you feel about him, but I want you to trust me when I say that right now, he's the best person to watch over Alex."

Lightning flashed across the western sky, and the first big drops of rain began to pelt the window.

"I'm not saying you aren't capable of protecting your sister, but this—" She paused to search for the correct words. "Whatever is going on in Jefferson, I feel—well, I'm not sure what I feel, honestly. Just be careful, sweetheart, and I'll see you soon."

Emily closed her phone and stared at the blank screen for a moment before slipping it back in her bag. Settling into her seat, she sipped her coffee and watched the rapidly approaching storm darken the outside world.

eight

THE JEFFERSON POLICE DEPARTMENT'S IMPOUND YARD was little more than a bare dirt lot surrounded by a razor wire–topped chain-link fence. A large metal building had been erected to one side of the lot and served as the office for the yard manager and a garage where vehicles could be taken apart, inspected, and processed for evidence.

Harvey's gaze roamed the lot, searching for his target. The forensic techs were all inside the garage. Even if one of them came out and saw him, he was leading the investigation into the shooting. He had a right to examine the evidence and doubted that any of them would challenge him. In a far corner reserved for cars impounded by his department, he found the vehicle he'd been seeking.

Sabian's green Jeep Grand Cherokee looked forlorn with its missing back glass and tailgate riddled with bullet holes.

He sidled up to the driver's-side door and cast

another cursory glance across the lot to be certain he was indeed alone. Satisfied, he pulled a white cotton handkerchief from his pocket and used it to cover the door handle as he lifted it. The last thing he wanted was for someone to find his fingerprints where they shouldn't be.

The door opened, and he checked the lot again. Still he saw no one.

Using the handkerchief, he opened the center console and dropped a small zip-top Baggie containing a small amber vial among the various receipts and wadded napkins.

Sweat beaded his brow and upper lip. His mission was almost over. Now he just had to leave without—

"Sheriff Manser?" a woman's voice asked from behind him.

Harvey's heart kicked into high gear. He jumped, and the back of his head struck the metal frame of the open door. "Ah, damn it!" Clutching his head and blinking rapidly to clear the stars bursting in his field of vision, he whirled to face the new arrival.

A petite woman in a white jumpsuit, blue foot coverings, and latex gloves stood at the rear of the Jeep. "Oh, my God," she said, and came toward him. "I didn't mean to startle you. Are you okay?"

Harvey waved her away. "Yes, yes, I'm fine. My head's a lot harder than it looks."

"I am *so* sorry. I just wasn't expecting anyone to be back here."

"That's all right." He checked his head and was pleased to see that there was no blood. "I wanted to look things over for myself, just a quick look," he lied, when she opened her mouth to ask a question.

"Well, I don't think that's such a good idea," she said. "We haven't even started processing yet, and—"

He spread his hands, palms up. "Say no more. I understand. Like I said, I just wanted a quick look." He nodded as he passed her. "I'll be on my way."

Harvey wanted to run but forced himself to maintain a steady stroll, pausing beside a bullet-riddled car once in a while and making a show of inspecting some small detail. He used those moments to look back at the tech.

She wore a puzzled frown, but she'd closed the Jeep's door without looking inside.

When he reached the exit gate he checked again, and she was gone. He heaved a sigh of relief and rubbed the knot rising on the back of his head. His mission hadn't gone according to plan, but at least it'd been accomplished.

He lit a cigarette and then whistled a tune between puffs as he proudly walked toward the Municipal Center and dreamt of his hero's destiny.

Alex sat in the morgue's employee lounge and waited for Doc Hancock to render his final judgment.

He nodded to himself before ripping the blood pressure cuff from her arm. "You seem to be recovered from your little fainting spell. How do you feel?"

"Fine," she said hoarsely, and Varik handed her a half-empty bottle of water. Ever since she'd awakened screaming nearly an hour ago, her voice had been playing hide-and-seek. It alternated between normal, hoarse, and nonexistent. Doc Hancock had forced her to remain on the paisley sofa, sipping water and nibbling crackers.

"How's the throat?" he asked. His fingertips were cool against the soft flesh of her neck as he lightly probed for swelling.

She shrugged with her good shoulder because she could tell her voice had disappeared once again. Her wounded arm had been immobilized in a sling after Doc Hancock had taken it upon himself to not only re-dress the seeping wound but also suture it closed.

"Any pain?"

She shook her head.

"Humph," he grunted. "Darnedest thing I've ever seen." His eyes flicked to Varik perched on the arm of the sofa beside Alex. "You ever heard of a vampire losing their voice after fainting?"

"I assure you, Doctor, this is new to me as well as to you," Varik answered. He smiled down at her when she put down the water bottle and met his gaze. "But I think I kind of like her this way. Less arguing."

Alex smacked his thigh with her empty bottle. "Fuck you," she mouthed wordlessly.

Varik laughed.

Beethoven's Fifth Symphony filled the room, and Alex pulled her cell phone out from where she'd tucked it inside her sling. Checking the caller ID, she frowned and handed it to Varik, mouthing, "Tasha."

He walked a few feet away before answering.

"Alex," Doc Hancock said, as he began gently examining her arm. "What happened to you during my report? I've never seen you react that way."

She sighed and rolled her good shoulder in a silent "I don't know." She remembered being in the autopsy room, listening to him present his findings, and then everything turned hazy until she'd woken up screaming on the sofa.

An uneasy feeling gnawed at her. She knew she'd been dreaming, but whenever she tried to summon the dream, to examine it, it skittered away, leaving her frustrated and on edge. She pulled Varik's denim jacket higher beneath her chin, finding comfort in his scent of sandalwood and cinnamon.

Varik returned, and she could feel his excitement beating against her. "Tasha has a lead on a missing vampire."

"Missing?" Alex croaked.

"A foreman at Morrison Distribution says one of his forklift operators hasn't shown up for work in over a week. He opened the guy's locker and found a vial of Midnight."

"Ah, shit," she mumbled.

Doc Hancock cleared his throat. "Well, that's my cue to leave the two of you alone." He began gathering his medical supplies. "Call me if that arm bothers you or if you start feeling light-headed. Otherwise, *try* to take it easy."

Alex gave him a lopsided salute. "Aye, Captain."

He patted her head and shuffled for the door.

Once the door had closed behind the doctor, Varik

picked up where he'd left off. "In addition to leaving Midnight behind in his locker, our missing vampire, Gary Lipscomb, listed Eric Stromheimer as an emergency contact."

Alex gaped at him. "Are you serious?"

"Tasha's having Lipscomb's car towed to the JPD impound lot as we speak."

She struggled to gain her feet and scowled when he extended a hand to help her. Rather than flail about the sofa because she was minus one arm, she clasped his hand, and he pulled her effortlessly to her feet and into his arms. His warmth surrounded her, offering her shelter from the chaos swirling in her mind.

The scent of sandalwood and cinnamon mingled with jasmine and vanilla, made her heart race, and brought on a flood of memories. She remembered how her skin burned from the heat of his hands as he carried her to bed for the first time. He sat beside her at a restaurant, laughing at a shared joke. Morning sunlight danced along the edge of the diamond ring she'd woken to find on her finger.

She saw the heat in his eyes and knew he was also thinking of the past. The blood-bond pulsed with life. It would be so easy to lift her mental shields, to allow him access to her most intimate thoughts. "Varik," she murmured, "I—"

His finger settled on her lips, quieting her.

She shuddered as he traced the outline of her mouth. Suddenly she wanted to recapture those memories, make them come alive once again. Fear and expectation shivered her spine and weakened her legs. She leaned forward, rising up on the tips of her toes as his head bent down to meet her, and held her breath.

His lips brushed hers, soft, tender, uncertain. His fingertips trailed over her scar.

Sensations raced along her skin, prickling her flesh. Alex moaned and dropped the barriers dividing their minds. Memories of their past, seen from her perspective as well as his, raced through her consciousness and fed the growing need within her.

He groaned with a special hunger born of six years' separation and slipped his arms around her waist.

Not to be outdone, she pulled Varik toward her, deepening the kiss. She felt his desire melding with her own rising passions. He wanted more. *She* wanted more.

Alarms clamored in her mind. Something wasn't right. It was all happening too fast. Her mental shields slammed into place once more.

His embrace tightened, crushing her to him, in an effort to substitute physical closeness for the sudden lack of the blood-bond.

Her arm, trapped between them, screamed in protest, and she broke the kiss, gasping in pain. "I can't… We can't."

Varik sighed and rested his head on her good shoulder, panting. "I know. I'm sorry. I don't know what came over me."

"It's the bond." She drew in a ragged breath as he stepped back to look at her and eased the pressure on her arm. "I opened it. I'm sorry. I lost my head. I—*we* can't afford to let that happen again."

He nodded. "You're right," he whispered, and kissed

her forehead. "We have to focus on other matters, and then we can focus on us."

"There isn't going—" Her words died when she looked up into Varik's kaleidoscopic gold-and-brown eyes. Her stomach lurched. "I'm going to be sick."

Varik swept her into his arms and carried her down the hall to the women's restroom. A couple of startled women shrieked and ran as he helped her into a stall.

Her prediction proved correct. Everything she'd eaten since waking returned, and she continued to dry-heave for several minutes. It wasn't until she tried to stand that she realized Varik had stayed, holding her hair back.

He helped her to rise and then walk to a sink.

Alex splashed cold water on her face and rinsed her mouth. She grabbed several paper towels and patted her face dry. Her liquid-amber eyes met Varik's in the mirror as he exited the stall. "Thanks," she whispered hoarsely.

"Are you okay?"

She nodded. "I think so."

"If I'd known kissing you would have that effect, I would've reconsidered."

"It wasn't you, Varik." She watched his reflection in the mirror. He crossed the room to stand behind her, raising his hand as if to grab her arm.

The memory of a headless corpse reaching for her flashed through her mind. She batted the hand away. "Don't touch me."

"What's wrong?" Varik took another step toward her.

Alex closed her eyes, trying to shut out the memory. "It wasn't real. It wasn't real." She repeated the phrase like a protective charm, but the images refused to dissipate.

Stone monoliths. Storm clouds. Trembling earth. Headless corpses. Trapped in an unending maze. Her father standing before her.

Hands grabbed her arms.

She screamed.

"Alex!" The hands shook her. "Snap out of it."

Her eyes opened. Varik stood in front of her, worry and fear etched on his face. Movement behind him drew her attention.

A half-formed shadow pulsed and undulated in the far corner. It elongated, taking on a humanoid appearance, and began to solidify. Swirling dark mist lightened and turned to flesh as the shadow became the motionless visage of a headless corpse.

Varik glanced over his shoulder. "What? What do you see?"

"Death," she whispered.

Varik stared at her. "Alex—"

"What is going on in here?" Doc Hancock's eyes blinked behind his soda-bottle glasses as he entered the restroom.

"A little misunderstanding, nothing more," Varik said calmly.

Alex watched as the vision of the corpse faded, leaving only a faint scent of decay in its wake.

"Misunderstanding, my ass," Doc Hancock said, pointing to Alex. "She's scared shitless. Again."

Varik half turned to face the coroner. "And you think I'm to blame?"

"If the shoe fits."

"Stop it," Alex demanded, her voice once again little more than a rasp in her throat. "Varik was helping me."

"From where I'm standing, it looks more like hurting," Doc Hancock responded.

"Doctor, if I intended harm to anyone in this room, I'd have done it by now." Varik smiled, showing his fangs fully. "And you wouldn't have been able to stop me."

Doc Hancock tensed.

"That's enough, Varik," Alex whispered. Her legs felt shaky, but she pushed him away. She had to defuse the tension before it spiraled out of control. Using the sink as support, she faced Doc Hancock fully. "I slipped," she lied. "I fell and hit my shoulder on the side of the sink. That's why I screamed. Varik was just helping me."

Doc Hancock glanced from her to Varik, leaning against the partial wall between two stall doors, and back to Alex. "You expect me to believe that?"

"Yes," she hissed.

He continued to stare.

"Varik isn't stupid enough to attack me in a women's restroom."

"Thanks, I think," Varik mumbled.

She shot him a withering glance. "Stay out of this, please."

He held his hands up in mock surrender.

"Do you trust him?" Doc Hancock asked.

Alex considered her response. *Did* she trust Varik?

She thought he was an ass by default, and he'd done things in the past that weren't easily forgiven. But he hadn't given her a reason not to trust him since coming to Jefferson. It killed her to admit it aloud, but she looked at him and their eyes met. "Yes, I do."

Something passed behind Varik's eyes, some emotion she couldn't quite interpret, and then was gone.

Doc Hancock sighed. "All right, if falling is your story, I have no choice but to accept it." Shaking his head, he turned to leave. "However, I'd appreciate it if you'd keep the noise level down. This is a morgue, after all."

Alex watched the door shut slowly behind the coroner. She hated lying to him. Doc Hancock had been one of the few humans who'd openly accepted her when she moved to Jefferson, and she genuinely liked him. Some things, however, were beyond the doctor's understanding or need to know, and her sudden onslaught of visions was one of them.

Varik came to stand in front of her. "Did you mean that?"

"What?"

"That you trust me."

"For now, yes. But you have to do something for me. Two things, actually."

His face grew guarded. "What?"

"First, get me the fuck out of this morgue."

"And the second?" He gently took her elbow, steadying her as they walked.

"Leave my investigation alone."

"Sorry, no can do. Damian's orders. You're stuck with me."

"Can't blame a girl for trying."

Varik snickered. "It was a good try."

Alex gritted her teeth to keep from saying what she was really thinking. In truth, she was glad he was staying. Until she could decipher the meaning behind her visions, she needed him. She leaned against him, against his warmth, and only then realized she'd been shivering as though she were standing naked in a snowstorm.

He closed the tailgate of his truck and lowered the hatch on the camper, securing it with a twist of the handle. The meeting was scheduled for eight o'clock. He had enough time to shower, drive into town, and then when the meeting was over, dispose of the body he'd loaded in the truck before reporting for his shift. That meant he'd have to take his uniform with him and change later. Good thing he'd packed a clean pair of coveralls so the blood he'd have to wash off later should be minimal.

"Cleanliness is next to godliness." He recited the adage that had been one of Claire's favorites.

He peered through all the windows on the truck's camper shell. The extra tint he'd added months ago kept the contents from being visible. He'd also taken the added precaution of wrapping the corpse in tarps and covering those with assorted scraps of lumber, trash, and tools. Even if someone looked through one of the windows, he doubted they'd be able to discern the outline of a dead vamp.

Satisfied with his work, he whistled a tune as he trotted up the front steps. He blew a kiss to Claire's picture hanging on the living-room wall and began stripping as he walked through the house. He was completely naked by the time he reached the small bathroom.

Steam rose from the hot-water tap, and he adjusted the temperature to his liking. He had one foot in the tub when he remembered he'd left the photo he always carried of Claire in the bedroom. Humming, he ignored the puddles he left on the hardwood floor from the water dripping from one leg. He slipped Claire's photo into a protective clear plastic container and returned to the bathroom.

He balanced the photo's container on the shelf he'd installed at the opposite end from the showerhead. He stood under the water's spray and rubbed soap over his body as Claire watched.

Memories of the vamps he'd killed played through his mind. The first had been Trent Thibodaux, the one whose body he'd purposefully kept anonymous. As far as he knew, the Enforcer bitch still hadn't identified Thibodaux.

The second was Grant Williams and then Eric Stromheimer. Fourth had been Gary Lipscomb, the vamp he'd loaded in his truck and planned to dispose of tonight.

He thought of the vamp he'd killed earlier in the day—Scott Adams—and smiled. He was becoming more efficient at killing them. He held the power of life and death in his hand. He chose the time and place of each demon's demise.

Humming, he continued to spread the soap, keeping his gaze fixed on Claire's photo. The desire in her frozen eyes seemed to grow brighter. His body began to respond in turn.

A cool breeze seeped around the edges of the curtain, carrying the scent of lavender.

He paused and closed his eyes, feeling the coolness creep up his legs. He backed farther into the warm spray until the water trickled over his shoulders, running in rivulets down his chest to his swelling penis.

The smell of lavender grew stronger, overpowering his senses.

He stood under the pounding water, stroking himself.

Visions danced before him. Claire's hair bounced in time to the motion of her body as she rode him in the early-morning light. His hammer struck a sharpened cross. A plume of fire and smoke erupted from a gun's barrel. Claire was on her knees before him. She braced herself against the headboard, arched her back, and drove her hips back to meet him, moaning his name each time he thrust into her.

The visions exploded as he climaxed. He slumped against the tiled wall, legs rubbery and groin throbbing. Surrounded by the scent of lavender and fading memories of Claire, he wept.

An older-model Lincoln Town Car, which had once been gray but now sported more rust and dirt than paint, sat under the glare of floodlights in the center of the JPD impound garage. Forensics technicians wearing white Doughboy suits moved around the car, snapping photos, removing layer after layer of trash from the car's seats and floorboards, and documenting every step of their process.

Techs examined each piece as it came out of the car. They were looking for blood or some clue that would lead them to the car's owner. They tagged and separated anything that appeared to have even a single drop of blood on it.

Alex stood at a table and sifted through the remains of Gary Lipscomb's life: fast-food bags, empty drink cans, used vials of Vlad's Tears, and various other paraphernalia belonging to the missing vampire. She was working through the "No Blood" pile. The thick latex glove she wore over her left hand made her sweat, and the combination of perspiration and pressure from the glove's tightness made her knuckles throb. She used the edge of the table to push the sleeve of her sweater up to her elbow and kept picking through the obvious trash.

A door opened across the garage, and her eyes met Varik's. She looked away, finding a discarded sale ad to study, and swore softly as she felt heat rising in her cheeks. Ever since their kiss at the morgue, she'd alternated between feelings of shame and euphoria.

She couldn't deny that Varik had always had a certain affect on her, but the fact that she hadn't been able to stop thinking about the kiss filled her with guilt. She needed to get her head back in the investigation and find whoever was behind the murders before they struck again.

"Merry Christmas." Varik dangled a newly purchased fast-food bag in front of her.

The smell of fresh fries and grilled meat made her stomach grumble. She tossed the ad aside and snatched the bag. She hadn't eaten in hours, and lack of food was making her grumpy. "Thanks," she mumbled, hooking a stool with her foot and dragging it from beneath the table.

"You're welcome." He set the accompanying drink on a shelf beside her, but not before he stole a sip of the dark, bubbly liquid.

She used her teeth to grab the edge of her glove and pull it off.

Varik plucked the limp latex from her mouth. "You could've asked for help with that."

"I'm stubborn when I'm hungry."

"I've noticed."

She slapped his hand away from her fries. "Try that again, and you'll draw back a nub."

Chuckling, he faced the table and began rolling up his sleeves. "Finding anything?"

"Nothing substantial," she said, cramming three fries into her mouth. "And if you're going to play with evidence, you should be wearing gloves."

Varik stepped around her and stretched to pluck a pair of gloves from the box on the shelf behind her, brushing against her back.

She tensed at his touch.

"You're blushing," he whispered in her ear.

She hated the satisfaction in his voice. She had a choice to make—either face him now and show him that what happened meant nothing to her or run away and risk losing every remaining shred of her dignity. Her voice sounded strained as she fought to keep from storming out of the garage. "Are you going to help or flirt?"

With his face inches from hers, he grinned. "I can't do both?"

"You're good at multitasking, but—"

"I'm good at a lot of things," he said with a suggestive wiggle of his brows.

She growled a warning.

"Okay, okay. I'll behave. But you can't tell me you didn't *want* me to kiss you."

"In your dreams," she muttered around a mouthful of hot fry mush. She couldn't deny that his words held some truth, but she wasn't about to give him the pleasure of confirming it.

"I think you still want it."

"I do *not.*"

He inhaled. "I can smell it on you, Alex...the desire."

Jasmine and vanilla swirled with sandalwood and cinnamon in an intoxicating combination between them. It called to her, teased her with promises of ecstatic pleasures. Muscles in her lower abdomen tightened in anticipation. She pulled away from him, from the call of their combined scents. "I'm warning you, Varik. Drop it or get the hell out of here."

He straightened, a knowing smirk frozen on his face, and stuffed two stolen fries in his mouth before snapping his gloves in place. "Freddy and Reyes have started processing the evidence from the first three crime scenes," he said, as he began picking through the trash.

Grateful for the change of subjects, Alex sipped her drink before responding. "Have they found anything yet?"

"No prints on the driver's licenses or leather pouches. Freddy *was* able to find a partial stamp embossed into the leather. It's in the pouch's interior and obscured by a seam, but he thinks he may be able to use that to trace the leather."

"Since the pouches appear to be hand-sewn, if he traces the leather, he should be able to find either a local supplier or one that's shipped to someone in Jefferson recently."

"Exactly." Varik thumbed through an ancient copy of *Playboy* and then moved on. "Reyes is examining the cross-stakes. He's trying to match up the carvings to specific tool marks or identify stray hairs that may have gotten trapped in the varnish. It's slow work, but hopefully it will lead us somewhere."

"And Tasha?"

"Gone; said something about a meeting she couldn't miss."

Alex bit into the greasy burger and frowned when she tasted tomatoes. She picked the offending vegetables from the remainder of the sandwich and dropped the slices into the paper bag beside her stool.

"Congratulations on your big Midnight bust, by the

way," Varik said, as he examined a receipt. "I heard it made the Bureau newsletter."

"Thanks," she mumbled with her mouth full of burger. She washed it down with a sip of her drink and continued. "But that article was a little biased. The DEA played a much bigger role in helping break up the ring."

"Enforcer Sabian," a technician called.

Alex shifted on her stool, sipping her drink.

"We're ready to start printing the car."

Alex set her drink down on the shelf and dropped the rest of her fries into the bag she'd placed on the floor. She wiped the grease from her hand as she joined the techs by the car, where they lightly sprinkled a fine powder over the doors, windows, and steering wheel. Their fuzzy brushes worked back and forth in swirling circles.

"Looks like a couple of good prints here on the door and the wheel." Tony Maslan, chief crime scene investigator for the JPD, pointed to the areas with the prints.

She squinted and moved closer. "All I see are smudges."

"They're a little hard to see, but they're there. I'll lift them and run them through IAFIS and VIPER, see if we get a match."

"Great."

IAFIS—the Integrated Automated Fingerprint Identification System—was maintained by the human-run Federal Bureau of Investigation in Washington, D.C., and allowed for an automated search of more than fifty-five million human subjects. VIPER—the Vampire Identification Patterns and Enforcement Resource, a twin of

IAFIS—housed the records of millions of vampires who'd either committed or been the victim of a crime, and was maintained by Enforcers in Louisville.

Latent prints were routinely submitted to both resources in order to establish the identity of the individual who'd left the print. Before the creation of VIPER in the early 1990s, many vampire fingerprints were overlooked by humans as either smudged or unusable. The ridge patterns for vampire prints were much lower than humans', making their fingerprints hard to detect.

"We've cleaned out most of the car's interior. Want us to pop the trunk?" Tony asked, as he walked past her with what appeared to be a long metal rod.

"Sure." She followed him to the back of the car.

He placed one end of the rod against the trunk's keyhole and shoved it into the hole with a loud pop. He removed the rod, lifted the trunk, and whistled. "There's something you don't see every day."

Hundreds of clear vials, dozens of bottles of aspirin, syringes, rubber tubing, and Baggies containing brightly colored pills filled the trunk.

Alex gaped at the unexpected find. "Son of a bitch." She glanced at Varik as he abandoned the table and came to stand opposite Tony. "Our missing vampire appears to have been running a Midnight operation out of his trunk."

They moved back to let a tech with a camera snap several pictures.

"Looks like he was doing a decent business, judging from the number of empty vials," Varik said.

Tony and the camera-wielding tech left, called away

by another, and Alex stepped up to the car. "It's like pulling weeds. Get rid of one and two more pop up in its place."

Varik lifted a Baggie of pills from the trunk. "This is definitely Ecstasy." He tossed the bag back into the trunk. "Only things missing are the blood and garlic. But was he selling it locally or shipping it out?"

"We'll have to check into it, but this could easily explain his disappearance."

Varik walked around to the side of the car. "Business deal gone bad?"

"It's happened before, so we can't rule it out."

"Any chance he was involved with the ring you busted up?"

"I don't remember his name coming up in the investigation, but it's possible. We never did apprehend the main supplier. Hell, we couldn't even get a name, no matter how many deals we made."

"If Lipscomb's disappearance is the result of a deal gone badly, then we've been chasing our tails."

"Damn," Alex whispered, leaning over the trunk to get a better look. "If that's true," she said to Varik as she teetered on one foot, "then I'm going to be so pissed— whoa!"

Her weight pitched her forward. She extended her hand to catch herself before she slammed her injured arm into the side of the car. The bare skin of her palm landed on a stack of aspirin bottles. Images flooded her mind.

A young vampire sat at a kitchen table, surrounded by empty and half-filled vials. Stephen stood behind the bar at Crimson Swan, cheering as a player made a touchdown on a televised football game. A shadow loomed in a doorway, and fire erupted from the barrel of a pistol.

Pain seared her chest. Her breath stopped, and the world turned black.

The Holy Word Church wasn't a huge church. In fact, it wasn't a "church" in the conventional sense, because the small congregation met in a converted farmhouse on the outskirts of Jefferson. A wraparound porch and plantation shutters made for a quaint outer façade. However, the interior of the two-story home had been gutted and converted to a small sanctuary and even smaller offices. The only room that remained virtually untouched was the kitchen in which Tasha sat, sipping chamomile tea and listening to the latest of Nathaniel "Tubby" Jordan's rants.

"Decadence, open sexuality," Tubby said, as he shifted his bulk to the edge of his seat. His jowls flapped as he spoke, and his face had taken on an unhealthy red. "Why, Mary Mason found a three-year-old boy trying to bite a girl's neck in the church nursery last Sunday. Boy said he was *playing vampire*."

"Kids have been playing vampire or doctor for years," Tasha said. "It's an innocent game."

"Innocent! Ha! You of all people should know there is nothing innocent about those vamps!"

"What's your point, Tubby, if you have one?"

"My point is that ever since that bar—that den of

iniquity—opened, more of those Hell-spawned blood-suckers have moved into Jefferson."

Tasha sighed and sipped the chamomile tea Tubby had offered upon her arrival. It was an old argument, one she'd heard before from others, but none were as animated as Tubby. She didn't think there was enough chamomile in the world to calm Tubby once he was in full swing, railing about the imagined evils flowing through the doors of Crimson Swan.

"They're morally corrupting our youth!"

"Who is?" she asked.

"Vampires! Especially that Sabian vamp."

"You mean Enforcer Sabian?"

"No, the other one." He waved away her question. "Whatever its name is."

"Stephen Sabian?"

"That's the one. I, along with some of my flock, were over there this morning—"

"I heard, and I thought I told you to stay away from the bar."

He fixed her with a disapproving look. "I go where the Lord leads, Tasha. Those vamps are pushing drugs, and not just Midnight. Now I, and a lot of other folks around here, want to know what you're doing about it."

"We've been over this before, Tubby. Crimson Swan is a legal business with all its permits and paperwork in order. There is no evidence of drug activity. Stephen Sabian—"

"The Sabians are evil—the devil incarnate." He struggled to his feet. "Both of 'em!"

Tasha pinched the bridge of her nose in a dual effort

to block the overpowering smell of his cologne and to stave off a building headache.

Tubby and others had brought repeated proposals before the Jefferson town council to have the bar's license revoked, and they were voted down every time. In the past few months, Tubby had turned his attention to her, trying to convince her that Crimson Swan was involved in illegal activity. Even if Stephen was involved in something, which she doubted, it wasn't her jurisdiction. All vampire-related crimes were Alex's exclusive territory.

"Do you have any evidence that Stephen or *anyone* at Crimson Swan is doing something illegal?"

"They're vampires! What more evidence do you need?"

"Something that'll hold up in court and isn't simply your prejudicial judgment."

"Prejudicial—" His jowls trembled. "How am I supposed to get evidence if I can't go there? Isn't that *your* job, anyway?"

"Crimes, or *potential* crimes, involving vampires are Enforcer Sabian's territory, not mine. You know that."

"Which makes it the perfect setup for that brother of hers to deal drugs willy-nilly out the back door!"

"And you're accusing a federal officer of misconduct *and* a major cover-up, neither of which I can do anything about without solid evidence!"

Tubby huffed and whirled away only to turn back a moment later. "Why *do* you work with that vamp? I thought you were scared of vampires."

"I am," she answered quietly.

"Then why—"

"Because, unlike some people, I choose to face my fears. Familiarity alleviates fear."

"It also breeds contempt." He sat down again. "Tell me, Tasha, how much respect do you think those vamps really have for you, for any of us? Why, just look at what happened today at Maggie's Place."

"What makes you think vampires had any role in that shooting?"

"Look at the victims, Tasha. All of the dead are humans; so are a majority of the wounded. Only vamp injured was Sabian."

"Maggie's Place is predominantly a human establishment. Very few vampires even go there. Alex was in the wrong place at the wrong time."

"Or maybe she was there as a shill," Tubby said. "Maybe she was the convenient token vamp present so as to cast doubt on the rest of them."

Tasha gawked at him. "Will you listen to yourself? You sound like some kind of paranoid whack-job who's one step away from stockpiling weapons and army rations because of an imagined impending apocalypse!"

"The apocalypse *is* coming, Tasha. Mark my words. For them, humans are nothing more than forbidden fruit waiting to be plucked."

"They have a right to survive."

"Do they?" Tubby placed his fleshy hands flatly on the table and leaned forward. Another wave of cologne beat against her. "You'd kill a mosquito that landed on your arm. How are vampires any different?"

Tasha glared at him, remembering the way Alex had

looked at her while at the Stromheimer scene the previous night. It was the same way a half-starved man would look at a hamburger.

"The Lord liveth, *Lieutenant*, and the Lord shall smite them," Tubby murmured.

She stood to cover the shudder than ran down her spine. "Is that a threat?"

"No, merely paraphrasing the Good Book. Judgment Day is coming, Tasha, for *us* as well as the vampires. Where are you going to stand when that day comes?"

"I think it's time for me to leave, *Reverend*."

"As you wish, but I hope you'll at least consider what I've said."

"I'll take it under advisement."

"Would you care to stay for our weekly prayer service tonight?"

"No, thank you. I have to get back to the office." She gathered her jacket and purse.

"I understand," Tubby responded. "The Holy Word Church doors are always open if you ever need to talk, Tasha."

"Don't hold your breath on that," she muttered.

"We'll be praying for you."

Tasha left the kitchen without acknowledging his final comment and entered the sanctuary, where several members of the church had started gathering. Their conversation stopped, and they watched her with guarded eyes as she passed through the large room. She couldn't help but compare their looks to those she'd received while at Crimson Swan. She was the outsider in both places, and it made her skin crawl.

Even though she thought some of Tubby's concerns were valid and knew that he sometimes took liberties with the boundaries of their tenuous friendship, she couldn't drop everything in order to investigate his latest allegations.

Outside, she hurried down the steps, head down and jingling her keys, anxious to be away. She rounded the side of the porch and was taken aback when she bumped into a warm body.

"Excuse me," she and the man she'd nearly run over apologized simultaneously. Tasha jerked back in surprise. "Darryl?"

Darryl Black, formerly of the Jefferson PD and who now worked with the Nassau County Sheriff's Department, smiled lazily. His dark hair was shaggier than she'd remembered it, and fine lines creased the edges of his hazel eyes. "Evening, Lieutenant."

Tasha returned his smile. "It's been a while since I've seen you. Is Harvey treating you decently?"

"Can't complain. I've been mostly working the night shift, but it suits me fine. It's better than sitting at home."

She nodded in agreement. "What brings you out here?"

He bobbed his head toward the church. "Prayer meeting tonight."

"I didn't know you attended Holy Word."

"I don't; well, not officially. I just come to the prayer meetings occasionally." He focused on her once more. "And you?"

"Tubby and some others were at Crimson Swan this morning. I was just following up on a few things."

"Is he spouting more of his conspiracy theories?"

Tasha rolled her eyes. "Lord, yes, and wearing too much cologne again. I swear the fumes must be rotting his brain or something. Now he's accusing Alex of both corruption and of covering up the fact that Stephen's a Midnight dealer."

Darryl chuckled. "Don't let him get to you. He means well, but—"

"But he can worry the horns off a goat," Tasha supplied. She patted his arm. "Listen, it's been great seeing you, but I have to run."

"Yeah, I should get inside before Tubby eats all the Oreos."

Gravel crunched beneath her feet as she strode across the makeshift parking lot. Darryl had been one of the finest cops in the JPD until he found a pink slip included with his last paycheck, a casualty of the latest round of citywide budget cuts. At least he'd found a niche within the sheriff's department and seemed happy with the move.

She was on Sawyer Mill Road and had just entered the Jefferson city limits when the call came across the radio of an officer down at the impound lot. She flipped the switches to activate her lights and siren, leaving thoughts of Darryl Black and Tubby Jordan in her wake as she sped through the darkening twilight.

nine

"ALEX!" VARIK GRABBED HER SHOULDERS AND PULLED her out of Lipscomb's trunk. He eased her down onto the garage's smooth concrete floor.

Technicians stopped their work and rushed forward. He held his hand up to ward them off. "Stand back."

They stopped a few feet away, their eyes and mouths gone wide. His gaze flicked to his bloody hand.

"Shit," he hissed, and began checking Alex for visible wounds. Her amber eyes were open and staring, but she wasn't breathing. Her skin was cool and growing colder. His hands passed over her chest and stopped. "Oh, no. No, no, no." He gripped the collar of her sweater and ripped it open.

Blood welled between her breasts and pooled in the hollow of her neck before spilling over her shoulder and onto the floor.

"Jesus," one of the techs whispered. "Looks like she was shot."

"Come on, baby. Don't do this to me." Varik found

her pulsing heartbeat, but it was thin, weak. "Damn it." He looked up at the techs. "Call an ambulance! Now!"

He didn't wait to see who responded but laid Alex flat and began CPR. His hands compressed her chest for a five-count, and then he blew into her mouth, trying to encourage her to breathe. "You're not going to die on me. Not like this," he mumbled, doing another five-count of chest compressions.

Tony knelt beside him. "I didn't hear a shot. What the hell happened?"

"It's a psychic wound. She's reliving Lipscomb's death."

"Holy fuck. What can we do?"

Varik checked Alex's pulse. It was still there but weaker. She was fading. "Goddamn it." He snapped the gloves off his hands. "You are *not* doing this to me. I won't let you."

"Whoa!" Tony grabbed Varik's arm as he raised it and opened his mouth, flashing his fangs. "What are you doing?"

"Saving her life." Varik snarled, jerking his arm free. "She'll die just like Lipscomb if I don't do this."

"There has to be another way. What if I—"

"You're human. It won't work."

"The hospital can—"

"They can't deal with this! Alex needs a connection to this physical plane."

Tony chewed his bottom lip, staring at Alex.

"I'm the only chance she's got," Varik whispered.

Tony stood and stepped back, mumbling, "Lieutenant Lockwood's going to have my ass for this."

Varik bit into the soft flesh of his wrist. His fangs pierced the skin and muscle beneath, puncturing the veins. He ignored the pain as the warm flow of blood filled his mouth. Gently cradling Alex in his arms, he held his bleeding wrist to her mouth as if offering a bottle to an infant. "Drink, baby. Come back to me."

Alex felt nothing. Darkness blinded her. Silence deafened her. Then she was floating.

She looked down and saw Varik giving someone CPR. Blood stained the woman's chest and the floor beneath her. His movement seemed agonizingly slow, as if he were working underwater. She watched with curious detachment until she realized *she* was the woman. "What the fuck?"

Looking around, everything in the garage wavered as if she was viewing it through heat waves rising from sunbaked asphalt. Colors were muted, pale shadows of themselves. She saw Tony as he rounded the side of the car and could see his mouth moving as he talked to Varik but heard no words.

A chime drew her attention, and she was no longer floating but standing. The chime sounded like distant crystal bells and filled her with a sense of peace. Something wasn't right. How could she be standing beside Varik and lying on the ground at the same time?

The chime sounded again, urging her to seek it. She felt weightless. Her feet rose from the floor, and she drifted over the car, leaving Varik behind, searching for the source of the crystalline bells. She landed in front of the car and heard the chime again. This time it was louder, behind her. She turned.

A man leaned against the trash-filled table. His casual stance seemed ill matched with the formality of the dark suit he wore.

"Daddy?"

"Hey, Princess." Bernard Sabian's deep voice still carried the Irish lilt that had never given way to the Kentucky drawl she and Stephen possessed. "It's been a while."

Alex nodded, unable to speak.

A smile showing perfect human teeth brightened his pale face.

"Is this real?" she asked, looking around.

"I'm afraid so."

"Where are we?"

"Beyond the Veil that separates the physical world from the spirit realm. This"—he gestured to the surrounding room—"is sort of a no-man's-land in between the two planes, the Shadowlands. Anyone from either side can enter it, if they know the way and have good reason to do so."

"And you have a reason?"

He nodded. "I came for you."

Her throat contracted painfully, choking her.

The edges of his form shimmered as he closed the distance between them.

"I miss you." She forced out the strangled words.

He stopped and brushed a lock of hair behind her ear. "I know, Princess. I miss you, too."

She sobbed and moved into his open arms. The pain of decades of separation left her as they embraced.

He stroked her hair and held her close. "We don't have a lot of time."

"I'm dead. We have plenty of time."

"No, you're not."

"What do you mean?" Alex pulled away enough so that she could look up into his face. His dark green eyes, so very much like her own, stared down at her. The sorrow she found within them frightened her. "Daddy, what's—"

He gripped her elbows and moved her to arm's length. "This isn't your time. You're not meant to die like this."

"I don't understand."

"In a few minutes, you're going to be back in your physical body, but I have to tell you something first. I need you to listen to me very carefully. Okay?"

Alex nodded.

"You have to step down from this investigation."

"What? Why?"

"I can't tell you that. I can only tell you that no good will come from your continuing. I never meant for you to walk the path of shadows, as I did."

"What does that mean?"

"It means that I don't want to see you hurt, which is precisely what will happen if you continue."

"I'm not stepping down." Anger replaced the joy she'd felt at seeing her father. "How could you even ask me to do that?"

"Princess, you have to—"

"No." She pulled away from him. "I became an Enforcer to stop murders like these—like *yours*—from happening."

"You don't understand—"

"Then explain it to me."

He shook his head. "I can't."

"Why not?"

"Alexandra, please—"

The edges of her father's form wavered, and Alex felt heavy, as though a massive weight had been dropped on her shoulders. She looked around the garage. Colors were brighter, richer, and objects seemed more solid. "What's happening?"

"I can't hold you here any longer. You're transitioning back to your physical body."

"Alex." Varik's voice drifted up from the back of the car. *"Come on, baby. Come back to me."*

"No! I don't want to go back," she cried.

"You have to, Princess." Her father began to fade. "This isn't the place for you. You're not ready."

"Daddy!" She reached for him, and her fingers slipped through his hands. "What aren't I ready for?"

"That's it. Come back." Varik's voice grew louder.

"Daddy! Don't leave me again!"

"I love you, Princess." Her father's voice was little more than a hushed whisper as he faded from view.

She stared at the empty air where he'd vanished. He was gone. Again. Silence enveloped her, and the world melted around her, plunging her into shadows. She spun out of control through darkness until she slammed into something hard.

The bubble of silence collapsed, and sound rushed in with a cacophony of sirens. Lights danced before her eyes in a confusing ballet. Panic clawed at her. Voices surrounded her, menacing in their foreignness. But one voice cut through the confusion.

"That's it. Come back to me, baby," the voice whispered in her ear.

The salty metallic taste of blood filled her mouth, and she swallowed. Brief flashes of memory sparked through her mind: A woman with black hair pulled into a tight bun leaned forward and kissed her cheek. A door crashed open, kicked off its hinges. A shotgun aimed at a fleeing figure. The recoil of the blast knocked her back.

She returned to the present to find movement all around her. Voices spoke in a language she couldn't understand. The sour stench of fear mingled with the coppery smell of blood.

Blood. *That* she understood, and it excited her. All coherent thought fled before a tide of primal instinct.

The source of the blood—her prey—tried to pull away. She gripped it tightly, refusing to let it go.

"That's enough," the voice whispered.

She smelled sandalwood and cinnamon. Vampire. A male, and he wanted what was rightfully hers. He couldn't have it. It was hers. She'd *make* it hers. A warning growl rumbled deep in her throat, and she shook her head. Her teeth dug into fleshy tissue, tearing it. More blood flowed into her mouth in a warm rush.

"Enough!" The prey jerked free.

Alex bolted forward, snarling, and pushed her prey to the floor. She straddled it and plunged her fangs into the soft tissue of its neck. Blood, sweet and hot, pumped into her mouth. The sharp tang of fear mingled with sandalwood and cinnamon, and she moaned in pleasure, reveling in the heady scent.

Hands gripped her shoulders, her sides, trying to pull her away. Indistinct shouts faded into the background, replaced by two rapid heartbeats.

Her mind focused on the heartbeats.

Alex! No!

A voice shouted inside her head, accompanied by the image of a man lying on a bloodstained floor with her straddling him, feeding. Uniformed police and paramedics pulled at her, trying to pry her away from the man's—from Varik's—throat.

Stop! Varik shouted in her mind.

The two heartbeats overlapped, merged, and became one.

Pain seared her neck. She released him, screaming and clawing at the scar on her neck. The humans surrounding her parted, and she stumbled a few feet away before collapsing to the floor. She gasped for air and choked on the blood in her mouth. Gagging and coughing, she rolled onto her side and curled into the fetal position. Tremors racked her body. Muscles tightened and unclenched in painful spasms.

"Easy, easy." Varik's voice was both a whisper in her mind and a deafening shout in her ears. His hands on her bare shoulders were like cold fire, soothing and burning simultaneously. "She needs a blanket."

There was movement to her left as she struggled to

escape his grip. She felt him pull her back against his body, against his warmth. She shivered. "What..."

"Shh, it's okay," he said in that echoed whispering shout. "You're okay."

The weight and warmth of a blanket surrounded her, invited her to explore its depths. Her eyes closed, and the thought of sleep flitted through her mind in a voice that mingled Varik's with her own. The sensation of rising into the air pulled her eyes open.

Varik was holding her as he climbed into the back of an ambulance. He laid her down on the stretcher and sat on the small bench beside her.

She seemed to be in two places at once. She looked at him but saw herself lying on the stretcher in her mind. "Varik," she croaked and grabbed his blood-soaked shirt. "What...happened?"

The doors slammed shut, and a paramedic jammed a needle into her arm. The siren wailed to life, and the ambulance lurched forward.

Alex felt a warm rush in her veins as the IV began flowing. Her eyelids drooped, and she fought to keep them open.

Varik's voice whispered in her mind. *Blood-bond.*

She tried to scream, to lash out, but couldn't move. Her eyes closed, and she once again drifted in darkness.

He whistled as he opened the gates to Jefferson High School's football field. He unfolded a map and used the truck's headlights to illuminate it. The positioning of the body had to be precise. If it wasn't, all his work would be meaningless. He'd carefully chosen the sites. All were equidistant to a central point, to the focus of his rage.

He stuffed the map in his coverall's pocket and climbed into the truck. He drove onto the field to the selected spot by the bleachers and parked. Using an old gas station receipt, he spat out the gum he'd been chewing since he left the Holy Word Church's prayer meeting and dropped the sticky wad into the truck's ashtray.

The Holy Word's weekly meetings offered him cover as well as served as cover for the Human Separatist Movement's strategy-planning sessions. While he wasn't an HSM member, he agreed with much of their beliefs, even if he did prefer the philosophy championed by two other anti-vamp groups, Blood Brothers and Kill All Bloodsuckers—"Kill 'em all and let Satan sort 'em out." While HSM preached separation between humans and vamps, Blood Brothers and KABS both wanted to see vampires eradicated, believing them to be an affront to nature and to God's design. Violent confrontations between the groups and vamps were common, especially in larger cities.

He continued to whistle while he opened the camper's hatch and dropped the truck's tailgate. Lugging a vampire's corpse up to the top row was going to be a bitch, but he didn't have to report for his shift until ten. He had time.

"Hammer . . . stake," he muttered, checking the contents of a backpack he'd thrown in with the corpse. It was too risky to leave the stakes in the vamps' chests when he transported them. One wrong bump and the corpse could shift and dislodge the stake or, worse, break it. If a stake broke, revealing its secret too soon, he and Claire couldn't be reunited. Timing was the key. Sabian had to know he'd done what she couldn't— avenge Claire. Sabian had to be present, and she had to believe he'd taken away that which she held most dear. Her world had to be shattered, the same as his had been. Only then could he and Claire finally be together again.

Of course, trusting that the Enforcer bitch would fig- ure things out in time was a gamble, but a necessary one. She'd made him suffer for far too long. He wanted to return the favor.

He shouldered the backpack, grasped one end of the tarp secured around the corpse, and tugged.

The body inched forward, and he tugged again. He repeated the process until it reached a tipping point and gravity took over, dumping the bundle onto the field. The impact loosened some of the bindings, reveal- ing a pallid foot.

He scrambled into the back of the truck to rummage for the coil of rope he always kept handy. If he looped the rope under the corpse's arms and made a rough har- ness, lifting the body up the bleacher stairs would be much easier.

As he squatted in the truck's bed, he glanced out one of the camper's side windows and froze.

A flashlight bobbed along the fence lining the oppo- site side of the field. The light paused and cut in his di- rection, and he heard the squeak of a gate's rusty hinges.

He mouthed silent curses. Sweat beaded on his

upper lip and dripped down his temples. He'd watched the school's nighttime security guard's routine for weeks, learning the pattern. The guard wasn't scheduled to check the athletic area until much later.

"Hey!" the guard called from midfield. "No one's allowed back here after hours."

He tensed in the darkness provided by the camper shell. The voice was female, a different guard from the one he'd watched. Mouthing more curses, he searched the truck's bed for a weapon, something he could use to incapacitate the guard while he finished his work. His hand closed over the straight end of a crowbar. His heart pounding, he hunkered down in the truck, covering himself using the wall of the camper on the same side from which the guard approached.

The guard's flashlight swept the ground, illuminating the foot peeking out from the tarp.

He heard the guard curse and quicken her pace. He tightened his grip on the crowbar and tried to ignore the sudden pressure in his bladder. His mouth felt dry even though he was perspiring, and he wished he hadn't gotten rid of his gum.

The guard's silhouette came into view. She stopped by the open tailgate, focused on the tarp lying on the ground at her feet. "Oh, my gaa—"

He waylaid her with the crowbar, striking her in the side of the head, and she never finished her exclamation. He jumped from the truck as she crumpled and accepted more blows onto her helpless form.

———

Alex blindly ran through a never-ending labyrinth. A single pinpoint of light danced on an invisible wind before her, drawing her along the path, guiding her steps. Guttural whispers and screams echoed in the dark. Shadows, barely discernible in the gloom, pressed close. Hands reached for her. She forged ahead, focused on reaching the light, spurred by her father's voice.

"Alexandra, hurry."

"Daddy!" She stumbled when phantom hands pushed her, and she lost sight of the light. Turning in a circle, she shouted into the darkness. "Where are you?"

"Come to me, Alexandra. Come to the light."

Faces floated before her, screaming their eternal torment. The smell and taste of blood overwhelmed her, suffocated her, and made her gag. The hands pushed her, and she stumbled.

Panic threatened to consume her. She had to find the light, to escape. "Leave me alone!" Her words wrapped around her, cutting her flesh. The phantoms laughed, and she screamed.

"Alexandra!"

"Daddy!"

The phantoms hesitated, seemed to back away and melt into the void once more. The light returned to her right, brighter and closer than before. She ran toward it, and as it grew larger, shades of gray and blue filtered into the darkness.

A shadowy form appeared in the light, and her father called to her. "They're coming! Run!"

Alex lunged forward. Screams engulfed her and pierced her heart, making it falter. Fingers dug into her arms and legs. Claws raked her sides, tearing her flesh. Phantom bodies slammed into her, pulled her hair, trying to drag her back from the light. She reached for her father's outstretched hand.

His hand closed over hers. Warmth enveloped her and drove the shrieking phantoms into the darkness as he pulled her into the expanding light.

"Daddy," she said, and fell into his arms.

"Shh," he murmured, and held her close. "It's okay. You're safe now."

She breathed in his scent and clung to him, happy to be reunited with the man who'd meant so much to her and who'd been taken away far too soon. Slowly she became aware of her surroundings, of the waning light overhead and the soft breeze ruffling her hair. She pulled away and looked around. "Where are we?"

"Same place as before," he answered. "The Shadowlands between the spirit and physical worlds."

Alex looked at the field around her and the trees in the distance. Colors were muted, as if she was seeing everything through a thin fog. Rows of headstones extended before her like marching soldiers. Recognition weighted her shoulders and turned her skin to ice. The same cemetery had haunted her dreams for years. The place where—

"I brought you here because I knew you'd be safe."

She faced her father. "Safe from what? What were those things attacking me?"

"It doesn't matter. They can't harm you here."

"It matters to me. What's going on, Daddy?"

"Princess, please—"

"Don't 'Princess, please' me. I'm not a child. I want answers."

He looked at her, his green eyes contemplative, and he smoothed a narrow black tie over his pristine white shirt.

"Please, Daddy," she said, "I want to know what's going on. Why am I here? Did you pull me through again?"

He sighed and looked away. "No, I didn't, not this time."

"Then how—"

"I told you before that anyone could access this place"—he gestured to the surrounding graveyard—"if they knew how." He looked back at her. "You're apparently a quick study."

"I haven't studied anything. I was reviewing evidence, then I—" The vision of fire erupting from a gun barrel wavered before her.

"You connected to the consciousness of a dead vampire. You followed him, and that opened the doorway."

"I don't understand. What doorway?"

"The dark labyrinth, the path of shadow. That was the entrance to the true spirit world."

Alex crossed her arms over her chest. Recalling the hands that pulled at her, she stroked her upper arms in an effort to dispel the chill that lingered. "What were those things that attacked me?"

"Lost souls denied entrance into the eternal rest of the spirit world. They wander the maze, preying on others. They'll try to trick another soul into giving up its rightful claim to rest. If they can convince a spirit to trade places, they can cross over and leave the other soul to wander."

"Why would they be denied?"

He shrugged. "Any number of reasons. Maybe they were a bad person in life, or maybe they feel that some injustice has gone unpunished."

"Why did they attack me?"

"Because you're still living. You haven't truly crossed over. They can sense that, and they want what you have. They want life."

"Lost souls," she repeated. Another chill crept over her, this one from within. "Daddy"—her voice shook as she spoke—"why are you here?"

"Alexandra—"

"Why haven't you crossed over?"

"I can't," he whispered. "Not yet."

"Why not?"

"I have unfinished business."

"What does that—"

"I'm a lost soul, Princess."

"No," she whispered, shaking her head. "That's not true. You can't be." He reached for her, and she pulled away. "It's not true!"

"It is. I chose this, Alexandra. Do you understand me? I gave up my claim to rest. I traded places with one of those wandering souls. I *chose* this."

"But...why?"

"I had my reasons."

"What—"

"I can't explain them. I wish I could, but you'll just have to trust me."

The gentle breeze that had been blowing since their arrival died, only to return a moment later, stronger and with an ominous feeling, as though a storm followed in its wake. Alex looked to the horizon and saw a dark vortex churning in the distance. "Daddy, what is—"

"We have to hurry." He grabbed her hand. "This way."

Alex followed him, stumbling over the uneven ground. The wind picked up and howled in her ears. Small bits of debris flew past them as they ran. She glanced over her shoulder and saw the vortex barreling toward them, closer, roaring with all the fury of an awakened monster. "What is that thing?" she shouted over the howling wind.

"A sweeper," he shouted back. "It finds unregistered consciousnesses and forces them back through the Veil."

"What do you mean by 'unregistered'?"

"Minds that aren't dead but have broken through the Veil." He tugged on her arm. "Hurry!"

Alex lost her footing and fell to the ground. She felt herself being pulled backward into the approaching tornado. Her hands clawed at the earth. "Daddy!"

"Alexandra!"

The vortex claimed her and spun her into the air. Her screams were drowned by the wind's angry howls. She was tossed about and buffeted, carried higher and higher.

Something brushed her hand and then darted before her eyes, a bright streak of orange and black. She looked up from the center of the vortex to see bright blue skies filled with hundreds of butterflies. The tiny insects dove into the swirling mass of clouds and debris, latched on to her, and carried her upward.

A single monarch butterfly alighted on her hand. Its wings opened and closed slowly. As she and her tiny winged chariots burst into the radiant skies above the storm, the scent of sandalwood and cinnamon permeated the air.

She looked down at the spinning funnel and saw her father staring up at her. The tornado veered away from him, churning through the cemetery but leaving no visible destruction in its path.

She and the butterflies climbed higher, and the intoxicating aroma of sandalwood and cinnamon grew stronger. The wings of the single insect resting on her hand brushed her skin in a feathery touch, pulling her attention away from the receding ground. It beat its wings, stroking her hand, and she heard a voice whispering in her mind.

"Please wake up, Alex."

"Varik," she answered.

Varik held Alex's hand, lightly stroking his thumb over her knuckles' ridges. White gauze spiraled up his arm where he'd bitten himself, and a bandage covered the bite on his neck. Even though vampires healed much faster and cleaner than humans, both wounds had required stitches and would most likely leave scars.

"Guess you owed me, huh?" He raised her hand and

kissed it, hoping for a reaction, some sign that she knew he was there.

Her breathing was slow and steady, and the color had returned to her cheeks. A monitor beeped and the black cuff on her arm inflated, automatically checking her blood pressure. They were in a small windowless treatment area in the emergency room. The doctors didn't think she would need to be admitted, but until she regained consciousness, they were keeping her under observation.

He brushed the hair away from her face, watching her eyes move beneath the closed lids as if she was dreaming. "I'm so sorry, Alex." His whispered words echoed in the dimly lit room. The monitor beeped again, and the black cuff deflated with a soft hiss. "I didn't want this to happen."

Her chest injury had been a psychic wound, not physical. She'd channeled Gary Lipscomb's final moments and the result had been a stigmata, a sympathy wound. Because it'd been fatal for Lipscomb, his death had threatened to take Alex as well.

Psychic wounds were the body's reaction to the shared trauma. By forcing her to drink his blood, Varik managed to pull her back, to save her, but he knew she wouldn't see it that way. Even though he'd saved her life, she'd focus on the resulting strengthened blood-bond and blame him for it, and he'd be lucky to get out of the room with his skin intact.

The ability to tap into another vampire's death memories, as Alex had done, was rare. Varik had known only one other vampire who'd possessed the talent.

That's how he'd known to use blood to anchor Alex's consciousness to the physical world, to keep Lipscomb's death from pulling her down with it.

Minutes slipped away with nothing but the steady beep of the monitors to mark their passage. He could sense Alex's presence in the back of his mind. Until the bond had been reestablished, he'd sensed her occasionally, seen the odd flash of what she saw or heard a stray thought, unless one of them deliberately opened the barriers separating their minds, as Alex had done when he kissed her.

Now her mind buzzed within his like a barely audible radio station. He couldn't hear her thoughts, but he could sense her emotions. Fear and confusion masked the anger writhing beneath the surface. Anger directed at him.

The door opened behind him. The scent of musk and cloves filled the room, and Varik tensed as Stephen rounded the foot of the bed.

The blond vampire's eyes were twin nuggets of amber rimmed in the crystal blue of a cloudless sky. He looked at Alex and then settled his hate-filled gaze on Varik. "I told you to stay away from my sister."

"If I had, she'd be dead now."

"Stay. Away. From. Her."

"I heard you the first time. In case you haven't noticed, there's a killer on the loose. I'm helping Alex—"

"And you're doing a bang-up job, aren't you? She's lying in a hospital bed. You nearly killed her—again."

Varik struggled to keep his own rising anger at bay.

"It was a psychic wound. She was reliving the death of one of the murder victims."

"Doesn't matter. You were there when it happened. Ever since you showed up, Alex has had more trouble than help from you."

"Believe whatever you want, Stephen, but I'm telling you the truth when I say I'm only here to help."

Stephen clenched his fists and blood rose to color his face in bright pink splotches. "You're here to finish what you started in Louisville. All you want is to—" He stopped abruptly, staring at Varik. His gaze danced over the bandages on Varik's arm and neck, and then darted to Alex and back. "You son of a bitch," he breathed. His eyes narrowed and he leapt across the bed, clearing it in a single graceful movement.

A fist connected with Varik's jaw and sent him tumbling over in the chair. Stephen's weight crashed into him as he fell and knocked the air from his lungs.

"You bound her—again!" A hail of fists punctuated each word. "You goddamned son of a bitch!"

Varik gasped for breath as someone pried Stephen off him. Hands gripped his arms and waist, pulled him up from the floor, and helped him sit in the righted chair. He tasted blood, and his face and sides hurt, but sweet air once again flowed into his lungs. A warm trickle snaked down his neck from the now exposed bite and soaked into his shirt.

Stephen continued to hurl curses and insults at him from across the room. Several members of the hospital's staff blocked his path, and a couple of vampire orderlies restrained him, keeping him from lunging at Varik. "He bound her! She didn't want it!"

Varik touched his lip and flinched. His left arm hurt from trying to fend off the blows, and he tucked it close to his body. He could tell that a few of the stitches in his wrist had weakened and that the wound had begun bleeding again.

Stephen had surprised him twice since his arrival, unacceptable for a former Hunter, and it was time to make good on his promise. He pushed himself out of the chair. "Let him go."

The two orderlies holding Stephen glanced at each other. One looked over his shoulder. "You sure about that, sir?"

"Let him go," he repeated. "No one intervenes this time."

"We can't—" one nurse began.

"That's an order," Varik said. He nodded to the vampires holding Stephen.

The orderlies shared a look.

One shrugged. "His funeral, man."

They released Stephen, and he charged forward.

Varik sidestepped the rush. His uninjured hand gripped the younger vampire's throat, stopping him in his tracks. Stephen's eyes widened, and he clawed at Varik's arm, drawing blood. He tried to speak but managed only a strangled gurgle.

Movement caught Varik's eye, and he looked at the staff who'd inched forward. He shook his head, and they backed away.

Stephen gasped, and his struggles slowed.

"I told you before, Stephen, you *had* your freebie." His muscles tensed and bulged. He drew Stephen closer. "I said I wouldn't be so charitable the next time." His fingers tightened, slowly choking off Stephen's air supply.

"Varik."

Alex's hoarse whisper echoed in both his ears and his mind. He looked down at her, met her dark green eyes as she reached for him. His anger evaporated. He shoved Stephen away and grabbed her outstretched hand. "I'm here, baby."

She swallowed visibly and winced. "Water."

Varik stepped over the prone and coughing Stephen, and grabbed a plastic pitcher filled with half-melted ice. He poured water into a small cup and slipped a straw into it. "Here," he said, and sat on the side of the bed.

Her hand closed over his while he held the cup and straw. She sipped the water and then nodded that she'd had enough.

"How're you feeling?" He set the cup down on a wheeled tray table.

"Like shit."

"Well, you kind of look like shit." He tried to smooth her hair back, but she blocked his hand.

Her eyes never left his. "You okay, Stephen?"

Stephen groaned and coughed from his position on the floor. "Just peachy."

"Alex, I—" Varik stopped when she held her finger over his mouth, mirroring his own gesture from earlier at the morgue.

She looked past him to the knot of hospital staff near the door. "A little privacy, please?"

They all looked to Varik, and he nodded. They turned as a group and filed out. "Holler if you need us," one of the orderlies said, and pulled the door closed behind him.

Varik met Alex's gaze. His heart lurched at the cold hatred he saw reflected in her swirling eyes. "Alex—"

"Don't you *dare* speak to me."

"But—"

She shoved him off the bed. "Shut up!"

His foot slipped, and he landed on the floor beside Stephen. He hissed as his already bruised ribs protested the rough treatment. A warm coppery taste told him that his lip had ruptured again. Her words rang in his ears and echoed through his mind. He felt the wave of her emotions—anger, fear, betrayal—crash into him, and it left him gasping for breath.

Her hands clawed at her temples. "I can hear you in my head. Feel your pain like it's my own."

Sadness—her sadness—overwhelmed him. He pushed against the tide and managed a weak whisper. "It's the blood-bond."

"I didn't want it. You *knew* that! How could you do this to me?"

Varik swallowed the lump in his throat. "It was the only way I could save you."

"I didn't ask you to save me!"

He watched as Stephen struggled to his feet and sat beside Alex, comforting her. He had to reason with her, make her see that he'd had no choice. "Will you please listen—"

"Get out." Her words were muffled against Stephen's shoulder.

Varik rose slowly, stiffly. "Alex—"

"Get *out!*" She threw the plastic cup at him.

Water splashed his face, and the cup bounced off his chest. He staggered under the weight of her anger. They both needed time to adjust and accept what'd happened. He'd back off and let her cool down for a while.

He reached for the door, and Damian's words drifted through his mind before he could stop them: *You'll have to take over the investigation.*

Alex gasped behind him.

He looked over his shoulder at her stricken face.

"You . . . *bastard.*"

ten

TASHA ENTERED THE EMERGENCY ROOM AND FLASHED her badge to the desk clerk. "Lieutenant Lockwood. I'm looking for Enforcer Alexandra Sabian."

The clerk pressed a button beneath her desk's edge and a pair of metal doors opened with a loud buzz. "Down the hall, take a right, and listen for World War Three."

"Excuse me?"

"They've been arguing for about half an hour now. Security tried to break it up, but after seeing three vampires ready to kill each other, security backed out and let them have the room."

Tasha hesitated but then made the decision to see it for herself. She followed the clerk's instructions, and as soon as she rounded the corner, she heard Alex shouting and a loud crash. She cautiously opened the door.

"You son of a bitch!" Alex roared, and threw a plastic pitcher at Varik, who was using a bedpan for a shield, as the two circled a gurney. "You planned this, didn't you?" She threw a box of latex gloves at him. "Didn't you!"

"No, of course not." Varik kicked the pitcher out of his way and ducked to avoid the sailing box that showered the room with gloves. "If you'd just let me explain."

"What's with the ruckus?" Tasha asked, edging into the room to stand beside Stephen, who was watching the fray from the relative safety of a corner.

"Varik's kicking Alex to the curb."

"You arrogant asshole!" Alex threw a jar of cotton balls at Varik.

He batted it with the bedpan and forced Tasha and Stephen to duck when it exploded against the wall next to them.

"You used me!" Anger made Alex's voice tremble. Monitors beeped wildly, reacting to her elevated pulse and heart rate. A broken IV line dripped onto the floor, creating a widened puddle under the bed.

"No, I didn't," Varik countered. "You misunderstood—"

"You said you were taking over." Alex ripped the remaining IV tubing from her arm. "I heard you."

"Damian's words, not mine."

"But you agree with him. Don't try to deny it." Her eyes narrowed, and she sneered. "I can sense it in you, Varik."

"Fine, I won't"—he spread his arms wide—"but you should also know that I want you on the case. Damian ordered me to take over if it became apparent you couldn't handle it anymore."

Stephen shook cotton balls from his curls and folded

his arms over his chest. "Since when do you care about following orders?"

"You stay out of this," Varik snarled, using the bedpan as a pointer.

"Or what? You'll kill me?"

"No. I don't do that anymore."

"Oh, really? Then what do you call that little stunt of yours? Remember? When you had your hand around my throat!"

"Self-defense."

Stephen lurched forward.

"Knock it off!" Tasha grabbed his arm. "I don't know what's going on here, but fighting isn't getting anyone anywhere."

"I'm not giving up the investigation," Alex said hoarsely. She rubbed her chest and winced.

Varik, across the room, flinched at the same time.

Tasha's gaze flickered between them. Something Alex had said gnawed at her. "What did you mean when you said you could 'sense' Varik's agreement?"

All three vampires noticeably tensed.

"Does this have something to do with that blood-bond thing?"

"How do you know about that?" Alex's amber eyes darted from Tasha's face to Stephen and narrowed. "*You* told her?"

"She came to Crimson Swan asking questions about him," Stephen said, pointing at Varik. "She said she didn't trust him. I told her she shouldn't, and yes, I told her about what he did to you."

Fury raged in Alex's eyes. "You had no right, Stephen. No right!"

"What was I supposed to do? Lie?"

"I went to him, Alex," Tasha said, feeling as though she needed to be on the defensive. "He didn't want to tell me—"

"But he did anyway, didn't he?" Alex's fists clenched tightly, and her body shook. She pinned Stephen with an icy glare. "I can't believe my own brother would betray my trust."

"I was trying to protect you."

"I don't need your fucking protection."

"Obviously you do, since you allowed yourself to be blood-bound!"

"Allowed myself? You think—"

"He's in your head. Messing with your mind or—"

"I reestablished the bond!" Alex thumped her chest. Both she and Varik flinched in pain.

"That's just great! I get the breath choked out of me for defending your honor, when I could've saved myself the trouble had I known my sister was a goddamn whore!"

Silence filled the room, drifting in on the wake of Stephen's words. Tasha shifted her focus between the siblings until Stephen stepped forward, the knowledge that he'd crossed a line evident on his face.

"Alex—"

"Get out," his sister growled.

"Alex, please—"

"Stephen"—her voice was a barely audible rasp—"you're my brother. I love you, but if you don't leave right now, I swear I'm going to rip your balls out through your eye sockets."

He stiffened. "You don't mean that."

Alex charged him, and Tasha scurried to avoid being caught between them. The two vampires crashed into the door. It groaned from the force of their impact, and dust drifted from the ceiling tiles like a fine mist.

Tasha remained motionless in the corner and watched as Varik tried to pry the siblings apart. Alex released Stephen, stalked to the opposite side of the room, and punched the cinder-block wall. Dust and brick chips flew into the air, and a fist-sized hole appeared.

Alex stood in front of the hole with her back to the room, sucking in air and releasing it in harsh puffs.

No one moved as the seconds ticked away. When Varik finally moved to Alex, Tasha joined Stephen. The expression on his face was unreadable. He met her gaze briefly before opening the door and leaving without a word.

Tasha held the door open, watching him walk away. She looked to Alex and Varik. He saw her and jerked his head to the side, silently indicating that she should go as well.

She left the room, closing the door softly behind her. She passed through the emergency-room waiting area and exited the hospital, seeing no signs of Stephen.

Her cell phone rang as she opened her car's door. "Lieutenant Lockwood," she answered wearily.

"Fire proceedeth out of their mouths and devoureth their enemies," a distorted voice said.

"Who is this?"

"Judgment shall come to pass on those who spill the blood of God's children."

"This is Lieutenant Tasha Lockwood of the Jefferson Police Department. Who—"

"We know who you are, Lieutenant. We know where you live."

Fear uncoiled in her belly and wrapped around her spine. "What do you want?"

"Cooperation. We'll be in touch." A series of clicks played in her ear, and then silence.

Tasha checked the caller history, but the call registered as "unknown." She hailed JPD's dispatch operator on the radio. "Have someone pull the records on my cell phone, and I also want cars sent to two thirty-one Mimosa Street."

"Two thirty-one Mimosa?" the operator repeated. "Isn't that your—"

"Yes, damn it! That's my house. Just get someone over there."

"Cars are on the way, ma'am."

Tasha tossed the radio mike aside. She felt sick. She flipped the switches to activate her lights and sirens, and sped from the hospital's parking lot. One word repeated in her thoughts: "cooperation." What the hell was that supposed to mean? Cooperate with what or with whom?

As her car rocketed through the night, she tried to shake the fear loose from her spine, but it remained firmly lodged in place. She realized the madness that had thrown her life into chaos would never stop, not as long as she worked with vampires, and the first seeds of hate began to sprout in her heart.

"Just put the stuff in the truck, Bill." Harvey thumbed the ashes from his cigarette. "And quit your bitching."

They'd planned this for months. More vamps were coming to Jefferson every week, drawn by the blood bar. Not all of them stayed, but that didn't really matter. All that mattered was that tonight would see the end of their invasion. Humans would regain their town and be able to live in peace once more. If only Bill would be quiet and load the truck.

"Are we sure about this?" A sealed five-gallon bucket slipped from Bill's grip and landed heavily on the tailgate of the truck. "Do we really want to—"

"I told you to quit bitching." Harvey ground the cigarette butt beneath his heel. "You had your chance to back out."

"Yeah, but—"

"Shut up, Bill," Martin Evans said from the bed of the truck. He slid the bucket into position with the others. "We all agreed we wanted the vamps out of Jefferson. Now's our chance."

"I know, but this—" Bill shook his head. "What if somebody gets hurt?"

"Goddamn it!" Harvey advanced on the smaller man. "They're vamps, Bill. Bloodsuckers! They're stealing our lives, our souls—"

"Yeah, but what if there are humans in—"

"They made their beds. I can't help that."

"Harvey—"

"Anyone siding with the vamps deserves the same fate."

"But—"

"I've had enough of your bellyaching. You agreed to the plan."

"I know. It's just—"

Harvey poked the smaller man in the chest. "You showed up tonight, and you *will* go through with it, or so help me"—his hand rested on the butt of his pistol—"I will strike you down for the craven coward you are!"

Bill paled. "You wouldn't."

"Try me." Harvey stepped back. "Now get back to work."

Bill dashed away.

He glanced at the silent Martin. "That goes for you, too."

"You got it, boss."

Harvey reached for the crumpled pack of cigarettes in his shirt pocket. He licked his lips and inhaled the earthy scent of fresh tobacco. Fire erupted from the tip of the disposable lighter. He lit the cigarette, stared at the blue-and-yellow flame dancing over the silver metal of the lighter, and smiled. Tonight he'd send those damn vamps where they belonged.

Straight to Hell.

Varik opened Alex's Crimson Swan apartment door and helped her over the threshold. The doctors in the emergency room had cleared her to go home, but she was still a little shaky. He was reluctant to leave her, despite her prior insistence that she would be all right on her own. At least she'd stopped being pissed at him and shifted her anger to Stephen.

Alex tottered away from him by using the back of the leather sofa as a handrail. "Have a seat," she said, assuaging his unspoken concerns. "I'll be back in a few minutes." She moved slowly as she passed through the bedroom area and disappeared into the bathroom.

He heard the muffled sound of running water as he closed the front door and hung her keys on the hook next to it. Looking around the tiny apartment, he took in the ramshackle appearance and sighed. This was not the neat Alex-style environment he remembered.

Clothing littered the floor and spilled from boxes, refugees from her water-damaged apartment. The dark-brown leather sofa divided the studio's common space into two rooms. A folding table with two chairs served as the dining area between the living room and the small kitchen. A profusion of take-out menus clung to the refrigerator with magnets from various local businesses. A calendar that advertised a car-repair shop and featured landscape photos was tacked to a cabinet door.

Moving into the living room, bare white walls surrounded him on all sides, and the furniture consisted of the sofa and a side table with a lamp. A television sat in the far corner on a rolling stand that also housed electronic equipment.

Two bookcases flanked the television and drew his interest. One case was empty, but the other held a mix of books, DVDs, and CDs. Judging from the water spots and warping of book covers, he guessed these were items salvaged from Alex's other apartment. He glanced over the book titles, mostly mysteries and a few romances. There'd been a time when the mere mention of a romance novel would send Alex screaming from the room.

He moved on to the DVDs and smiled. At least some things never changed. The films were mostly black-and-white classics starring Bela Lugosi, Boris Karloff, and Vincent Price. The music was a little more eclectic than he remembered, featuring everything from Beethoven to Rob Zombie.

The sound of running water stopped, and he settled into a corner of the sofa to wait. His gaze continued to roam around the apartment. The only decorative item in the room aside from the shoji screen blocking his view of the bed was the small half-geode on top of the television. Amethyst crystals glittered from within the depths of the split stone sphere. He recognized it as a prized possession that had belonged to Alex's father.

A large black-and-tan cat jumped onto the back of the sofa and stared at him. Its golden eyes were rimmed in green, reminding him of Alex's eyes when she was facing blood-hunger or really pissed off, which seemed to be most of the time when he was around. The cat yawned and stretched before hopping to the cushion next to him.

Varik remained motionless while the cat sniffed his fingers and jeans. It climbed into his lap and smelled its way up his shirt to his face. Whiskers tickled his chin as the cat investigated his hair. It blinked at him, licked its nose, and then settled onto the cushion beside him, front paws on his thigh and head held high with closed eyes, purring contentedly.

"I see you've met Dweezil." Alex entered the room carrying a hairbrush, a cordless phone, and trailing the scent of soap. She had changed into a pair of black jogging shorts covered by an oversized University of Louisville T-shirt, and a dark-blue towel wrapped around her head like a turban.

"I think I've been claimed." He brushed at the trail of hairs left on his shirt.

"Dweezil would claim a skunk if he thought he could get food out of the deal." Alex tucked one leg beneath her as she sat down on the opposite end of the sofa and laid the brush and phone on the coffee table.

"How's your arm?"

She rolled up her sleeve. Emergency-room doctors had removed Doc Hancock's stitches. An angry red welt sliced across the outer edge of her biceps, but it was healing well and would be just another scar in a few days. "Much better. At least I can move it now without it hurting too much."

"And your chest?"

"Bruised but manageable."

"That's good."

They sat in silence for several minutes. The only sounds within the apartment were the faint rush of heated air from the overhead vents and Dweezil's contented purring.

Varik tried not to stare at Alex's bare legs, tried not

to acknowledge that his body was responding to her presence the same way it had years ago. The kiss they'd shared, followed by the renewing of the blood-bond, had stirred the memories locked within his mind. Sitting in her apartment, immersed in her scent, made him want to pull her into his lap, cradle her in his arms, and feel her heart beating in time with his.

"Stop it," she hissed, massaging her temples.

"What?"

"Thinking about us. Just having you here is distracting enough. I don't want to hear your lewd thoughts as well."

He chuckled. "If you find my presence distracting, that must mean you've thought about me."

"Thought of how to get rid of you."

"Ouch, that hurt."

Alex rolled her eyes and pulled her turban loose, releasing the scent of jasmine and vanilla along with her damp hair. She folded the towel, dropped it into her lap, and grabbed the brush from the coffee table. "You'll mend."

"You want to tell me about your vision during the autopsy review?"

"I'm not sure how to explain it."

Varik's hand dropped to Dweezil's head and scratched behind the cat's ears as he waited for her to continue.

"It was the body." She tossed the brush and towel onto the coffee table. "It sat up, but it's what came after that I don't know how to explain."

"There is another way for you to tell me," he said softly.

"The blood-bond."

He nodded, stroking Dweezil's back and smiling wryly when the cat lifted its haunches to follow the curve of his hand.

Alex chewed her bottom lip, flashing her small fangs.

He watched her draw her knees up to her chest and wrap her arms around her legs, curling her body into the upright fetal position he recognized as her way of trying to protect herself from unpleasant memories. He could sense the fear and doubt hanging around her like storm clouds.

"All right, I'll show you," she said, and then muttered, "I can't believe I'm doing this." She brushed a lock of hair away from her face. "What—I mean, how do we do this?"

Varik picked up Dweezil and gently set the cat on the floor. He shifted on the sofa until he faced Alex fully. "I'm not certain. I've never been blood-bound before."

"That makes two of us."

"It's your memories that you want to share, so you should be the one to open the bond." He moved closer to her. "Remember when we were at the morgue?"

"I'm not kissing you."

"No, but I think it may help if we're touching."

Alex hesitated and then shifted so her knees were no longer drawn to her chest. She folded her legs into a lotus position, and he mirrored her. They inched toward each other until their knees touched. He held out his hands, and after a moment's pause, she laid hers in his.

"Close your eyes," he instructed. "Think of what you saw in the morgue and then lower your mental shields. I should be able to see what you saw."

She nodded and closed her eyes.

He could feel her trembling and knew she was anxious. His natural instinct was one of protection. He wanted to shelter her from what frightened her, but the source was within her, out of his reach.

When he lowered the barriers dividing his mind from hers, he felt no welcoming warmth. Her memories remained locked.

"It's not working," she said, and pulled away. "I can sense your mind. I know you lowered your shields, but something is blocking me."

"Try again."

"This isn't going to work, Varik."

"Yes, it will."

"No." She unfolded her legs and rose. "I think you should just leave."

He grabbed her waist, pulled her into his lap, and kissed her.

Alex broke the kiss. "You son of a bitch!" Her eyes were a swirling maelstrom of emerald and amber. She pushed against him, but he held her fast and wouldn't let her escape. "Let me go!"

Varik kept one arm around her waist and used the other to halt the blow she aimed at his face. "Not until you try again," he growled. He couldn't force his way into her mind. To do so would be the equivalent of rape under vampiric law. She had to share her memories willingly, but nothing prevented him from manipulating her. "If I have to piss you off in order for you to do that, then that's what I'll do."

She stopped struggling but continued to glare at him, breathing heavily. "You'll leave if it doesn't work?"

"The apartment, yes. Jefferson, no."

"Promise you'll forget this whole bond business if this doesn't work?"

"Scout's honor."

"You're a lot of things, Varik, but a scout isn't one of them."

"No, but I *am* a man of my word." He released his hold on her waist, but when she sprang to her feet, he stopped her from returning to her seat on the sofa. "I think we need to be closer this time."

"Closer? How the hell do you expect—" Her voice died as he stood, and she began shaking her head. "No way. Forget it."

"Alex, it's—"

"I'm not kissing you, Varik!"

"Would you rather sit on my lap again?"

"No."

"Then I suggest you get used to seeing me here, because I'm not leaving until you try again. That's our agreement."

"You said nothing about—"

"I'm not saying we have to kiss, Alex, but think of when we were at the morgue, how easy it was for you to open the bond when we were that physically close."

Color painted her cheeks red. "Don't remind me."

Her head rolled back, and she stared at the ceiling for a moment before looking at him again. "Let's just get this over with."

Varik spread his arms, and she stepped into his embrace. Her arms slipped around his neck. A tremor ran the length of his body when her fingers brushed the bandage covering the wound where she'd bitten him.

The desire to kiss her again nearly overwhelmed him, but he resisted the urge and tried to ignore the swelling erection trapped in his jeans. Gazing into her eyes from only a few inches away, a painful stab of regret speared his heart, and she winced, having felt it through the blood-bond.

She stiffened and tried to pull back. "Maybe this wasn't such a good—"

The barriers separating their psyches vanished. Varik gasped as images filled his mind. He was part of the scenes playing out across his consciousness but was also distant. He saw three headless corpses reaching for him and Alex simultaneously. He both ran through and flew over the erupting monolith maze. He watched as Bernard and Alex ran to evade a massive tornado and also ran alongside them. He and Alex were swept away by the twister and carried into a brightening sky.

"*Varik,*" Alex whispered against his chest and in his mind.

Jasmine and vanilla combined with sandalwood and cinnamon, rocking his senses. The blood-bond forged deeper into their minds, parading memories before them.

Alex's fifth birthday, only months before her father's murder.

Varik lying in wait for a rogue Hunter, his grip tight on a knife's handle.

Alex in her teens visiting her father's grave, kneeling beside the headstone and weeping.

Varik standing on a river's edge, watching the flow drag a body downstream.

Part of his mind awoke, suddenly aware that he and Alex were no longer standing. He slumped on the sofa while she straddled him, kissing him passionately, and him her. Panic seized his brain for an instant until the blood-bond offered up new images, thoughts dredged from one of their subconsciousnesses.

He lay naked on the floor as she moved over him with her head back in the throes of ecstasy. The vision shifted. He moved over her with her hips bucking to counter his every thrust, never breaking contact.

The still-conscious part of him stirred again as his hands slipped beneath Alex's shirt to cup her breasts. His palms caressed her hardened nipples, and she moaned, his name rolling from her lips to set his skin aflame.

This isn't right, his mind screamed. He felt Alex pause, and it was the refuge he needed to break the blood-bond's hold on them.

She cried out as he slammed shut the barriers between their minds, cutting off the bond's flow of memories, emotions, and desires. She clawed at the side of her head, then stilled. Her body fell limp, and she slumped against him.

"Alex?" His voice sounded harsh in the quiet of her apartment. "Baby?"

She groaned and rolled off him. "What happened?"

"The blood-bond," he replied. "It overwhelmed us."

She groaned again. "My head. It tingles."

A prickly sensation similar to what he felt when his foot fell asleep and returned to life throbbed in his head, making his eyes tear. "Mine, too."

Alex curled up on one end of the sofa. "Is this supposed to happen?"

He slid to the opposite side, putting as much distance between them as possible, and massaged his forehead. "I don't know."

Minutes passed in silence, and Varik worked to keep his mind free of all thought. Thinking hurt his brain. His eyelids drooped with weariness. His head lolled on his shoulders, and he jerked awake. Yawning, he forced himself to stand. "I should leave."

Alex didn't answer.

Alarmed, he turned to her and then relaxed. The sound of her steady breathing let him know she'd fallen asleep. He gently lifted her into his arms.

She mumbled incoherently as he carried her to the bed.

He laid her down, and she rolled onto her side and once more curled into a tight ball. He covered her with a blanket and, as an afterthought, he kissed her cheek.

She sighed in her sleep.

Dweezil jumped onto the half-wall serving as a headboard and blinked at him.

"Take care of her for me," Varik whispered, stroking the cat's head.

Dweezil warbled softly and leapt onto the bed. He placed his paws on the curve of Alex's waist between her ribs and hip. He rested his head on his paws, and his golden eyes closed.

Varik watched the cat guarding the woman they both loved. He crept to the door, opened it, exited, and then reached through a small crack to turn off the light before closing the door fully. He tested the knob and was satisfied to find it locked automatically.

His footsteps echoed heavily in the tower's stairwell. He stepped into the alley behind Crimson Swan, and the cold night air wrapped around him, bit his exposed flesh, as he recalled the shared memory of Alex's vision.

Warm air rushed from his Corvette's vents but didn't alleviate the chill that continued to make him shiver as he watched the tower fade into the darkness behind him.

Tires screeched on pavement as Tasha braked hard in front of her home at 231 Mimosa Street. She sprang from the car as a marked unit slid to a stop behind her vehicle. Drawing her Beretta, she motioned for the two uniformed officers to circle around to the back of the single-story bungalow.

She had to resist the urge to rush up the front steps and throw open the door. No lights burned within the house's interior. She frowned. She always left the porch light burning and a lamp on in the living room.

Moving rapidly but with caution, she mounted the front steps and crossed the small porch. Glass crunched underfoot. She glanced up. Someone had shattered the overhead fixture and bulb. *Not good.* She pressed her back to the wall beside the door's hinges. From her vantage point she could see that the door was slightly ajar.

Panic threatened to overtake her senses. She stilled her breath, willing herself to be calm. She eased the door open with her foot while raising her arms in front of her to bring her weapon into a ready position.

Silence filled the house, and shadows enshrouded the foyer. Tasha stepped into the gloom, hugging the walls. She methodically moved through the small entryway and deeper into the interior. She met up with the uniformed officers in the kitchen at the rear of the house. Seconds ticked away as they searched each room before declaring it empty.

Tasha sighed heavily, removed her handheld radio from her belt, and signaled an all-clear with dispatch. She thanked the uniformed officers for responding, said it was probably some neighborhood kids playing a prank. She didn't believe it, but there was no evidence that anyone had been in the house. Aside from the broken porch light, nothing was missing or appeared out of place.

The uniformed officers left reluctantly. She promised to call if anything happened and thanked them again. As she closed and locked the front door, a mirror that had been obscured by the door when she entered caught her eye.

Tasha saw the writing scrawled on the glass surface,

but her brain refused to process the information. She stepped closer, and the words seemed to spread across her face. Finally, her brain awoke and the words on the mirror became clear.

JUDGMENT DAY COMES. COOPERATE AND LIVE. INTERFERE AND DIE.

He'd killed the security guard at the high school. It hadn't been his intention to kill her, but she'd seen his face. If he simply knocked her out and left her locked up somewhere, she'd eventually be found and would identify him. He couldn't let that happen. He'd beaten her with a crowbar and stashed her body in an equipment shed.

Once that was done, he'd positioned the vamp's corpse behind the top row of the football-field bleachers. Using a hose behind the equipment shed, he'd washed the blood from his hands, cleaned the gory bits from the crowbar, and gathered the tarps. He changed into his uniform and drove to work.

Now the game was getting interesting.

He cruised Jefferson's streets, humming along with the music in his head, waiting. He checked his watch. Any time now the show would start.

eleven

STROBING BLUE AND WHITE LIGHTS DANCED OVER THE manicured lawns of Mimosa Street. Neatly trimmed hedges transformed into menacing blobs behind which shadows darted, chased by the lights. Curious faces pressed against windows. Braver souls congregated in driveways and beneath sprawling bare oak tree branches.

Tasha sat at the circular dining table in a home she once considered her haven from the madness of the outside world, with a cup of herbal tea clamped between her hands to keep them from shaking. One uniformed officer stood in the doorway between the dining room and the hallway leading to the foyer, where forensic techs worked.

She wanted to run screaming from the house that someone had violated. It took all her strength to not break into hysterics, but falling apart wouldn't help find who'd threatened her. She had to remain calm.

A hand brushed her shoulder. "Lieutenant?"

Tasha followed the line of the arm attached to the hand and was greeted with Harvey Manser's grim face.

Harvey pulled out the chair beside her and sat. He folded his hands on the table in front of him. "Tasha," he said gently, "I'm real sorry about all this, but I want you to know that I'm going to do everything I can to find the bastards."

She stared at him, her brain sluggishly deciphering his words. When she finally spoke, her voice was a harsh whisper. "You're leading the investigation?"

"Given the circumstances, it's best for someone outside of the JPD to oversee it. I know it's hard, but I need to ask you some questions."

Tasha sipped her tea and nodded.

"You said you received a phone call earlier?"

"That's right. Caller said essentially the same thing as the message on the mirror. The voice was distorted somehow, like something mechanical."

"Maybe one of those voice-changer toys that are always popular around Halloween?"

"Yeah, could be."

"Is there anyone you can think of who'd want to hurt you? Someone with a grudge?"

"I'm a cop, Harvey. Take your pick of about six thousand Jefferson residents." She sipped her tea. "Could this be tied to the vampire murders somehow?"

Harvey scratched his balding head. "Maybe. We'll look into it."

"I should call Alex. Maybe she could—"

"Tasha, you know how the vamps work. They look after their own and to hell with us humans."

"I know, but I thought that since the FBPI has that mobile lab in town, maybe they could find something our guys miss."

Harvey fidgeted in his seat. "Unless it's proof this is tied to the murders, they aren't going to touch anything we dig up here. Best to just let me and my boys handle this."

Tasha began to protest, but a deputy appeared in the doorway. "Sheriff?" She and Harvey looked to him, and he shuffled his feet. "Sorry to interrupt, but you got a phone call."

Harvey sighed and patted Tasha's arm as he stood. "I've got to take care of this, but don't you worry. Everything's going to be okay. I promise."

Tasha watched him retreat down the hall with the deputy in tow. She stared at her reflection in her teacup and silently prayed for Harvey's promise not to be an empty one.

Where was everyone?

He didn't see signs of anyone taking their positions, and the clock was ticking. The vamp would be home soon. If they missed their opportunity—

The cell phone hooked to his belt vibrated. He pulled it free and answered.

"The girl wasn't part of the plan," a gruff voice said.

His heart faltered and threatened to stop. "What girl?"

"Tasha Lockwood, you idiot," Harvey Manser

snarled. "Someone broke into her house, threatened her."

He breathed a sigh of relief. His secret was safe for now. "It wasn't me. Talk to Tubby. Maybe he knows something."

"I just did. He says he doesn't know anything."

"What about Martin and Bill? Have you talked to them?"

"No, but I will. Where are you?"

"On my way to Crimson Swan, like we planned. You?"

"The same. You're to observe and record only. Do not interfere. Are we clear?"

"Yes, sir."

"Fire proceedeth out of their mouths."

"And devoureth their enemies," he completed the biblical quote.

"Amen," Harvey intoned, and the line fell silent.

He returned the phone to his belt and steered his car down Jefferson Boulevard toward the blood bar. He'd suggested the biblical passage as the Human Separatist Movement's code for Judgment Day. Since the inspiration for ridding Jefferson of its demons was the Lord's act of casting Satan and his minions into the lake of fire, he thought it was fitting.

The fact that Tasha Lockwood had been threatened bothered him. He'd always liked Tasha despite the fact that she associated with that vamp bitch Enforcer. The lieutenant had always been decent to him, especially after Claire died.

He waited in the shadows alongside the strip mall

on the opposite side of Jefferson Boulevard from Crimson Swan. From here he could remain hidden but still see the action as it unfolded. His role was simple: observe the passing of judgment, and if needs be, he could stop anyone who may try to prevent HSM from carrying out their task. Otherwise, he was an observer and nothing more.

No vehicles were parked in the bar's lot, not even the owner's pickup. That would change. He'd been observing the vamp's comings and goings. It usually returned late after escorting one of the human whores to her home. He was certain the vamp and donor were more than employer and employee. Not that it would matter after tonight.

He didn't have to wait long before he saw shadows darting along the bar's walls and ducking around corners. HSM members were moving into position, waiting for the vamp to arrive.

Minutes ticked away. Finally, a blue Dodge pickup appeared, moving slowly down the boulevard. He picked up the camcorder and began filming.

The truck turned into the bar's lot and parked beneath a streetlamp. The demon's golden curls shone under the fluorescent light as it locked up the truck. He could hear it whistling while it strolled along the sidewalk toward the alley behind the bar, heading for the private entrance in the rear.

A shadow broke away from the side of the building. The vamp spun to face the attacker. More shadows peeled away from the darkness. They surrounded and descended on the vamp. Shouts and curses echoed in the night. The vamp lashed out at two rushing attackers, and they dropped to the pavement, unmoving.

He watched the fight and offered silent encouragement.

Another set of shadows leapt into the melee. The vamp whirled to face them, and another shadow materialized from the darkness of the alley. It assumed a shooter's stance and raised its arms. No gunshot sounded, but the vamp cried out in pain nonetheless. Its back arched, and its limbs jerked spasmodically. It fell to the ground and the shooter shadow advanced.

The vamp tried to rise. The shooter shadow halted, and he heard the distinctive rapid clicking of a Taser. The vamp shrieked and writhed on the ground.

He smiled.

Using a Taser to subdue the demon had also been his idea. It'd come to him after reading a forensic science article regarding vampires' heightened sensitivity to electrical currents. A genetic fluke left them with higher levels of iron in their bodies. The article stated that Tasers could be used effectively to subdue vamps, a handy tip when faced with a bloodsucker hyped on Midnight.

The shooter shadow was now standing over the unmoving vamp. The other shadows were gathering around, supporting those who had taken the brunt of the vamp's counterattack.

A van emerged from behind the bar, and a side door slid open. The shooter shadow knelt down and jammed something into the vamp's arm. The shooter then stood and gestured for the others to load the vamp into the van.

He watched the van leave the lot, turning toward the interstate. It sped beneath the overpass, heading past Maggie's Place and into the rural county. Phase one of Judgment Day was over.

Crashing glass and the *whoosh* of igniting flames pulled his attention back to the bar.

The shooter shadow, his balding head gleaming, triumphantly stood in the center of the parking lot as the others darted around the building. They lobbed makeshift torches into windows. Buckets of accelerant were tossed in through the broken windows. Flaming bottles smashed against the front doors and walls. They even torched the vamp's truck.

He settled into his seat and smiled. As he watched the inferno devour Crimson Swan, he couldn't help but feel as though he were at the movies with Claire sitting beside him, and he wished he'd brought a bucket of popcorn.

Alex bolted from the bed. Her gaze darted around the darkened room. Her ears strained to catch the faint noise that had awakened her.

Dweezil yawned, and then his head bobbed as he sniffed the air.

Click-click-click. A muffled cry.

She crept through the studio apartment and pressed her back to the wall beside the window overlooking Crimson Swan's parking lot. She caught the corner of the blinds with her finger and peered into the night. Her blood turned to ice.

Stephen lay immobile on the pavement. A gang of shadows slowly converged on him.

Adrenaline surged into her bloodstream and revived her tired and dulled senses. She crossed the studio to the bedroom and reached for her FBPI-issued Glock G31 .357-caliber sidearm on the side table. She pulled three fifteen-round-capacity clips from the drawer and retrieved a leather shoulder holster from behind the corner of the shoji screen. She slipped it on while stuffing her bare feet into her hiking boots.

She slid one of the clips home in the Glock and chambered a round. The two remaining clips were secured in the carrying case on the right side of her holster.

The sound of a racing engine pulled her back to the window. The shadow gang roughly hoisted Stephen into the rear of a van.

"Damn it all to hell!" she shouted, and sprinted for the door.

A small explosion shook the building.

Dweezil and the smoke alarm over her head both screeched their displeasure. The smell of burning pine and the chemical sting of diesel soon permeated the air.

Black smoke seeped around the apartment's windows and curled under the door. It seared her lungs, and she coughed violently as she thumbed on the safety and stowed her Glock in her holster. Tears blurred her vision as she grabbed her badge from the nightstand.

Dweezil howled as another thunderous boom vibrated

the floor beneath her. She dropped a blanket over him and scooped him into her arms. Crimson Swan was on fire, and they had to get out quickly. She threw open the apartment door. More smoke rolled in, blinding her.

Coughing and holding on tightly to the howling, blanket-wrapped Dweezil, she hurried down the stairs.

Flames raced along the walls and the open doorway leading to the bar. They rolled along the ceiling like the rippling skin of a dying beast. She heard the glasses behind the bar shattering from the heat. Bottles of alcohol exploded in tiny fireballs. She winced when she noticed the framed Bela Lugosi poster, bubbling and peeling as the fire closed around it.

The stairs leading to Stephen's loft above the bar were already blocked by flames and debris. She stood in their shared entrance, momentarily frozen with indecision.

A beam collapsed within the bar, sending a shower of sparks and molten glass into the tower's stairwell.

Dweezil howled and tried to climb out of the blanket.

"Hush," she said, tightening her grip. "We're getting out of here."

She could feel her skin beginning to blister. Her lungs ached from the superheated air. Her eyes watered from the smoke. She reached for the outer steel door and screamed as the hot metal burned the palm of her hand.

"Damn it!" She kicked the door, but it refused to open. She kicked again.

The whine of fatigued metal spurred her on.

She kicked again.

The door shuddered but didn't give way.

She screamed in frustration. She kicked a final time, and the door flew off its hinges.

Flames burst through the open door, seeking new fuel. Alex ducked to the floor, seeking cleaner air. Fire curled up the door's frame and along the ceiling. An opening formed, and with a desperate shout, she leapt into the blaze.

She landed heavily and staggered away from the burning building. The alley was a kaleidoscope of flickering light and shadows. Stephen's attackers were undoubtedly still in the area. Tears filled her eyes, and she couldn't distinguish between a natural shadow and a possible assailant. Holding Dweezil also made it impossible for her to carry her weapon at the ready. She could only hope she slipped past the arsonists unnoticed.

She made it to the corner of Crimson Swan and braced herself against the rough brick. Coughing, she loosened her grip on the blanket.

Dweezil peered out from his shelter. His green-and-gold eyes reflected the fire raging behind her. He hissed and struggled to break free.

She tightened her grip. "Not yet." She coughed. She wiped her eyes against a corner of the blanket. "It's still not safe."

The cat howled in protest.

"Oh, be quiet." Alex pushed away from the wall.

As she rounded a Dumpster, something hard slammed into her stomach, knocking the air from her lungs. She twisted to land on her back, trying to keep from crushing Dweezil. The cat rocketed from the blanket with a screeching howl and leapt for the safety of the Dumpster.

Alex struggled to regain her breath. Starbursts strobed before her eyes. A figure appeared over her, holding an aluminum bat in its hands.

Cruel, dark eyes blazed with hatred as they stared down at her through the holes of a blue-and-gray ski mask. "Not so high and mighty now, are you?"

Air filled her lungs. "Who—"

A foot crashed into her side. "Don't interrupt me, bitch!"

Alex coughed and tasted blood.

"Didn't anyone teach you it's bad manners to interrupt when others are talking?" He knelt beside her; his rough hands slipped beneath her shirt. "Got a message for you and your friends."

She seized his wrist and squeezed. Bones cracked and flesh bruised.

Her assailant cried out and swung the bat, striking her healing bullet wound.

Pain flared along her arm, numbing it, and she was forced to relinquish her hold.

"Fucking bitch," the hooded man snarled, and jabbed her in the face with the bat's rounded end, slamming the back of her head into the pavement.

A dark screeching mass flew over her and attached itself to the man's hooded face. He screamed and reeled away.

Shadows crowded into the edges of Alex's consciousness. She heard Dweezil's howl and felt his furry body sweep past her outstretched hand. Through blurry eyes she caught a glimpse of dark hair and bloody scratches as her assailant ran by her. Her vision cleared briefly as an image of Varik asleep in a hotel bed filled her mind.

Varik. She directed her call along the blood-bond's path.

His slumbering mind latched upon hers and awakened. His eyes opened, and he sat up, searching for her. Surprise turned to horror and fear. *Alex!*

Help me. She tried to sustain the connection, but the image faded and darkness claimed her.

Harvey stood next to his car, watching the crews trying to salvage what they could of Crimson Swan. Outwardly, he kept a grim face for the rescue teams and camera crews. Inwardly, he jumped for joy with each fiery column that continued to leap skyward.

"Looks like a total loss, huh, Sheriff?" Deputy Case said from beside him.

"Yep, looks that way."

Part of the roof collapsed, followed by gasps and screams from the crowd behind the hastily erected police barricade. He smiled, then coughed to cover it, trying to keep from appearing too happy with the bar's destruction.

"You think everyone got out?" Deputy Case asked, blowing into his cupped hands to warm them.

Harvey shrugged. "If not, we'll hear about it soon enough," he said, looking over the crowd.

More shouts and screams from the crowd pulled his

attention back to the fire. An exterior wall collapsed in a column of fire, sparks, and smoke, sending firefighters in a mad scramble to get out of harm's way.

Thick smoke wafted across his face. He reached into his pocket for his handkerchief, intending to use it as a makeshift mask, but the pocket was empty. He patted his other pockets, growing increasingly alarmed as he failed to locate it.

"Problem, Sheriff?" Deputy Case inquired.

"I can't find—" A horrific realization settled over him. His handkerchief. He'd been using it at the impound yard, but he didn't remember putting it in his pocket when he left. He must have dropped it when the tech startled him.

"Can't find what?" Deputy Case asked.

"Nothing. It's not important," he lied.

How could he have been so stupid as to forget his handkerchief? Maybe the techs would think it belonged to Sabian or was a stray bit of garbage. He clung to that thin hope and lit a cigarette with shaking hands.

Varik's Corvette jerked to a halt beside the entrance of Crimson Swan's parking lot. He jumped from the car and ran toward the flames.

He ran blindly around fire trucks and the men working to kill the blaze. He leapt over snaking hoses and dodged streams of water. His heart slammed against his ribs in a furious rhythm fueled by adrenaline and fear. The image of a battered Alex lying in an alley was already fading from his mind.

He charged into the alleyway and skidded to a halt, listening, but heard only the steady splashing of water, the distant *pop* of exploding liquor bottles, and the shouts of firemen. "Alex!"

No response.

Sweat dripped into his eyes, and he angrily brushed it away. He reached out to her with his mind. No welcoming warmth greeted his probing senses. Nausea twisted his insides. "Alex! Where are you?"

A faint noise stopped him in mid-stride. He took a deep breath and waited, hoping to hear the noise again.

Nothing.

He took another step. "Alex?"

A fresh shot of adrenaline jolted his heart when he saw a pale hand covered in blood. His feet raced over the pavement, and he dropped to his knees beside Alex.

She lay on her side. Fresh blood coated her face and arms. Blisters ruptured under his fingers as he gently rolled her over, searching for a pulse and finding the slow, steady rhythm.

"Alex? Baby?" He stroked her swollen cheek and felt something shift beneath her skin. Anger bubbled to the surface and burned away his fear.

Dweezil emerged from beneath a nearby Dumpster. The cat climbed onto her chest, curling his tail around his feet, and bunched up until he resembled a ragged black-and-tan meat loaf. He blinked at Varik and mewed, long and sorrowfully.

Varik scooped Alex into his arms. The cat protested the change but didn't move. Carrying them both, he hurried back toward the parking lot and more approaching sirens. "I'll find whoever did this, baby," he vowed. "I'll find them and I'll fucking cut out their hearts."

Emily Sabian steered her rental car off Interstate 55 and skidded to a halt in the center of Jefferson Boulevard. "Oh, no," she breathed.

Flames engulfed Crimson Swan. Fiery fingers scorched their way up the building's sides and waved at her from windows. The bell tower leaned precariously to one side. Showers of embers erupted from its interior like macabre Roman candles.

"Stephen." She hit the gas, and the car sped forward. "Oh, Alex."

Police cars and fire trucks blocked the street. She pulled onto the shoulder behind a row of sheriff's department cruisers. Emily sprang from her rental and dashed toward the blaze, shouldering her purse as she ran.

A Nassau County deputy standing in front of a police barricade waved for her to stop as she neared the fire. "Sorry, ma'am. Authorized personnel only. No civilians allowed inside the perimeter."

"You don't understand," she said breathlessly, while rummaging through her bag. She extracted her wallet and flipped it open to show her Kentucky driver's license. "I'm Emily Sabian." She pointed over the deputy's shoulder to the blaze. "Crimson Swan is my son's bar."

The deputy studied her identification and then her face before shaking his head. "Sorry, but I can't let you through."

"But my son! My daughter! Were they in the bar? Are they hurt?"

"I can't tell you anything. You'll have to wait."

"Now, you listen to me," she said, and leaned over the wooden barricade. She poked the deputy's brass nameplate pinned to his shirt. "I want to know where my children are, Deputy Black, and if you don't let me through, I swear—"

"Emily!" someone shouted from behind the deputy.

She glanced over the officer's shoulder, and relief washed over her. "Varik!" she called, and waved to him.

"It's all right," he told the deputy as he approached. Light from the blaze reflected off the silver badge clipped to his belt. "You can let her through."

Deputy Black scowled but moved aside.

Emily ducked under the barricade and rushed to meet Varik. She wrapped him in a quick embrace and then stepped back, searching his soot-streaked face. "Alex and Stephen—where are they?"

Varik slipped his arm around her waist and guided her away from the blaze, toward a silently waiting ambulance. "Alex was in the apartment in the bell tower when the fire started." He gave her a reassuring squeeze and forced her to keep walking when she tried to stop. "She got out, but whoever set the fire attacked her in the alleyway behind the bar."

"How badly is she hurt?"

"Minor burns and blisters, cuts from exploding glass, bruises." They'd reached the ambulance, and he turned to face her. "She's got a nasty black eye and most likely a fractured cheekbone."

Emily's heart dropped into her stomach. "And Stephen?"

Shouts from the blaze distracted them. The leaning bell tower succumbed to gravity's pull and fell into the heart of the inferno. Firefighters scrambled to escape the flaming rubble ejected into the parking lot like earthly meteors.

"Varik?" She touched his arm, pulling his gaze back to her. "Where's Stephen?"

Emotions swam in the depths of his golden eyes. A muscle jumped along his jaw.

Despair swept her up into its unforgiving tide. Tears trailed over her cheeks, and she clasped her hands in front of her. "No, please. He couldn't have been in there. No!"

Varik wrapped her in his arms, stroking her tangled curls. "We don't know," he whispered. "We just don't know. The bar was closed, so Alex is the only witness. She hasn't—"

Emily pushed him away and angrily wiped her wet cheeks. "I want to see Alex."

He nodded and knocked on the ambulance's rear door. It opened, and he gestured for the paramedic inside to step out. "Enforcer Sabian's mother wants to see her."

The paramedic glanced at Emily and hopped down to the pavement. "I gave her something for the pain. She's resting now, but she really needs to go to the hospital for X rays."

"Has she said anything?" Varik asked.

"Nothing coherent."

Emily accepted Varik's hand as she climbed into the ambulance. The bright overhead light made her squint and shield her eyes. She perched on the edge of the low built-in bench and shuddered.

Alex lay on her left side on a gurney, with a large black-and-tan cat curled up in her arms. Bruises covered the upper portion of her right arm. The recent bullet wound streaked across her biceps, a red slash in a field of purple. The right side of her face was swollen and a mottled blue and red. An IV line pumped fluids into her system. Her breathing was slow and steady, but Emily heard a slight wheeze when she exhaled, signs of mild smoke inhalation.

She gently kissed the top of her head.

Alex twitched in her sleep. "Come back," she muttered.

"Shh," Emily murmured, smoothing Alex's hair away from her face. "Momma's here. I'm here, sweetheart."

"Daddy." Alex groaned and reached for something in her sleep. "Don't leave me."

Fresh tears stung Emily's eyes. Her son was missing and her daughter was in pain. She clasped Alex's searching hand and wished that just this once, it was she whom Alex called for in her sleep.

Alex stood in the den of her childhood home and knew she was dreaming again.

Sunlight poured through the windows to her right, illuminating the ornate blue-and-white wallpaper.

Hardwood floors creaked beneath her feet as she moved in a slow circle. A tufted gold sofa stood at an angle to the heavy console-style television. Two matching chairs faced each other over the coffee table, and knickknacks covered every available horizontal surface.

Soft music, a scratchy version of Billie Holliday's "Blue Moon," drifted into the room from the record player in the corner. She smiled and scanned the room once more. Her gaze fell on the calendar above the record player and her smile faded.

The days of the week had been ticked off with neat black *X*'s, and today—the date in the dream—was March 16, 1968. The day her father's body was found.

Alex looked at the windows again. The sunlight was waning with the afternoon's slow demise. She shook her head. She no longer wanted to be here. She didn't want to see, didn't want to remember.

The front door in the unseen foyer burst open, and a child screamed for her mother.

Footsteps hurried from the back of the house. "Alexandra!" Emily Sabian called, rushing through the den.

Alex watched as her mother disappeared into the foyer only to reappear a second later carrying a hysterical five-year-old girl. Emily sat on the edge of one of the chairs, holding her daughter in her arms. The young Alex clung to her mother, sobbing uncontrollably, tears streaming down her scarlet face.

"No," the older Alex whispered. "I don't want to remember this. Wake up." She pounded her fists against her thighs. *"Wake up."*

"Honey," Emily whispered, fear making her voice tremble. "Honey, what's wrong?"

The younger Alex pointed to the windows, her voice hitching with hiccups and sobs. "Da-dad-daddy!"

Older Alex hugged herself, wanting to look away, to shut out the memory-turned-nightmare.

Emily stared at the window, and all color drained from her face. "Honey, what about your daddy? Do you know where he is?"

Older Alex nodded along with younger Alex. "Cemetery," they whispered in unison.

"Where in the cemetery, honey?"

The dream wavered, and the scene shifted from the interior of her childhood home. Alex found herself standing in the fading sunlight of a Kentucky spring afternoon. Gravestones surrounded her on all sides in endless rows, and an unworldly calm pressed down on her, weakening her knees. She could still hear her younger self's sobs echoing through the cemetery. She sank to the ground, staring at the body in front of her.

Her father's once sparkling green eyes, now silvered with the film of death, were wide and staring. Blood stained the collar and front of his crisp white dress shirt. The wooden stake protruding from his chest cast a long shadow over his face.

She heard her mother's anguished wail in the distance, and Alex screamed with her.

twelve

october 15

TASHA RUBBED HER HANDS TOGETHER, TRYING TO WARM
them. The rain began during the early-morning hours
and had been a steady downpour ever since, bringing
with it a cold wind blowing in from the north. She
leaned against the trunk of her car, huddled in her
fleece-lined jacket topped by a bright yellow poncho,
and watched the firemen sifting through the still-
smoldering ruins of Crimson Swan.

Two exterior walls remained standing, but the others had collapsed when their supports succumbed to
the flames. Piles of bricks and charred cinder blocks
formed a new jagged foundation. Steel girders broke
through the skin of ash like the twisted and broken ribs
of a monstrous demon.

A blaring horn made her look toward the street. Cars
slowed on Jefferson Boulevard as morning commuters
and rubberneckers excitedly pointed to the wreckage.
Uniformed police waved traffic around the emergency
equipment.

Satellite news trucks filled the gaps between the emergency vehicles. Reporters lined the sidewalk, facing the street, with the bar's burned-out skeleton behind them. The media began arriving as soon as word of Crimson Swan's destruction and the subsequent disappearance of Stephen Sabian spread. The two events combined with a potential serial killer using Jefferson as a dumping ground sparked their imaginations. The facts that Alex had been injured in the blaze, Emily Sabian had arrived in the middle of the night, and the FBPI had a current "no comment" policy only fueled their speculation.

Across the street, a crowd of onlookers gathered in front of the strip mall, some cheering and clapping in obvious delight while others stoically watched the residual chaos.

Tasha shook her head. "Get a life, people," she muttered, and blew into her frozen hands, wishing for a warm cup of tea. She could understand the jubilation some of Jefferson's residents would feel over the blood bar's destruction, but understanding didn't equal condoning criminal behavior.

Squealing brakes made her turn quickly toward the street. Two black Ford Expeditions made a quick U-turn in the center of the street, jumped the curb, and pulled into the bar's already crowded parking lot.

Tasha jammed her hands into her jacket pockets. The hairs on the back of her neck stood on end as the Expeditions' doors opened and several men climbed out of each. She counted four in the lead vehicle and six in the other. The silver badges around their necks identified them all as Enforcers.

She'd been expecting them. News of Stephen's kidnapping traveled quickly, and seeing as the Sabians were considered the vampires' version of the Kennedy family, the FBPI wasn't interested in taking chances on local law enforcement screwing up. Since a mobile lab was already on-site, Varik had briefly explained that more Enforcers were being pulled from the Jackson field office. She watched as they unloaded equipment with the speed and efficiency of a military unit but shifted her focus to the vampire approaching her.

He was tall, well over six feet—closer to seven—and his skin was the lustrous hue of polished ebony. Dark eyes scanned the bar's remains and then settled on her.

Every fiber of her body screamed for her to run, but she held her ground.

"Lieutenant Lockwood?" His voice was a deep, resonating bass that vibrated the air around her.

She nodded.

"Chief Enforcer Damian Alberez with the Federal Bureau of Preternatural Investigation," he said, extending his hand.

Tasha grasped his hand and was relieved to see that hers didn't tremble. Varik said Alberez had flown in from Louisville at the personal request of Emily Sabian to take over the investigations into Crimson Swan, Stephen's kidnapping, the murders, and even the shooting at Maggie's Place. Tasha wasn't happy about being forced to the sidelines yet again, but faced with his imposing stature, she was reconsidering her plans to fight to remain in the investigative loop. "Good to meet you, Chief. Varik told me you were coming."

"Where is Enforcer Baudelaire?"

"He set up Alex and her mother at one of the local hotels." She watched him surveying the area like a wolf assesses a herd of elk, searching for weakness, and again felt a strong desire to run. "He said he would stay with them until you ordered otherwise."

Alberez grunted. "What's Enforcer Sabian's condition?"

"Moderate smoke inhalation, minor burns, hell of a lot of bruises, and some small scrapes. The assailant clocked her face pretty well and chipped a cheekbone. Doctors said she'd be fully healed in a week or so and released her."

"And her brother?"

"Aside from the ransom note, no word." She produced a small clear plastic evidence bag containing a crumpled and bloodstained note that Varik had given to her. Uneven and broken letters scrawled a message across the page: *We have your brother. All vampires leave town or he dies. You have until midnight, October 16.*

Alberez took the note and looked it over. He snapped his fingers, and one of the Enforcers near the SUVs hurried to his side. "Get this to the lab. I want to know everything there is about it, especially if that's vampire or human blood."

"Yes, sir," the Enforcer responded, and sprinted for one of the Expeditions. He leapt into it and backed wildly out of the lot, then sped toward downtown.

"I have my people searching the alley where Alex

was found per Varik's instructions," Tasha said, once Alberez focused on her again. "We're working on the assumption that whoever attacked her and left the note is involved with Stephen's kidnapping and possibly the murders."

"Is that the alley?"

Tasha glanced over her shoulder, following the line of his arm as he pointed. "Yes."

He snapped his fingers again and gestured toward the alley.

Four Enforcers picked up what looked to Tasha like heavy steel suitcases and hurried away. Two more had donned hip waders normally used for fishing and were already picking their way through the debris field of Crimson Swan. The others were busy setting up the framework for a command tent.

She returned her attention to Alberez, gearing up for the fight she was destined to lose. "I've got a forensic team scouring the area. Why don't you let my guys handle it, since they're already knee-deep in it?"

"I'm sure your people are capable, Lieutenant, but the destruction of a blood bar, attacks on a federal agent, and the disappearance of Stephen Sabian—combined with the recent murder of vampires *and* a mass shooting—make this a federal case."

"So, you're going to sweep in here and throw my people under the bus."

"I'm not throwing anyone under the bus."

"Then let my guys work the scene. They've been here since last night. At the very least, allow them to work with your people and let Harvey keep the shooting."

He shook his head. "I'll be happy to share any information we gain from the evidence we gather, but this and the diner shooting are now federal investigations. The best thing for you and your people to do is clear out. Let us do our jobs." He half turned as one of the other Enforcers approached. "Excuse me, Lieutenant."

Tasha watched the two Enforcers walk away, deep in conversation. She saw her forensic team emerging from the alley with looks ranging from disbelief to anger on their grime-streaked faces. She yanked her car door open and climbed in. If she couldn't work the scene, then she'd go where she could work.

She navigated her car through the throng of reporters and into traffic along Jefferson Boulevard. She'd head back to the department and go over the files again. Maybe she'd get lucky and find something they'd missed.

Her radio crackled. "Dispatch to Lieutenant Lockwood."

She picked up the mike and pressed the broadcast button. "Lieutenant Lockwood, go ahead."

"We just received a call about a body over at the high school."

Ice water pumped into her veins. "Another shooting?"

"Negative. Caller said it's a vampire, like the others."

"Damn it," she muttered, and then responded over the radio. "On my way, and call Enforcer Baudelaire. I'm sure he's going to want to see this."

"Affirmative. Dispatch, out."

Tasha dropped the mike and flipped on her lights

and siren. Her hands clutched the steering wheel until her knuckles turned white. "Fucking vamps. When the hell is this going to end?"

Varik unlocked the door of the Governor's Suite and pushed it open with his foot. Alex had lost all her clothing and supplies for Dweezil in the fire. He'd gone shopping while she was still asleep and picked up a couple of outfits for her, as well as stuff for the cat. The luxury hotel in the heart of downtown Jefferson wasn't happy about having an animal in the room, but his status as the FBPI's director of special operations didn't leave much room for argument.

He still had a room reserved at a cheap hotel near the interstate, but he'd checked Alex and Emily into the suite under assumed names. Flashing his FBPI creds to the manager at four in the morning had deterred the man from balking at the falsification of records. Once they were settled in the bedrooms, he'd collapsed on the couch for a few hours of sleep.

As he fumbled with the bags and door, Emily appeared from one of the bedrooms and hurried to him. "Here, let me help." She grabbed the fast-food bag dangling from his mouth and the cardboard tray filled with steaming coffee cups. As she turned away, she asked of no one in particular, "Why do men have to load themselves up so? You could've made two trips."

"Efficiency," he answered. He dropped onto the couch the discount-store bags looped over his arm and clutched in his hand. Wiggling his fingers, he was relieved to have the blood flow restored.

Emily paused in her emptying of the fast-food bag's contents. "Has there been any word on Stephen?"

"Not yet, but Damian's in town. He's at Crimson Swan now."

She nodded. "It was kind of him to come."

Varik snorted and joined her beside the small dining table. "You didn't give him much option to refuse." He picked up a lukewarm hash-brown patty and bit into it. "'Get down here and find my son or so help me, I'll rip your fangs out myself and shove them up your ass,'" he quoted with a smile.

Emily's status as the widow of Bernard Sabian gave her a great deal of political clout with the upper echelons of vampire society, including FBPI brass. She didn't use it often, preferring to remain in relative obscurity, a fact Varik had always admired.

Emily blushed as she continued to pull food from the bag. "I may have been a bit abrupt."

"Abrupt?" Varik laughed. "You were brilliant. I only wish I could've actually seen Damian's face."

"I'm just worried about Stephen." She looked at a closed bedroom door. "And Alex."

Varik sat down and plucked one of the coffee cups from the cardboard tray. "Is she still asleep?"

Emily sat across from him with a sigh. "You're blood-bound to her. You tell me."

It was Varik's turn to blush. He could sense Alex's mind within his own and knew from the steady humming, like the sound of a distant beehive, that she was sleeping. When awake, the humming would rise and fall in pitch, depending on her mood and what she was thinking, but he could hear her thoughts or see her memories only if they both lowered their mental guards. After last night, he didn't think she would be eager for that anytime soon.

"For the record," Emily began, as she poured creamer into her coffee, "I just want you to know that I tried to convince Alex to stay in Louisville, to work things out with you."

"I know."

"She refused to listen to me."

"She refuses to listen to most people."

Emily smiled. "She's a lot like her father in that regard." Her gaze darted to Alex's door and back. "She still doesn't know about you and—"

"No," Varik answered quickly, "and I want to keep it that way. It'll be difficult because of the bond, but you thought it best that she not know her father was a Hunter."

She clasped and unclasped her hands. "I may have been wrong about that. Stephen told me Alex was having visions."

Varik nodded.

"What if the Special Operations unit wants her?"

"That won't happen."

"Being in Special Ops nearly killed Bernard."

"No, Emily, it *did* kill him." He reached across the table and gave her hands a reassuring squeeze. "But I'm not going to let that happen to Alex. As long as I can maintain an inner shield in my mind, Alex won't know about Bernard. I can do it. I had plenty of practice working with him."

Emily's lips thinned, and she stared out the window, her blue eyes growing distant.

Varik finished his hash-brown patty and reached for a sausage-and-egg muffin. He'd been young when he first met Bernard Sabian. He and Damian were selected for a new Hunter program utilizing vampires with strong psychic abilities referred to as Talents. Varik, Damian, and several others with virtually no psychic abilities were called Nils, and served as protectors for the Talents and hunted down the vampires that the Talents determined had violated vampiric law.

Varik had proven himself especially adept at tracking other Hunters. He rose through the ranks and was eventually paired with Bernard Sabian, the strongest of the Talents, as a specialized team tracking corrupt Hunters. Bernard would enter into a trance, sometimes for hours, and when he awoke he would have one or two names for Varik. While Bernard remained safely in Louisville, Varik would then track down the designated Hunters, determine if they'd turned rogue and jeopardized the vampire community's veil of secrecy. If so, he eliminated them.

This part Alex knew, that Varik had hunted other Hunters. However, she didn't know that it had been her beloved father who'd sealed the fate of so many during the near century they worked together. It was a secret Varik bore and would give his life to keep her from learning, for with that knowledge came an awareness of other secrets, darker and more deadly. Secrets Bernard had died protecting. Secrets he would now work to keep from Alex.

Beethoven's Fifth Symphony played in the distance, muffled by the closed door of Alex's room.

"Shit." Varik leapt from his chair. He could already feel her mind stirring within his own. "I forgot to take away her cell phone."

He reached the door as the music died. Hand on the knob, he debated opening it. He didn't have to debate long.

The knob jerked from his hand, and Alex barreled into him, cell phone glued to her ear. They stumbled over and around each other.

"Damn it to hell, Varik!" Alex swore and staggered away. "Watch where you're fucking going."

"Alexandra!" Emily exclaimed. "That is no way—"

"Save it, Mom," Alex grumbled, as she grabbed the last coffee from the cardboard tray. "I'm not in the mood."

Emily crossed her arms in front of her and returned to staring out the window.

Varik tried to pluck the cell phone from her hand, and she growled at him. He propped his foot against the wall between the two bedrooms and leaned back. If she wanted to talk on the phone, he wasn't going to argue with her. He couldn't hear the conversation, but judging from the scowl on Alex's face and the intensity of the blood-bond's hum in his mind, the news wasn't pleasant.

Alex gulped down several mouthfuls of steaming coffee. "Yeah, I got it," she said hoarsely into her phone.

"Tell them not to touch anything. We'll be there as soon as we can." She closed the phone and tossed it onto the couch among the plastic bags filled with clothing.

"That didn't sound good," Varik said, eyeing her warily. The right side of her face was swollen, and the area under her eye was a mixture of vibrant blues and greens. More bruises and scrapes covered her arms, which were still a bright pink from the heat of the fire. It would take days for all of her injuries to heal and the bruises to fade.

Alex drained the large coffee cup in three more gulps. "Jefferson police found a body at the high school."

Emily gasped. Her eyes were a swirling mix of sky blue and darkest amber. "Is it—" Her question trailed away.

Alex toyed with her cup. "I don't know," she admitted quietly. "We won't know until we get there."

"What's this 'we' business?" Varik asked. "You aren't going anywhere."

"Like hell I'm staying here."

"Look at yourself, Alex. You can barely stand up straight. There is no way I'm letting you anywhere near a crime scene."

Alex glanced at her mother and then crossed the room to him. She grabbed his arm and shoved him toward her bedroom. "Inside," she hissed.

He allowed himself to be forced into the room before turning to face her.

"Someone has to stay with Mom," she said tersely, as

she shut the door behind her. "She can't be left alone, not with Stephen missing."

"Agreed. You'll stay."

"I'm going."

"How do you plan to do that? Your Jeep is still sitting in the impound yard, and you're not riding with me."

"I'll take Mom's rental."

"Not if I take the keys with me."

"Damn it, Varik! This is still my investigation."

"Not anymore," he retorted. "Damian's in town, and as of this morning, he's assumed command of all open Bureau cases, including the arson, the murders, Stephen, and the diner shooting."

"The diner isn't even a federal case!"

He shrugged. "Damian seems to think it's related in some way. He's taken it from the sheriff and brought in a bunch of Enforcers from the Jackson office."

"That's just great!" Alex threw her arms up in frustration. "What the hell am I supposed to do now?"

"Enjoy some quality time with your mother and get some rest."

"Excuse me?"

"You heard me. Damian has removed you from active duty."

"He did what!"

"You and Emily are to stay here, while—"

"This is bullshit!" Her eyes had bled to amber, and she paced the floor like a caged animal. "I am *not* going to just sit here while Stephen is out there!"

"Alex—"

"I saw them, Varik!" She pounded her chest, and

tears slipped down her cheeks. "Don't you understand? I *saw* them take Stephen! I tried—I *wanted* to save him, but the fire—" She sobbed and doubled over, clutching her stomach.

Varik pulled her into his arms, cradling her as she wept and clung to him.

"I couldn't save him." She forced the words out. "I wasn't fast enough. I couldn't—"

A new round of sobs racked her frame, and he held her tightly, stroked her hair, and wished he did have psychic talents so he could steal away her pain.

thirteen

EIGHT LIFELESS EYES WATCHED HIM PREPARE FOR HIS latest triumph.

The smell of wood stain failed to cover the darker smell of blood. He'd cleaned the floor after each kill, but nothing got rid of the smell completely. The cross in his gloved hands was almost finished. Once the stain was set, he could start working on his new addition. Glancing at the crumpled form wrapped in plastic and hidden beneath a faded blue tarp, he couldn't suppress a grin.

His gaze flicked to the photo of Claire from their wedding anniversary, the one he carried with him everywhere. He'd propped it up against the large jars lining the overhead shelf before starting his work on the cross. Claire's eyes shone brightly with her approval. Surrounded by the trophies of his kills, she smiled at him. He blew her a kiss and returned to his work and memories of the previous night.

The vamp bar had ignited like a house of cards and

burned as brightly as the sun. He could feel the town being cleansed of the bloodsucking infection. Everything was going as he'd hoped. He had only to see that Enforcer bitch suffer a little longer and then his anger, his need for vengeance, would be satiated.

He hadn't always been angry. He'd been happy once. With Claire. She'd been his rock, the stabilizing force in his life. He thought they'd always be together.

Then she was taken from him.

It was late, and she'd been leaving The Stakehouse, the blood bar in Natchez where she worked as a waitress. Jefferson was located about an hour or so east of the Mississippi River town. He didn't like her driving home that far late at night, even though she worked there only on the weekends. She'd laugh and tell him that he worried too much.

But his worrying had proven correct.

Claire left The Stakehouse at about midnight on October 1, 2005, and never made it home. Four days later her body was found dumped on the side of Highway 84, halfway between Natchez and Jefferson. She was naked, bruised, battered, and bloodless. Dozens of bite marks and puncture wounds had marred her once beautiful form.

The case was kicked over to Alexandra Sabian because of the obvious vampire involvement. She'd promised him for months that she would find Claire's killers. She was committed to seeing justice served. She wouldn't rest until Claire's killers had answered for their crimes.

He should've known it was all a lie. He should've

known better than to trust a fucking vamp to hunt down one of its own.

Sabian's phone calls became less frequent until they simply stopped altogether. When he called her, she said she was sorry but there wasn't enough evidence to charge anyone, wasn't even enough to provide viable suspects.

The case had grown cold. Sabian moved on to other investigations. He'd been left in the darkness with only Claire's memory.

His anger simmered beneath the surface. He started investigating Claire's murder for himself. He traveled to Natchez on his days off and weekends, asking if anyone remembered seeing her.

No one talked at first. He hadn't expected them to. They were vampires, and vampires looked after their own kind.

That's when he met Tubby Jordan, and the reverend had introduced him to someone who remembered Claire, remembered the vamps who followed her when she left work. He'd been given a name—Trent Thibodaux, who supplied him with the names of his accomplices through the aid of torture before he killed the vampire. He'd tracked them all down, but he saved Alexandra Sabian for last. He wanted to see her writhe and suffer the way he'd suffered. Her unwillingness to pursue Claire's killers was the ultimate betrayal, and now, with the help of Tubby and HSM, he was going to see it happen.

After all, it was the Human Separatist Movement, an organization in which Tubby proudly proclaimed membership, that showed him the true nature of the vampire—evil Hell-spawned demons bent on ruling over humans. They were Satan's army in the flesh, and HSM would be both the hand and the sword of God that sent them back to the abysmal fires.

He dipped a rag into the pot of stain on the workbench before him and smoothed it over the carved stake. He used a second rag to wipe away the excess, wiped it away in the same manner he'd see the vamps wiped out of Jefferson.

He checked his watch and smiled. The present he'd left at the high school would've been found by now. He could almost smell the terror rippling through the vamps as word spread that another corpse had been found.

The cross in his hands was nearly complete. Once it was finished, he'd be able to start working on the body of the vamp he'd killed yesterday. It would be his greatest work yet and would serve as the killing blow to Alexandra Sabian.

Eight lifeless eyes and Claire stared at him with pride as he hummed and continued to stain the wooden cross.

"What are we going to do?" Bill Jenkins asked, his fingers drumming the Holy Word Church's kitchen tabletop. "The cops are bound to—"

"We're not doing anything," Martin interrupted, glancing at Harvey. "Right?"

Harvey looked around at the faces gathered at the

table and wished he could light a cigarette. "As far as metro police and the vamps know, none of us are involved in the fire."

"That's great, but what about the vamp we shoved in the van?" Bill asked.

"What about him?" Martin retorted.

"We don't know where he is," Bill hissed. "The plan was to bring him back here, hold him until the vampires left town, and then let him go." He threw his arms wide. "But he's not here! No sign of him or the van! It's like they fucking disappeared."

"Do *not* curse in the house of the Lord," Tubby Jordan said, twisting in his chair to settle his bulk in a more comfortable position and kicking up the stench of his cologne in the process.

"Sorry, Reverend," Bill muttered. "I'm just worried, that's all. Seems like nothing is going the way we planned it."

Tubby nodded. "What do you propose we do? Do you want us to go to the Enforcers and tell them that the vampire we kidnapped has been kidnapped from *us*?"

Bill sighed and chewed on an already ragged thumbnail.

"Think of the situation this way," Tubby said. "We now have what the politicians call 'plausible deniability.' Even if the vamps do figure out we set fire to the bar, we can honestly say we don't know the whereabouts of Stephen Sabian."

"He's got a point, Bill," Martin said, nodding. "As long as none of us confess to arson, Harvey can run interference with the JPD and the vamps. Right?" He looked to Harvey for confirmation.

Harvey sighed. "I'll do what I can, but there's still the not-so-small matter of someone threatening Lock-wood last night."

"It wasn't any of us," Tubby said defensively.

"I know that, but someone did it, someone who knew about Judgment Day."

"Maybe Darryl—" Martin began.

Harvey waved away his argument. "I talked to him. He says he didn't do it. I also talked to the others, and none of them claim to know anything about it."

The mood in the room turned from somber to suspicious. Each of them sent cautious glances at the others and looked away quickly when caught.

"What if—" Bill started, paused, and then began again. "What if we have a spy in HSM?"

A ripple of shock followed by unease shook Harvey. He hadn't considered that possibility, but it actually made sense, given the strange turn of events with the missing van. But who?

A dozen men had been involved in Judgment Day, most of whom Harvey had known his entire life. They'd all lived in Jefferson, and he found it hard to believe that any of them would betray their mutual cause, or threaten a woman, for that matter. Destroying the heart of the vampire community was one thing, but there were lines even they wouldn't cross.

He didn't believe anyone he'd known for so long or who upheld the same beliefs as he did would betray their group. The only exceptions were Tubby and Darryl

Black. Tubby was a newcomer to the town, but aside from having an unnatural love of cheap cologne and sweets, the reverend's background was spotless. He'd checked.

Darryl, on the other hand, had moved to Jefferson from somewhere in southern Louisiana about ten years ago, met and married a local woman, and joined the JPD. Despite Darryl's history in Jefferson, he and Harvey hadn't run in the same circles until recently.

Thinking of Darryl, Harvey frowned. Something niggled at his brain.

Darryl was working the night shift again last night. He'd arrived late, an unusual occurrence for him, and had been pale and withdrawn. Deputy Case had noticed a few spots that appeared to be blood along the hem of Darryl's khaki uniform pants. When asked about it, Darryl had said he'd hit a deer on the way in to work and had moved the carcass off the road. Harvey hadn't thought much of it at the time, but when he'd left the department after clocking out for the evening, he'd seen no damage to Darryl's pickup. If Darryl had hit a deer as he claimed, there should have been at least a dent in the front fender or a busted headlight.

Uneasiness filled him, and Harvey checked his watch and stood. It was already well past mid-morning, and he had his own damage control to perform at the impound yard. As he'd expected, the vamps had taken over the Maggie's Place shooting. He'd lodged a good argument for show, but in the end, he'd turned everything over. He wanted the vamps to investigate the shooting and find the present he'd left for Sabian in her Jeep. What he didn't want them to find was his missing handkerchief. "I've got to get back to the office."

The men said their good-byes, and Harvey departed with a promise to give the spy idea more thought.

He sank into the driver's seat of his county cruiser and started the car's engine. Darryl still bothered him, and suspicion gnawed at him. As he drove away from the Holy Word Church, he decided that he'd drive out to Darryl's later and talk to him. It was the only way he could be certain his self-reassurances weren't anything more than bald-faced lies.

When Varik arrived at the high-school football field, Tasha hadn't been surprised that he'd taken one look at the scene and called for Bureau backup. Now, aside from the coach who'd discovered the body, she was the only human inside a perimeter of yellow crime scene tape.

Chief Enforcer Alberez had arrived a short time ago and begun questioning the coach, who was still very visibly shaken.

Tasha kept one eye on the coach and his inquisitor and the other on Varik as he and a forensic tech worked the scene. The Enforcers were allowing her to observe but not participate in the evidence-gathering process. This was a federal case now. Her role as the liaison officer, as well as her prior involvement in the investigation, made it necessary for her to be there. It didn't mean they had to let her do her job.

She stood to the side, using the wooden bleachers to

increase her field of vision. The other bodies had been left in a supine position, lying on their backs. This one was different.

First, the killer had taken the time and effort needed to drag the corpse to the top of the bleachers. Second, the body had been left in an upright position. Heavy nylon rope encircled the victim's arms and legs, which were spread wide between two upright support beams for the commentator's booth, where the announcers sat during games. Everything else remained the same. No blood trail leading to the nude corpse of a male vampire. A cross-stake driven through the victim's chest, and no head on the body.

"These kinds of cases always creep me out," Freddy, the FBPI forensic tech working with Varik, said, as he snapped a series of photos with a digital camera. "Why do I always get assigned to the sicko cases?"

"Just lucky, I guess," Varik answered. He plucked the leather pouch from around the cross-stake, opened it, and dumped the contents into his gloved hand.

Freddy snapped several photos of the contents. "What is that?" he asked, pointing to one of the items.

Tasha moved closer as Varik lifted the small silver object. "It looks like a four-leaf clover charm."

Varik nodded. "That's exactly what it is." He examined the charm closely. An emotion flittered across his face, too quickly for Tasha to identify. His hand closed over the charm. "Didn't the other pouches contain items personal to the victims?"

"Two did," she said. "Stromheimer's wedding ring

was included, and Williams had a bloody photo of him and his girlfriend. The first body didn't have anything."

"So, the clover may be special to this vic," Freddy surmised.

Varik didn't answer immediately, and appeared lost in thought.

Tasha opened her mouth to question him. He seemed to shake free of whatever memory had gripped his mind and held up a Mississippi driver's license.

"Well, now we know what happened to Gary Lipscomb." He turned the license around for Tasha to see.

A photo of a smiling vampire stared at her. She read the information from the license. "Gary Lipscomb. Age one hundred and nine. Address is three-oh-eight-one Cabot Lane, Jefferson." Her gaze flickered to Varik. "Cabot Lane is in the county, outside of city limits. The other vics lived here in town."

Varik returned the license and two bloody fangs to the pouch. The clover charm he slipped into a separate evidence bag.

"Killer's deviating from his established pattern." She glanced at the corpse. "That's not a good sign."

"I don't think it's a deviation," Varik countered. "Lipscomb worked in Jefferson. His car was found at his job site. I think the killer either lured Lipscomb away from his car or picked him up somewhere else here in town."

"But where?"

"Crimson Swan would be the most likely place."

"And it was just torched."

"Convenient, no?"

She shook her head. "No, planned."

A techno beat sounded from Varik's belt, and he checked his cell phone. He stepped a few feet away before answering.

Tasha watched as Freddy and another Enforcer carefully severed the bonds supporting the body. They worked in unison to hold it upright for a moment, and then gently laid it on a wooden bench. She flinched when Freddy pulled the stake free and placed it in a flat white box.

Varik returned as Freddy and the other Enforcer were prepping a black body bag. "Looks like we may have gotten a break."

"What happened?"

"Owen Gibson, the truck driver seen arguing with Lipscomb a couple of weeks ago, just turned himself in to the Nassau County Sheriff's Department."

Alex paced the length of the hotel suite, turned, and retraced her steps. She hated being out of the loop, feeling useless. Worry gnawed at her. Where was Stephen? Was he okay? Was he even alive?

She replayed the scene from the previous night through her mind, trying to remember some detail that would help lead her to Stephen's kidnappers. The memory kept shifting to her final confrontation with her brother in the hospital. She'd been so mad, so hurt by what he'd done. Guilt weighed heavily on her shoulders. If anything happened to him—

"You're going to wear a hole in the carpet," her mother said from her seat on the couch.

She glared at the blond-and-silver curls piled high on the back of her mother's head and kept moving. "How can you be so calm? Aren't you worried about Stephen?"

"Of course I am, but is pacing the floor or wringing my hands going to bring him back? No, it's not." Her mother answered her own question.

Alex reached the window and paused, looking over the rain-slicked pavement of the hotel's parking lot. Part of her recognized the truth in her mother's statement, but she still felt as though she'd failed Stephen. Yes, she was the younger sister, but she was also the Enforcer, the family's protector. She should've been able to prevent Stephen from being taken, and she hadn't.

Beethoven's Fifth Symphony filled the room.

Alex checked the display on her cell phone and flipped it open. "Varik, is it—"

"It's not Stephen," he said, by way of greeting.

Her shoulders slumped in relief. She caught her mother's gaze and shook her head. "Who is it?"

"Gary Lipscomb."

"Ah, fucking hell."

"Tasha and I are on our way to the sheriff's department now. You remember the BOLO we sent out for Owen Gibson?"

"The truck driver who'd argued with Lipscomb. Yeah, I remember."

"Gibson just turned himself in."

Alex nearly dropped the phone in her haste to reach the exit. "I'm on my way. I can be there in—"

"You're staying where you are."

"Like hell I am."

"You're not part of this investigation anymore, Alex. You can't be present when we interview Gibson."

She began pacing in a circle in front of the door. "Then let me sit in the video observation room."

"Alex—"

"You need me on this," she said quickly. "I saw Stephen's kidnappers, and—"

"They wore masks! You can't possibly identify any of them."

"But I saw one of them in the alley when he attacked me! Dweezil scratched his face."

Varik blew his breath out in frustration.

Alex felt the sting of unshed tears. "Please, Varik," she whispered tightly. "Stephen's my brother. I have to do *something*."

The silence stretched out, and then finally broke. "All right," Varik said. "You can sit in the video room, but that's it. You will *not* interfere with the interview in any way. Understood?"

"Perfectly."

"Damian's going to have my fangs for this," he muttered, and ended the call.

Alex grinned and shouted triumphantly. She spun to face her bewildered mother and suddenly felt like a teenager again when she asked, "Mom, can I borrow your car?"

"Stay here," Varik said, pointing to the table in front of Alex. "I don't want you to so much as step a toe out of this room."

They were in the video observation room for the Jefferson Police Department. A row of monitors glowed softly in the dimness, and each showed a different interview room, but only one was occupied.

Alex stared at the man on the screen in front of her. "I want to talk to him," she said. "I—"

"Am no longer a part of any official investigation," he finished her sentence and pushed her gently back in her seat.

"Damn it, Varik. I can help!"

He placed one hand on the table, the other on the back of her chair, and leaned into her personal space. "You really want to help?"

She raised her chin defiantly. "Yes."

"Then for once in your life, *trust me.*"

Her eyes were a swirling mix of emerald and amber, and she appeared to be mounting a comeback, but she surprised him. She seemed to deflate and crossed her arms in front of her, dropping her gaze and nodding in acquiescence.

Tasha entered the room, and Varik backed away from Alex. "Am I interrupting something?"

"No, I was laying down the ground rules. That's all," Varik replied.

"I see," Tasha said, and took a seat beside Alex.

He picked up a notepad and pen from another table. They were more for show than use because of the video recorders, but if Gibson confessed to anything, he'd need to get it in writing.

"Varik?"

He paused in the doorway and looked at Alex.

Emotions passed behind her eyes, and the blood-bond hummed in his mind. She didn't have to say anything for him to understand what she wanted to express. He directed a single thought along the bond: *You're welcome.*

She smiled weakly and then focused on the monitor in front of her.

Varik closed the door and walked the short distance to interview room five, where Owen Gibson waited. He breezed into the room with an air of nonchalance. "Hello, Mr. Gibson," he said, as he laid the notepad on the table and sat down across from the truck driver. "I'm Enforcer Varik Baudelaire, and I want to thank you for coming in today."

"Humph," Owen Gibson snorted. "Didn't have much choice, did I? I show up for work and find out the feds are looking for me. Boss threatened to fire my ass if I didn't get it straightened out." He picked at the edges of a jagged cuticle. "So, what's this all about?"

Varik studied the man and thought he looked more than a little like a grizzly bear. He was tall and carried at least fifty extra pounds around his waist. The fresh stains on his Harley-Davidson shirt stank of beer, as did his breath, although he'd tried to conceal it with liberal amounts of breath mints. Greasy brown hair was slicked back into a messy braid that snaked around his neck and ended in a bright red elastic band. A thick dark beard streaked with gray covered most of his face, but a pair of bright green eyes stared out from under the equally bushy brows. Faded tattoos adorned his forearms, one of a winged heart and another of a skull impaled by a spike.

Varik smiled, flashing his fangs, which caused Gibson to squirm in his seat. "I have a few questions regarding a case I'm working."

"The dead vamps?"

"You're familiar with the case?"

"I heard about it."

"Do you know a vampire by the name of Gary Lipscomb?"

Gibson blinked and laced his fingers together, stilling his hands on the tabletop, before shaking his head. "I don't know any vamps by name."

"He works for Morrison Distribution. You had an argument with him a couple of weeks ago. Called him a 'damn bloodsucker' and blocked his forklift."

"If you say so. I don't remember."

"What started the argument?"

"I said I don't remember."

Varik pursed his lips and remained quiet. He waited to speak until Gibson wriggled with impatience. "Here's my problem, Owen. I have a warehouse full of witnesses who are willing to swear that you had an altercation with Gary Lipscomb, and unfortunately, Mr. Lipscomb's dead, so he can't tell us his version of the story."

Gibson began shaking his head vigorously. "You're not pinning a murder on me. I haven't killed anybody, human or vamp. Hell, no."

"You argued with the victim. Now he turns up dead after being missing for several days. You can see where we might find all this puzzling, Mr. Gibson."

"I can explain that, the argument."

Varik inclined his head slightly and positioned his pen over the notepad, waiting.

"It's like this, okay?" Gibson sat forward, hands gesturing. "I got to Morrison Distribution to pick up a load of sporting equipment and I was running behind schedule. The vamp loading the truck—"

"Gary Lipscomb."

"I didn't know his name. All I knew was he wasn't loading the stuff quickly enough. I was falling further behind because of it. I may've said some things in the heat of the moment, but I didn't kill anyone, swear to God."

Varik scribbled a few notes, buying himself time. "How do you feel about vampires in general, Mr. Gibson?"

"I, uh . . ."

"Do you like them? Hate them?"

"I don't really know any. Personally."

"But surely you have an opinion."

"Yeah, of course, but—"

"You know what I think? I think you don't like vampires much, and when Gary Lipscomb screwed with your schedule, you got mad."

"Now, wait a second. You're getting this all wrong. I—"

"You look like you've seen some action. I'm willing to bet you even enjoyed killing Lipscomb."

"I didn't kill him!" Gibson roared. "Yeah, I don't like vamps much. I think they're unnatural, but I *am not* a killer."

" 'Unnatural'?" Varik asked.

"The Bible says that we—humans—are made in God's

image, and I don't think He'd create something that's sole purpose is to devour, to destroy, that image."

"If God didn't create vampires, then who—"

"Satan," he said, and spread his arms wide, as if that explained it all. "He created—no, *spawned*—vampires in the pits of Hell and sent you demons here, to earth, to create chaos and discord among humans."

Varik stared at him and reassessed his previous evaluation. Instinct still told him Gibson wasn't a killer, but he most certainly was a nutcase.

"It's all here." Gibson pulled a crumpled pamphlet from his back pocket and tossed it on the table.

A logo featuring a stylized samurai sword cutting through the equally stylized letters HSM glared up at Varik from the glossy paper. "Human Separatist Movement?"

Gibson nodded.

Varik picked it up and unfolded it. The cover showed a cartoon of a human mob cheering as one man drove a cross-shaped stake through a bat-winged vampire's heart. An image of Gary Lipscomb's body drifted before his mind's eye. "Where did you get this?"

"I don't have to tell you—"

"Where did you get it?" He shouted the question.

Gibson recoiled. "From a guy at a diner here in town, Maggie's Place."

"Who was it? What's his name?"

"The cook. I think his name was Bill."

Varik scooped up the pamphlet and left the room without saying another word. He saw Tasha standing in the doorway of the video room, staring down an empty hall. "What's going on?"

"Alex," Tasha answered. "She just ran out of here like her ass was on fire."

"Ah, shit," he breathed, and sprinted down the corridor.

fourteen

"HAM SANDWICHES WITH MAYO, SWISS CHEESE, AND homemade sweet pickles make the best lunches," Darryl Black said, settling into his recliner. He balanced the plate of sandwiches on top of his glass of Mountain Dew and worked the lever to elevate the folding footrest. Once comfortable, he punched the power button on the remote that he'd duct-taped to the chair's arm so he wouldn't lose it.

The small TV flickered once, then twice, before coming to life. He bit into the corner of the first sandwich and watched a replay of the Crimson Swan fire on the news.

"Authorities are still investigating the apparent arson of Jefferson's only blood bar," a male voice-over said.

Darryl applauded when the tower fell in a spectacular show of flames and sparks.

The video switched to a studio view of the news anchor. "In addition to Crimson Swan's destruction,

Stephen Sabian, the bar's owner and the son of murdered university professor Bernard Sabian, is missing.
Anyone with information regarding either of these
events is being asked to call the Jefferson Police Department or the FBPI's national toll-free hotline."

Darryl made a rude hand gesture at the reporter and
lowered the volume when the broadcast cut to a commercial.

He smiled at the picture of Claire hanging on the
wall next to him. "Well, what do you think, sweetheart?"

The floorboards creaked and popped behind him. A
shadow passed over Claire's photo, moved along the
wall, and merged with those behind the television. The
screen flickered, and the hiss of static filled the room.

He sighed and took a bite of his sandwich before
looking to the portrait once more.

Claire's brown eyes bored into him, their warmth
turning to accusation.

"You're not happy."

The TV screen flickered.

"What did I do, or not do, this time?"

The screen became a fuzzy field of black-and-white
snow. It flashed twice, accompanied by a snippet of
sound. *Stake. Rest.*

He swiped a hand over his face. "All right, all right. I
get it. Let me finish my sandwich and I'll take care of it."

The screen flickered once and returned to normal.

Darryl took two more bites of sandwich. The crumbs
fell onto his navy jumpsuit and turned a pale pink before changing to dark red as they soaked up trace

amounts of blood. He brushed the crumbs away, his gaze drifting back to Claire's picture as it always did.

The accusation was gone from her eyes, leaving only the silent adoration of a wife for her husband.

Alex could feel Varik's mind pressing against her own, searching for a way past the barriers she'd erected to block the blood-bond. She didn't have time to deal with him. The window in which to find and recover Stephen safely was closing. After listening to Owen Gibson's inane prattling and admission that the cook at Maggie's Place had given him Human Separatist Movement literature, she wanted to have a little chat with said cook.

She left the JPD in her mother's rental car and drove across town to the diner, which was still cordoned off with yellow tape, but two cars were parked in the back. She had no way of knowing if one of them belonged to the cook. She'd just have to take her chances.

She parked beside the cars and got out, leaving her cell phone behind but making certain her Glock was readily accessible beneath the denim jacket Varik had bought for her. Approaching the rear entrance cautiously, she could hear the rustling of papers coming from inside.

The heavy metal security door was open. Alex stepped into the gloomy storeroom and skirted the wall in an effort to remain in the darkest shadows. More rustling of papers filtered through the open doorway of an office, along with the sound of struggling machinery.

"Fucking piece of shit," a man's voice muttered from inside the office, followed by the slap of flesh striking hard plastic.

Alex crept to the office door and peered around the corner. She instantly recognized both the smell and the girth of Tubby Jordan even though he was bent over, trying to free a stack of papers that had gotten jammed in a shredder.

Arms grabbed her from behind, pinning her own arms and lifting her off the ground.

She roared and kicked at the legs of the man holding her.

Tubby Jordan appeared in front of her, his eyes wide. "What are you *doing*? Let her go!"

Alex arched her back, driving her head into the face of the man behind her. She both felt and heard a sickening crunch and then smelled fresh blood as the man released her with an anguished yelp.

"You bitch!" her assailant cried. "You broke my fucking nose!"

She stepped out of either man's reach and drew her Glock.

The man with the broken nose rushed her. His momentum carried them to the floor. They rolled, each trying to gain the upper hand as well as control of the gun.

Alex could hear Tubby shouting in the background. Instinct kicked in, and she sank her fangs into her assailant's forearm.

He screamed and jerked away.

Blood filled her mouth. Memories that were not her own flooded her mind. A group of men sitting around a table. Stephen's gold curls shining under the glow of a streetlamp as he fell to the ground, crying out in pain. Flames erupting from the shattered windows of Crimson Swan.

The visions faded, and the world around her fell silent. Mr. Broken Nose was no longer on top of her. She blinked, looked around from her supine position on the floor, and her heart stopped.

Varik stood nearby with Broken Nose, who cradled his bloody arm to his chest, firmly in hand. His golden eyes were fixed on her, his expression a carefully constructed mask of neutrality. Tubby Jordan cowered in the office doorway under the watchful glare of another Enforcer. Standing at her feet, glaring at her with barely contained rage, was Damian Alberez.

Tasha left the Municipal Center's main lobby, pulled a set of keys from her jacket pocket, and was greeted by a mob of reporters armed with microphones.

"Lieutenant!" one shouted. "Is it true that the FBPI is replacing Enforcer Sabian?"

"Have there been any ransom demands made for Stephen Sabian?" another asked.

"Has the FBPI made any progress in finding the shooter of the Maggie's Place massacre?" a third demanded.

"No comment," Tasha answered, and repeated it several times as she tried to break out of the throng. She finally succeeded and hurried to reach her car before the reporters caught her again.

Slipping into her unmarked cruiser, she gripped the steering wheel until her knuckles turned white. When she'd first agreed to work with Alex, she'd thought it was a perfect opportunity not only to conquer her fear of vampires but to show her hometown that human-vampire harmony was possible. Now she realized she'd been deluding herself.

Tasha started the car's engine and backed out of the space. She turned onto Jefferson Boulevard, her mind traveling in circles. She'd learned more about vampires in the past few days than she had in the six years she'd worked side by side with Alex. It was as though someone had taken the wool from over her eyes. She'd considered Alex a friend, but she realized she'd been used, not for blood but for resources. With more Enforcers in town and their subsequent assumption of investigative powers, she was being tossed aside like an empty Vlad's Tears vial.

She pulled into a reserved parking space close to the Nassau County morgue's front entrance. Disgusted by her past behavior, she climbed out of the car and jammed her hands into her pockets. The rustling of crumpled paper made her pause halfway to the door.

Tasha pulled out a wrinkled note bearing the logo for the Human Separatist Movement and recalled Owen Gibson's statements to Varik. Vampires were demon-spawn sent to create discord among humans. They'd certainly managed to disrupt her life.

She turned the note over and saw the same scrawl-ing handwriting as had been on her foyer mirror: *3:00 today. We'll be in touch.*

She hurriedly stuffed it back into her pocket. Someone was playing games with her. The question was who. It seemed that the only way she could find out would be to play along.

Even though her original fear of vampires was turning darker, angrier, she couldn't label it hatred. Not yet. She wasn't willing to align herself with HSM and jeopardize her career, even though she knew some of Jefferson's police force were already members. She should consider distancing herself from the Enforcers after this investigation was over. Maybe that would help her to refocus her life and bring the chaos to an end.

She entered the morgue and nodded to Jeff, Doc Hancock's assistant, seated at the front desk.

"Hey, Lieutenant," Jeff said brightly. "I was just about to call you. Dr. Hancock's got the results on those bodies from the high school."

"Did you say 'bodies'?"

He nodded. "Gary Lipscomb and Nichelle Adams."

"Who is Nichelle Adams?"

"Security guard for the high school. She was found stuffed in an equipment locker after you left the scene. Weren't you notified?"

Tasha sighed. How many more people were going to die before this all ended? "No, I wasn't. It's the Bureau's case, not mine."

Jeff motioned for her to follow him, and the two of them pushed through a pair of large steel doors marked

RESTRICTED in red letters. "How's Alex?" Jeff asked, as they entered the corridor outside the autopsy room.

Tasha shrugged. "Don't know. Don't care."

Jeff glanced at her. "You two get in a fight or something?"

"I'd rather not talk about it."

He gestured to the autopsy room's double door. "Doc's in there finishing up some notes."

Tasha nodded her thanks and entered the room, leaving Jeff in the hallway.

Nassau County's coroner perched on a tall stool beside an empty steel table, pen poised over an open file folder. Doc Hancock's owl-like eyes focused on her. "Lieutenant Lockwood," he said, and set down his pen. "I'm glad you're here. I was about to have Jeff fax over my reports on the latest victims."

She took a deep breath, inhaling the chemically clean scents of bleach and alcohol, and asked, "What can you tell me?"

"Ran the prints of both victims through IAFIS and VIPER to confirm their identities. Lipscomb's prints were on file from a DWI arrest in Natchez last year, and Nichelle Adams was a security guard for the school, so that explains hers being in the system."

Tasha accepted his handwritten reports. The tight scrawl resembled a foreign language, but years of reading bad handwriting helped her interpret the notes. "Lipscomb was shot and staked, like the others."

"Then decapitated. Definitely the work of the same killer."

She scanned the second report. "Adams was beaten?"

Doc Hancock bobbed his head. "Severely, but there were no signs of sexual assault. Mostly blunt-force trauma, but I did find a few stab wounds. Judging from the damage to the surrounding tissue, I'd say you're looking for a slender but heavy instrument with some kind of pronged, wedge-shaped tip."

"Did you find *anything* that might lead us to this guy? Prints? Skin under the fingernails?"

Doc Hancock shook his head. "The rain washed away any trace of physical evidence left on Lipscomb's body." He pulled a plastic zip-top bag sealed with red tape from the bottom of the stack of reports and handed it to her. "However, when we went to examine Adams, we found this in the folds of her clothing."

Tasha examined the blood-stained block. "A pack of gum?"

"It may or may not belong to the vic, but I thought the Bureau's forensic tech may be able to lift a print from it."

"Yeah, maybe. Anything else?"

"One more thing." He handed her another report. "Report on some Taser confetti found at the Crimson Swan scene. It was sent to me by mistake."

Tasha took the paper and scanned over it.

"I think you'll find it traced back to an interesting source."

Taser confetti consisted of small paper dots imprinted with a tracking number that scattered over the area where the probes were initially fired. The number could be traced back to a particular weapon and to whom it was sold. She checked the report a second time before looking to Doc Hancock. "Is this correct?"

"Verified it over the phone."

"Mind if I hang on to this?"

"Don't see why not. Like I said, it came to me by mistake."

Her hands shook as she folded the paper and slipped it into her pocket.

"You want to take copies of my reports back to the Enforcers?"

"No, I have to follow up on this Taser thing. Just fax everything else to Enforcer Baudelaire at the precinct."

"Will do."

"Thanks, Doc," Tasha said, and turned on her heel. She exited the autopsy room and headed for her car.

And to have a little chat with Harvey Manser.

"What the hell were you thinking?" Damian's deep voice rose with each word.

Alex shrank into the couch in the hotel suite she shared with her mother. Varik and Damian had escorted her back to the hotel while Tubby Jordan and Martin Evans, the man whose nose she'd broken, had been taken into custody by the Enforcers for questioning after it was discovered they were in the diner shredding HSM documents.

The question most concerning Alex now was her own fate. She'd bitten a non-donor human and ingested his blood. She'd broken the most sacred of laws, the Blood Law: "Never take by force from one what is freely offered by others." It was a crime punishable by death under vampiric law. Her only shot at avoiding a capital charge was to plead her case and hope Damian took pity on her.

"Of all the stupid shit you could've pulled," Damian railed, "you had to go and bite a human!"

"It was just a little bite," she said. "In self-defense."

"Excuse me?" Damian whirled on her. "Did you say something? I sure as hell hope not, because I don't remember giving you permission to speak yet, Enforcer Sabian."

Alex clenched her teeth to keep from telling him to piss off.

Varik stepped between them. "Ease up, Damian," he said calmly. "She knows what she did was wrong."

"Does she? For that matter, I ought to ship the both of you off to Alaska for screwing up a murder investigation!"

"Varik didn't—" Alex's voice faded away as Varik talked over her.

"If that's what you really want to do, then by all means, go right ahead." Varik shrugged. "I could spend my weekends ice fishing."

"I'm warning you, Baudelaire. I'm in no mood for your shit."

"And I'm in no mood for yours."

"Stop it." Emily finally spoke and struck the windowside table with her open palm. "All of you, just stop it. This bickering isn't going to accomplish anything useful, and it certainly isn't going to help any of you find Stephen."

Alex met Varik's gaze and then looked away. Her mother was right, as usual. Stephen should be their primary focus. According to the note Alex had been given, the kidnappers wanted all vampires out of Jefferson by midnight or they'd kill Stephen. She felt a fresh stab of guilt pierce her chest. If only she'd gotten to him sooner...

Damian jabbed a finger at her, but his voice was calmer when he spoke. "*You* had no business going anywhere near that diner."

Varik backed off and leaned against the wall, arms folded over his chest and one foot crossed in front of the other. His stance was one of indifference, but his eyes were bright gold and remained locked on Damian like twin lasers.

"I know that," Alex said through clenched teeth. "But Owen Gibson said the cook at the diner had given him HSM material. I don't know why, but I got it in my head that that son of a bitch knows where Stephen is."

"Bill Jenkins wasn't even at the diner."

"I know that *now*, but I also know the two who were there and HSM are involved."

"Yes, but Jordan and Evans both claim not to know anything about the kidnapping, the fire, the murders, or the shooting."

"Evans is lying," Alex muttered.

"You would know, wouldn't you?" Damian asked, glaring at her.

She couldn't meet his gaze. The coppery bite of Evans's blood still lingered in her mouth and increased her guilt.

Damian swiped a hand over his face and sat down across from her. "Biting Evans is the least of your problems, anyway."

Her head snapped up. "What does that mean?"

Damian produced a small zip-top bag containing an amber vial from his jacket pocket. "This was found in the center console of your Jeep." He dropped it on the coffee table in front of her. "Care to explain it?"

Alex frowned and used a corner of her shirt to cover her thumb and index finger as she picked up the bag. Dark liquid sloshed within the vial, and a teardrop superimposed over a crescent moon adorned the cap. "It's Midnight."

"No shit, Sherlock," Damian retorted. "What's it doing in your vehicle?"

"I've never seen this before." She handed the bag to Varik, who'd joined her on the couch. "You can't possibly think it's *mine*?"

"No, I don't," Damian said, and pulled another bag containing a wad of cloth from his pocket. "We also found this."

"That looks like a man's handkerchief."

"It is."

"Where did it come from?" Emily asked, moving from the window table to stand beside Damian.

"One of JPD's forensic techs saw Harvey Manser near your vehicle yesterday."

"The sheriff?" Varik asked.

Damian nodded. "Any ideas why he'd want to set you up, Enforcer Sabian?"

"Other than my being a vampire and his hatred of all vampires? No, can't think of a single reason."

"Don't get cute. This is a serious situation. If one branch of human law enforcement is actively trying to set you up for a fall, then we have to assume metro police may be in on the conspiracy as well."

Alex gaped at him. "You can't be serious."

"I'm very serious." He picked up the bag containing the vial of Midnight. "As of this moment, all communication between our people and the local agencies is severed. Until we can get this mess under control, neither of you"—he pointed to Alex and Varik—"are to breathe a word of this or anything else related to an ongoing investigation to Lieutenant Lockwood, Sheriff Manser, or any of their officers. Is that understood?"

"Yes, sir," Alex and Varik answered simultaneously, followed by Varik asking, "What about the kidnappers' demands?"

"We're working on a plan to bus vampires out of town and to a temporary shelter in the country. It's just a precaution in the event we can't find Stephen before the midnight deadline," Damian answered.

The trilling notes of a futuristic ringtone filled the room. Damian unclipped his phone from his belt and answered it as he walked into one of the adjoining bedrooms.

Alex's mind spun. She couldn't believe Damian was organizing a vampire exodus and had severed ties with the JPD and the sheriff's department. Even though he'd brought more Enforcers to Jefferson as well as set up a mobile lab, the Bureau *needed* cooperation from the locals to find Stephen as well as remove a large vampire population from their homes. Without it, she feared all investigations, especially that of Stephen's disappearance, would grind to a halt.

She glanced at her mother, standing beside Varik, as the Enforcer seemed to slip something into her mother's hand. Frowning, she opened her mouth to speak, but Damian returned with a spring in his step, blocking Alex's opportunity.

Emily thrust her hand into her pocket, and Varik stepped away.

"Baudelaire," Damian called, directing his path toward the exit. "We need to get over to the lab. Reyes found something on the cross-stakes."

Varik fell into step with Damian.

"Hang on a second," Alex said. They stopped, and she hurried forward. "What about me? What am I supposed to do?"

Damian pointed to the couch. "Sit. Behave." He opened the door and stepped into the hallway, calling over his shoulder, "Move it, Baudelaire. I don't have time for dillydallying."

Varik paused with his hand on the open door. He used his other hand to brush Alex's cheek lightly. "I'll let you know what we find out."

Her lips thinned, but she nodded. She was out of the official loop but would be able to learn everything Varik did through the blood-bond, if she was willing to risk opening it again.

He turned to leave, and she grabbed his arm.

"What was that thing you gave Mom?" she asked quietly.

He gave her a quick peck on the forehead and smiled before jogging down the corridor to catch up with Damian.

The door closed automatically, and Alex returned to the suite's sitting area, lost in thought. Had she seen what she thought she saw? Was her mind playing tricks on her?

Her mother sat on the edge of the coffee table, elbows on her knees, staring at something in her hand. She looked up when she heard Alex settling on the couch and once again shoved whatever it was into her pocket.

Alex stuck out her hand. "Hand it over."

Her mother sighed. "I don't know what you're talking about."

"Bullshit. I saw Varik give you something."

"Alexandra, I will not have you speaking to me in that tone."

"Then answer me. What did Varik give you?"

Her mother produced a wad of paper and dropped it into her hand.

She stared at the crumpled five-dollar bill. "Money? He gave you money?"

"Change from breakfast."

Alex thought of the coffee and fast-food biscuits she'd eaten that morning. Heat rose in her cheeks, and she handed the bill back to her mother.

"Honestly, Alexandra, everything Varik does is *not* a conspiracy against you." Her mother returned the money to her pocket as she rose and headed for her bedroom. "You may want to take his advice and trust him once in a while."

Alex felt the sting of her mother's words as she listened to the ringing silence around her. Dweezil jumped on the coffee table before her and began licking his paw and swiping it over his face. She watched the cat's bathing ritual while thoughts of her father, her mother, Varik, Stephen, and a thousand other issues traveled through her mind, gradually growing more organized until she was fidgeting in her seat and staring at the exit.

Eventually her mother returned from the bedroom and sat in the chair across from Alex. Her blue eyes—so much like Stephen's—pinned her in place. "You're up to something."

Alex cleared her throat and picked at a loose thread on the hem of her shirt. "No, I'm not."

"Oh, don't lie to me, Alexandra. I'm your mother. You're plotting something. I can see it in your eyes. You're thinking of going after Stephen."

"Mom, you heard Damian. I'm in a shitload of trouble because of what I did today." The thread she'd plucked began to unravel her shirt's hem. She dropped it and wiped her palms along her thighs. "Besides, I'm under orders to sit and behave."

Emily reached for her hand and pulled Alex to her feet as she herself rose. "I'll be sure to tell Damian that when he calls to check on you." She smoothed Alex's hair behind her ears. "Now go find your brother."

———

Tasha's cell phone rang at precisely three o'clock, just as the note had promised. "Lieutenant Lockwood," she answered after three rings.

"You're being screwed by the vamps," a digitized voice announced.

"What do you mean?"

"Alberez and his minions have severed all communication with your department."

"He can't do that. We're assisting—"

"The Enforcers have also taken a portly friend of yours into custody."

"Tubby." Tasha gasped.

"If you want to save him and yourself, Lieutenant, you will do exactly as we say."

With the twin snakes of fear and hatred gobbling her spine and sapping her will, Tasha listened as the voice laid out her instructions.

fifteen

HARVEY EYED THE PHONE AS IF IT WERE A RABID DOG waiting to pounce on him. A cigarette smoldered in the ashtray in front of him, untouched. Bill had called and told him Tubby and Martin were picked up by the vamps for questioning. Bill was worried that he and Harvey would be next. He'd told Bill to pack his bags and leave town.

A bone-chilling sense of dread filled him. He couldn't leave. His absence would be too noticeable. He wasn't able to retrieve his handkerchief from the impound yard before it was turned over to the Enforcers. It would be only a matter of time until they traced it back to him, along with the bottle of Midnight he'd planted in Sabian's Jeep. He had to figure a way out of that mess. Plus, he had unfinished business with Darryl.

Raised voices outside his office had him envisioning a troop of Enforcers storming the department, and he reached for his sidearm. His door burst open, and Tasha

Lockwood entered, followed by a harried-looking Deputy Justin Case.

"I'm sorry, Sheriff," Deputy Case said. "I tried to stop her, but—"

"You can't barge in here like this, Lockwood. What if I was conducting an interview or something?"

"Then I'd be the first to alert the media that you were actually doing what the taxpayers *pay* you to do." She sat in the chair opposite from him and crossed her legs at the knee.

"Now wait just a damn minute—"

Tasha talked over him. "You and I have a mutual problem, Harvey, and I suggest you take this opportunity to consider your options."

Harvey's eyes narrowed. Something had changed in her. He couldn't put a finger on it, but it was there nonetheless. He waved away Deputy Case. Once the door was closed and they were alone, he leaned back in his chair and lit a cigarette. "All right. I'm listening. What's this mutual problem?"

"Vampires."

He couldn't suppress his laughter. "*You*, the fucking liaison officer, have a problem with vamps? What's the matter? Did they spike your tea with blood or something?"

"No, they used me and my department to do grunt work and then kicked us to the curb. The FBPI has severed communication with the JPD, as well as your department."

"Good riddance, I say."

"You don't get it, do you, Harvey? They severed communication with us—with humans—because they suspect someone with ties to one of our departments is involved in burning down Crimson Swan and Stephen Sabian's kidnapping."

"I don't know what you're talking about, Lieutenant, but you can't waltz in here and accuse me and my men of misconduct."

"You're right." She produced a folded piece of paper and held it up for him to see. "This is a report I received this morning regarding a Taser that the Enforcers suspect was used to kidnap Stephen."

"Fascinating."

"The tracking number on the confetti traces back to one purchased by your department a few months ago."

Harvey swallowed the lump forming in his throat. "You're thinking one of my men was involved?"

"No, I think *you* were."

"Me?" He laughed to cover his rising panic. "Do you honestly think I'd have a hand in arson?"

"Honestly, I wouldn't put it past you to sell your own mother if you thought it'd be to your advantage."

"Now, listen here, Lieutenant. I've had enough of your—"

"Cut the crap, Harvey. Everyone knows you hate the vampires and that you'd love to see them out of Jefferson."

He eyed her for a moment as he puffed his cigarette. "I'm not the only one, though. Am I?"

She wiggled in her seat, running her fingers over the creases in the paper. "No, you're not."

Harvey felt a smile tugging at the corners of his mouth. "Why are *you* here and not the Enforcers?"

She stood and slipped the paper onto his desk. "Let's just call it a warning, from one human to another." She opened the door and closed it softly behind her.

He waited to be certain she was gone and that no one came in after her. He picked up the paper and scanned it. The coldness he'd felt in his bones began to spread outward like a disease. The implication of her words and the evidence in his hands hung in the air like ghosts sent to torment his soul, and Harvey trembled in their wake.

Varik bounded up the steps of the mobile lab, anxious to learn what Reyes had found.

The Bureau's mobile forensics lab was a forty-foot converted recreational vehicle. Overhead storage cabinets and workstations lined both sides of the interior. Separate areas had been designed for maximum efficiency in the analysis of evidence, such as firearms and the chemical analysis of narcotics, latent fingerprints, audio/video analysis, and questionable documents. The lab also featured an on-site command center with satellite links to the Bureau's central crime lab in Louisville and a small lounge area for the techs to have meals and sleep in shifts.

Bags and boxes secured with red tape marked EVIDENCE in large block letters had overtaken most of the storage areas and spilled over into the lounge. Reyes and Freddy appeared more haggard than they had when he last saw them, but both were excited by his and Damian's arrival.

Freddy reached them first. "I've been working on the Crimson Swan fire," he said, and gestured for them to accompany him to a workstation equipped with a laptop computer, several video monitors, and other assorted technical devices Varik couldn't identify. "We learned from our friends in Jefferson metro that Stephen Sabian had some kind of video surveillance system on the bar's exterior, as well as within the private donor rooms. A prudent measure, all things considered."

"Your point?" Damian asked, an edge of irritation in his voice.

"*This* is my point, sir." Freddy lifted what appeared to be a large chunk of black-and-gray lava rock.

Varik frowned. "What is it?"

"The protective layers surrounding a solid-state hard disk used by Crimson Swan to store video surveillance footage. Top-of-the-line stuff. You see, when this bad boy is exposed to more than a few hundred degrees of heat, the case starts to melt, which seals all the vents and stuff for the disk inside. It basically turns into a rock, encasing the disk and protecting the data."

"Is the footage usable?"

"Oh, yeah. Once I chiseled through about seven or eight layers of melted plastic and steel, I managed to extract the disk. I've already transferred some of the data to here." He patted the laptop.

"Please tell me you have video of the kidnapping and arson on there," Varik said.

Freddy grinned and set the melted casing aside and tapped a series of keys on the laptop. A menu popped up on the screen. He highlighted and clicked on one of the items and stepped back.

A new window opened, and a silent black-and-white video began rolling. As Varik and Damian watched, Stephen Sabian's truck pulled into a parking space. He got out of the truck and walked toward Crimson Swan.

Suddenly a gang of hooded shadows descended on him. They watched the screen as he fought back, was overwhelmed, nearly escaped, and finally was felled by a Taser-wielding member of the gang. A van appeared. Stephen was hurriedly stowed inside, and the van disappeared.

Some of the gang's hoods had been lost during the scuffle, and their faces were visible on the video. Varik recognized Martin Evans as he lit a rag stuffed in the neck of a bottle and hurled it at a window. One of the members who retained his hood appeared with more bottles, and Varik guessed the man to be Tubby Jordan from his size and rolling gait.

Flames began to leap from broken windows. More bottles shattered against the walls, the accelerants within coating the bar's exterior and burning.

The video froze, and the screen turned black. Freddy pressed a button and shrugged. "That's all I have so far. I should have more in a few hours."

"That's enough to play for our guests and get a confession." Damian clapped the tech on the shoulder. "Good work."

Freddy beamed. "Thank you, sir."

Varik and Damian moved farther into the lab, and Reyes greeted them both before plunging into his findings. "I couldn't believe it, but once I discovered the trick, I was able to piece everything together."

Varik watched with mounting curiosity as Reyes laid the three cross-stakes from their murder victims on one of the workstations. Beautifully carved with climbing vines and blooms and stained a rich cherry color, the metal-tipped stakes gleamed under the lab's fluorescent lighting.

Reyes lined up each stake arm-to-arm and stepped back, smiling. "What do you see in the arms?"

Damian and Varik leaned in, searching. After a moment, Damian shook his head. "I don't see anything but a bunch of damn flowers and vines."

Varik stepped closer. His finger hovered over the right arm of the first cross and traced over both arms of the second and third. "There's a message hidden in the carvings."

"Yes!" Reyes exclaimed. "I didn't see it at first, but I noticed subtle differences in the carvings on each one. It wasn't until I lined them up that I was able to read it."

The vines and blossoms covering the crosses stood in relief against the background. He followed the letters formed by the negative spaces between the raised flora with his finger for Damian's benefit. "*For Claire Elizabeth B*—The final word isn't complete."

"That makes me think there's another body we haven't found yet," Reyes said.

"Ah, shit," Damian muttered. "So, who—"

"Excuse me, sir," Reyes interrupted, "but there's more, and honestly, this is the part that creeps me out."

Varik folded his arms over his chest and watched as Reyes picked up each cross-stake in turn and removed the metal tip.

"The legs of the crosses are hollow," Reyes said, holding the third aloft for Varik and Damian to see the small cavity drilled within the wood. "That's why they have these metal tips, to protect the wood from splintering in the wound track and contaminating the messages *inside* the stakes."

"What messages?" Damian asked.

Reyes produced three newspaper articles that had been encased with some form of clear laminate. "These were rolled up inside the stakes, one in each. The protective film is standard clear Con-Tact paper like you'd use for lining shelves in your kitchen. It's cheap, readily available, and the paper remains flexible enough to be rolled up."

Varik moved closer to Damian in order to see the articles. He read the first headline, dated March 17, 1968, in Louisville, and felt as though he'd been punched in the gut. *Beloved University Professor Found Slain.* The second article, from the same newspaper, was dated a few days after the first. *Gruesome Murder Leaves City Stunned.* The date of the final article was more recent, October 7, 2005, and from the local paper, *The Jefferson Daily Journal. Local Woman Brutally Murdered, Left on Roadside.*

"Third one is about a local woman, Claire Black, who was killed by vampires and dumped on the side of a highway," Reyes said. "The case was given to Enforcer

Sabian, but it never developed, due to a lack of evidence and suspects, although one vampire was named, Trent Thibodaux, as a 'person of interest.'" He bunny-eared quotation marks in the air. "Thibodaux was never listed as an official suspect, and as far as I can gather from searching the Bureau's records, it's a cold case."

"Claire Black," Varik repeated, and pointed to the crosses. "*For Claire Elizabeth B,* with the last word unfinished. That can't be coincidence. Did this woman have any family here in town?"

"A husband, Darryl. He was a patrolman with the JPD but was laid off because of budget cuts. He works for the sheriff's department now."

"We need to talk to him," Varik said. "Having your wife's murder go unsolved for years must be hell."

"There's one other thing," Reyes said, and held up a pack of gum coated in black fingerprint dust. "This was found on the body of that security guard at the high school. I found a partial print and ran it. Care to guess whose name popped?"

"Darryl Black," Varik responded.

"Bingo. On a hunch, I ran the prints from John Doe Vampire through VIPER again, this time with Thibodaux's name."

"Did they match?"

Reyes grinned. "Perfectly. Turns out Enforcer Sabian picked him up a few years ago as part of that Midnight bust."

"Why didn't the previous search turn up Thibodaux's name?"

"According to the case log, Thibodaux rolled on his

buddies and was given immunity as part of a plea deal so long as he agreed to work for the Bureau as a confidential informant. His record was removed from the general search pools. The only way to compare his prints to John Doe Vampire was by accessing Thibodaux's file directly, and I had to have a name in order to do that."

"Surely Alex would've recognized his name as being connected to the Claire Black case."

"The record shows that she did, but Thibodaux maintained his innocence on the murder. Without physical evidence tying him to the body, she had no choice but to let it go and run with the drug charges only."

Varik ran a hand through his hair and sighed. "The murders aren't about running the vampires out of Jefferson like the kidnappers' note claims. This is personal. Darryl Black is targeting the vampires who he thinks killed his wife."

"Not so fast," Damian said, tapping two of the newspaper articles against his open palm. "If this is about revenge for his wife's murder, why would these be here? They're about Bernard Sabian's murder."

Reyes pointed to the two 1968 articles. "Read the back."

Damian flipped them over, and Varik's blood turned to an icy sludge.

The same handwritten note had been printed in fine block letters in red ink. *An eye for an eye. Suffer and die, bitch.*

"Alex," Varik whispered.

Having spent the better part of an hour trying to weasel information out of the Enforcers processing the scene at Crimson Swan and meeting with no success, Alex had decided to try the direct approach. She knew Tubby Jordan and Martin Evans were being sequestered in the holding area used by prisoners who were transferred from the jail for court appearances. Evans was unlikely to be willing to talk to her after she'd bitten him, but she was hoping Tubby would be more cooperative.

She mounted the steps leading into the Municipal Center lobby. She could feel the weight of Varik's mind pressing against hers and knew he was checking on her. In response, she clamped her mental shield tighter and was rewarded by feeling the pressure ease.

Tasha appeared from around the side of the building and stopped when she saw Alex. "What are you doing here? I thought you'd been replaced."

"Only temporarily," Alex replied but made no attempt to explain her presence.

The women stared at each other for a moment. Tasha's gaze dropped to the ground, and she moved toward the lobby. "I have to go."

"Tasha, wait."

She paused but didn't look up.

"I wanted to thank you for helping me with the murder investigation. I had no way of knowing what Damian would do once—"

"Bullshit!" Tasha's head snapped up, and the venom behind her words took Alex aback. "You feds are all the same. You use us locals to do your damn dirty work and then toss us aside whenever it suits you. You treat us like second-rate rent-a-cops and take all the glory for yourselves, but not this time. This time it's going to be different."

"I have never treated you like that, or any other cop in Jefferson, for that matter."

"Really? What about Harvey? You've complained about him at every opportunity."

"Harvey's a fucking asshole and is trying to set me up to look like a Midnight user!"

"Here we go again. The mean humans are picking on the poor defenseless vampire!"

"Are you insane?"

"Maybe I am, but isn't it funny how you never questioned my abilities, or loyalty, when it was just the two of us working this case. Now, suddenly, when there's a whole crew of Enforcers in town, I'm not good enough."

"What the hell is wrong with you? I never said you weren't good enough!"

"You didn't have to say it. You implied it."

Alex felt a tugging on the blood-bond. Varik had surely felt her rising irritation and anger. "Bloody hell," she muttered, trying to block his mind from hers. "I don't have time for this right now."

"Oh, I'm sorry to have disturbed you," Tasha said icily. "If you'll excuse me, Enforcer Sabian, I have things to do."

"Tasha, wait!"

The lieutenant stormed away, flashing a rude hand gesture over her shoulder as she entered the building.

"Damn it!" Dropping her mental barriers, she

reached out to Varik and felt the warmth of his mind brush hers. She shuddered as the bond equalized between them. *We have a problem.*

What's wrong?

Alex shivered as his words forced themselves into her consciousness. *I think Tasha's going to do something to screw up the investigation.*

She felt the magnitude of her words sinking into his mind. *Why would she do that?* he asked.

Because I may have inadvertently insulted her.

Varik mentally groaned. *What did you do?*

Alex allowed the memory of her conversation with Tasha to drift to the surface.

Shit and damn it to hell. The force of Varik's anger rocked her and made her head pound. *I have to tell Damian about this, and I want you to go back to the hotel with Emily, which is where you're supposed to be anyway.*

I need to find Stephen, Varik.

You're off the case, Alex.

Thank you very much for reminding me.

Varik's irritation at having sensed her thoughts about conducting her own investigation grew. *You said you trusted me.*

The memory of standing in the women's restroom at the morgue welled up and twisted Alex's conscience.

Did you mean it?

She closed her eyes. *Yes.*

Then trust me to find Stephen. If anything happened to you ... The bond warmed with the glow of his emotions.

Alex sent a mental nod of acquiescence and felt a rush of relief from Varik before he closed the bond.

Once again alone inside her mind, she took a shuddering breath, knowing her window of opportunity to find Stephen on her own had narrowed but hadn't slammed shut entirely.

"I'm sorry, Varik," she whispered, "but Stephen can't wait."

She walked into the Municipal Center and headed for the restricted area.

An Enforcer met her as she passed through a set of doors and entered the corridor leading to the prisoner holding area. He shook his head when she flashed her badge. "Sorry, ma'am, but I can't let you pass."

Alex's eyes flickered to the photo ID he wore on a chain around his neck. The green stripe along the right edge of his photo marked him as a recent graduate of the FBPI training center located on a portion of the more than one-hundred-thousand-acre base of Fort Knox, south of Louisville.

She smiled sweetly. "I just wanted to see a friend. Can't you give me a few minutes?"

"My orders are from Chief Enforcer Alberez himself."

She pouted and sidled closer, inhaling deeply, taking in his natural scent of cedar and allspice. Her own scent of jasmine and vanilla filled the space between them as she swept her hair over one shoulder.

The Enforcer inhaled, and his gray eyes began to shift to a pale bronze.

Her fingertips traced the line of his biceps bulging underneath his white button-down shirt. "He doesn't have to know," she murmured. "It could be our little secret."

He swallowed loudly and gently removed her hand. "I don't think so. Orders are orders, ma'am."

Alex sighed and moved away. "I understand. You're just doing your job, like I'm doing mine."

"Yes, ma—oof!"

Her foot slammed into his solar plexus and sent him flying into the corridor's opposite wall. She followed him, delivered a right hook to his face, and swept his legs with her own. He hit the tile floor with a loud *smack*. Her final kick landed in his groin. His face paled, then turned bright red as he curled into a tight ball with his hands between his legs.

Alex brushed her hair from her face, breathing heavily. "I only need a few minutes, but you had to do it the hard way."

He groaned in pain.

"Sorry, buddy, but I *did* try asking nicely," she said, and sprinted down the hallway.

Attacking a fellow Enforcer compounded the trouble she'd face when all this was over, but she was beyond caring. Her career meant nothing if she couldn't bring Stephen home. She'd seen the fear and desperation in her mother's eyes. If Stephen died, it would devastate Emily. Alex couldn't live with knowing she might have been able to prevent that if only she'd tried harder.

She turned a corner and reached the first of the holding cells. Steel-reinforced doors with thick shatterproof windows lined both sides of the hall. Most of the cells were empty, but a few held prisoners in bright orange-and-white jumpsuits waiting for late-afternoon court appearances. At the end of the corridor beside an emergency fire exit, she found the cell she wanted.

Tubby Jordan sat on a low concrete bench, his face buried in his hands.

Alex pressed the red button on the intercom next to the door. "Where's my brother?"

He didn't move.

"Talk to me, damn it!"

"Why should I?" His question was muffled by his hands.

"You're a minister. You're supposed to help people."

Seconds ticked away. His shoulders began to shake. Sounds like muted sobs filtered through the intercom. Then Tubby lifted his head and roared with laughter.

Alex stared at him as if he'd lost his mind.

He rose from his seat with a fluidity and grace she'd never seen in him prior. His pudgy face was fixed in a mask of savage cruelty as he examined her through the window with hate-filled eyes. His normally mellow voice deepened and held a hardness at odds with his soft appearance. "Tell me again, Enforcer Sabian, why I should help you. I haven't laughed that much in years."

Her eyes widened as the scent of his omnipresent cologne seeped through the door. It had lost the chemical sting of a manufactured fragrance, leaving the pure, natural earthiness of licorice and orange peels. "You've been masking your scent with cologne."

"Vile stuff." A malicious grin split his face. "But effective, wouldn't you say?"

Her gaze dropped to his perfect human teeth.

"Modern dentistry is a wonderful thing, isn't it?"

"You're a vampire."

"Ding, ding, ding! And she wins the booby prize. By the way, how's your arm?" He mimicked shooting a gun with his fingers.

Disbelief gave way to anger. "You killed all those people at Maggie's Place."

"Oh, you're a smart one."

"Why?"

"To sow discord, my dear. You can't build a fire without killing a few trees."

"You torched Crimson Swan and set up the Human Separatist Movement to take the fall."

"Humans are stupid. Always looking for the easy way out. Promise them a fucking Utopia and they'll blithely follow anyone. It's pathetic. However, I must admit, while it *was* my idea to set up the Human Separatists as patsies and to snag that brother of yours, incinerating the bar wasn't."

"Why Crimson Swan? Why Stephen?"

Tubby bobbed his head and rolled his eyes. "I don't think I want to answer those questions."

Alex smacked her palm against the window. "Answer me!"

He laughed. "No. I won't tell you why, but I *will* tell you who suggested it."

"Who?"

"Someone you know all too well, Enforcer. Someone who has a major bone to pick with you. Like I said, humans are stupid. All I had to do was give him the name of a vampire who was rumored to have been involved with his wife's murder. Just a *rumor*, and poof!" He mimicked an explosion with his hands.

"Claire," she whispered. "Darryl Black. But why—"

He laughed. "I can tell from the confusion on your face that you're not sure whether to believe me or not. Well, maybe this will help." He leaned forward conspiratorially. "The name I gave Black was Trent Thibodaux. Ring any bells?"

"He was one of the Midnight dealers I arrested," she said slowly. "He rolled on his suppliers, but—"

"But he never gave up the big boss, even after turning into a snitch," Tubby finished. "However, I'd heard through the grapevine that he was reconsidering his position, was thinking of turning in his old boss."

"It was you," Alex whispered. "You were the one we were trying to get."

"Guilty." He spread his arms wide and then let them fall to his sides. "So, now you see why I couldn't let Trent turn me in. If he had, all my carefully laid plans would've backfired. I told Trent's name to Black and then sat back to watch the puppet dance. He didn't disappoint, because as it turns out, he also took care of a couple of Trent's buddies. Saved me the trouble."

The horrible realization that four vampires were dead, that Crimson Swan and Stephen had been targeted because she'd failed in her job, crushed her.

Tubby grinned at her. "I told you humans are stupid."

Alex heard voices echoing down the corridor. The Enforcer she'd beaten up must have recovered and was now raising the alarm. Her time was up. "Tell me where Stephen is."

"Say please."

"When Hell freezes over."

"Tsk, tsk." His breath fogged the glass between them. "Wrong answer."

The smell of bitter almonds was faint but detectable and unmistakable as Tubby doubled over in pain, clutching his stomach. Alex shook the locked door and growled in frustration, watching as the poison Tubby had somehow ingested worked through his system.

Inside the cell, Tubby collapsed on the floor beside the concrete bench. His breathing was ragged and labored. Bright red spots covered his skin and were spreading rapidly. "No use," he said weakly. "Cyanide and strychnine. Suicide pill. I'm as good as dead."

"Why?" Alex demanded over the intercom. "Why do this?"

"To hurt you."

"Where's Stephen?" She pounded on the door with her fists. "Where is he?"

Tubby began shaking uncontrollably.

"No!" She watched helplessly as a gray mist rose to hover over the convulsing vampire.

He stilled, and the mist coalesced, taking on the ghostly visage of Tubby Jordan. It moved away from the lifeless shell and faded into the wall.

"There she is!" a voice cried from behind her.

Alex saw three Enforcers barreling down the corridor toward her. She hit the release bar on the emergency exit and crashed through the door as fire alarms blared overhead.

Legs churning, she didn't pause to see if the Enforcers were chasing her. They would be. Her heart pumped madly and seemed to be in a race with her feet. She jumped a low wall only to discover the sheer drop on the other side too late to correct her course.

She landed on her feet with a loud grunt. Her ankles protested the impact and the return to motion as she sprinted up the service ramp and around the side of the building toward the parking lot. The sound of heavy boots hitting pavement let her know she wasn't alone, and it gave her renewed speed.

Reaching the parking lot, she managed to fish the keys to her mother's rental car out of her pocket without dropping them. She never slowed and vaulted over the car's hood.

The three Enforcers chasing her weren't far behind.

Alex scrambled into the car and jammed the key in the ignition. She threw the transmission into drive and stomped the gas, and tires squealed as one of the Enforcers launched himself onto the trunk.

The blood-bond pulsed and beat within her head like a drum line. She could feel Varik calling to her. The car careened around a light pole, throwing the hitch-hiking Enforcer into the side of an SUV.

A black Corvette screeched to a halt in front of the exit, blocking it. Varik climbed out and waved at her to stop.

She gunned the car's engine and swerved around him. She fought to maintain control of the fishtailing vehicle. It jumped a curb and narrowly missed a low retaining wall before spinning to a stop in the street.

"Alex!"

Her eyes met Varik's across the distance. Guilt stabbed her heart and she opened the blood-bond for the briefest of moments. *I'm sorry.*

"Alex!" he shouted, and ran toward her.

The warmth of Varik's mind pressing against hers disappeared as she sealed the bond. She could feel him trying to find another way into her mind, and she reinforced the wall she'd erected between them.

The car shot forward, leaving Varik behind. She was throwing away her career, and possibly her life, by going rogue. She refused to drag him down with her.

Tubby was dead. He hadn't told her Stephen's location, but he'd given her a name.

And that was all she needed.

sixteen

"OUR PRIMARY OBJECTIVE IS TWOFOLD," DAMIAN WAS saying, as Tasha scanned the faces of Enforcers gathered on the steps of the Nassau County Municipal Center in a hastily called planning session. "Retrieve the rogue Enforcer, Alexandra Sabian, and bring Darryl Black in for questioning."

Tasha couldn't help but feel partly responsible for Alex's sudden change. It hadn't taken long for Varik and Damian to mobilize their men into a task force, but Alex had a head start.

The Jefferson PD wasn't a part of the team being sent after Alex, since the Bureau had severed their ties. She wasn't there to join the hunt. She was there to relieve her own guilt. While she didn't expect Varik or any of the Enforcers to understand why she'd given evidence to Harvey, she felt she had to confess. Her conscience wouldn't let her rest otherwise.

She found Varik in the crowd and watched as he silently stood next to Damian, who continued to lay out the group's plans. Worry hunched his shoulders, and his dark eyes seemed haunted, their depths veiled in shadows. The memory of handing over evidence to Harvey hovered before her mind's eye, and she looked down at the pavement.

When she looked up again, the group was disbanding, checking weapons and body armor as they headed for their Ford Expeditions. Clearing her throat, she approached Varik, who was adjusting the straps of his body armor.

He glanced at her as she approached.

"I need to tell you something," she said in a rush. She felt as though she were drowning in her guilt, and she folded her arms in front of her, hugging herself.

Varik straightened his shoulders and faced her squarely.

"I—I..." She paused, took a steadying breath and released it slowly. "I broke the chain of evidence. I gave a Taser report to Harvey, knowing it implicated someone in his department—most likely Darryl—as an accomplice to Stephen's kidnapping."

He closed his eyes. A muscle jumped along his jaw. Tension pulled his spine into a rigid line. When he looked at her again, his eyes were the color of molten gold.

She waited for him to scream at her, to punch her, to do something, but he simply stared at her. "Varik, I know what I did was out of line, but I can—"

He held up his hand to stop her. "I don't care why you did it, Lieutenant. All I care about is stopping Alex before she causes more damage." He stepped closer, violating her personal space, and his voice dropped to a deadly whisper. "However, if anything happens to her as a result of your actions, there will be nowhere on this earth you can hide from me."

Tasha stood in his shadow, trembling and unable to respond.

"Let's go, people," Damian's booming voice echoed over the parking lot. "Move out!"

She watched as Varik climbed into the backseat of the lead Expedition. The heat of his threat, of his *promise,* continued to burn into her brain long after the Enforcers had disappeared.

Her betrayal of her oath as a police officer wouldn't go unpunished. Tubby Jordan had already paid the price for her treachery. More blood was going to be shed before this ended. That blood would be on her hands, and she could already feel it staining her soul.

Harvey lit one cigarette from another and looked at the closed front door of Darryl's house. He still sat in his car, gathering his thoughts.

The paper Tasha had dropped on his desk when she'd come to see him—no, to *threaten* him—felt like a weight in his pocket. He snorted with the memory. She'd been the last person he'd ever expected to turn against the vamps, but apparently something had changed between her and Sabian. Whatever that something was, he wasn't fool enough to forsake his good fortune.

He opened the car door and climbed out. Smoke

swirled around him as though he'd come from the pits
of Hell. He adjusted his belt and checked to make sure
his gun and handcuffs were within easy reach.

While Harvey had been careful not to have any direct physical evidence personally tying him to the
arson, he hadn't considered Darryl's brazenness in providing him with a Taser stolen from his own department. He'd trusted Darryl to provide an untraceable
Taser and the son of a bitch had betrayed him and the
HSM cause. It was the only explanation for Lockwood's
report. The Enforcers knew by now that he'd planted
the Midnight in Sabian's Jeep and would be coming for
him.

Everything was falling apart, and it was Darryl's
fault.

Harvey mounted the stairs and stepped onto the
faded blue porch boards. The screen door creaked as he
opened it and knocked on the closed wooden door.
Smoke from his cigarette curled upward and tickled his
nose.

"Darryl? You home?" He knocked on the door again.
He listened for footsteps or some other sign of life
within the house.

Silence.

Harvey tossed his cigarette into the yard and
reached for the doorknob. His other hand rested on the
butt of the Browning nine-millimeter at his hip. He took
a deep breath and opened the door.

Shadows shrouded the interior. Newspapers, empty
beer cans, boxes, and used paper plates littered the living room. The only clean spot was along one wall, where

a photo of Claire Black in her wedding gown and veil hung above a makeshift shrine. Cheap bookcases flanked the television and overflowed with an assortment of magazines, books, and forgotten mail.

"Darryl?" Harvey called, slipping into the dim room and allowing his eyes to adjust. "You in here?"

A noise deeper inside the house made him freeze. Cold sweat trickled down his back as he tried to identify the source. He sighed. It was just the refrigerator's compressor. He turned his attention to the shelves beside the TV.

Most of the mail was junk, credit card offers and advertisements. He riffled through a stack of pornographic magazines before selecting the most recent issue. He flipped through the pages, admiring the glossy photos of bare-breasted women and lingering over the more graphic shots before turning the magazine to gaze upon the glory of the centerfold.

Disgust and horror raced through his veins. The centerfold was a buxom blond-haired woman with small fangs and eyes the color of polished brass. But it wasn't the photo that had dampened his enjoyment.

Someone had drawn cross-shaped stakes between the woman's breasts and wide-spread legs and scribbled over her neck with a red marker so that it looked as if her throat had been slashed. Frenzied, handwritten words surrounded her: *Slut! Die, bitch! Vampire whore!*

"My God," Harvey whispered, and threw the magazine away from himself before looking over the shelves.

Textbooks on forensic science, medical references, how-to manuals for carving wood, and anatomy guides lined the shelves. Bibles of varying sizes and colors were interspersed among the other books. A large scrapbook was jammed into the top shelf.

Harvey pulled the scrapbook free and opened it with trembling hands.

Newspaper clippings detailing Claire's murder were pasted to the stiff black sheets. One of the articles sported a photo of Alex Sabian with a caption stating that still no arrests had been made in the case after three months. Someone—no, not some*one, Darryl*—had used a red marker to scribble "Fuck you, bitch" over the picture.

Harvey turned the pages. The articles about Claire dwindled and were replaced with articles focusing on Sabian, her brother, and Crimson Swan. Every photo of the two vampires had been scribbled over with curses or drawings depicting violence. Intermixed with the articles were computer printouts about the 1968 murder of Bernard Sabian.

Highlighted passages in some of the printouts detailed facts about the decades-old crime. A stake in the heart. Decapitated. Body dumped in a cemetery. University professor. A silver shamrock charm clutched in his hand.

Handwritten notes in the margins revealed Darryl's elaborate plot to exact revenge on Alex Sabian for her failure to bring Claire's killers to justice. The recent murders mirrored different aspects of Bernard Sabian's murder. His stomach churned, and he slammed the book closed.

The scrape of boots on hardwood floors made him

stiffen. The sound of a bullet being chambered behind him was unmistakable. A bead of sweat rolled down the center of his back. He spun around.

Darryl stood in the doorway that led to the back of the house with a pistol in his hand, aimed at Harvey's chest. A crazed glint shone in his hazel eyes. "Evening, Sheriff," he drawled. "I wasn't expecting company or I would've cleaned."

"What the hell do you think you're doing, Darryl?"

"Looking out for what's mine."

"Put that thing away before someone gets hurt."

Darryl shook his head and smiled. "Can't do it."

"Listen to me, Darryl." Harvey fought to keep his knees from buckling. "You don't want to do this. Killing me will send you straight to the state penitentiary."

"I don't think so."

"This isn't what Claire would've wanted."

"How would you know? She talks to me, Harvey, gives me signs. A man knows what his wife wants."

Harvey blinked and then noticed the blood staining the front of Darryl's jumpsuit. His chest constricted, and he felt short of breath. "What have you done, Darryl?"

"Nothing that wasn't necessary. 'Separation by any means necessary,' right? I thought you of all people would understand that." The smile faded from his lips. "Guess I was wrong."

Harvey's eyes widened. "Darryl, don't—"

Pain seared his leg. He screamed and crumbled to the floor. Blood, hot and sticky, poured from the hole where his left knee had once been. Fragments of bone protruded from the gaping wound, and darkness crowded at the edges of his vision.

"Sorry about that, Harvey," Darryl said as he knelt beside him and relieved the sheriff of his weapon. "But I can't have you running back to that Enforcer bitch and telling her what you've seen."

Harvey gasped and writhed on the floor. He watched as Darryl raised the pistol once more. "No—"

The hot steel of the gun's barrel struck his temple, and the world turned black.

Fading sun filtered through the trees like a chaotic strobe light. Wind rushed past the car's open window and brought a mixture of scents: the sharp bite of hot asphalt, the bitter tang of smoke from someone's fireplace, and the clean smell of pine after a storm.

Alex's silver badge lay forgotten next to her cell phone on the passenger-side seat. Part of her knew she'd crossed a line and returning from it might not be possible, but the rage that held her in its sway was stronger than reason.

Darryl Black was the man responsible for Crimson Swan's destruction and had at least played a role in Stephen's abduction, even if he wasn't the mastermind of the plot. Instead of venting his anger on her directly, he'd targeted the one person she trusted most in the world.

Now she was going to make him pay.

Beethoven's Fifth Symphony played as she swerved around a pickup. Her cell phone bounced to the floor when the car's tires skidded off the pavement and lost traction in the loose gravel along the road's shoulder.

"Damn it," she muttered, and righted the sedan. She wouldn't be much use to Stephen if she got herself killed.

Classical music continued to filter up from the floor, and she ignored it. She knew it was Varik. The blood-bond vibrated within her mind, its pitch high and urgent. She ignored it.

She wanted revenge. She wanted—

Justice, a voice echoed in her mind.

"I'm coming, Stephen," she whispered. "I'm coming."

Emily sat on the couch in her empty hotel suite, a pillow clutched to her chest for comfort, and staring at her cell phone. Dweezil lay belly-up under the coffee table, snoring softly and paws twitching, in the throes of kitty dreams.

She envied the cat. She hadn't slept since arriving in Jefferson. Worry for her children kept her going. She couldn't rest until they were safely returned to her.

And they would return to her. Both of them. She couldn't bear considering the alternative.

She opened one clutched hand to reveal a small plastic bag sealed with red tape. A silver shamrock charm slid along the bottom of the bag when she held it up for closer inspection. A few light scratches marred the charm's surface, and the loop intended for a chain at the top of one leaf was broken.

Emily reached beneath the neckline of her blouse and pulled free a delicate silver chain. A silver four-leaf clover charm dangled before her, and she held it beside the charm in the bag.

The two were identical.

Dread filled her. The one she wore had been the charm Bernard held in his hand when Alex discovered his body. It had been a symbol of his affiliation with the Hunters, with his being marked as a Talent.

Had the vampire whose body was left at the high school been another Talent? Another former Hunter? There were too many questions she couldn't answer, but the sense that Alex was in danger rooted itself in her mind and heart.

She hid her necklace away and returned the bag and broken charm to her pocket. Clutching the pillow tightly to her chest and thinking of Alex, she sighed. "Oh, Bernard, she's so much like you, and she needs you badly."

For a brief moment, Emily thought she smelled tobacco, coffee, and chalk—scents heralding Bernard's presence—but then the moment passed, and she was left alone to stare at a silent phone and wait with only the ghosts of the past to keep her company.

Varik listened to the rapid ringing in his ear, wishing for Alex to pick up. "Goddamn it to Hell." He snapped his cell phone closed. "She's not answering."

The driver of the Expedition took a curve a little too

fast, and Varik found himself pressed between the rear passenger door and Damian.

"Did you really expect her to answer?" Damian asked, as he straightened up and once again adjusted the straps of the bulletproof vest that barely covered his broad chest.

"No." Anxiety made his stomach churn, and it worsened as he watched Damian pull a pump-action shotgun from the Expedition's cargo area and began loading it. "What are you doing?"

"Going after a murder suspect and a rogue Enforcer." Damian twisted in the seat once again and secured the shotgun in the cargo area.

"This is Alex we're talking about, Damian."

The big Enforcer settled in the seat once more with a .357 Glock in his hands. "She's gone rogue. We may not have a choice."

"I always have a choice." Varik stared at the firearm in Damian's hand. He felt the weight of his own pressing against his right hip like a cancer he couldn't excise.

"Fine, suit yourself." Damian slipped the Glock into its holster and secured it to his belt. "But when you get yourself shot or staked, don't come crying to me."

Varik continued to stare. The memory of a vampire running away from him, rocked by a shotgun blast, flitted through his mind.

It was supposed to have been a simple job. Track down a group of rogue vampires and eliminate them, but the information he'd been given was faulty. The rogues weren't at the house, hadn't been for weeks. One of their friends had come looking for them and ran when he saw Varik. The kid was innocent, scared, but Varik hadn't known that, and he'd killed a vampire barely out of his teens. An official investigation had cleared him of any wrongdoing, but he'd never forgotten it, and it'd been his last kill.

"Earth to Varik," Damian said. "Get your mind out of the past and into the present."

Varik raised his eyes to meet Damian's stare. "Do you really think Alex will do it? Kill Black, I mean."

"If it were *my* brother who was missing, Black would be one dead motherfucker."

"I know her, Damian. She's not a killer."

"You'd better hope you're right."

"Almost there, sir," the driver reported.

Alex didn't want to talk to Black. She wanted to kill him. Varik knew that, had felt it through the bond. He'd seen Alex when she was pissed off, but the rage that consumed her now was something else.

Enforcers don't kill people. We uphold the law. Alex's words rang in his ears.

Sighing, he pulled his Glock free of its holster, released the clip, and made certain it was fully loaded. He reinserted it and double-checked the safety before securing it once again.

He couldn't let Alex kill Black. He just hoped he wouldn't have to hurt her in the process.

Live oaks covered with Spanish moss dotted the expansive yard and shaded a large metal storage shed. Security lights attached to poles in the front yard washed the house in bluish-green light, and yet the single-story clapboard house was half covered in the new night's shadowy embrace.

As Alex parked behind Harvey Manser's marked cruiser, killed the rental car's engine, and stared at the house, a memory came to life. It'd been years since she'd been to Darryl Black's home. Where it had once been a shining example of domestic bliss, it was now twisted into a nightmarish parody of its former self.

The crisp white paint she remembered was grayed with age and peeling away in strips. Green shutters flanking the windows hung at odd angles, barely able to maintain their grip on the wall. Windows that had glowed with warmth were dark and cold, dead eyes reflecting the broken soul within.

Gravel crunched under her booted feet. A breeze picked up her hair and whipped it around her face. The smell of blood and gunpowder hung in the air. Keeping a wary eye on the shed, she drew her Glock and thumbed off the safety. She cautiously approached the house steps and climbed, senses on full alert, searching for any indication of Harvey's or Darryl's whereabouts.

The front door was open, and the smell of blood and gunpowder intensified. She entered the shadows of the living room, crouching low to make herself a smaller target, and swept the room right to left with her Glock held at the ready. Nothing moved within, and she eased through to the next room. Systematically she checked each room and found no one.

Returning to the living room, she noted the shrine to Claire and the fresh pool of blood on the floor. She squatted beside the crimson puddle and dipped the tip of her finger into it. The thickened consistency told her it hadn't been spilled more than an hour or so prior. But was it Darryl's or Harvey's?

If she placed the drop on her tongue, she'd see the memories locked within it. It would be easy to determine its origin and possibly gain more answers, like where Stephen was being held.

She wiped her hand on her jeans, cleansing it of the blood. She'd already bitten one human against his will, and she refused to compound her damnation by adding another violation to the list of Enforcer misconduct.

As she stood, she saw a blood-splattered scrapbook lying facedown on the floor. She picked it up. Horror rocked her as she flipped through page after page of articles detailing her life, her father's murder, and Darryl's quest for vengeance.

The final computer-printed article regarding her father showed his University of Louisville faculty photo. Her fingertips trailed over it, and longing filled her heart.

Pervasive, bitter cold pierced her. Her breath left in a rush. The world spun away. When it returned she found herself standing beside Harvey, the scrapbook in his hands instead of her own.

Darryl faced him from across the room, a Beretta aimed at the sheriff. She watched as he squeezed the trigger. The bullet flew in slow motion and penetrated Harvey's leg at the knee. He cried out as his legs gave way and he collapsed. The scrapbook tumbled from his hands.

The book hit the floor, and Alex staggered back from it, returning to reality in a disorienting swirl of colors and sensations. Usually she received only vague impressions of people, places, or events when touching an object. The full re-creation of the scene she'd witnessed left her mind reeling.

When the world stopped spinning, she was surprised to find a woman dressed in a flowing white gown standing before her. Her gaze darted from the woman to the portrait above the shrine and back. "Claire?"

Her sorrow-filled eyes bore into Alex. Then she turned her head to reveal the vine-wrapping cross tattoo on her neck. She raised her arm, pointing to a blank wall, and returned her pleading stare to Alex. An ethereal voice permeated Alex's mind.

Stop him. Please.

Claire faded into the shadows, and Alex dashed from the house.

seventeen

HARVEY AWOKE TO PAIN. HIS LEG FELT AS THOUGH someone had poured acid on it. A sharp stinging blow landed on his swollen cheek. He flinched.

"Wakey wakey," Darryl said in a singsong voice. "Wouldn't want you to miss the best part."

The smell of blood and chemicals permeated the air, making him gag. He tried to sit up and alleviate the pain radiating up his leg, but his wrists were shackled above his head to a thick wooden post. He looked at the wad of bandages and tourniquet encapsulating his leg and leaned over as far as he could and vomited.

"Son of a bitch," Darryl mumbled, jumping out of the way. "That's going to take forever to clean."

A painful spasm traveled up his ruined leg and sent his head spinning. Darkness encircled him, but he fought to remain conscious. "You fucking shot me."

Darryl grinned. "Well, I can't have you running off to tell the vamps about my little hobby."

"Hobby? You're a goddamned murderer!"

"I prefer to think of it more as a public service. Isn't that what you told Lieutenant Lockwood?"

"You're insane."

"No, I'm doing what should've been done when those goddamn demons killed my Claire." Darryl cocked his head as if listening to an inner voice. "It's time."

"Time? What are you—"

Harvey saw the table bearing a golden-haired body as Darryl retreated to another room within the large metal building. The workbench was filled with tools, wood shavings, and crosses in various stages of completion. A broad-bladed double ax hung horizontally above the work surface. Finally, his gaze settled on the wide bracketed shelves, the four large jars, and the heads perfectly preserved and suspended in a clear liquid.

A barrier deep inside his psyche shuddered, snapped, and Harvey was set adrift on a strange ocean from which there could be no return.

Alex slowed as she neared the shed. Keeping to the darkest shadows, she crept forward and crouched beneath a window. Light and the sound of someone whistling spilled through the small opening. With her back braced against the wall, she rose slowly and peeked inside.

Darryl Black whistled softly as he rinsed a pair of pliers under the faucet in a sink to her left. Glass jars and racks of vials lined the open-fronted shelves to either side of the sink.

The faucet shut off, and she ducked down, out of sight. Footsteps and the cessation of Darryl's whistling made her breath catch in her throat. She chanced another quick peek through the window.

The room was empty.

She felt a tug on the blood-bond, and the scent of cinnamon and sandalwood swept over her. The bond surged to life, beating in time with her racing heart, and Varik's voice filled her mind, calling to her.

Go the fuck away. She sent the thought over the bond along with a mental shove, pushing him out of her mind.

Alex! Back off! Varik's mental shout reverberated in her head. *Damian and I are—*

Fuck you, Varik. She thrust his thoughts aside and sealed the bond between them. She could feel him pounding at the thick wall she erected, trying to reconnect with her, but he was a distraction she couldn't afford to entertain.

Her time to confront Darryl was ending. She darted to the corner and quickly checked to be sure her pathway to the door was clear. It was. She skirted around the building and paused by the door. She'd have only one chance to stop Darryl. Steeling her nerves, she tightened her grip on her Glock, eased the door open, and slipped inside.

Darryl held a cross-shaped stake over a golden-haired vampire's chest. His other hand raised a heavy mallet in preparation for delivering a fatal strike.

"Swing that mallet and all you'll have left is a fucking stump," Alex said, aiming her Glock.

He didn't flinch or move. Slowly he turned his head and pinned her with a malevolent scowl.

She saw him tense and took a half-step forward. "Try it and I swear Claire won't recognize you in the after-life."

"You've got no right to speak her name, demon." His voice was a tense, harsh growl.

"This is between you and me, Darryl. Let Stephen go."

Confusion momentarily flashed in his eyes, only to be replaced with grim determination. He tightened his hold on the cross-stake. Shaking his head, he planted his feet. "Get thee behind me, Satan."

Roaring, he swung the mallet and Alex pulled the trigger.

Gravel pinged against the bottom of the Ford Expedition as it barreled up Darryl Black's driveway. Varik didn't wait for the vehicle to reach a full stop before leaping out. He hit the ground running. "Alex!"

The rapid pop of multiple gunshots split the cold night and made his heart stutter.

"No!" he screamed, and charged the metal shed, following the noise. He pulled his Glock free and primed it as he ran, fear and adrenaline giving his feet wings.

He could no longer hear gunfire as he reached the shed. Without slowing, he kicked the door. Wood splintered and flew inward like shrapnel. "Alex!"

Fluorescent lights damaged by bullets buzzed, hummed, and flickered overhead, creating a dizzying strobe effect. A body lay on a table, a cross-stake protruding from its chest. Harvey Manser sat in a corner, his wrists shackled to a wooden post and blood staining the floor beneath him.

Sounds of a struggle issued from the shadows beyond the table. He rushed forward to find Alex straddling Darryl Black on the blood-covered floor. The man was screaming in a combination of rage and pain, his mangled hand pinned by Alex's knee. She knocked a Beretta from his free hand, and Varik lost sight of the weapon in the chaotic flash of light and shadows. Black dodged a punch aimed at his head, then sank his teeth into Alex's arm. She howled and jerked away.

"Alex!" Varik shouted, and wrapped his arms around her, pulling her backward and off Black.

"Let me go!" she screamed.

Varik pulled her toward the exit. "You can't do this, Alex."

"He killed Stephen!"

Varik glanced at the bloody body on the table. Golden hair framed a pallid face. Unseeing eyes stared into the heavens. "Alex—" Movement to his right drew his attention back to Black. "Shit," he breathed, and spun, holding Alex tightly to his chest.

The gunshot sounded like a bomb in the confines of the metal shed. Pain seared his chest, and his left arm numbed. Alex slipped from his grip. The force of the bullet knocked the air from his lungs, and he crashed into a wall before sliding to the floor.

Gasping for breath, he reached for Alex, but she sprang away from him. He tried to call to her, but pain robbed him of his voice. He watched, helpless, as Alex charged into battle without him.

The gunshot deafened her. She felt Varik's body jerk against her and smelled fresh blood and charred flesh. She continued the spin Varik had begun and found Black holding his reclaimed Beretta in a shaky hand.

He drew a ragged breath and spoke: "And ye shall tread down the wicked, for they shall be ashes—"

Alex slammed into him, grabbing his arm. The gun fired into the floor. Her voice was a harsh whisper. "Thou—"

She clenched her fingers. The bones in his arm snapped, and he screeched. "Shalt—"

His howls of pain died as her fist connected with his throat.

"Not—"

He gagged.

"Kill!" Her final punch sent him crashing through the metal wall and into the night.

She ran to the hole made by Darryl's body and peered into the darkness. Flickering light from the interior strobed over his bloody and battered form. A broken two-by-four timber, once part of the wall's frame, now pierced his back and protruded through his chest. Wide eyes, devoid of life's spark, stared into the black, star-filled heavens.

Behind her, Varik groaned and struggled into a sitting position.

Alex moved toward him.

He was pale, and his left arm dangled uselessly at his side. "Fucking A," he groaned. "That burns."

"Are you—"

A flash of light seen from the corner of her eye turned her head. Time slowed. Sounds grew distorted and movements sluggish.

The ghostly vision of Claire stood in front of the table. A shadow formed beside her, stretching, roiling, and morphing into Darryl Black.

She watched, enthralled, as Darryl swept Claire into his arms. Claire appeared to be laughing, her face radiant, as Darryl lifted her and twirled in place. When Alex's eyes met Claire's, she once again heard the woman's voice in her mind.

Thank you.

The ethereal lovers spun and danced their way through the table and disappeared in the shadows.

Alex blinked, unsure of what she'd witnessed. The flickering lights overhead highlighted the golden hair of the vampire still lying on the table. "Stephen," she whispered.

Her approach was unsteady. The need to know drove her to place one foot in front of the other.

Gaze firmly fixed on the cross-stake, she reached the table. Her eyes closed. She no longer wanted to see.

"Alex."

Varik's call sounded distant to her ears, but it drew her out of her shell. She looked down at the body, and an anguished sob ripped from her throat.

Time restored itself. There was movement all around

her. She heard someone calling her name and ignored it. "It's not Stephen," she cried. "It's not him!"

She sounded her frustration, fear, anguish, and relief in a primal wail. Her legs buckled and folded under her. She collapsed on the floor and sobbed into her blood-streaked hands.

"Alex." Varik's soft voice echoed in her ears and in her mind, cut through her stupor, pulled her back into herself.

She looked at him and blinked, uncertain if what she saw was real.

He held a pale, blood-splattered hand out to her. "Come on, baby," he whispered. "There's nothing more you can do here. Let the Enforcers do their job."

Alex saw the blood on her hands, and they began to shake.

A strong arm wrapped around her, lifted her to her feet, and sandalwood and cinnamon enveloped her. Hot tears tracked down her cheeks. She clung to Varik as he led her into the shadows of a faded day.

Stars shone brightly in the clear sky over the scene of Darryl Black's final stand. A cold northern breeze wound its way through bare oak branches. The trees voiced their displeasure in low groans and high-pitched creaks.

Tasha leaned against the hood of her cruiser, arms folded over her stomach, trying to find some comfort and warmth in the flood of lights around Darryl's house and the surrounding grounds. But no comfort came as she watched Darryl's body being loaded into a hearse for his final trip to the morgue.

None of the Enforcers were talking as they went about their business of collecting evidence. The house had been ruled an official federal crime scene. The vampires had closed ranks around one of their own, and Tasha and her men weren't needed.

However, despite everything that had happened, the JPD and the Nassau County Sheriff's Department considered Darryl one of *theirs,* and many who'd known Darryl had gathered outside the FBPI perimeter, watching in silence.

Tasha stiffened as another body was wheeled from the metal shed and loaded into a second hearse. She guessed it was the body of the as-yet-to-be-identified vampire. How could Darryl, someone she'd known and trusted with her life more than once, be capable of such inhuman cruelty?

Paramedics pushing a gurney emerged from the shed. Even from a distance, she recognized the gleaming hairless dome of Harvey Manser as they loaded him into an awaiting ambulance. Its lights and sirens flared to life seconds later. Within moments, she and the others gathered alongside her watched the ambulance speed down the gravel drive, turn onto the narrow unpaved county road, and disappear.

Tasha sighed. Harvey was an arsonist and kidnapper. Darryl had been a murderer. Tubby had poisoned himself while in custody. She obviously didn't know anyone as well as she thought, not even herself, since she was guilty of tampering with evidence.

Another flurry of activity at the shed pulled her from her musings.

Alex emerged with Varik beside her, supporting her with his right arm. The other was held tightly against his chest and drenched in blood. They climbed into the back of a second ambulance, and the doors closed, sealing them away from prying eyes.

"Lieutenant Lockwood," Chief Enforcer Damian Alberez addressed her as he strode across the yard.

Tasha stood up straight.

"Come with me."

She ducked under the barricade and fell into step with the vampire. "Are you going to tell me what happened in there?"

"Enforcer Sabian did her job," he replied tersely, and kept walking.

"That's all you're going to say?"

"Nothing else needs to be said, Lieutenant." He halted beneath a towering sycamore tree, out of hearing distance for any of the humans sequestered behind the tape and even most of the vampires roaming the grounds.

The ambulance bearing Alex and Varik began to roll down the drive. Its red and white lights cast eerie flickering patterns on the ground. They watched as it made the turn and headed toward Jefferson.

Wind rustled the few dried and curled leaves that still stubbornly clung to the branches above her. "What happens now? Does Alex get reinstated?"

"That's not for me to decide. For now she'll continue

to be on paid suspension, pending the outcome of an official investigation."

Tasha snorted and shook her head. "So, she kills a human, wreaks havoc through the entire town, attacks fellow Enforcers, and gets away with it?"

"I didn't say she would get away with anything, Lieutenant. Her fate is yet to be determined."

"In the meantime, she walks away from all this, totally unaffected."

"I wouldn't go that far. Taking a life isn't easy. It can have unforeseen consequences."

"Yeah, I guess that's something you'd know about, huh?"

He shrugged.

Tasha felt restless. She needed to get away from this place, away from the vamps and their bureaucracy.

"Lieutenant," he called to her as she brushed past him.

She waited.

"I understand you knew Black, worked with him, but Stephen Sabian is still missing." He faced her. "As liaison officer, you have an obligation to assist the Bureau in our efforts to find him."

Tasha opened her mouth to reply, and a curious thing happened. She laughed. "Oh, *now* you want our help?" Her laughter turned harsh. "With all due respect, Chief Enforcer, you and all the rest of you fucking vamps can get bent. You want to find Stephen Sabian? Find him yourselves."

She stormed away, ignoring his repeated calls for her to come back. "Let's go, boys," she said loudly as she neared the barricade. "We've got our own people to protect. Let the feds have their fun."

Officers drifted to their cars and trucks. She slipped into the cool interior of her car. She'd had enough of vampires for one day, maybe even for her entire life. She maneuvered through the orderly mass exodus and onto the narrow gravel road.

The night seemed more ominous as she drove back to Jefferson. In her mind, gunmen and vampires lurked behind every tree. A rock kicked up by a passing car struck her windshield with the sound of a gunshot. Her pulse jumped.

She was close to town but didn't want to face the harsh lights of the hospital, waiting for word on Harvey's condition. The source of the threats she'd received was still a mystery. She had no idea who was behind them, but knowing that she was the one ultimately responsible for Harvey being in the hospital was more than she could bear.

She pulled into a dimly lit parking lot on the outskirts of town. Her hands shook, and she stared at the cracked windshield. She had to get ahold of herself.

A flickering sign in a window across the parking lot beckoned. Bars had never interested her, and she'd always considered herself a teetotaler, preferring tea to coffee and soda to alcohol, after seeing the effects alcohol had had on her mother. But times had changed.

She had changed.

She killed the engine and stepped into the night. Jamming her hands into her jacket pockets, she picked her way through the crowded lot.

Tasha paused at the door, uncertain. Someone roared in laughter inside. The sound was pleasant, warm and entirely human. That's what she needed. She needed to be with her own kind, with other humans. She held her breath and opened the door.

Smoke and the smell of beer assaulted her. Music pumped from the jukebox next to the chicken wire–encased stage across the room from the entrance. Two pool tables were crowded into a small room to the right of the stage. Outdated license plates and faded advertising signs decorated the bead board–paneled walls. Heads turned to check out the newcomer, and a few nodded greetings.

Tasha wove through the tables and took a seat at the bar, keeping her eyes downcast, not making eye contact with anyone. She wanted to be with other humans, but conversation seemed like a chore.

"Looks like you've had a rough night, honey," the woman behind the bar said, setting a paper napkin and a bowl of popcorn in front of Tasha. "What can I getcha?"

She looked at the rows of glistening bottles lining the wall. Her mind blanked, and she simply stared. "I don't know," she muttered.

The bartender arched a thin black eyebrow that had been drawn way too high on her forehead. "Hmf. I got just the thing for ya, honey."

Tasha watched the woman blend liquids from several bottles and add a dash of cranberry juice in an ice-filled glass before straining it into a shot glass.

She set the dark red final product down with a smile. "Slam that back, honey. It'll take the edge off."

Tasha picked up the glass and eyed it. Taking a deep breath, she brought it to her lips and drank it down in a single gulp. The cold liquid burned her tongue and throat. Coughing, she struggled to draw another breath while the woman cackled with high-pitched laughter.

"Good, ain't it?"

Tears gathered at the corners of Tasha's eyes, and she wiped them away. The burning in her throat spread out to encompass the rest of her, calming her frazzled nerves. She nodded. "What was that?"

"My specialty. I call it a Vamp Fang 'cause it's cold as hell and it'll bite your ass if you drink too many."

"Appropriate."

The woman grinned. "Want another?"

The damn vamps had been biting her ass for a long time—what was once more? At least this way, she had a chance of not remembering it in the morning. Sighing, she passed the glass back to the woman.

Alex paced the full length of the emergency room's waiting area, turned, and retraced her steps. She could feel her mother's eyes on her as she moved. She reached the opposite wall and turned to start the circuit again.

"What's taking so long?" she demanded as she passed by her mother for the hundredth time. The plate-glass wall and door that separated the waiting room from the nurses' and receptionist's shared desk allowed her a full view of the rest of the emergency room.

"I'm sure the doctors are working as quickly as they can."

Varik had been carted off to have his arm looked after. The bullet intended for her had struck his arm just below the shoulder. A few inches higher and it would have been a head shot.

The waiting-room door opened, and she spun around, ready to pepper the doctor with questions and demands, but stopped when a woman with short black hair entered. "Janet."

"I heard you found another body," Janet Klein, full-time bartender and part-time donor for Crimson Swan, said in a shaky voice. "And an Enforcer had been wounded. I figured you'd be here, and I wanted—I *needed* to know if—" Her brave façade broke, and she dropped into a chair, weeping.

Alex exchanged a confused glance with her mother.

Janet sniffled loudly and angrily brushed at her reddened cheeks. "I'm sorry. It's just I keep thinking that Stephen wouldn't have been attacked if he hadn't taken me home that night. When I heard that—" Her voice broke. "When I—"

The truth of Janet's appearance hit Alex. This woman, the human before her, was in love with Stephen. Janet freely displayed the emotions she herself had been keeping tightly reined in. She knelt in front of her. "It wasn't Stephen we found," she said softly.

Janet sighed in relief and then burst into another round of tears. "Then he's still out there, and it's all my fault!"

Alex cupped Janet's hands in her own. "No, it's not.

It's not anyone's fault. It simply is what it is. But we're going to find him. Do you understand me?"

Janet nodded.

"We're going to bring him home," Alex said, with more force.

Her mother sat in the chair beside Janet and took over for Alex, talking to the distraught woman in a soothing voice.

Alex stood and moved to the back of the waiting room, drawn by the bitter scent of coffee. Her hands shook as she poured the thick brown liquid into a small insulated cup and added sugar and cream. She stirred the coffee and thought of Varik.

He'd come for her tonight, blindly charged into an unknown and dangerous situation. She could've lost him at the very moment when she was once again becoming accustomed to his presence.

The memory of Darryl's and Claire's ghosts dancing as they faded from view swam before her. They'd both been overjoyed to be reunited for eternity.

She'd been given a second chance with Varik, and she'd squandered it. She'd been petty, defensive, and stubborn. Her selfishness had nearly killed him.

A warm hand on her shoulder massaged the tension in her muscles, and she inhaled deeply. Sandalwood and cinnamon. Varik. She spun to face him.

Heavy bandages covered his left arm, and it was held in place with a sling, but he was smiling. "I'll be fine in a week or so," he answered her unspoken question.

She stepped into his one-armed embrace and fought to keep her tears from falling. She listened to the steady rhythm of his heartbeat, the perfect match to her own. "It's my fault," she murmured against his chest.

"What do you mean?" he asked softly.

"If I'd caught Claire Black's killers, none of this would've happened."

Varik squeezed her to him. "You did the best you could."

"But it wasn't good enough, and now look at how many people have died or been hurt because of it."

The waiting room's door opened. A muscular vampire Alex recognized as the security guard Stephen had hired for Crimson Swan entered, and Alex's heart dropped into her shoes.

Janet stood and gave him a quick hug. "It wasn't him, Josh," she said. "It wasn't Stephen."

"What's wrong?" Varik asked softly, when Alex pulled away from him.

Josh released Janet. "That's good. That means he's—"

Alex grabbed Josh's arm and hurled him into a chair.

Chaos erupted, with Varik rushing to her side, Janet screaming, Alex's mother pulling the girl into a far corner, and Alex grappling for Josh's throat. "Where's Stephen? Answer me! Where is he?"

"You're fucking crazy!" Josh screamed. "Get her off me!"

Varik peeled her off the larger vampire. "Alex!"

"Look at his face!" Alex broke free of Varik's hold on her arm. "Look!"

Deep and long scratches covered one side of Josh's face.

"He's the fucker who attacked me at Crimson Swan."

Josh bolted for the door.

Varik stuck his foot in his path, and Josh crashed through the glass, landing hard on the tiled floor.

Emergency staff and security appeared from all corners. Varik moved between them and Josh, holding up his badge. "Federal Bureau of Preternatural Investigation," he announced. "Nothing to see, folks. Just apprehending a suspect."

Josh groaned and flipped over onto his hands and knees, attempting to rise.

Alex grabbed his neck and his arm, forcing him to his feet, and rushed him out of the hospital. She pinned him face-first into a brick wall, twisting his arm behind his back in an unnatural and painful position. "Where's Stephen?"

"Fuck you," he muttered.

She kicked the back of his knee. He dropped like a stone, and she smacked his head into the brick. "You want to play rough? We can play rough, asshole."

"Alex." Varik's voice held an edge of warning.

She flashed him a withering glance and leaned over Josh's shoulder, whispering in his ear. "I'm going to ask you one more time. But you should know, if you don't answer, I've already killed once tonight, and I have no qualms about offing a piece of shit like you." She increased the amount of pressure she exerted on Josh's arm, and he yelped in pain. In a louder voice, she asked, "Where is Stephen?"

"Two-seven-one-three Grazzier Lane," Josh gasped. "In the barn."

The barn doors collapsed under the weight of a massive iron battering ram.

"FBPI!" a chorus of voices shouted. Enforcers swarmed into the building. "Get down! Everybody down!"

Startled men were forcibly taken to the ground. The Enforcers moved systematically through the structure, searching, and calling out when they came up empty.

Varik, accompanied by Alex and Damian, strode into the barn last. He surveyed the area and the men now lying on the ground. Midnight drug dealers had been posing as members of the Human Separatist Movement in order to use HSM as a cover for their illicit drug trade.

"We've got him!" a voice called from somewhere in the loft area. "Southwest corner!"

"Stephen!" Alex shouted, and sprinted for the stairs with Varik and Damian on her heels.

Varik reached the loft two steps behind Alex. He slowed and allowed her to go forward alone.

"Stephen!" she cried, and dropped to her knees beside his bound and unmoving form.

Varik and the other Enforcers hung back as Alex smoothed the matted curls away from her brother's bruised and battered face. His clothing was soiled and torn. Bruises and deep cuts covered much of his exposed skin.

"Stephen?" Alex called, and her voice was thick with tears.

He groaned weakly.

"It's me. It's Alex."

Stephen's lips moved. "About time you showed up," he said in a barely audible whisper.

Medics arrived, and Varik gently pulled Alex away so they could begin assessing Stephen's condition.

She flung her arms around his neck and buried her face against his chest, weeping.

He stroked her hair and held her, repeating softly, "I'm here, baby. It's over now."

eighteen

october 18

TASHA NURSED A CUP OF PEPPERMINT TEA WHILE silently staring at her desk. The fallout from the Darryl Black investigation was only beginning to surface, and she wondered how long she'd continue to sit in her office.

Three days had passed since Alex's confrontation with Darryl and the discovery of Stephen Sabian in a barn on property owned by Tubby Jordan, who Tasha was shocked to learn had been a vampire passing as a human. In those three days, Bill Jenkins had turned himself in to the Jefferson Police Department and confessed to his role in the arson of Crimson Swan. Martin Evans and six other humans were also charged with arson.

The FBPI had arrested four vampires posing as members of the Human Separatist Movement and charged them with kidnapping, drug manufacturing, trafficking, and a host of other felonies. In the interest of maintaining good public relations with the Jefferson Police and Nassau County Sheriff's departments, they agreed to drop federal hate-crime charges against the arsonists in exchange for their testimonies against the impostor HSM members in the kidnapping of Stephen Sabian.

The Midnight dealers had been driving the van used during the kidnapping, so it was easy for them to whisk Stephen away to a different location without Harvey or the others being the wiser. Tubby had masterminded the kidnapping so as to use Stephen as leverage against Alex. While the initial demands had been for all vampires to leave town, Tubby's ultimate goal was to drive Alex away. His plan had backfired.

Harvey remained in the hospital, listed in stable condition. The doctors had been able to repair his leg, and physically he was on the mend. Psychologically, however, the man was a goner. He mostly stayed in a catatonic state, not responding to any outside stimulus, but every so often he had brief periods in which he would scream continuously and seemed to be fighting to awaken from some horrific nightmare. The doctors couldn't explain his condition, and until Harvey's mind returned from whatever dark place it'd fled, he wasn't being charged with any crimes.

All of Darryl's vampire victims had now been identified: Trent Thibodaux, Grant Williams, Eric Stromheimer, Gary Lipscomb, and Scott Adams. Once they had names and dug into their backgrounds, they'd discovered all had a connection to Claire's murder and Alex. Thibodaux had been arrested by Alex but was working as a confidential informant for the FBPI office out of Natchez as part of a plea deal.

Williams and Stromheimer had been named and in-
terviewed as potential witnesses in Claire's case because
they'd been two of the last people to see her alive. Lipscomb had bought Midnight from Thibodaux in the
past, and Adams was a small-time dealer that Alex had
begun investigating before Darryl started his murder
spree. The time between Claire's murder and Darryl's
rampage had been long enough that Alex hadn't
thought to connect the two.

Then there was her own fate to consider. When the
word got out about what she'd done, her career would
be over, and that frightened her to her core.

A knock on the door pulled her from her musings.
"Come in."

The door swung wide to admit Varik Baudelaire, his
left arm in a blue and white sling. "Is this a bad time?"

Tasha glanced at the file in his free hand. Ice settled
into her bloodstream. She set her teacup aside before he
could notice how her hand shook. "Is that the final report?"

Varik closed the door and settled into the chair
across from her. He laid the file on her desk. "That's the
final report on the Crimson Swan arson and all the subsequent events."

She picked up the file and thumbed through it. She
had to give the FBPI credit for one thing. They were efficient. "Diesel fuel–soaked rags around the perimeter,"
she read from the section regarding the arson, "and
more fuel splashed on the outer walls and through the
windows, combined with the alcohol inside the bar itself, equals total destruction."

"That confirms what Bill Jenkins and the video told us."

She stopped on a page in the file, not understanding what she read. She looked up at him. "This says—"

"That the Taser report was discovered in Sheriff Manser's pocket after his arrival at Jefferson Memorial," Varik finished her sentence. He grimaced as he shifted his injured arm. "He must have picked it up after you *accidentally* dropped it in his office."

"But I didn't—I mean, I told you—"

"I know what you told me. Alex asked me to keep it out of my official report, and I did."

"Why?"

"Because, like Alex, I don't think a good cop deserves to have her career destroyed for a momentary lapse in judgment."

"But Harvey. What if he—"

"That's a subject for later discussion, should the need ever arise."

Tasha laid the report aside, astounded. She'd been given a get-out-of-jail-free card courtesy of the very woman whose brother, only a few days prior, Tasha had refused to help search for. "What's going to happen to Alex?"

"There'll be a hearing."

"And then?"

"The matter will be dealt with accordingly."

She knew vampires had strict laws governing human interaction. Alex had crossed more than a few lines in her quest to find Stephen. Part of her wanted to point fingers and place blame, but Tasha thought of what she would've done in the same situation. She didn't think she would've acted much differently than Alex had.

"I should be going," Varik said. "I still have a few things to take care of before I leave town."

"You're going back to Louisville?"

He stood up and extended his hand. "I'm going back to retirement. I'm too old for this shit."

Tasha clasped his hand. "I thought that after everything, you and Alex..."

He paused with the door half open. "So did I," he murmured. His eyes grew distant for a moment, and then he seemed to come back to himself. With a final nod, he left and the door closed with a soft *click*.

Tasha picked up her tea and thought of what had just transpired. Alex had asked Varik to falsify official records in order to keep Tasha out of legal trouble. As long as no one uncovered the truth, she was safe as far as the law was concerned, but she knew the truth, and she'd have to live with it.

Liquid sloshed onto the desk as her hands trembled at the thought of ever facing Alex again.

Emily Sabian was happy. As she strolled down the fourth-floor corridor of Jefferson Memorial Hospital, she hummed an Irish ballad Bernard had taught her long ago.

Her children were safe again. At least for the time being. Alex still faced an FBPI investigation, and Stephen had an extended recovery time looming ahead of him due to his injuries. However, both were alive and, for the most part, whole.

She had no doubts that Stephen would mend, but Alex concerned her. Her daughter was in pain, and Emily couldn't alleviate it. However, Alex wasn't the only one suffering.

Emily had visited Varik and returned the silver shamrock charm he'd slipped to her. She'd told him that it was identical to the one she wore that had been Bernard's. He thought it odd that Gary Lipscomb would have a charm used by the Special Operations division to indicate Talents. There was no record of Lipscomb having been a Hunter, a part of the FBPI after its establishment, or having any psychic ability at all. How the charm came into his possession was a mystery.

Varik hadn't asked about Alex, but Emily could tell Alex occupied much of his thoughts. When she suggested that Varik simply call Alex and arrange to meet before he returned to Louisville, he shook his head, saying, "I tried. She refuses to accept or return my calls. I can't even reach her through the bond. No, I won't force her to see me when she doesn't want it."

Emily left him and returned to the hospital, happy to have her children safe but also sad that one remained in misery because of pure stubbornness.

Laughter greeted her when she opened the door to Stephen's room. "What's all this?"

"Gifts from my admirers," Stephen replied, gesturing with his one usable arm at the balloons, flowers, and cards filling the room.

"Admirers?"

"Apparently my brother is some kind of previously unknown stud muffin," Alex said from her perch on one of the windowsills overlooking a park behind the hospital. "He gets his picture plastered all over the news, and he's suddenly receiving marriage proposals from as far away as Kansas."

"Yeah, but that one was from a guy in prison." Stephen shook his head. "No, thank you."

"Well, there's only one proposal you need to worry about," Janet Klein said, as she adjusted his pillow.

Beneath the fading facial bruises, Stephen blushed as Alex laughed.

"What proposal is that?" Emily asked.

Stephen reached for Janet's hand, and she readily gave it, along with a broad smile. "Since I'm officially homeless, Janet's offered to let me move in with her once the doctors clear me for release."

"I see," Emily said, sounding skeptical of the arrangement.

"He'll be in good hands, Mrs. Sabian," Janet said. "I'm not just a bartender. I only do that so I can pay my way through school. You see, I'm studying for a degree in physical therapy, so I'd help Stephen with whatever he needs when they send him home."

"Oh, I'm not worried about that," Emily said with a dismissive wave. She focused on Stephen. "You have months of recovery ahead of you. You're going to require more blood and more frequently."

"It's okay, Mom. The hospital's going to send me home with a supply, and Janet is a certified donor. I'll be fine."

"You're perfectly capable of making your own decision, Stephen, so long as you've explained to Janet the risks of a human living with a vampire."

"I understand the risks, Mrs. Sabian," Janet said. She smiled down at Stephen. "I think he's worth it."

Stephen tugged on her arm, pulling her toward him, and kissed her.

Alex hopped down from her perch and left the room.

Emily followed her down the hallway to a small waiting area beside the elevators. "Is something wrong, honey?"

"No," Alex answered a little too quickly. "I just thought the lovebirds could use some space. That's all."

Emily watched Alex closely and knew why her daughter's face was forlorn and her eyes haunted. "Varik's leaving today."

Alex flinched.

"Have you spoken to him?"

"He left me a voice mail earlier. Asked me to come by his hotel room." She crossed her arms in front of her and walked to a narrow sun-drenched window. "But I'm not going."

"Why not?"

"It's . . . complicated."

"Of course it's complicated. You and he are blood-bound, and nothing's going to change that. Avoiding him isn't going to make the bond, or your feelings for him, go away."

"I know. I'm just so confused, Mom. I've spent the past six years blaming him for the attack and the bond.

But then he came here and *I* attacked *him*. I reestablished the bond."

"And now you understand that it was never his fault. He, and you, were both doing what is instinctive."

Alex turned from the window, unshed tears in her eyes. "What would you do, Mom?"

Emily cupped her daughter's face and marveled at how much she really did resemble Bernard, in so many ways. "If I were given a second chance to be with your father, the man I loved for over two hundred years, I wouldn't waste it by hiding in a hospital."

Alex stood frozen in front of Varik's hotel-room door, hand poised to knock. Her mother's words had made sense when she stood in the hospital waiting room. Now that she was here, she was having doubts.

"Just knock on the damn door," she whispered to herself. She tapped lightly on the door, waited two heartbeats, and turned to leave, telling herself he wasn't there.

The door opened behind her. "Alex?"

She could feel the heat rising in her face when she turned back to find him standing in the doorway, wearing nothing but a towel around his waist and his hair dripping water onto the blue industrial carpet. "I, uh, if this is a bad time, I can come back..."

"No, please"—he stepped aside—"come in. I've wanted to talk to you."

She skirted past him and into his room. The smell of sandalwood and cinnamon hit her hard, and the muscles in her lower abdomen fluttered in response. Her pulse jumped, and she purposefully sat in one of the chairs next to the small, round table rather than on the still-rumpled bed. A suitcase lay on the floor, half filled with clothes. "I got your message."

"I was beginning to think you weren't coming," Varik said as he leaned against the far wall, cradling his left arm to his chest.

"I wasn't."

"What changed your mind?"

Alex smirked. "Mom."

"Ah." Varik grinned. "Emily can be very persuasive. You should've heard what she said to Damian to get him down here."

"I can imagine."

An uncomfortable silence settled between them. Everything in the room smelled of him, and it tugged at Alex's memories of the good times they'd shared.

"Ever since I came to Jefferson, we've been dancing around our past," he said softly. "The other night, when—" He fingered the bright pink scar forming on his shoulder, and it pulled at her conscience. "It got me to thinking—"

She nodded. "I know. We need to talk about the blood-bond."

"No, actually, I wanted to give you something." He stepped to the nightstand and picked up a long silver chain before moving to stand in front of her.

"What—"

He dangled the chain so the ring at the end glittered in the sunlight coming from the window behind her.

"Oh, my..." She took the chain holding her engagement ring from him and looked up at him. Dark currents of emotions swirled in his color-shifting eyes. The same jumbled emotions churned within her. "You kept it. Why?"

"It was the only thing you left behind. The only piece of you I still had."

The blood-bond suddenly opened, and years of pent-up emotions raced through her. Anger, regret, anxiety—all collided within her and swept her away in their powerful ebb and flow. She tried to rein in the turbulence, to retain control. She could no longer tell where her psyche ended and Varik's began.

Thoughts of how she'd fled Louisville whirled around her. She'd been terrified of the blood-bond. Running had been the only solution for her. She'd assumed Varik hated her for leaving, that he'd moved on with his life.

But he hadn't. He'd stayed away, giving her the distance she wanted. Not because he hated her, not because he moved on, but because he loved her and he wanted her to come back to him. Freely and without regrets.

The revelation shook her to the core. The world tilted, and she felt as though she were standing on the edge of a yawning void.

"Varik"—she stood to face him squarely—"why are you giving me this? I'm not going to marry you."

"I know, but I gave it to you. I want you to have it."

"I don't understand."

"I love you, Alex." His warm fingers touched her cheek. "I've never stopped loving you."

She looked into Varik's golden eyes, drank in the calming effect of his touch. "I never stopped loving you, either."

A new emotion sped across the bond and entered her, chased away her doubts, and stole her breath.

His lips seized hers, and she moaned, dropping the chain and ring. Memories of their shared past sped through her mind like a film on fast-forward. Years of loneliness and longing fell to the side, replaced by a sense of belonging and heady desire. A need to be touched, to be held, to be loved, consumed her. Her arms circled his neck, and she pressed closer to him.

Varik groaned, and his arms threatened to crush her. A thousand tiny electric currents zinged through Alex's body. Muscles in her lower abdomen tightened in anticipation. A deep ache settled between her thighs as she felt his towel slipping. Part of her prayed for it to remain in place, and part of her screamed for Varik to rip it away.

Varik broke the kiss long enough to literally sweep her off her feet and lay her on the bed, peel away the towel, and stretch out next to her.

She ran her hands over his smooth torso, over his defined abdominal muscles, his sculpted chest. The logical part of her mind screamed at her to stop, and she hesitated. She felt him tremble, felt his sudden uncertainty through the bond.

"Alex," he whispered, "are you—"

Desire reasserted its control over her, and his question ended in a strangled groan as her fingers teased his coarse hair and brushed against his swollen, throbbing flesh. The uncertainty she'd sensed in him vanished, and he recaptured her lips with a hungry growl.

Her skin prickled where his hands touched her as he undressed her. Heat from Varik's body beat against her. His hand cupped her breast, and she moaned when he broke the kiss, only to arch her back with a loud gasp as he pulled her swollen nipple into his mouth, grazing the tender flesh with his fangs, teasing her with his tongue.

"Varik." She sighed, wrapping her legs around him, arching against him, wanting him inside her.

He entered her with a kiss, filling her with his entire length in a single flex of his hips.

Alex bucked her hips, matching him stroke for stroke. Their breathing was labored and frantic as they moved against each other. The bed creaked and groaned in time to their rhythm. Pressure built between her thighs and erupted in a blinding wash of vibrant colors. She clutched him to her and bit his shoulder, tasting blood.

Varik gasped, and it turned to a triumphant shout as he exploded within her.

She felt his fangs pierce her shoulder, sending another shock of pleasure through her body.

He collapsed on top of her, shivering and gulping down huge breaths of air.

Alex, her thoughts scattered, stroked his back, playing with his long, still-damp hair, enjoying the small tremors that continued to shake her. She moaned when he withdrew, not wanting to part, but he pulled her into his arms, and she nestled in by his side.

"Somehow I don't think this is what Mom had in mind when she suggested I come talk to you," she said, her voice echoing against Varik's chest.

He snorted. "It's not exactly what I had in mind, either, but I'm not complaining."

She smiled and snuggled against him. His fingers traced lazy circles on her bare shoulder. Her eyes drooped, and sleep pulled at her. For once, she didn't fight it.

nineteen

ALEX DREAMT.

She was four years old again. She stood next to an iron railing and looked out over the Grand Canyon. An old stone watchtower stood nearby, a lonesome sentinel guarding against a forgotten invader. The hot August sun burned her skin and made sweat bead along her exposed shoulders and arms. A raven flew overhead. Its shrill caw echoed as it dove into the canyon. A shadow fell over her, and she looked up.

"Here you go, Princess." Her father handed her a rapidly melting ice-cream cone. "Whew, look at your shoulders. We better get you out of the sun."

The melting ice cream was both warm and cold on her lips as he led her into the shade of a tree near the watchtower. "Where's Mommy and Stephen?"

Bernard settled on the dry brown grass and pulled her into his lap. "They'll be along soon."

She smiled and nestled closer to his chest, inhaling

his scent of coffee, tobacco, and chalk. She could hear and feel his heart beating next to her.

Couples and families walked by them, lost in their own conversations. Ravens hopped along the ground, searching for leftover bits of picnics or insects. Alex licked her ice cream and watched a bright orange-and-black butterfly flit along the underside of the tree's branches. It beat its wings, looped, and whirled in a mad dance.

"Look, Daddy," she said, smiling and patting Bernard's face with a sticky hand. She turned to make sure he was watching. "Look at the butter—"

Bernard's emerald eyes were wide and staring, now silvered with death. His mouth hung open in a silent scream. Blood coated the front of his white button-down shirt.

"Daddy!"

Alex awoke with a start, the dream falling away in a confused blur. Dim light filtered through a window to her right. Slowly her senses and memory returned. She glanced at Varik, lying asleep next to her. Brushing the hair from her face, she sat up, careful not to wake him, and slipped into one of his white T-shirts that had been tossed on the floor.

She rose and moved to the window, staring at the moonlight filtered by the thin white draperies. Her brow furrowed. Something wasn't right. She glanced around the room, trying to locate the source of her anxiety.

It was the colors. Even in the moonlight, she should've seen the brightly colored diamond pattern of the carpet as though it were daylight, but they were muted. All the colors were muted, and she realized she wasn't truly awake. She was once again beyond the Veil and walking in the Shadowlands.

"Alexandra," her father's voice called to her from outside the room.

She glanced at Varik's sleeping form in the bed.

"Alexandra." Her father's call was more insistent.

"I'm coming," she said, and crossed the room. With one last quick look at the bed, she slipped out of the room.

The corridor beyond was empty and seemed to stretch forever in front and behind her. Doors lined both sides, each with a different number, some with large X's painted over them in bright red. Each door had a small crystal, glowing with a soft white light, embedded in the wall to one side. She stepped away from her door and looked both ways but saw no sign of Bernard. "Daddy?"

"I'm here, Princess," he said from behind her, startling her. He smiled when she turned to face him. "It's time."

"Time? Time for what?"

"For me to explain everything to you."

"What is this place?" she asked, gesturing to the corridor. "Why are we here?"

"This"—he nodded and looked around him—"is your entry point to the world beyond the Veil. It has many names, but I call it the Hall of Records. Each of these doors can take you to a different place, a different time. Think of it as a universal archive for souls and their memories, but only vampires, not humans. We can only access the archive of our own kind."

Alex spun in place. Having access to other people's memories? People she'd never met and may never meet? What he was suggesting was beyond her comprehension.

"You don't have to understand it all right now," he said, his green eyes dancing with delight. "You just have to know this place exists, and this should be your starting point whenever you want to cross the Veil. You're safe here. It's a neutral zone. Nothing can harm you here."

"How did you find out about this place?"

"I've known of it for a long time, long before you were born." He smiled. "I always hoped to have a child who could access it. I'm really proud of you, Princess."

"Yeah, too bad you weren't around to teach me about it before now." Her words sounded bitter, even to her ears.

His smile faded. "I'm sorry about that, Alexandra. Fate can be a cruel mistress."

"Fuck fate!" Her shout echoed throughout the corridor. "Why did you leave? Why did you leave me?"

"I didn't have a choice, Princess." He gripped her arms and held her in place as he spoke. "I didn't want to go away, but I had to. There are things in your world and in this one," his eyes moved to indicate their surroundings, "that simply aren't meant to be known."

"What are you talking about?" She pulled away from him and began looking at the various doors. "Which door is yours, Daddy? Which one will take me to the day you were killed?" She walked down the hall. "Which one?"

"You can't access mine, Alexandra."

She whirled on him, years of frustration erupting within her. "Why not? What don't you want me to know?"

He sighed and moved to one of the doors with the big red X. "Doors marked in this way are barred, Princess. No one can access them, for one reason."

She stared at him and the door. Understanding came to her slowly, and she sank to her knees. "It's because you're a lost soul. Isn't it?"

He knelt in front of her. "Yes."

Alex closed her eyes and fought back her tears. "Why, Daddy? Why did you choose this?"

"The reason doesn't really matter anymore."

"It matters to me!" She looked away from him. He'd told her she had this ability, one that could help her to finally solve his murder, to put his soul to rest, only to strip her of any hope of actually accomplishing it.

"Alexandra," he touched her arm, "listen to me. I don't have a lot of time left. I can only come to this place for short periods, and there's a lot I still have to tell you."

She brushed away the tears on her cheeks and nodded. "Can you tell me what happened to me the other day? Was that really Claire Black's ghost I saw?"

He nodded. "You were able to see her because she chose to reveal herself. She must have trusted you to do the right thing, otherwise she wouldn't have done it."

"And the vision of Darryl shooting Harvey? That was because of my psychometry?"

"Yes, and that's why you connected with Gary Lipscomb so easily."

"The psychic wound," she murmured.

He nodded again. "Now that his murderer has been stopped, his and the others' souls are at peace. You won't see them again."

"Will that happen—psychic wounds, I mean—every time I connect with a victim in that way?"

"It could, but the blood-bond you have will offer you some protection from it."

"But Varik can't access this place, can he?"

"No, he doesn't have the same gift as you, but he can and does act as an anchor for you. Just as your mother did for me."

Alex stared at him in confusion. "You and Mom were blood-bound?"

"For nearly two hundred years. I can still feel her"—he touched his temple—"here. That's how I know she's okay."

"I didn't think a vampire could survive the death of a bond-mate."

"It takes a very strong will to resist the call of death." He smiled. "Which is why I loved your mother so."

A crystalline chime sounded from overhead. Alex glanced up at the ceiling, only then noticing that it appeared to be a star-filled night sky. "What was that?"

"My time's up." He rose slowly, helping her to her feet. "I have to return to my world, and you have to go back to yours."

"But you haven't told me how to access this place."

"It's simple, Princess." He led her back to the door to

Varik's hotel room. "Visualize a door in your mind. Will it into being, and open it. It should bring you here."

"But how do I know where the doors lead?"

He touched the crystal next to the door. A beam of light shot upward and then expanded to show a list of names, dates, and places scrolling across a spectral screen. "Access the main directory. It will tell you everything you need to know."

The crystalline chime sounded again, and Bernard's outline wavered. "Time to go, Princess."

Alex reached for the doorknob and turned it. "I love you, Dad—"

He was gone.

When Alex awoke again, true moonlight lit the room around her, and the smell of sandalwood and cinnamon clung to her. She rolled onto her stomach, reaching for Varik, and grabbed a handful of empty pillow.

She heard his voice then, muffled, coming from the bathroom. Curious, she tapped the blood-bond. She felt a brief surge of anxiety, and then it was gone, stymied by the wall Varik erected between them.

Climbing out of bed, she pulled on one of his white T-shirts and paused as a feeling of déjà vu passed over her. Shaking her head as the bathroom door opened, she stood and turned to face him with a smile.

The look of concern on his face changed her smile to a frown.

"What is it? What's wrong?" she asked.

"That was Damian," he said, sinking onto the bed, turning his cell phone over and over in his hands.

Damian had left Jefferson the day after she'd killed Darryl Black, summoned back to Louisville and FBPI headquarters. "What did he want?"

He didn't answer.

"Varik?"

He seemed to struggle with a decision, uncertain, and then sighed. "Damian says they're going to launch a full investigation into every case you've worked since coming to Jefferson."

Alex's breath left her in a rush. Investigations of that scope happened only if they believed an Enforcer to be corrupt, compromised in some way. Compromised Enforcers weren't tolerated any more today than they had been before the formation of the FBPI, back when the Hunters were still the only means of law enforcement among vampires. Charges of corruption carried only one penalty—death. She sat on the bed next to him, stunned.

"I shouldn't have told you."

"No, I'm glad you told me. It's just..." She loved being an Enforcer, but she'd allowed the pressures to crack her, and far too many had paid the price for it. How was she supposed to get through a corruption investigation?

Varik pulled her in tight next to him. "We'll get through this. You'll see."

"I thought you were going back to Louisville."

"Jefferson still needs an Enforcer, and since you're

suspended while the investigation is pending, Damian's reassigned me."

"You're staying?"

"Only if you really want me here."

She slipped her arms around his waist and laid her head on his uninjured shoulder. "Stay."

"See? I told you you'd realize you couldn't live without me."

Alex smiled but didn't respond. Outside, a cloud drifted across the moon, blotting out its light and plunging them into a shadowy darkness from which she wondered if they'd ever return.

*Look for more of Alexandra Sabian's dangerously
sexy adventures in the hotly anticipated sequel*

BLOOD
SECRETS

by Jeannie Holmes

Coming soon from Dell Books
Turn the page to take a look inside....

prologue

NO MOON SHONE IN THE SKY WHEN HE DUMPED THE body. He hardly recognized the mangled mess before him as the vibrant young woman he'd known. Hair the color of new pennies turned black with dried blood. A dull silver film encroached the sparkling jade of her eyes.

Her jaw was marred by a dark smear as he traced its gentle curve. He pulled back and stuck the digit in his mouth, coating his tongue with her blood. An electric charge jolted his spine. Memories that were not his own flickered through his consciousness, playing scenes from her life on the movie screen of his mind, until the film stopped in a crimson moment of violence.

The rags he'd used to wipe down the trunk and hide his fingerprints fell from his hand and greedily absorbed the blood pooling beneath the remains. Using his elbow, he slammed the trunk closed, blotting the macabre view from sight.

A falling star streaked across the glittering sky. He

closed his eyes and made a wish he'd made a thousand times before. The vision of his wish coming true filled his mind.

"Soon." His whisper, a blade, sliced through the silent night. Without a second glance at the trunk-turned-tomb, he walked away.

november 17

ALEXANDRA SABIAN SEARCHED THE HALL OF RECORDS for clues that would lead her to a killer. The only problem with her search was that she had no suspects, no witnesses, and the body had been buried for forty years.

Her father, Bernard Sabian, had been murdered in the spring of 1968, when she was only five. Someone had left his staked and beheaded body in a cemetery near her childhood home.

Simply because he was a vampire, like her.

At least that was her theory.

The large screen before her was projected by crystals housed in a black granite access terminal. Names scrolled by in one column while the adjacent column held a series of numbers showing the location of a door that led to that person's memory.

In the two weeks since she'd discovered she could access the Hall of Records—a metaphysical storehouse for the memories and experiences of every man, woman, and child who'd walked the face of Earth—she'd been searching through the records, trying to locate her father's. She hoped once she did that she would uncover the clues she needed to find his killer.

The screen flashed from white to red and bold black letters appeared: ACCESS DENIED.

"Damn it," Alex muttered and dropped her head into her hands. Every time she searched for her father's name she met the same result.

Sighing, she looked up and around the Hall. It had transformed since the first time she'd entered. What had been a single endless hallway had become a huge ornate multilevel rotunda. Countless doors lay hidden in shadows on each level of the massive round building. Large golden Corinthian-style columns supported each level, and she craned her neck to count ten floors before the top-most levels became lost in darkness. The only light came from the screen in front of her and the softly glowing crystals beside each door. Although moonlight streamed through a circular opening in the apex of the rotunda's unseen dome, none of it reached the lower levels.

"All I need are some crickets chirping in the background," she said to no one. She turned her attention back to the screen, ready to try a different approach to her search.

Somewhere in the distant shadows overhead, a door opened and closed.

Alex jerked. While she'd known others could access the Hall, she'd never been present when it happened. She waited to see if someone appeared or if she heard footsteps.

No noise broke the silence. No one showed themselves.

"Hello," she called. "Is someone there?"

Only her echoed voice answered.

Frowning, Alex peered into the gloom overhead. Had she imagined it?

A persistent, steady beeping sounded from her wrist. She checked her watch and sighed. It was time to leave the Hall behind.

She rose from her seat and headed for the simple wooden door behind her. The Hall wasn't a place located on the physical plane but rather was located in the Shadowlands, a sort of neutral zone between the physical world and the realm of the spirit. Light flooded the rotunda as she opened it and stepped through.

The light surrounded her, warm and welcoming. The moon had reigned over the Hall, but once outside, Alex found herself in a flowering meadow kissed by sunlight. Looking over her shoulder, no building was visible—only the door through which she'd exited the Hall.

"Curiouser and curiouser," she muttered and then smirked at the reference to *Alice in Wonderland*. Sometimes she definitely felt like Alice tumbling through the looking-glass.

Parting the Veil that separated the physical from the spiritual required concentration. She sighed and closed her eyes, pushing aside the random thoughts that crowded her mind.

Her physical body lay in a hotel room in a meditative trance. Once awake, she would be groggy and disoriented, like someone coming out from under anesthesia.

In order to shift her consciousness from the Shadow-lands back to the real world, she had to remember details of the room.

Gradually she recalled the feel of the bed beneath her, the coolness of the air, and the hum of machinery from the nearby elevators. The sensation of a yawning pit opening beneath her made her stomach roll. She'd learned to keep her eyes shut tightly against a kaleidoscopic whirlwind of colors and shadows as she passed through the void and returned to the physical plane.

Alex slowly awoke from the dreamlike trance in which she'd fallen and alarms immediately sounded in her mind. Her skin prickled under the gaze of an unseen observer.

Darkness cloaked her surroundings. Disoriented, she searched with her senses, probing the night for signs of life. She steadied and measured her breathing as her eyes adjusted to the gloom. The greenish glow of a security light bathed the window beside the bed on which she lay and cast strange shadows on the wall.

Without turning her head, she looked around the small hotel room trying to make sense of what she saw. One of the shadows in a far corner shifted and her focus zeroed in on it. She eased her hand beneath her pillow, reaching for her loaded Glock G31 .357-caliber pistol.

The shadow detached from the wall and moved toward her.

Alex sat up quickly and aimed her pistol at the shadow as it launched itself onto the bed. Her finger found the trigger.

The shadow landed beside her with an inquisitive warble.

"Damn it, Dweezil," Alex whispered, jerking her finger from the trigger as the large Maine Coon cat swished its tail over her bare legs. She secured the gun's safety and laid it on the nightstand.

Dweezil head butted her empty hand and purred.

She chuckled and scratched behind his large tufted ears. "Don't scare me like that. I almost shot you."

His eyes flashed iridescent green in the light filtering through the window. He winked at her as if to say "Gotcha," before moving to the spare pillow and curling into a tight ball.

"Crazy cat." Alex yawned and glanced at the time displayed on the digital clock on the nightstand.

It was almost four o'clock in the morning. She could still manage a few hours of real sleep before her meeting. Straightening the oversized University of Louisville T-shirt she wore, she walked into the bathroom and blinked against the harsh light before closing the door to insure Dweezil didn't join her. Answering the call of nature didn't require a fuzzy audience, though he begged to differ at times. His objections usually manifested as fuzzy paws waving at her from beneath the door.

As an Enforcer with the Federal Bureau of Preternatural Investigation, it was her job to police the vampire population of Jefferson, a small town in the southwestern corner of Mississippi. At least it had been until two weeks ago when she turned rogue, abandoned her oath to uphold the law, and incurred the wrath of Chief En-

forcer Damian Alberez. She'd been placed on adminis-
trative suspension and ordered to remain within the
city limits until the Bureau summoned her to their
headquarters in Louisville, Kentucky, to face an official
inquiry before the Tribunal, the vampire equivalent of
an internal affairs committee. She was being charged
with numerous violations of the Enforcer code of conduct, the most serious being corruption, which, if
found guilty, carried a mandatory death sentence.

She was scheduled to meet with Damian and a special investigator assigned by the Tribunal to examine
not only her recent actions but also every case she'd
worked since moving to Jefferson six years ago. It wasn't
a process she looked forward to enduring.

As she washed up, Alex checked her reflection in the
age-spotted mirror above the sink. The bruising that
had covered her ribs, stomach, and the right side of her
face had finally disappeared but the fractured cheekbone hadn't fully healed. She could still feel the sore-
ness when she smiled, not that she had much reason to
smile lately. A bright pink scar ran diagonally over her
right bicep, the result of a sniper's ballet grazing her
arm.

Another scar marred the left side of her neck, a
jagged slash starting behind her ear and extending to
her collarbone. She fingered the scar, a permanent reminder of a chapter in her life she thought was behind
her. Fate, however, had other plans for her.

"Snap out of it, Alex," she told her reflection as she
pulled loose the band securing her hair in a low ponytail. She gathered the shoulder-length-tangled auburn

mass at the nape of her neck and looped the band around it once more. "What's done is done."

She opened the door and was greeted by the first crashing notes of Beethoven's Fifth Symphony.

Dweezil chirped his displeasure as she dived across the bed to reach her cell phone.

"Sabian," she answered breathlessly on the second ring.

"Dreaming of me again?" a man's voice purred in her ear.

Alex rolled her eyes. "You wish."

Varik Baudelaire laughed. "Well, you can't blame me for asking when you answer the phone like that."

"I know you didn't call at this hour to flirt." She could hear distant voices over the line and the sound of dried leaves rustling in a breeze. "Where are you?"

"Nassau County Community College campus, outside the women's dorm," he answered.

"Crime scene?"

"That's what I'm trying to figure out. You've been keeping track of the Mindy Johnson disappearance?"

"The girl that went missing three days ago. Yeah, I'm familiar."

"Her car just turned up. We're processing it now."

"Why call me?"

"I need you here."

"I'm suspended, remember?"

"Not anymore. I already cleared it with Damian."

Alex's eyebrows rose and she checked the clock again. "How long have you been there?"

"Since a little after one."

Three hours on scene was a long time to process a car. "You said you were trying to figure out if you had a crime scene. What do you mean?"

Varik sighed and the weight of the past few hours seemed to be carried in the sound. "Open the bond and I'll show you."

Six years ago, they'd been lovers, engaged to be married, until he attacked her, savaging her neck and giving her the scar she now unconsciously traced with her finger. He'd taken her blood and forged a psychic bond between them. Time and distance had weakened the blood-bond but two weeks ago, she'd turned the tables and attacked him, restrengthening the bond.

Alex drew a steadying breath and lowered the mental barriers she'd erected to protect her mind from Varik's. The low-level hum she always heard in the back of her mind grew louder, accompanied by a pressure comparable to a mounting headache. Her awareness expanded until it met a warm tide of thoughts and memories, and her consciousness merged with Varik's.

Images, sounds, and smells assaulted her: a three-story brick building, snippets of conversations, the clean scent of rain, a Honda Accord with its driver's-side door open and engine left idling. The final vision focused on a small figure, a doll clothed in a white dress lying in a sea of darkness. Along with the doll came a wave of emotions ranging from disgust to anxiety to recognition.

Alex latched on to the sense of recognition, pulling on it like a loose thread, following it back to its source. Alarm and anger pulsed through the bond and left her reeling when Varik threw up his mental barriers, severing the connection. She fought against the vertigo that threatened to overwhelm her and raised her own psychic shields once more.

"How soon can you be here?" Varik asked.

She evaded his question. "What's the significance of the doll?"

"I don't know."

"Like hell you don't. You recognized it. What's going on?"

"I said I don't know, Alex."

"Yes, you do. I sensed it in you."

Silence filled the line.

"Damn it, Varik. If you want me to help, then you have to talk to me."

"We'll talk when you get here."

"Varik—"

"When you get here," he snapped and ended the call.

Alex stared at her cell phone for a moment before closing it in frustration. "You're damn right we'll talk," she grumbled, rolling over the bed to gain her feet.

As she dressed, the image of the doll remained fixed in her mind's eye. She felt none of the emotions she'd sensed from Varik upon seeing it. Why wouldn't he tell her anything over the phone, or more important, through the blood-bond? What was it about this doll that had him so spooked?

"Only one way to find out." She shrugged into a dark brown leather jacket and secured her Glock in a holster at her hip. Grabbing her keys beside the television, she ran a hand over Dweezil's back. "Guard the place and behave yourself."

The cat yawned and rolled onto his back, exposing his fuzzy belly, which she quickly scratched and was rewarded with a low, rumbling purr.

Alex stepped into the brightly lit hotel hallway and made certain the door locked behind her. She stalked past the other rooms containing sleeping patrons and waited for the elevator.

Her apartment had been damaged in a fire a few weeks prior and wasn't ready for her return. She'd been staying with her brother, Stephen, in a studio apartment he rented out over Crimson Swan, Jefferson's only legal blood bar for vampires. However, arsonists led by the now former sheriff of Nassau County, Harvey Manser, had destroyed the bar, leaving her homeless once again.

The hotel room in which she was staying had originally been reserved by Varik. Her suspension from the Bureau left the town without an Enforcer so the Bureau had assigned Varik as her temporary replacement and had provided him with a short-term apartment. He, in turn, had given his hotel room to Alex. She'd offered to reserve her own room but he'd insisted, claiming that the room was already paid for in advance.

She didn't believe his story, just as she didn't believe that he didn't know more about the doll than he was claiming.

The elevator arrived and the doors slid open. She pushed the button that would take her to the lobby.

As the doors shut, another door opened and closed

somewhere in the distance, bringing to mind her encounter—or lack of an encounter—in the Hall of Records.

Machinery whirred overhead and, while the elevator descended, she was on edge. Dread settled over her like a shroud and she couldn't shake it.

The elevator reached the first floor and the doors opened to reveal a well-lit, empty lobby.

Alex silently chided herself as she passed the vacant front desk. She was allowing the events of recent weeks to get to her. Now she had an opportunity to make up for some of her mistakes.

And yet when she stepped into the rainy predawn gloom, the sense that some unseen menace lay in wait, watching, quickened her steps until she was running when she reached her dark green Jeep Grand Cherokee.

She climbed inside the SUV and locked the doors. Her heart beat was deafening in the confines of the cab. She glared at herself in the rearview mirror and muttered, "Get a hold of yourself. You're acting like a frightened school girl."

Pushing aside the anxiety that still swirled around her like a palpable cloud, she fired up the Jeep's engine and guided the vehicle out of the parking lot, determined not to squander the opportunity she'd been given.

And determined to stop jumping at shadows.

Basements weren't possible in southern Mississippi for two reasons: a high water table and a layer of shifting clay within the ground. That was why so many old houses had immense attic space to compensate.

Above or below ground didn't matter to him though. All he needed was privacy and the attic offered it.

The doorway was well-hidden. He'd made certain it wouldn't be noticed by the casual observer. Not that he had many visitors.

A door in the second-floor hall opened to stairs that led to a portion of the attic. A very small portion used for actual storage. The rest of the attic could be accessed by a false panel concealed behind an oversized print of Marcel Duchamp's *Nude Descending a Staircase, No. 2*. The Cubist painting depicted both a woman and a staircase that were all blocks and overlapping angles with little separating the moving nude figure from the irregular background.

The irony was too much. He laughed every time he opened the panel and climbed the hidden stairs, as he did now. Reaching the top step, he entered the wide expanse that was his private heaven.

Shelves containing his most precious collection lined the walls. Bins filled with all the bits needed to create his masterpieces were arranged in a neat row on his workstation. Lamps hung overhead and bathed the table in soft light.

He pulled a rolling stool from under the table and sat down with a sigh. It felt good to be returning to work. He pushed a button on a remote control and the opening overture for *Carmen* filtered through concealed speakers. His eyes dipped shut. The music surrounded him, caressed him, and lulled his senses into a calm.

Tonight had been a very good night. He'd seen *her*. It had been a brief glimpse only, but it had been enough to rekindle his desire, to assure him that his work was not in vain.

He'd even heard her voice. Her sweet, angelic voice calling to him, seeking him out.

Opening his eyes, he removed the protective drape from his current work. It was crude but the subtle features were taking shape in the face. Each doll he created was perfect, an exact copy of the Living Doll he'd seen long ago. Each imbued with the vital essence he hoped would bring her to him.

His gaze flickered across the attic to his latest acquisition.

She stared at him, eyes wide and wild. She hadn't struggled in the same manner as her predecessor so the bindings were minimal. Bands across her forehead and throat kept her head immobile. Her arms lay naturally along her sides with black straps holding them securely in place at the elbows and wrists. A special harness crossed over her shoulders and then over her stomach. More straps held her thighs and shins in place. She said nothing even though her mouth remained uncovered.

He smiled and picked up the new doll's head from the table.

This one was special.

This was the one that would finally bring the Living Doll to him.

This was the one that would make her his.

Forever.